Contributing Author: Gretchen Nobles

Cover design by Bespoke Author

To anyone who has ever lost their way, may you find the strength and courage to trust that the path will open before you.

CHAPTER 1

I've been called many things in life, but never by a name that felt like it belonged to me. There were times when it made me so angry I wanted to lash out, and other times when the weight of it made me so sad I wished I could just disappear. To be forgotten. Perhaps I never grew accustomed to untangling such sentiments, but my life certainly hadn't prepared me for understanding emotions. It never seemed like a skill worth mastering. Still, with the morning sun at my back, staring down at the grave marker of my wife and daughter, I was faced with the name I hated for years. Colter. Elise Colter. That name marking the resting place of the only woman I'd ever loved made me feel broken. Or blessed? Maybe it was a touch of both. Nevertheless, the fact that Elise had so willingly agreed to take such a ridiculous name made me feel fortunate to be her husband.

Since her passing, I'd taken the wagon into town twice a week to visit her grave. Some days, I'd sit there in silence, sometimes stand and say a prayer, and at other times, I'd talk to Elise as if she were right beside me. I made it a habit to keep her up to date with what was happening with the sheep or about the coyotes that kept sniffing around the ranch, or I would simply assure her that I was eating enough. She was generally concerned with such things. And, if I happened to overhear any gossip as I passed through town, I also made sure to share that with her. I couldn't give two figs about all the townsfolks' secrets and scandals, but Elise always enjoyed hearing the unseemly tales of the men and women of Virginia City. So, I made it a point to show up once or twice a week to tell her everything I'd learned. It had been my routine for well over a year now.

If I'd had my way, Elise would have been laid to rest on our land, but Elise had different views. She left no doubt about her wishes. She insisted that she be laid to rest in town, in the church cemetery, like a proper lady. And, as much as I disliked spending time in town, I vowed to her that

I would respect her wishes. The women at church took up a collection and had a nice headstone made for Elise. I think it's what she would have wanted. Even though I laid our daughter to rest with her, I decided against inscribing her name on the stone. She was never properly given a name, and it didn't feel right to name her without Elise having a say.

Elise never shied away from the name Colter. She concluded that the name belonged to me regardless of how I came to possess it, and because she loved me, she also loved my name. I was envious of how she introduced us whenever we met new folks. The name Elise Colter left her mouth with an air of honor, as if the name meant something. I wasn't able to duplicate her self-assuredness, but it was always comforting to be near it and borrow some of the dignity she felt. Unfortunately, the feeling was always short-lived, and now it was gone altogether. Without her unwavering confidence, my typical doubts about my own worth were stronger than ever. No matter how many times I stood there, looking down at her final resting place, the reality of her absence was always like a weight on my chest. Elise was gone. She died giving birth to our only child. They're both gone now, and I was left to carry on alone and find a way to navigate the remainder of my days. For now, I am merely existing. It seemed like any chance I had at happiness was buried in that cold ground with them.

The only thing I disliked more than my last name was when it was mentioned in tandem with my first. Moses Colter. As a child, I spent a fair amount of time despising the name and found myself in quite a few scuffles as a result. But as the years passed, I learned to accept it. It sounds simple enough, but learning to play the game with the cards you're dealt can be difficult to overcome.

Not that I've ever been one to moan or whine about it, but my life didn't have such a stable beginning, at least not the parts I can recall. Truth be told, several years of my childhood have escaped my memory altogether. As far as I'm concerned, my life began in 1848, just outside of Jonesborough, Tennessee, when I was seven years old. The particulars surrounding my discovery and subsequent rescue are foggy at best, but growing up, I heard the story many times. A young deputy from Jonesborough named Wesley found me that night. He and another deputy were traveling by horse, making their way home from a quick trip to Elizabethton. It was a quiet evening, calm and clear. The sun was low in the sky, settling in behind the hills as the lawmen rode in silence. As the story goes, the men were only a few minutes outside of town when Wesley heard a commotion in the river not too far off the trail. Assuming it was likely a deer or a dog, Wesley was curious enough to check out the ruckus while his companion continued on his way.

To Wesley's surprise, it wasn't a deer, dog, or any other wild creature he discovered but a young boy. He was a feral-looking creature in his own right, grunting and writhing around in the shallow waters as if fighting for his life against some unseen foe. Deputy Wesley leaped from his horse, waded into the river, and grabbed the boy. Grabbed me. Despite my young age, I fought like a wounded grizzly. I kicked, screamed, clawed, punched, and bit poor old Wesley until he finally managed to wrestle me down onto the rocky riverbank. It soon became apparent that Wesley had gotten the better of me, and all the fight in me gave way to exhaustion. The next thing I knew, Wesley was pulling me off the back of his horse and ushering me through the front doors of the Grace House Orphanage. I slowly regained my sensibilities as I walked into the orphanage with Wesley's large hand clamped firmly on my shoulder.

"Well, what on earth do we have here?" a kind-looking old man said, peering at me over his spectacles. He wore his night clothes and carried a lantern, which he held to my face to get a better look.

"I'm not really sure," Wesley said, nudging me closer to the lantern's glow. "I found him throwin' a fit in the river just outside town."

The old man squinted intently through the dim light. "What's your name, son?" he asked. I didn't answer. I didn't know how. "Are you lost? Hungry? You must be hungry. Where are your folks?" Again, I offered nothing, but even still, he smiled at me with warm, gentle eyes. "If I knew your name, it might help me find out where you belong. Or at least I'd know who to call when it's time for breakfast."

Wesley spoke up. "Best I can tell, he was abandoned. I've never seen him before, and I couldn't find anyone camped nearby. Could be he followed the river down from one of the mining towns, but there hasn't been any report of a missing child. Other than that, we've had some outlaws moving through the area. Maybe they dumped him. It wouldn't be the first time somebody snatched a kid to buy some time."

The old man studied my face as if trying to decide what to do with me. "Found him in the river, you say?"

"That's right," Wesley said. "Just a mile outside of town. Pulled him out of the Colter while he did his best to beat the fool out of me. He finally got so tired he passed out, and I brought him to you."

"An orphan abandoned and then discovered in the river," the old man said, tilting his head to one side and grinning like he'd heard a joke. "So, you're our very own Moses of the Colter River." And since it was necessary, and seeing as I had no recollection of my proper name, I was officially given residence at Grace House Orphanage under the name of Moses Colter.

Before long, I had learned the rules and expectations of the orphanage. Having three meals a day, a bed to sleep in, and other kids to play with, I was more than happy to oblige. The kind older gentleman who took me in ran the orphanage with his wife. James and Charlotte Peabody housed ten other orphans in addition to me. They fed us, made sure we bathed, taught us how to read and write, and tried their best to curb our wild tendencies in hopes that we may one day become respectable adults.

Of course, children would come and go. Some of the older kids would even run away at times, but other forsaken young souls in need of care soon replaced them. On rare occasions, some of the children were adopted, usually by families in need of able-bodied young boys to help with their farming. So, while I enjoyed my time with the Peabodys, I learned not to grow too attached.

The one constant in my life was my friend, Andrew Harlan. Everyone called him Drew for short. He was around the same age as me but had been at the orphanage since he was a baby. Like many others, Drew's parents had come to America, looking to head west, stake a claim, and create a new life. Unfortunately, they didn't make it far before encountering a small party of Shawnee. One of Harlan's guides lost his cool and fired on the Indians, inciting their rage and resulting in a full-on attack. It didn't end well for the Harlans and their guides. By the time the fighting stopped, not a Harlan was left alive. None except Drew, that is. No one knows why the Shawnee didn't kill him or decide to keep him, as had been known to happen. But when the law finally found the wagons, the Shawnee had long since gone, along with the settlers' supplies and horses. Little was left behind but a pile of bodies and a crying baby boy.

Drew and I were as inseparable as young boys can be. We spent every waking moment together, sniffing out adventure and dreaming about traveling the world. There wasn't a single morning that didn't start without laughter and Drew's mischievous grin, which never failed to put everyone at ease. I admired Drew. He was wild and unpredictable, a loyal friend who never backed down from a challenge. His confidence and zeal for life gave me an ideal to latch onto – a way of viewing the world that was exciting and never lacking purpose. Drew was more than my friend; he was my brother. He gave my days at the orphanage meaning beyond just existing.

We both took to our lessons quickly, working diligently to master each skill introduced. Of course, our hard work wasn't driven by an innate thirst for knowledge. We found that the sooner we mastered a lesson, the sooner we could return to our play. Consequently, we learned a great deal about reading, writing, and a little arithmetic. At the time, we didn't realize how fortunate we were to be learning such things. Many boys our age weren't afforded the opportunity to spend time on academic pursuits. The demands of a family business, whether farming, ranching, or trade, were better served by developing muscle and skill rather than brains and learning. Mr. and Mrs. Peabody often told us that the acquisition of intellect was far superior to that of physical prowess, but I don't suspect they ever spent much time running a farm.

CHAPTER 2

We followed a familiar routine at the orphanage. The morning bell would ring, and we'd wake up, make our beds, and get cleaned up for breakfast. There were chores, school lessons, and a bit of time for recess and roughhousing. It was a good life for a kid. Apart from the ever-present sense of being unwanted lingering within each of us, everything ran smoothly. It was a constant, silent struggle that lived just beneath the surface. Even in the happiest times, it was there, waiting to remind you that you were alone. That no one wanted you. Not in the way we all dreamed of anyway. But I did have something worth caring about. I had friends and people who took an interest in me and cared for me. I was content.

I had been at Grace House for nearly two years when everything in my world changed. I can still see the faces of the other kids gawking at me with eyes as large as wagon wheels. They tried their best to convince me that I'd hit the jackpot. We each dreamed about it but chose not to believe it would happen. Still, it was happening for me. I was the lucky one. But the empty feeling in my chest made me doubt whether or not luck was the right word for it.

The familiar routine of the day had begun, starting with kids pulling their shirts on as they ran to the dining hall for breakfast. As was our custom, Drew and I sat beside one another, lapping up our portion of porridge and bread. Laughter and chatter echoed through the room, along with the sounds of spoons scraping bowls and cups of milk hitting the table more forcefully than necessary. Drew was in an especially good mood because he'd heard that a horse trader was passing through town. He loved horses and had even managed to charm Mr. and Mrs. Peabody into letting us walk to the livery stables to see them. The deal he'd managed to strike was simple enough – finish all chores by noon, and we could leave after lunch.

"When the sheriff came by, I heard him tell Peabody that this trader might have some really rare breeds," Drew said with bright eyes. "You think they'll have any Arabians? I've always wanted to see an Arabian."

"I don't know much about horses," I said. "I like white ones, though."

Drew shook his head in disappointment. "Look, you can't be a real cowboy if you don't know nothin' about horses."

"But I'm not a cowboy," I said with a grin.

"Not yet," Drew said, raising a finger. "First things first. Wait here." Drew jumped up from the table and raced away. He was hardly gone a second before returning to his seat with a book in hand. "Here," he said, "this is mine, but you can borrow it." He placed the book in my hands but immediately pulled it away. "I said you can *borrow* it. Understand?"

"Yeah, yeah," I said, snatching the book with a smirk. It was well worn with a leather-bound cover, far too nice a book for an orphan to have. Embossed into the worn brown leather were the words, *A Practical Guide to Horse Breeds of the World*. "Woah, thanks," I said as I thumbed through the pages.

Drew grinned and puffed out his chest. "Well, if we're gonna get out of here and make a name for ourselves one day, you at least need to know *something* about horses." Drew took the book from me. "Here, let me show you my favorite." He flipped through the pages with the ease of someone who knew exactly what he was looking for. After a moment, he found the page and tapped his finger on the image of a majestic-looking creature. "Look at this one. This here is a solid black Thoroughbred." His eyes darted from me back to the image. "This is the horse I'm gonna have someday. From what I hear, they can run all day and never get tired. Just think, if we had a couple of these, we could take off, and no one would ever catch us."

He closed the book and handed it back to me. "You keep this for a while. Learn about the different breeds and settle on a favorite. We'll save every penny we get, and one day, we'll meet with a horse trader and buy one of our very own."

It seemed like a far-fetched idea, but I smiled and nodded all the same. "Sounds good, Drew. It's a plan."

Suddenly, the door to the dining hall swung open, and I instinctively placed the book in my chair and quickly sat on top of it. I'm not sure why that was my initial reaction. We were allowed to have books, but in the orphanage, you learn to protect everything you have. There were very few things we could call our own, and when you had something of your own, no matter how small or insignificant it might seem to others, your natural inclination was to keep it safe.

Mr. and Mrs. Peabody entered first, smiling and gesturing around the room to the young woman who followed closely behind. She was a vision of elegance and wealth, and the room fell silent upon her entrance. I'd never seen anyone dressed so richly in my life. Her dress was emerald green with a white lace collar and cuffs and looked like it had never had a stain. Her long red hair was tied up in a bun, and I could smell how clean she was from across the room.

"Who is that?" I asked Drew. His gaze was fixed on her like she was a coon in a chicken coop.

"That is Josephine Ashbourne," Drew whispered. "Her husband is Augustus Ashbourne, and they are some of the wealthiest people in the state. They own Ivywood Plantation. It's a big operation. They grow tobacco."

"Does she come here much? I've never seen her before."

"Not much," he went on, keeping his eyes on Mrs. Ashbourne. "Every couple of years, she'll drop by, take a look at us orphans, and decide if she wants to take any of us home with her. Sometimes she does, sometimes she don't."

"What does she want kids for? Don't she have any of her own?"

Drew shrugged. "Some say she comes to gather kids to help work her fields. I don't think that's true, though. She never takes any kid who doesn't want to go with her. I think she's just rich and bored."

"Do some kids say no?"

Drew huffed. "Maybe once, but I don't know anyone who wouldn't want to live in a big ol' mansion with rich folks." He paused. "But I wouldn't worry about it too much. She'd never pick kids like us anyway. She prefers her orphans to be a little more well-mannered."

Mrs. Ashbourne was there most of the morning, but Drew and I didn't pay her much attention. We raced through our chores with little else on our minds besides the exotic horses waiting for us at the stables. With great effort and speed, Drew and I completed our tasks with half an hour to spare before lunch. We raced back to our bunks to look at the horse book when the bell rang. "It's too early for lunch," I said. "We better see what's goin' on."

Mr. and Mrs. Peabody were joined in the dining hall by the elegant Mrs. Ashbourne. "Right this way, children," Mr. Peabody called out. "All of you line up against the wall now. Mrs. Ashbourne would like to take a good look at you."

We did as we were told and stood, shoulder to shoulder, as Mrs. Ashbourne walked up and down the row, whispering questions to Mr. and Mrs. Peabody. After a moment, they stepped away and had what seemed to be a very pleasant conversation, with Mr. and Mrs. Peabody smiling and nodding. When they returned, Mrs. Ashbourne walked right up to me. With a warm smile, she knelt beside me. "Hello, young man," she said. "Is your name Moses?"

I nodded and shifted about nervously. "Well, speak up, boy," Mrs. Peabody interjected.

"Yes," I said, "Yes, ma'am, my name is Moses."

Mrs. Ashbourne smiled even wider. "Well, Moses, my name is Mrs. Josephine Ashbourne, and I am looking to adopt a child. Would that be of interest to you?"

I knew it was rude to stand there staring at her without speaking, but no words made it past my throat. "It's okay, Moses," she said. "You don't have to answer right now. I'll come back tomorrow when you've had time to decide."

I nodded, attempting to hide my uncertainty. "Thank you, Mrs. Ashbourne. I'll think on it."

With that, Mrs. Ashbourne stood up straight, thanked Mr. and Mrs. Peabody, and gave me a parting smile before leaving the room. The other children gathered around me in a whirlwind of excitement and congratulations. Such circumstances were rare, and the kids were beaming with joy for me – all but one. Drew was silent, staring at his feet. It was odd to see him that way since Drew was typically at the center of any celebration. But I assumed his hesitation was similar to mine. It's just as hard to be left behind as it is to go.

Mrs. Ashbourne's offer laid heavily on me. On one hand, she was offering me everything I could ask for – a family, a home, parents, a chance for a normal life. Something inside me yearned for the kind of warmth and gentleness she so readily displayed. On the other hand, was Drew. I didn't think it was possible to carry on in life without him. He was my friend. My brother. He was a constant confidant in a world that hadn't been so kind to us.

Later that night, Drew and I talked in our bunks before bed. Mr. and Mrs. Peabody had refused to let us go see the horses. They didn't want any opportunity for us to get in trouble before Mrs. Ashbourne returned. We were disappointed, but the genuine possibility of me leaving the orphanage took up most of the available acreage in our minds.

"Maybe she'd take both of us," I said.

Drew shook his head. "Nah, she don't want me. She wants you to be her son." Even though he attempted to be lighthearted, there was pain in his voice.

Minutes seemed to stretch into hours, and Drew and I sat there in silence, neither of us sure what to say. Finally, by force of will, Drew emerged from his bunk with a soft smile. "Go with her, Moses," he said. "You deserve this. You deserve a real family. We can still be friends." He motioned around the room. "You know where I live. You can come visit whenever you want."

Tears welled up in my eyes, but I forced them away. I didn't want to leave Drew, but deep down, I knew he was right. It was an opportunity anyone would want. I had no choice but to embrace such good fortune for the promise of a better life. The next day, with a heavy but determined heart, I bid farewell to Drew, my brother. I left with a handshake and a promise to keep our friendship alive.

CHAPTER 3

I wiped the dirt from Elise's grave marker and slowly walked toward my wagon. It was late morning by then, and the sun was high. The weight of my loss felt like dragging around iron chains, and with each step, I was reminded of the growing emptiness slowly overtaking me. The ache I lived with had become commonplace, a familiar companion occupying the space in my heart left by Elise.

As I moved through town, men and women passed me by, but no one spoke. Of course, they all knew me as a widower, but I suppose I put off an air that I wasn't looking for conversation. Those who didn't outright ignore me did their best to avoid eye contact, while others looked my way and offered a smile laced with pity. Part of me hated those looks, but I knew they meant well. Still, my overwhelming preference was simply to be left alone. But the lonely days were beginning to wear on me. I couldn't spend the rest of my life holed up in a ranch house, raising sheep. It all felt too meaningless. I had no one to care for, no one to provide for, and no one to leave anything of worth to after I was gone.

As I trudged along, the Rusty Nail Saloon caught my eye. I hadn't set foot in a saloon since Elise and I married nearly three years ago. More than once, she'd made it clear that she didn't care for such establishments, and I nearly changed my mind even as I climbed the creaky steps that day. However, I had spent the better part of a year mourning her passing and carrying on as if she still had an opinion about such things. Though I was fairly certain I was ill-prepared to do so, it was time to move on – or try, at least.

Inside the Rusty Nail, a few old men played poker while a few younger men leaned against the bar. Jimmy Tittle was the owner and was tending bar that day. He was a nice enough fella. A bit older than me, he looked like a man who'd experienced his share of troubles. What little hair he had,

Jimmy kept slicked back, only accentuating his lazy eye, which wandered wherever it pleased.

"Well, look what we have here," Jimmy said with a toothy grin. "If it ain't Moses Colter. It's good to see you, pal."

"Good to see you too, Jimmy," I replied. "Can I get a drink?"

"I'd say you deserve a drink," he said as he filled a shot glass and placed it on the bar. "I wanted you to know I'm real sorry about your wife and little one. I would've told you sooner, but I rarely see you around."

"Thank you, Jimmy," I said before downing the shot.

"It's a tragedy...a real tragedy."

I could feel the eyes of the two men at the bar upon me, and I glanced in their direction. One of them I knew was Sam Jeffers. Everyone called him Skillet on account of him being a cook in the war. He was broke and homeless, bumming enough change here and there to keep him well supplied with booze. But Skillet loved to talk.

A fella could quickly surmise that Skillet was one of those men who seemed lost after the war ended. He sacrificed three years and a left arm to the cause of the Union Army but never found much purpose after that. After his days as an enlisted man ended, Skillet moved from town to town until finally settling on Virginia City, Montana. According to Skillet, Montana was a territory that had very little to do with the war, and he needed a fresh start. It sounded nice but didn't make much sense to me. I couldn't see how Skillet planned to start anew, seeing as how he still wore his Union Coat every day. The buttons were stretched so tight they looked like they might give up at any second. I'm no expert on the thoughts of men, but I imagine it's hard to move on from something that once meant so much.

"Hey there, Moses," Skillet said with a grunt. "Can you spare a dollar?"

"Sure," I said, tossing him the coin. "Try not to drink it all in one place."

Skillet thanked me, stuffed the coin in his trouser pocket, and returned to sipping his drink.

"You always give money to bums?" the other man at the bar said with a scowl. "What are you rich or something?"

I didn't recognize him, but that wasn't unusual. Despite having gone to church with Elise every Sunday, I could count the people I knew in town on one hand. I kept to myself and didn't talk much. Anyone who felt familiar enough with me to speak did so of their own accord, not because I invited it. But I was sure I'd never crossed paths with this fella. He was probably passing through and decided to stop, and Virginia City was as good a place to visit as any. Lean and weathered, he had a stern look about him, but his mannerisms were deliberate and easy. He looked like he'd spent years in the saddle and slept many nights in the elements. He was dangerous. I'd encountered enough of his type to know that such men should be handled carefully.

Skillet began to protest the man's insult, but I interjected, hoping to steer him away from the conversation. "This here is Skillet," I said with a smile as I slid down the bar toward him. "He's a friend of mine. He's not a bum, but I must admit that he smells no better." Skillet huffed and went back to his drink. "And for the record, I may be many things, but rich ain't one of them."

The stranger killed his drink and turned to face me. "Name's Sutton," he said, reaching his hand out and shaking mine.

"I'm Moses," I replied.

"Moses?" he said with a mocking grin. "Like from the Bible?"

"Something like that," I said, returning to the bar.

"Well, Moses, maybe you can help me. I'm looking for someone. Been on the road for a while now."

"You a lawman?" I asked, glancing at the tied-down revolver on his hip. "Or a bounty hunter, maybe?"

He nodded. "Something like that."

"Well, I'll do what I can for you, but I don't know too many people. The list is pretty short outside of old Sam and Skillet here. I try to keep my head down."

"No worries, partner," Sutton said as he stood up and paid his tab. "It's a wise thing to do." He tossed an extra coin to Jimmy and nodded toward Skillet. "His next one's on me." He turned back just before walking out. "Ah, Moses, was it?"

"That's right."

"You wouldn't happen to know a scoundrel by the name of Andrew Harlan, would you? I was told he goes by Drew. Used to run with Smiling Jack Davis."

My heart pounded, and there was a pit in my stomach. It had been a long time since Drew and I had spoken and years since I'd heard the name

Smiling Jack. "Sorry, friend. I don't know anyone by that name," I said as confidently as I could.

Sutton smiled, tipped his hat to the room, and said, "Thank you, boys." Then to me, "And thank you, Mr. Colter. I'll leave you all be."

"Who was that, Jimmy?" I asked, staring after Sutton as the doors swung shut behind him. "He been around before?"

"No tellin'," Jimmy replied. "I know I ain't seen him in here before. How'd he know your name, anyway? You told him you was Moses, but he came up with Colter on his own."

"I'm not sure, but I'd be careful with him if I was you. Don't share too much if he comes back around askin' questions."

"No good bottom-feeder if you ask me," Skillet added. "Who walks in calling fellas a bum like that? He's lucky I don't carry my six shooters no more."

Jimmy ignored Skillet. "Do you know that Andrew Harlan fella he was askin' about?"

"I used to," I said. "But that was a long time ago."

"Understood," Jimmy said as he proceeded to wipe the bar. "Don't you worry one bit, Moses. He won't get nothin' outta nobody around here."

I left the Rusty Nail and continued on my way. It would figure the one occasion upon which I decided to engage socially resulted in a surly stranger digging for information. As troublesome as it was to learn he was hunting Drew, it was even worse that he also knew my name. As for him mentioning Smiling Jack Davis, that was a whole different collection of worries I chose not to fix my mind on.

"Mr. Colter, do you have a moment," a man called out. With a noticeable sigh, I turned to face Reverend Joseph Phillips, who was hurrying toward me. I wasn't accustomed to people approaching or engaging me in public, so I was immediately uneasy.

Reverend Phillips was a tall, thin man with a large nose and more hair on his face than his head. Though I had no desire to speak, the truth is, I liked the reverend. From what I could tell, most folks in town felt the same. My lack of enthusiasm was due to the fact that I'd already spoken to more people in one day than I usually would in a week. All I wanted was to get home.

The reverend and I had more in common than most in town. We had been inducted into a club to which no one sought membership. We were widowers. Jenine was his wife's name, and she died of pneumonia a couple of years back. It was soon apparent that Reverend Phillips handled his loss quite differently than I did. When Elise died, I pulled away from everyone. Being alone and quiet offered me a type of dull, predictable comfort. But not Reverend Phillips. He threw himself into his work when Jenine passed. And his work was shepherding the good people of Virginia City. It was a respectable life, but not one for me. I'd always been under the impression that good people didn't require shepherding nearly as much as the hellions. "Mr. Colter, I –"

"Oh, come on now, Reverend," I said. "We've known each other a while now. You can call me Moses."

"Yes, of course," he continued with a sheepish grin. "I haven't seen you around in a while, and when I noticed you passing through, I thought...I should check on Mr. Colter and see how he's doing."

"Well, thank you. I'm doing just fine," I said as I attempted to walk away. Reverend Phillips was persistent, though, and I blamed myself for the lack of conviction in my voice.

"I just wanted you to know that we at the church are devastated by your loss. Such tragedies are difficult to make sense of, but –"

"It's okay, Reverend. I appreciate you tellin' me, but I should be –"

"Now, the last thing I'd want to do is to impede upon your grieving process, but if there is anything I or the church can do to help you, please let me know. We're here if you need us."

As well rehearsed as his words came across, I believed him. From what I'd seen and heard of Reverend Phillips, he was a man of his word who genuinely cared about the people of this town. "I don't believe there's much to be done, Reverend, but I appreciate it all the same."

Again, I turned to leave, but Reverend Phillips wasn't satisfied. "You know, Moses, we'd all love to see you in church again. When you're ready, of course."

I lowered my head and nodded. "Thank you. I'll think on that."

"You're a good man, Moses," Reverend Phillips blurted out, tilting his head to make eye contact. "Don't you forget it."

I met his gaze and considered his words for a moment. "I don't mean no offense, Reverend, but the truth is...you don't have enough information to back such a claim. If you knew –"

"Oh, I know enough," he said without missing a beat. "I know that you, like the rest of us, are one of God's children. I know He brought you and Elise together and helped you find a new life here, and I believe our meeting today was a divine appointment." He paused a moment. I think he expected a response, but all I could think about was getting away from him without being rude.

"Look, Reverend, I've done things in life I'm not proud of, but those things happened, and I can't pretend otherwise. I wish it wasn't so, but I believe my actions have made my standing with the good Lord a little dicey at best.

"I know what I am. And I ain't never had any expectations of salvation or second chances. As far as I'm concerned, my wife was the living embodiment of both, but now she's gone. I always thought she could help me find my way if I was lucky. Now, I guess we'll just have to wait and see."

Reverend Phillips appeared genuinely pained by my words, but fortunately, he was a man who knew when to let things go. "I understand. I disagree with you, but I do understand. All I ask is that you do your best not to give up on the Lord. I don't care what you've done, and neither does he. I'm telling you, I can feel it. He has plans for you yet. Maybe you can't see it right now, but I *know* it's there. There's good in you. And if there's good in a man, it was put there for a reason."

I wanted to believe him, but in my experience, having hope never worked out too well. "It's a nice thought, Reverend. A nice thought indeed."

"One more thing, Moses, and then I'll let you go in peace," he said. "The last time we spoke, nearly a year ago now, you told me you were having some unsettling dreams. How's that going? Are they still troubling you?"

"Ah...no. The dreams just kinda faded away," I lied. "Everything has been goin' real good." Truthfully, I was having the same dream I'd spoken to Reverend Phillips about before. It was shortly before Elise died. They were coming on strong then, keeping me up nearly every night. Only by her prompting did I share it with Reverend Phillips in the first place. Now, they came about once or twice a week, always the same dream, always the same message.

"Well, I'm pleased to hear it," Reverend Phillips said. "Now, you go on about your business, and I'll be praying for you."

"Thank you," I said. "And don't feel like you have to wear your prayer room out on my account, Reverend. A more suitable prospect would likely get you a better return on your investment."

Reverend Phillips laughed. "Mr. Colter, I assure you I have multiple *investments*, and I expect all of them to pay off. I'll do my job and let the Lord do His.

I moved on, doing my best to ignore the man's words. Upon reaching my wagon, I found Hurley, my only mule, chewing grass and patiently waiting. With a pat on the neck, I went into my bag and found a carrot I'd been saving. I allowed Hurley a moment to finish before pulling myself into the seat. It was then I noticed a sign posted on the stable that read, *Horse trader in town this weekend*. A smile tugged at the corner of my mouth, and memories of Drew flooded my mind.

That Sutton fella shook me up, and I was worried for my friend. I didn't know what kind of trouble Drew had gotten into, but I hoped he was okay.

CHAPTER 4

I was nine years old in the summer of 1850. It was the summer I said goodbye to Drew and the Peabodys and went to live with the Ashbournes. As I climbed into the carriage, I tried to see my leaving the orphanage as a new adventure. It's what Drew would have done. However, my efforts were in vain because I wasn't Drew. Try as I might to convince myself otherwise, I was terrified to leave everything I knew. Mr. and Mrs. Peabody saw me off, but Drew had made it clear he wouldn't be there to watch me go. Since he was convinced we'd see each other soon, he refused to say goodbye. So I was surprised to see Drew rushing out with my bag before I left; otherwise, I might have forgotten it. "Don't do anything to mess this up," he whispered as he handed it over. "You just go in there, do what you're told, and enjoy bein' rich for a change. We're still gonna take off together one day. You wait and see. Only difference is, now you'll have enough money to buy those fancy horses for both of us."

The carriage wheels creaked over the uneven ground as I watched the scenery change outside the window. After a few minutes, we were outside Jonesborough and passing over the Colter River. Staring at that rushing water, I wondered how I ended up there the night Deputy Wesley found me. What if my real family was out there looking for me while I was on my way to join a new one? What if leaving the orphanage would make it impossible for my real family to find me? But I decided that if anyone out there *was* looking for me, they likely would have found me by now. I had to accept the truth. No one was coming for me. I was on my own.

Mrs. Ashbourne made an attempt at small talk as we traveled. She asked questions such as what my favorite color was, what I enjoyed doing, or what my favorite meal was, none of which I knew how to answer. She seemed especially impressed by my ability to read so well, and she had a book she asked me to read aloud. "That is simply wonderful," Mrs.

Ashbourne eventually interjected with a giddy grin and a clap of her hands. "You must be a brilliant young man."

No one had ever called me brilliant. Being told to shut my smart mouth was about as close as anyone ever got. And even though Mrs. Ashbourne seemed sincere, the compliment was uncomfortable. It was like putting on a shirt that didn't fit, one that hung loosely from my shoulders, causing more aggravation than protection.

"It won't be much longer now," Mrs. Ashbourne said. Then, her countenance changed, and her tone became serious. "Listen, Moses, there are things you should know before we arrive. It's nothing to worry about, but I thought you'd like to feel prepared. Is it alright if we talk about it now?"

I nodded. "Yes, ma'am." It didn't seem as if I had a choice. "We can talk now."

She sat up tall in her seat. "Well, I am entirely thrilled that you'll be coming to live with us, but I feel as if I should warn you that my husband, Augustus, Mr. Ashbourne, isn't the warmest of men. I assure you he fully supports my adopting you and bringing you into the family, but at times, his demeanor might strike you as indifferent. Just remember that it may take him a while to warm up to you." I sat in silence, unsure of how to respond to such information. "Oh, dear, I hope I haven't upset you," she said. "I'm just so excited to have you, and I want everything to be perfect."

"I'm sure it will be fine, ma'am."

"As am I," she said brightly. "You know, I have a son a little older than you. His name is Logan. I can't wait to see how well you two hit it off."

"Is he adopted, too?" I asked.

"No, Logan is the only child Augustus and I ever had. He's thirteen years old now. I'm sure he'll be simply thrilled to have a new friend." She raised her eyebrows and patted my knee. "A brother."

About that time, the carriage pulled up to a large gate, where two surly-looking men with rifles stood guard. "Good morning, Mrs. Ashbourne," one of them said as he peeked into the carriage.

"Good morning, Harold," she replied. "This here is Moses. He'll be moving in with us, so you'll see a lot of him."

"Moses," he said with an expressionless nod. He stepped away from the window and motioned the driver forward.

The carriage pulled up in front of the large plantation house, and I couldn't help but marvel at its magnificence. At my young age, everything about the place seemed larger than life. We stepped from the carriage, and Mrs. Ashbourne spread her arms wide and welcomed me home. The enormity of the mansion struck me first. The main hall sat high upon a grand shelf of steps, towering over the rest of the grounds. Opulent, white columns firmly held up the second and third floors, and the estate seemed to stretch on either side indefinitely. I had never seen such extravagance – such wealth.

Just as impressive as the mansion was the number of people it took to keep it running. The air was buzzing with activity, and the distant sounds of lively voices rang out over the warm summer breeze. I didn't fully grasp why this place operated with such urgency, but one thing was clear. This was not just a home; it was a business.

"Lisi," Mrs. Ashbourne called out to the young woman sweeping the front porch, "go and fetch Logan for me. I want him to come meet his new brother."

"Yesum," Lisi said with a nod as she put down her broom and passed through the large double doors into the home.

A moment later, a young boy with tousled blond hair, dressed nicer than any kid I'd ever seen, raced down the front steps with a huge smile. "Hello, Mother," he said, stopping before us and hugging her.

"Well, aren't you sweet," Mrs. Ashbourne said. "Logan, I want you to meet Moses. I've just adopted him from the Peabodys. He's your new brother."

"Hey there, Moses," Logan said as he reached to shake my hand. "Glad to meet you." He was nearly a foot taller than me and smelled as clean as his mother.

"Glad to meet you too," I said, unable to match Logan's enthusiasm.

"Isn't this wonderful?" Mrs. Ashbourne said, pressing her hands together. "Logan, why don't you show Moses around while I check on his room."

"Yes, ma'am," Logan replied. He placed a hand on my shoulder.

"And don't forget we'll be eating dinner at six o'clock sharp tonight," she said. "Make sure you wash up, dress nicely, and are on time. Help Moses, too. You know your father doesn't like to be kept waiting."

"Will do," Logan said. With an enamored grin, Mrs. Ashbourne proceeded up the staircase and hurried inside. No sooner had the doors closed behind her when Logan pulled his hand from my shoulder and sighed. He turned to face me, and the smile on his lips immediately soured. He was eyeing me like someone would a mangy dog. "When's the last time you had a bath?"

I shrugged. "A few days ago." Instantly, I was aware of how shabby my clothes were compared to Logan's.

"Well, you better take a bath before dinner, or Papa will kick you out of the house." He paused momentarily to stare at me with what I assumed to be contempt. "Come on, let's get this over with."

Logan led me through the grounds, making it apparent to anyone with a pulse how little he enjoyed doing so. I was fascinated with the work going on, the dedication of each man and woman, and the symphony of movement that permeated the plantation and kept the wheels turning. We walked along as Logan, with great disinterest, pointed out various elements of the plantation. There were the fields and the stables, the stretch of land being cleared for new crops, the barn where carriages were kept, and a group of ranchhands breaking horses. They were easily the most beautiful horses I'd ever seen. Drew would have loved it.

Every facet of the plantation operated with ease, free of squander. However, it was only when I got a good look at the tobacco fields that I discovered the actual workforce of the plantation. Rows upon rows of large leafy plants stretched further than I could see. It was the hottest part of the day, and the air was ripe with the scent of dirt and tobacco leaves. Men, women, and children toiled under the searing heat, their dark skin gleaming with sweat. They moved in rhythm, each individual playing their part to tend the precious plants.

Logan explained how far the fields extended on the property beyond our view when two young boys raced by us, nearly bumping into us. They were identical, shirtless and filthy, little more than sweat, dirt, and teeth, laughing and chasing one another. "Watch yourselves, you bally little devils," Logan yelled. The men closest to us looked up, clearly startled by Logan's outcry.

"Please, excuse them boys, sir," one of the men said as he walked toward us. He was impressively large but not like other large men I'd seen. This man was solid muscle, a body created from a lifetime of hard work. "Sorry, I'll tend to 'em."

"You better, Titus," Logan replied bitterly. Seeing such a large man shrink back from such a young boy was odd. "Or, by the Lord, you'll all get a good beating."

21

Titus dropped his head in a show of submission. "Yessir. I understand, sir."

Logan glared at the man with hate-filled eyes for what felt like an eternity. It was the first time I'd noticed the hellish fire dancing in his eyes. The first time, but not the last. "I want them boys whipped," he said coldly.

"Yessir," Titus said. His head was still low. "I'll see to it."

For a moment, we all stood in silence. It felt like the whole plantation had stopped, and all eyes were on us to see how this would play out.

Logan took a threatening step toward Titus. "What are you waiting for, you overgrown lunk? Do it. Do it now."

Titus's eyes widened. "You mean you want 'em whipped now?"

"Are you stupid?" Logan said. Then, to me, "Can you believe this idiot? Maybe he's been out in the sun too long. Maybe I should go tell Papa that his ruddy little kids are running wild around here, and instead of keeping them under control, this one's back-talking me."

"No need, sir," Titus said, backing away. He raised his voice. "Boys, get over here."

Everyone was watching to see how this sick show would play out. A huge pit formed in my stomach, and I wanted no part of it. "We should get going, Logan," I said. "Start gettin' ready for dinner."

"No," he answered, "You need to see this, and Titus needs to be reminded who's in charge here."

The young boys creeped out of the fields toward their pa. Their smiles and laughter were gone, replaced with tears and panic. With cracked voices, they both cried their apologies to Logan.

"Shut up," Logan yelled at them. "You should have thought about that before you nearly ran us over." Titus grabbed one of the boys, knelt, and turned him over his knee. "That's right, Titus. And you better do a dang good job of it. Cause I swear if you don't, you'll wish you had."

I looked on as a single tear leaked from Titus's eye. He wiped it away quickly, cast one more glance at Logan, and then whipped his boys worse than I'd ever seen any boys whipped in my life.

CHAPTER 5

After a slow, bumpy ride from town, I finally arrived home to find the ranch as empty and quiet as I'd left it. I pushed open the creaky front door, stepped inside, and was embraced by the oppressive solitude. I sat at the dining room table and stared at the bowl of leftover stew that had kept me fed for three days. It wasn't anywhere near as good as the stew Elise would make. Try as I might, I could never make it taste like hers. As my spoon clinked against the nearly empty bowl, I realized how much I missed the long-departed sounds of a life shared. The ghost of Elise's gentle voice and innocent laughter filled the empty room and intensified the hollowness inside of me.

As evening fell, the orchestra of crickets and frogs began their nightly concert, and I retreated to bed. I lit the lamp beside me, picked up my book, and found the spot where I'd left off. The book was a gift from Elise, the last gift she'd ever given me. I had put off reading it for some time due to the endless amount of work it took to run the farm on my own. Now, I treasured each word of it. She knew how much I loved reading, but it pained me that there was so much about me she never knew.

Instantly, my mind went to the regret I carried each day since the day we'd met. I can't explain why I never shared the whole truth about my past, but I did not. I was afraid. If Elise had known who I was and what I had done in my life, would she still have loved me? My heart whispered a tender "yes," but my mind shouted a deafening "no." How could she? The thought sat heavily on my chest. Can love be true when it's veiled in lies? I could only hope so.

Elise knew where I came from and how I was found in the Colter River and taken to the Grace House Children's Home. She knew I was adopted by the Ashbournes and afforded a life of wealth and comfort. What Elise never knew was why I left the Ashbournes and the ten years that followed. I told her that Drew and I struck out looking for more adventure than the plantation had to offer. That he and I explored the country, working whatever odd jobs we could, and saving all of our money. I never explained the nature of those "jobs" and that most of them were illegal. I used that money to help buy the ranch where she and I began our lives together. I couldn't bear her knowing that her new home was built with money taken from others. My shame compelled me to rewrite the painful parts of my past and kept me from showing Elise my true self. Like any good lie, there was enough truth there to fool myself into believing the past was better left in the past.

Through conscious choice, I kept an entire decade of my life hidden from her. To live with such deception, I told myself it was for her own good – that I didn't want to hurt her or burden her with the terrible truth about the man she'd married. The truth is, I was a coward. I was afraid that if Elise knew who I was, she would leave, and I would do everything I could to keep that from happening. What I now know and must face daily is that ignoring, denying, or lying about a thing doesn't cause the thing to fade away. It's always there, growing just underneath the skin like a parasite gnawing at your bones. It keeps you sick, and the only way to free oneself from such oppression is by exposing all of the ugly, festering wounds. I missed my chance.

Now Elise is gone. She's gone, and I'm left with a wagonload of regret and shame. Shortly after her passing, in an attempt to ease the burden I carried, I made a solemn promise. I swore to never deceive myself or others again. Although I found no pride in it, my life was my own. My story was mine, and I refused to live with the pain of pretending otherwise. I would rather face the possibility of loneliness and ridicule than live another day knowing I'm a liar. Despite that vow, I still felt the need to protect myself. I decided the best way to carry on was to live my remaining days in solitude. Were I successful, I'd be unable to hurt another living soul, and I'd never have to feel the pain of rejection or loss.

With a heavy sigh, I ran a hand through my knotted hair, put out the lamp, and drew the covers. "I'm sorry, Elise," I whispered, and my mind drifted back to Reverend Phillips' words. *He has plans for you yet.* Maybe there was some truth to it. Maybe there was some predetermined path I was meant to walk. Though the notion seemed ridiculous, perhaps there was a God who wasn't done with me yet. My spirit was troubled, but I finally succumbed to exhaustion. My mind drifted numbly while my heart clung to a lingering question. What could the good Lord possibly have in store for someone like me?

That night, the familiar dream returned as clear and sharp as ever. I stood at the front gate of the Ashbourne's property on a clear, cold night. The gates were wide open, and there wasn't a guard in sight. My gut feeling was that I was entirely alone. No men. No beasts. There was only me, the gravel drive at my feet, and the frigid, black sky above. Limestone crunched beneath my boots as I pressed on toward the mansion. My eyes were drawn to the sky. The boundless expanse was lit with countless stars as if the Almighty had scattered them across a midnight canvas. They showed themselves to me from unimaginable distances, filling my thoughts with the wonder of mysteries beyond. If I listened closely, I could almost hear those stars speak, whispering to me their ancient secrets, impressing upon me the notion that beauty exists even in the darkest of times.

As I approached the plantation house, the wind picked up. It howled through the grounds and the surrounding timber as I pushed my hat down and squinted into the night. Suddenly the wind stopped altogether, replaced with a dull, dreadful silence. In the stillness of the moment, the air grew thick and pressed heavily against my skin. I scanned the area for any sign of life, though there was none to be found. Still, I felt as if there were eyes on me, hiding in the shadows, watching. Waiting.

Without warning, the entire mansion burst into flames. There was no time to think or make sense of it. In one instant, there was nothing, and in the next, fire. Something flashed to my left, then to my right. I noticed that it wasn't only the mansion that had erupted into flames; it was the entire plantation. The barns, silos, servants' quarters, the corrals, and the tobacco fields all caught fire at once. I stood alone as the flames roared to life around me.

Horror and wonder overcame me at the thought of what could cause such immediate, all-encompassing devastation. It was beyond my comprehension. My legs gave way, and I dropped to my knees, shielding my face from the heat. Glancing at the mansion, I saw a lone figure descending the burning steps. My eyes watered from the smoke and heat, but I clearly saw that he too was engulfed in flames. The man didn't run from or fight the fire; he calmly moved toward me, unaffected by the heat and flames.

"Stand up, Moses," he called out as he approached. I did as he said. My eyes fought to adjust to the blinding light of the fiery figure before me, and I found myself face-to-face with Titus. His clothing, his skin, his body, all of him aglow with white-hot flames, but he gave no indication it brought him pain. Although everything around me burned, nothing was consumed. The entire plantation looked like it had been dipped in hell itself, but the fires laid nothing to waste.

"Titus, what's happening here? How can this be real?"

Titus looked at me with great concern in his smoke-filled eyes. He raised his arms and gestured to the burning plantation surrounding us. "This is more real than the air you breathe, Moses," he said gently. "We cried out, and the fire came, but faith shields us."

"I don't understand," I said, forcing myself to look into his burning face. "Where did all this come from? Why aren't you burning?"

Titus smiled and lifted a blazing hand to rub his chin. "The Maker's plan is greater than our struggle. We believe in you. We believe you will hear and obey."

In past versions of my dream, Titus would then turn and walk away. I would awake, breathless and confused, trying to forget what I'd seen. However, on this night, the dream didn't end. I waited for it. Expected it. Wanted it even. Titus did walk away, but I was still very much present.

"Titus, wait," I called out. He turned to face me. "How do I know what to do? What am I supposed to hear? What is it I'm supposed to obey?"

Titus fixed his fiery gaze upon mine, pausing momentarily as if trying to find the right words. "You will hear of the cries of your people, and their pain will burn within you. The words of both the wise and the fearless will move you to action and obedience. Once they have spoken, everything you need will be provided. The path will open before you. You will not go alone, and you will not be forsaken. *This* is truth." Titus climbed the steps and disappeared into the blazing mansion, leaving me alone as the world burned.

I awoke in my bed, gasping for breath. My heart pounded, and my lungs burned from the smoke. I still wasn't sure why those dreams plagued me, but one thing was clear. I could no longer ignore them.

CHAPTER 6

I woke up the next morning just before the sun broke the horizon. The hills outside my window were washed in a hazy gray, and the sky was turning deep purple. I stretched and quickly downed a cup of coffee before moving on to the chores awaiting me. One day on the ranch was not so different from another. There was an endless list of jobs, and the earlier I completed them, the better. I don't know why I continued to hold onto the practice of rising before the sun and rushing into my morning work. Not long ago, it would've afforded me more time to spend with Elise, but now, it only offered more time to sit and contemplate. In my experience, idle time alone with my thoughts drained my peace. It was like a front-row seat to a show replaying all of my life's regrets. On the other hand, familiarity brought a sense of normalcy, and I felt comfortable keeping up with my old habits.

After pulling on my boots and hat, I buttoned up my coat and stepped outside into the brisk morning air. The fresh scent of dirt, the thin layer of dew covering the earth, and the sweet smell of the ponderosa pines welcomed me like a close friend. I breathed deeply, filling my lungs with the quiet, peacefulness of the morning. I didn't mind the labor. My body had grown accustomed to it, and I worked most days, giving little thought to the tasks at hand. I never grew weary of the beauty of this plot of land and the timber and mountain ranges surrounding it. When I stopped to take it all in, I could scarcely believe I owned such a magnificent stretch of countryside.

The ranch was just over five hundred acres, which Elise and I purchased to raise children and sheep. At the onset, we had hundreds of sheep, a couple of dogs, and two hired hands to help with the labor. Since Elise passed, I sold almost everything and let the hands go. By the time I'd finished, all that was left was the land, one mule named Hurley, and a dozen sheep. Sometimes, I wonder why I chose to stay. I could've sold it all and moved on. But the hard truth is, I had nowhere to go and no one to go with. There was no desire to return to the life I'd known before Elise, and I could not imagine any life ahead without her. Despite that, restlessness was growing inside me, but I knew it wasn't a condition to be cured by cutting ties and wandering the country.

As the sun rose, the sheep began to stir, and their bleating mingled with the distant chirping of songbirds. Their wooly coats stood out against the darkness of the dawn in various shades of white, gray, and brown. I watched them graze peacefully in the dewy meadow. As dumb and defenseless as they were, I loved and cared for those sheep. My responsibility was to keep them safe, tend to their needs, and ensure they survived and were kept healthy. In return, they provided me with just enough high-quality wool to keep them fed and cared for. Still, the work kept me busy, and the ranch kept Elise's memory alive.

I filled their troughs with the last of the hay left over from winter and watched them feed for a few minutes before carrying on with my day. By the time I'd gathered my tools and supplies, the sun was up, and I spent the rest of the morning mending fences that had buckled to the wear and tear of time. It was a condition to which I could relate.

Soon, I fell into a mindless rhythm of placing the wood, driving the nails, and securing the wire. It was a rhythm that allowed my thoughts to roam, and as I worked, my mind drifted back to my dream. The images flashed through my consciousness as vividly as they had the night before. I reflected on the star-filled sky, the plantation set ablaze, the burning figure of Titus, and the message he shared. The words and images all tore through my mind with each blow of the hammer, and before long, I was exhausted from all the mending and pondering. The meaning of it all still eluded me, slipping away like smoke through my hands. Never before had something felt so elusive yet so urgent.

With my energy waning, it was time for a break and a bucket of water. I sat on the front porch in one of the rickety old rocking chairs and wiped the sweat from my face and neck. The sheep had returned to grazing, and the sun had burned off the morning dew. It felt good to rest. I leaned back and closed my eyes as the cool breeze whispered through the tall grass. Though my solitary lifestyle was lonely, there was comfort in the doldrums of ranch life.

I was pulled from my rest by the clomping canter of a horse approaching and saw a lone rider atop a blue roan headed my way. "Mornin' friend," the rider called out as he pulled to a halt before me. It was the same fella I'd seen at the Rusty Nail the day before, who introduced himself as Sutton.

"Mornin'," I said, rising to my feet. "You in some kinda hurry today? You were movin' pretty good there." It was the first time in some while that I missed having a gun on me. After Elise and I married, I did away with all of my weapons except for a shotgun, which hung on the wall near the front door. Honestly, I never missed wearing a revolver on my hip. Not until that moment, anyway. This man made me nervous.

Sitting up tall in the saddle, Sutton smiled and paused momentarily. "Nah," he said as he patted his horse. "This old boy here just loves to move, that's all." When you spend enough time with outlaws, you learn to recognize a dangerous man when you see one, and Sutton was dangerous. He was old enough to possess a respectable amount of wisdom and still young enough to be quick with his iron. There was an unsettling confidence about him, likely the result of cockiness, expertise, or both. Either was enough to give me pause. The same could be said for the sniper rifle fixed to his saddle. His eyes scanned the property. "Nice place you got here."

"I appreciate it. Look, I mean you no disrespect, sir, but can I help you with something?"

"Why, I sure hope so," Sutton said in an easy manner. "Like I told you before, I'm lookin' for Drew Harlan. It's just business, but it's important that I find him."

"And like I told you," I said firmly, "I haven't seen Drew in years. I'm sorry, but I can't help you. Besides, I don't even know you. I got no reason to help you."

Sutton nodded and patted his horse. "You are absolutely right, and I sincerely apologize," he said with a lazy smile. "I suppose the last few weeks of sleepin' rough have resulted in my apparent lack of manners. Forgive me. My name is Sutton – first name Gregory."

"I know your name. You told me yesterday. What I don't know is why you're looking for Drew, who you work for, and how you know who I am. You called me by name yesterday."

Sutton laughed aloud. "Nothing gets by you, does it, Mr. Colter? They told me you was a smart one. Maybe we should just skip the pleasantries and get right to it."

"That's probably for the best."

"I work for Smiling Jack Davis," Sutton said, his smile fading. "And I know you ran with him for years."

"I know him alright. And yeah, I did run with him, but that was a long time ago. Maybe you can explain to me how you're workin' for a man locked up in a state penitentiary."

"Oh, you didn't know? Jack was released a few weeks ago. It seems they let him out on account of good behavior." I couldn't help but chuckle at those words. Smiling Jack was a man possessed of a variety of giftings, none of which included good behavior.

"Look, I don't want nothin' to do with Smiling Jack," I said. "When he turned himself in, the gang broke up. Everybody went their separate ways and started new lives, so if he sent you to track us down, you tell him I'm good right where I am."

"It's Drew he wants," Sutton said soberly. "When Jack went away, Drew made off with five thousand dollars. He wants his money, or he wants Drew dead."

"How does he know Drew has his money? Any of his degenerates could've taken it."

"True, but Jack said Drew was the only one who knew where the cash was hidden." He paused. "Smiling Jack is set on finding him. You know he won't stop."

"Yeah," I said. Sutton was right. Smiling Jack was one of the most stubborn, persistent men I'd ever known. He would find Drew eventually. "Well, look, I still don't know where Drew is, mister. I ain't seen him for near on five years now."

Sutton stared at me for a moment as if trying to make up his mind whether or not I was telling the truth. "Alright," he finally conceded. "If you do hear from Drew, tell him it'd be best if he stopped running. I'll be in Bozeman for another week. I'm staying at the Bozeman Hotel. Maybe we can work something out with him, but it's only gonna be worse if he runs."

"Yeah, I got it," I said. "If I see Drew, which I doubt, I'll let him know."

With a click of his tongue, Sutton's horse turned and trotted off. "You have yourself a good day, Moses Colter," he called out.

I watched him ride away, knowing it wouldn't be the last time I'd see him. I'd rather not tangle with such a man if I could avoid it, but men like Sutton generally don't stop shaking trees until something falls out. *What have you gotten yourself into, Drew?*

CHAPTER 7

The fact that Logan Ashbourne could get away with behaving so cruelly toward Titus and his family was more than my nine-year-old mind could grasp. Logan was only a boy. It was unfathomable how he could be so brazen, forcing Titus to beat his boys while he watched with sick satisfaction. No one deserved such cruelty. Seeing it changed me. I wasn't sure what it stirred within me, but it was something akin to fear mixed with shame. The Ivywood Plantation operated by a set of rules that were foreign to me. And though I was only a boy, it was clear that I'd better learn them quickly.

I wrestled with my thoughts as I sat in my room, waiting for my first meal with the Ashbourne family. Logan and I returned from our tour of the grounds, and Mrs. Ashbourne showed me around their home. I'd never seen such opulence, and I certainly never thought I'd call such a place my home. Something about the whole thing didn't feel real to me. Mrs. Ashbourne assured me this was as much my home as it was theirs. However, my gut told me this was all temporary, and I'd better not get used to it.

After a few minutes, Mrs. Ashbourne showed me the upstairs bedroom, which she said was mine. I'd never had anything to call mine, much less an entire room. She informed me about my responsibilities around the grounds and, with great excitement, told me of a tutor she'd hired for my studies. Practically gushing, she finished by saying how fortunate we all were that I was now part of the family. Mrs. Ashbourne was kind enough, but nothing about the plantation felt like home to me, and I wasn't convinced that would change anytime soon.

Having bathed and dressed as instructed, I sat at the desk by my bed and pulled out my small pack of belongings. Right on top was a book I recognized instantly. It was Drew's book, *A Practical Guide to Horse Breeds of the World*. Without my knowing, Drew had slipped it into my pack before I left, which was surprising, seeing as how much Drew treasured his book. I rubbed my hand over the cover before cracking it open. Flipping through the pages, I noticed that Drew had folded down a corner of one. He had circled a picture of a black Thoroughbred running wild through a grassy field. His favorite. Next to it, Drew had scribbled a note in the margins. *"I figured you needed this more than me. This here is my horse, so you'll need to pick another one. Make sure it's fast. One day I'll show up to get you and we'll take off! Your pal, Drew."*

There was a knock at my door, and I slammed the book shut and stuffed it into my pack. "Come in," I said, standing up and sliding the pack under my bed. The door creaked open, and Logan entered.

"Hey, Ma told me to check on you and make sure you were getting ready for supper. Everything good?"

"Yeah, I'm good. At least...I think so."

Logan shrugged. "You look alive to me. Don't be late." He turned to leave, then stopped and looked back. "Oh, I almost forgot. Supper will be at a quarter past six instead of six o'clock tonight. Papa is running late. I was supposed to let you know."

"Got it. Thanks," I said as Logan left, shutting the door behind him.

I spent a bit more time looking at horses but kept a keen eye on the clock. At twelve minutes after six, my nervousness got the best of me, so I took one last glance in the mirror at my fancy new clothes and raced downstairs to supper. I dashed into the dining room and saw a long table full of food. At the table were Mr. and Mrs. Ashbourne and Logan, each seated in front of an empty plate as gentle music played in the background.

I noticed Mrs. Ashbourne first. Her eyes were diverted, and she stared blankly at the white plate before her. My eyes soon found Logan, who looked like he was doing his darndest to suppress a laugh. Then, I locked eyes with Mr. Ashbourne. He was a heavy-set man with a thick white mustache, thin white hair, and a round, red face. As he glared at me, I felt a wave of anger emanating from his being. I wasn't sure what I'd done to offend him, but there was no mistaking the vitriol bubbling within him.

"You're late," he said without breaking his glare.

Logan used his napkin to conceal his smile. "I'm sorry, sir," I replied. "I thought I was on time."

"My wife told me you were a smart young man," he said blankly. I didn't reply. "Well, speak up, boy? Are you smart or not?"

"I'm not sure if –"

"Be careful how you answer, boy. I can't have some buck wild, hillbilly orphan coming into my home and accusing my wife of being a liar. So, are you indeed smart, or is my wife a liar?"

I may have only been nine years old, but I was smart enough to know I'd better answer correctly. "I don't believe Mrs. Ashbourne is a liar, sir. If she says I'm smart, then I must be smarter than I know."

"You were made aware that dinner is at six each night. It is now six-thirteen, which means the three of us have been sitting here for thirteen minutes, staring at our plates, waiting for you."

Logan giggled.

"I'm sorry, sir," I said. "I guess I lost track of time."

"In my experience, smart people seldom lose track of time, young man. Barring an emergency of some sort, I am never late. My wife is never late. My son and employees are never late. And if you want to remain in this family, you will never be late again. Is that clear?"

"Yes, sir."

"Now, seeing as how I have no reason to doubt my wife's assessment, I've determined that you are at least intelligent enough to be on time for supper. Therefore, given your blatant disregard for our established dinner time, I am left to confer one of three things. You are either lazy, defiant, or unappreciative of the good fortune with which the Lord has seen fit to bless you."

"It won't happen again, sir."

"I'd like to believe you, but whether or not I can trust your word remains to be seen," Mr. Ashbourne said as he unfolded his napkin and placed it in his lap. "As for tonight, you go on back to your room. The three of us will be enjoying this lovely meal without you. You can try again tomorrow. If you're late again, I'll have Harold escort you back to the orphanage. That or I'll put you outside with the servants, and you can work for your dinner as they do. Now, off with you."

I went back to my room that night and lay on my bed crying for what felt like hours. I was angry at myself for believing that coming here was a good thing. Even worse, I let Logan play me for a fool. Sure, I could have sold him out and told his old man that he lied to me about changing dinner time, but that's not how we did things at the orphanage. We didn't rat.

Sometime later, as I lay on the floor staring at the ceiling, there was a quiet knock at the door. I half expected it to be Mrs. Ashbourne stopping by to console me, but it wasn't. It was one of the house servants, a young girl I'd heard them call Lisi. She cautiously peeked through the cracked door. "Mr. Colter?" she said, barely above a whisper. "Mr. Colter, can I come in?"

"Yeah," I said. "Come in. You can call me Moses."

"Yes, sir, Mr. Moses." Lisi stepped into the room and placed a tray covered with a white cloth on the desk by my bed. "I brung you some supper." She took one last peek into the hallway. "Eat what you want and leave the tray outside when you done. I'll fetch it 'fore anybody know it's there."

"I don't want to get you in trouble," I said.

Lisi smiled and offered a dismissive wave. "Don't you worry none 'bout that. I'll be just fine, and I ain't lettin' no young man go hungry if I can help it."

"Thank you, Lisi," I said. With a nod, she left and gently closed the door behind her. I ate quickly and placed the covered tray in the hallway, as Lisi said. After changing, I jumped into bed and pulled the covers over my head. I cried as silently as possible until sleep finally overcame me.

CHAPTER 8

Situated just off of Main Street in Virginia City was a small Methodist church. It was surrounded by large trees that kept the building covered in restful shade and cool throughout the summer. I hadn't darkened the door of the place since Elise died, but now things were different. My dreams had intensified, and I needed answers. Hopefully, Reverend Phillips wouldn't think me a fool for putting so much stock in these dreams. He was a caring sort, so I figured he'd at least be gracious enough to hear me out. I was uneasy but still surprised to find myself looking forward to the visit. While I'd never been in the church outside of a Sunday service, I still considered it a house of solace, a holy place for those seeking answers.

Once inside, it was almost as if I could hear the whispered prayers of the past, muttered throughout the years by men and women of faith. I was sure those men and women were far more attuned than I was at hearing and receiving answers to those prayers. The sanctuary was modest by most standards, unlike many cities' large, extravagant cathedrals. Still, the scent of polished wood and candle wax, along with the streaks of colored light that filtered in through the stained glass windows, instantly calmed me. In that regard, it rivaled any lavish city church I could ever visit.

Two rows of weathered pews lined the walls on either side of the church, with an aisle down the middle. I found a spot near the front and settled into the creaking pew. I had no sooner sat down when Reverend Phillips entered from one of the back rooms. He smiled, and his eyes lit up as he hurried toward me with his hand outstretched.

"Good morning, Moses," he said warmly as I stood to shake his hand. "Please, keep your seat." He sat down next to me. "I'm so glad you stopped by. What can I do for you today?"

My hands were fidgeting with the frayed edge of my coat. "I'm not exactly sure," I said. "I just need some help sortin' a few things out."

"I'll do what I can," he answered with a furrowed brow. "Go on."

"First of all, I want to apologize for lying to you the other day," I said. "You asked me about my dreams, and I told you they'd stopped. The fact is they've gotten worse, and I was hoping you might be able to help me understand them. Tell me why I'm seein' these things."

I spent the next few minutes describing the visions I'd had. I told Reverend Phillips about the plantation and the fire that erupted around me but consumed nothing. He listened intently as I shared about Titus and how he was also engulfed in a fire that did not appear to harm him. I told him everything I could remember except what Titus said. "*The words of both the wise and the fearless will move you to action. To obedience. Once they have spoken, everything you need will be provided. The path will open before you. You will not go alone, and you will not be forsaken.*" I kept those words to myself. For some reason, I felt they were meant for me alone – something to hold on to.

When I'd finished, Reverend Phillips sat silently for a moment. His hands were clasped, and his face twisted in deep concentration. "Thank you for sharing that with me, Moses," he said. "Dreams are a mysterious thing. They can carry messages, provide warnings, or reveal hidden truth that our conscious minds must wrestle with to understand."

I leaned forward with my elbows on my knees. "But what do you think it means, Reverend? Why am I seeing these things?"

He paused, carefully weighing his words. "I believe dreams are glimpses into our spirit. On one hand, they reflect our deepest desires and fears. On the other hand, I believe God can speak through our dreams. It can be a call to examine our lives and our choices. But, beyond that, it's clear to me that the good Lord can use dreams to move us to action – to shed light on our purpose."

I was beginning to think sharing everything with Reverend Phillips was a mistake. "But how can I act on something I don't understand?"

Reverend Phillips smiled and placed a hand on my shoulder. "You're off to an honorable start," he said. "You're taking this seriously and seeking the counsel of those you believe to be wise, not that I claim to embody such a virtue."

"So you can't tell me what they mean?" I said, trying to hide my frustration. I'm sure I wasn't doing so well.

Reverend Phillips took a settling breath before answering. "I always try to be careful not to play the role of prophet. It's dangerous to assume

I know any better than anyone else, to interpret for people what the Lord is saying to them. I'm just a man, and I could be wrong." I attempted to interrupt, but Reverend Phillips held a finger up and continued. "However," he said, speaking over me, "it seems to me that these dreams may be a way of calling you back to where it all began for you. Have you considered that Titus and his people may need help and that you're the man for the job? Maybe it's time for you to make a trip back home and visit those you left behind in Tennessee."

A wave of uneasiness overcame me at the thought of returning to that place. The past held painful memories I'd long since packed away, and the idea of revisiting them made my stomach churn. "I left Tennessee a long time ago, Reverend. I've spent years trying to forget that place."

He nodded reassuringly. "I, for one, can certainly understand how painful the past can be. Digging up old memories we've spent a lifetime trying to keep buried can be overwhelming, but it can also bring healing. Those things you feel are stirring inside of you for a reason. What if there are people who need you?"

I leaned back against the creaky pew and exhaled. "That's a big 'if' to carry. Even if it's true, which I'm not sayin' it is, who am I to help anyone? I can barely take care of my land and myself."

"Listen, my friend, none of us are capable. None of us are worthy. The best any of us can do is to decide to be open and willing. If you decide to act on what you believe, everything you need will be provided. The path will open before you."

The reverend's words struck like a lightning bolt through my chest. How was it possible he'd used those exact words? Titus's words. My heart pounded, and I was overcome with what I could best describe as vulnerability mixed with a healthy amount of fear and doubt. "I wish I could believe that, Reverend," I said. "And for all I know, you may be right. But if I'm supposed to pack up and hit the trail to Tennessee, I'm gonna need a little more clarity."

"And I'll pray you get it," he said gently. "Unfortunately, that's not always the case. Sometimes, we have to choose whether to act or not based on what we *do* know. The willingness to act without having all the information is what we call faith."

My mind drifted back to the plantation and the men and women I'd known. Some of them I cared for deeply, and some of them I'd just as soon put a bullet in. Undoubtedly, there were those who felt the same about me.

"What if I go back to Tennessee and find nothing? What if it turns out to be somethin' I made up in my head? What if there's nothin' there for me but pain and regret?"

Reverend Phillips' eyes gleamed with compassion. "You may be wrong. You may decide to make a trip that leaves you feeling foolish and naive, but there is comfort in such foolishness. The Lord honors the type of faith it takes to act and blesses us for it. Many people believe wisdom comes with age, but I've found that wisdom isn't measured by the number of years we've spent on this earth. Wisdom is found in the journeys we take throughout the course of those years."

His words resonated within me just enough to scare the devil out of me. "I don't know if – I guess I'm – I'm just not sure what I might find. At the risk of soundin' cowardly, the truth is…I'm scared to face the past."

"Fear is a natural part of any journey, Moses. All of us are afraid. You can be afraid of who you are, who you've been, who you might become, or what you're capable of. But don't forget the one who made you. He knows your fears and your weaknesses. Thankfully, He directs our steps and fills us with whatever we need to complete the jobs He gives us."

Reverend Phillips and I finished our chat, and I made my way to the front doors, just as confused as ever. The weight of uncertainty clung tightly to my heart, but something stirred within me. I knew it wouldn't be easily shrugged off. The thought of striking out on nothing more than faith seemed foolish. But a small part of me lurking in the depths of my soul was growing restless. It was a voice that echoed through my bones, asking, *What do you have to lose?*

As I reached for the door, Reverend Phillips called out to me. "Moses, if you don't mind me asking, what is it about the plantation house in Tennessee that makes you so hesitant? What happened there?"

I dropped my eyes and took a deep breath. The truth was dancing on my tongue, but I wasn't sure how honest Reverend Phillips wanted me to be. *What does it matter anymore?* I asked myself. *Tell him the truth. What do you have to lose?* "Well, Reverend, it's nothing to be proud of, but I killed a man there when I was seventeen. I ran for my life and never looked back."

CHAPTER 9

Reverend Phillips didn't take my confession of killing as poorly as I thought. I had to hand it to him. His eyes bulged only briefly, but he was disciplined enough to hide it quickly. Like a seasoned gambler, his face remained blank and unreadable. The reverend had such conviction and assurance when it came to matters of the Lord, and I suppose he was a gambler in a sense. He'd decided at some point to go all in with the big man himself.

Regardless of how he mustered such a neutral demeanor, Reverend Phillips looked me in the eye and said, "Well, I suppose that gives us a lot to talk about next time." There was no judgment in his tone or his eyes, and he gave a slight smirk.

I nodded to him. "Next time, then."

There was so much to think about on the ride back home, so I decided to turn my mind off and do my best to think about nothing. It wasn't a difficult task for me. I loved riding, and I loved the serenity of nature. I hadn't ridden a proper horse in a while. Maybe one day I could save some money and buy a new one. I didn't need anything special, just a good, sturdy horse with a nice temperament and a pretty coat.

I got home, cared for the animals, and finished my evening chores. The last good hour, right before sunset, was my favorite part of the day. It meant the workday was over, and it was time to relax. I missed those times with Elise most of all. We'd sit outside, stare at the mountains in the distance, and talk about plans for our future until the stars were out. Those were beautiful talks, filled with hope and excitement.

As I trekked back to the ranch, I paused at the sound of approaching hoofbeats. A figure on horseback topped the crest off to the east, but it didn't look like Sutton. Something about the rhythm of those hooves pounding the earth felt familiar. As the rider came closer, my attention was drawn to his inky-black beast of a horse. The rugged mount snorted, huffed, and kicked up dirt as if he wanted to race through the valley like a bullet through butter.

Then I saw the rider, smiling like an idiot and waving as he approached. He pumped his fist and yelped like a cowboy driving a herd, even though he'd never worked as a real cowboy a day in his life. As customary, it was impossible not to smile when he came around. He had that effect on most folks, though some found him irritating. Still, there was something humorous, ridiculous, and endearing about him all at the same time. I called out as he rode up, "Drew Harlan? Is that you?"

Chapter 10

By the time I turned twelve, I had accepted the Ivywood Plantation as my home. Mrs. Ashbourne did her best to take on the role of a caring mother, but I could never bring myself to refer to her as my ma. And though they adopted me, Mr. Ashbourne never gave me his name. Looking back, I'm sure that must have pained her, but to her credit, she never let it show. She ensured I was provided for and taken care of, and it was a perfectly acceptable expression of love as far as I was concerned.

Mr. Ashbourne was a different story. There was never any doubt about how the man felt as it pertained to me. It was almost impressive how he uttered so few words, only addressing me when necessary or when Mrs. Ashbourne forced him. I can't say it troubled me much since I spent most of my days trying to avoid him. I never understood why he hated me so much. I tried to do what Drew told me. I stayed out of sight and did as I was told. It seemed like a lot of anger for Mr. Ashbourne to hold for a boy whose only offense was being fifteen minutes late to dinner on his first day.

Then there was Logan. As much as neither of us wanted to admit it, we were family. I was the rescued orphan with whom Logan was frequently annoyed. And Logan was the psychotic older brother I never had. Since he'd recently turned sixteen, Mr. Ashbourne decided Logan should spend more time learning the family business. Logan was his heir and would take over the plantation after his father was gone. The only problem with the plan was that from the moment Mr. Ashbourne gave Logan his new responsibilities, limited as they were, Logan began to act as if the plantation was already his.

Mr. Ashbourne said it would be best if Logan began his education by becoming an official member of the security team. He was to shadow Harold Gullet, the Overseer of the plantation, who was in charge of security and protection. If Ivywood Plantation was a small town, Harold Gullet was its corrupt sheriff. He had a reputation for being cruel and stoic, and he loved a good fight. Anyone looking at him sideways after he'd had a few drinks was sure to find out how quick he was to go to fists.

Gullet was not happy when he found out another duty had been added to his plate. Babysitting is what he called it when no one else was around. He didn't care for Logan Ashbourne any more than the rest of us. And like the rest of us, he simply had to nod, smile, and indulge the little twit, if only to ensure his own wellbeing. Logan felt entitled to his newfound power and position and immediately sought to abuse it.

Alongside Harold Gullet and his thugs, Logan roamed the plantation on horseback like an undersized, overconfident gunslinger. There was never any doubt that Gullet was the boss of the operation. Still, Logan rode along with such confidence that someone who didn't know better might've thought he was in charge. Logan was an annoying little lapdog, yipping and yapping at every worker and hand while out on patrol. Of course, Logan knew very little about the actual work going on, but it didn't stop him from regularly barking commands.

At sixteen, Logan knew everything. Whether sweeping the porch, shoeing a horse, or harvesting tobacco, Logan believed wholeheartedly that he knew a better, more efficient way to accomplish each task. Everyone on the plantation, from Mr. Ashbourne to Titus' young boys, knew it wasn't true, but it didn't matter. Logan was bulletproof. His overbearing nature had gotten worse of late, but the laborers simply responded to his impudence with, "Yessir, Mr. Ashbourne," and they would carry on with their tasks as usual.

As with his father, I also did my best to steer clear of Logan, with the exception of our six o'clock dinner. I had no choice then. Dinnertime was an especially important event in the household. One night, we took our seats at the table as usual just as the grandfather clock in Mr. Ashbourne's study rang out the hour. Servants brought out all of the food at once. There was roast with gravy, green beans, sweet potatoes, and hot biscuits. We bowed our heads as Mr. Ashbourne recited the same prayer he said each night – something about being thankful for our blessings and the bounty before us. As soon as he said "amen," we all dug in.

Mostly, we ate in silence, except for Mrs. Ashbourne, who worked like a pack mule trying to drag a meaningful conversation out of us. I suppose it was her misfortune to share a table with three dinner companions who answered most questions with a grunt. It was a valiant effort, but she eventually gave up, and we returned to the sound of chewing and forks clinking against china.

That night, Mr. Ashbourne was the first to initiate a proper discussion when he asked Logan, "How are you getting on with Harold? Tell me what you've learned."

Logan shrugged and swallowed before answering. "It's goin' alright, I guess. I don't know if I'm learning much of anything except what *not* to do."

"What do you mean by that?" Mr. Ashbourne said, wiping his mouth.

"I mean, Gullet's okay," Logan went on. "He runs a tight operation and keeps the grounds covered well enough, but I don't think the workers respect him like they should."

"How so?" Mr. Ashbourne said with a furrowed brow. "Surely they aren't back-talking or slacking on their work. I know Harold well enough to know he wouldn't stand for that."

Logan shook his head. "No, they aren't that stupid. They're just lazy. They work too slow and take too many breaks, especially those in the tobacco fields. We might see our profits shoot up if Gullet was a little tougher on them."

"I see," Mr. Ashbourne said. "Perhaps I'll talk with Harold and see if we can do anything about that." He smiled at Logan. "Way to keep an eye on things, son. You'll make a great businessman one day."

Logan looked quite pleased with himself as we turned our attention back to the meal before us.

"Dear," Mrs. Ashbourne said to her husband. "Why don't you ask Moses how his work is going?"

My days were quite full. In the morning, I had schooling with our tutor, Mrs. Arnold, immediately after breakfast. Then, I worked outside with a different crew in the afternoons. I had already worked the stables, cleaning up and learning how to care for the horses. I'd spent time repairing fences, chopped wood from the land we'd been clearing, and next week, I'd be working with Titus and his boys in the tobacco fields. I enjoyed the labor and was much more comfortable with those working on the land than with those who owned it.

Mr. Ashbourne huffed and took a long gulp of water before resigning himself to speak. "And what have you been doing this week, Moses?" he said with little enthusiasm.

"I've been out at the clearing. I'm helping take down trees and chop firewood. It's hot, but it's fun."

Logan snickered to himself as he shoved a biscuit in his mouth. I wasn't sure what he found funny, but I knew it was likely something directed at me.

"It's *fun*, you say?" Mr. Ashbourne said. "I can't say I've heard too many young men refer to physical labor as 'fun.' You just make sure you aren't having too much fun while you're out there. This plantation is a business, and we rely on every cent of income this land provides. It's serious work. Important work. Not to mention, it's what keeps food on your plate."

"Yes, sir," I said.

"Besides," he continued, "just what is it you find so fun about it?"

"I like the work alright and learning how to do all the jobs. But mostly, I think I like the people. They're good folks."

Mr. Ashbourne carefully put his fork down and leaned in toward me. "Now you listen here, Moses. You are a member of this family, albeit an adopted one, but the workers still see you as something close enough to my son. You are not a sharecropper, a servant, or a slave, so I won't tolerate you acting like one. Those men aren't your friends. You can't get too close to the help, or they'll lose respect for you. And, if they don't respect one of us, it's only a matter of time before they don't respect any of us. Do you understand what I'm telling you?"

"I understand, sir," I replied.

"Good. You keep going out there and working. Do your job well because Lord knows we need as many hands as possible. But you keep to yourself and cut out the fraternizing. I'll have Logan keep an eye on you to make sure you act accordingly."

"Yes, sir," I said. I did understand, but I didn't agree. The men and women who worked on the plantation were some of the kindest people I had ever met. They taught me how to do their jobs and didn't treat me like a nuisance. And unlike Mr. Ashbourne, they seemed happy to see me when I came around. I'd be careful, but I wouldn't be unfriendly.

Later that night, as I sat in my room working on my spelling lessons, I thought of how the plantation workers were the closest thing to friends I had. Even though most of them were much older than me, they accepted me.

It didn't take long for my thoughts to drift to my old friend Drew, and I wondered how he was getting along. I hadn't seen him since I left the orphanage, which had been nearly three years. I wondered if he was still there or if he had managed to run off. I was tired, so I put my book away and blew out the lamp when my attention turned to a tapping sound on the window. I leaped from the bed, crossed the room, and lifted the window to see a young man standing below me with a handful of rocks.

"I told you I'd come visit," Drew said, looking up at me with a huge grin. "You probably forgot all about me."

"Yeah, right," I called down to him. "Drew, how did you get in here?"

"Don't worry about that. Just get yourself down here before you get me caught."

Chapter 11

It had turned out to be quite a week. Not only did I meet a bounty hunter and talk to Reverend Phillips about my dream, but now I faced the biggest surprise yet. I could hardly believe my eyes. Still, there he was, Drew Harlan, riding atop a magnificent black stallion. Neither of them garnered any lack of attention. Drew jumped from the saddle and spread his arms wide. He had new riding clothes, every piece bright and clean, from his hat to his boots, and looked far more polished than he actually was. His was quite the contrast to my moth-eaten work attire. Drew's gun belt was as dark as his horse, with ornately carved black leather holsters for each hip. The pearl-handled revolvers gleamed in the fading sunlight. Drew always knew how to make an entrance.

"Well, if it isn't Drew Harlan. That is you, ain't it, Drew?" I said jokingly as I stepped toward him.

Drew raced up, grabbed me, and pulled me in tight. "Moses, my old friend, it's good to see you." His voice rang with joy and excitement as he held me at arm's length and slapped me firmly on both shoulders.

It had been a while, but he was the same Drew I'd known since we were kids, ruddy and handsome. "I can't believe you're here," I said. "It's been so long now. How'd you even know where to find me?"

Drew flashed a mischievous grin. "Well, you know me, Moses. I have my ways of trackin' men down." He motioned to the ranch around us. "Plus, you haven't been exactly hidin' out. I have to hand it to you; this is a nice life you've gone and made for yourself here."

"Thank you, Drew. Caring for these sheep can be more work than it's worth sometimes, but you can't argue with the view."

"No, sir, you cannot," Drew said, staring out across the valley and the mountains beyond. Suddenly, a flash of excitement beamed upon his face as if he'd remembered something important. He ridiculously clapped his hands and rubbed them together. "Where is she? Where's that pretty little lady of yours? I can't believe you went and got hitched without telling me." He walked toward the house, calling out. "Come on out here, miss. I gotta lay eyes on you and meet the young lass who stole my best friend. Don't worry, now. I promise I'm not near as mean or ugly as the man you married. There's no need for concern."

"Drew," I called after him. "Drew, there's nobody –"

"Come on now," he continued, yelling at the front door. "I know you can hear me, lady."

"Drew, listen, I –"

"Oh, I'm sorry," Drew said, racing back to me. He lowered his voice, and his eyes grew wide. "I bet you got some little ones in there she's tryin' to put to bed. My apologies, Moses. I should've known to keep my big mouth shut. Sometimes, things just start comin' out."

"Drew, there's no one here." Drew stopped, and I finally got his attention. "My wife, her name was Elise. We were married two summers back, but she passed away last year."

We stood there in silence while my words hung in the air like a thundercloud. "Oh," Drew said, removing his hat and rubbing his forehead. "Moses, I'm a first-class moron. I'm sorry, brother. I didn't mean to –"

"It's okay," I said. "I know you didn't mean no harm."

"I didn't," Drew said barely above a whisper. "What happened, Moses? And, if you don't mind me askin', did you and the misses have any children before...well, you know."

"We had a child," I said. "Almost anyway. Elise was pregnant, and there were complications. She died giving birth." I paused. "It was a girl, but the baby didn't make it either. I buried them together in town."

"Good Lord," Drew mumbled, shaking his head. "That may be the saddest thing I've ever heard."

"It's alright, Drew," I said. "I'm gettin' along okay. These things happen. Me and Elise, we were happy. I didn't have her for long, but at least I had her for a while." I knew I was making too little of things and denying how much it still impacted me. It was something I did often when bad things happened. Painful thoughts aren't as painful if you can avoid them long enough. That's what I used to believe anyway. Now, I think those thoughts and feelings just pile up somewhere in a dusty corner of your heart until they can no longer be contained. I figured they'd likely spill out eventually, but it wouldn't be today.

Drew and I didn't share the same withdrawn disposition. He felt many things and felt them deeply. I always admired how little Drew cared about what others thought of him. He was comfortable with who he was. I never had to wonder what Drew was thinking or feeling. Whether laughing or crying, he did so with his whole heart.

With a hand on his back, I walked the distraught Drew over to the front porch. We sat down in the rocking chairs and continued our conversation. Drew felt awful for nothing more than being true to who he was, and he apologized far more than necessary. I thought I'd change the subject to ease his regret. Lighten the mood.

"I have to say," I began, taking in his polished appearance, "you sure look...different. Dare I say, a little too fancy feathered for your own good."

Drew glanced down at himself and chuckled, and his energy returned. "Yeah," he said. "I've been doing pretty good for myself. I worked as a scout and a guide for a few rich city folks for a while. And, recently, I've been runnin' bounties, believe it or not."

"What a world we live in," I said. "A former outlaw, hired to chase down present-day outlaws, all while dressed like a dime novel dandy."

"You go ahead and laugh," Drew said. "Get it all out. But, the truth is I'm darn good at it. Not to play my own fiddle, but I've earned quite the reputation as a hired gun. One of the best around these parts is what they're saying." He shrugged. "If you believe the rumors."

"Is that right? A gunman. One of the best?"

Drew nodded. "So, they say."

"Well, I'm happy for you," I said. "So you're good then? Everything's alright?"

"Right as rain, brother. Right. As. Rain."

"Uh-huh," I said, "You know, a fella came around here lookin' for you a couple of days back. Goes by the name of Sutton. Said he was working for Smiling Jack."

"I see," Drew said, diverting his eyes. "I hoped that wouldn't happen."

"Hoped it wouldn't, but figured it would, right? That the reason you're here now?"

"I am thoroughly offended by that," Drew said, slipping back into his jovial nature. "I haven't seen you for four years now, and the –"

"Five years."

"Four years, five years – who can keep up with these things?" he went on. "The point is, I ain't seen you since you took off, and they locked up Jack. You left me out on the trail with those degenerates of his. That I can forgive and forget, seeing the extenuating circumstances. But you are my best friend. My brother. And it pains me that the minute I show up, you start accusing me of bein' in trouble. Of needin' help. Of havin' less than honorable motives. It's hurtful, Moses. Downright hurtful."

"You stole the five thousand dollars from Jack, didn't you?"

"Stole is such an ugly word," Drew said. "I didn't *steal* his money. I...borrowed it. I thought I'd make a few lucrative investments while Jack was away. Besides, we all earned that money. I was shot at just as much as Jack, probably more. I always planned on payin' it back anyway; I just –"

"You just didn't figure on Jack gettin' out of prison early."

"Yep."

"Tell me about these lucrative investments you made," I said. "They include a Thoroughbred stallion, pearl-handled Colt revolvers, and some fancy new duds?"

Drew grinned. "How'd you know?"

"How much money you got left? You could give him what you have and try to work something out for the rest."

"That's a good idea," Drew said. "Very good, but see, I had a bad run at the blackjack tables a while back. Let's just say things didn't go exactly as planned."

"Meaning you lost all of Smiling Jack's cash," I said, "and now you've gotta go crawling back to him and hope he doesn't put a bullet between your eyes."

"That about sums it up," Drew said. "Of course, Sutton could always get to me first."

"What do you know about this Sutton?" I said. "He could be sellin' snake oil as far as I know, but he sure carries himself like a seasoned gunman."

"I ain't gonna lie," Drew said. "That Sutton is a scary fella. I never ran with him myself, but I've seen his work. Darn near shot up a whole town south of Harrodsburg, all just to bring in a bounty. Bad part was the fella he was after was a skittish little rabbit of a man. He was wanted for falsifying train tickets, for Pete's sake. The old boy was hidin' out in a room at one of the saloons when Sutton found him. Sutton went in, shot seven men, grabbed the pencil pusher, and high-tailed it out of town. Two of the men he shot weren't even armed. He was gone before the sheriff ever knew what happened. Of course, nobody saw nothin'."

"He doesn't sound like the kind of man you want tailin' you," I said.

"I'll figure it out," Drew said dismissively. "Besides, contrary to your unfavorable opinion of me, I didn't come here to burden you with my problems."

"I'm just givin' you a hard time. You know I'll help you any way I can."

"You got five thousand dollars?" he said with a chuckle.

"I got about a buck-fifty in a jar on the mantle. You're welcome to it. Money like that'll keep you stocked with coffee for at least two days."

Drew laughed. "Truth be told, I was passin' through on my way to Bozeman to meet with Jack and try to straighten this mess out. I heard you were close by, so I asked around town a bit, and here I am. I actually have some news for you."

"I can't wait to hear this," I said.

"I'm afraid it's not good news," Drew continued. "Or maybe it is for you. I'm not sure. I passed through Jonesborough a few months ago. I thought I'd ride by and see Mr. and Mrs. Peabody. You know, to let them see what a fine, outstanding citizen they raised. The whole place was gone, Moses. There was nothin' but an empty lot where Grace House used to sit."

"Do you know what happened?" I said, leaning forward in my chair.

"Well, you know me, I got to askin' around and found out that old man Peabody died a few years back. Old age, I guess. They told me Mrs. Peabody passed soon after. Didn't say of what. Anyway, they didn't have any kids to leave the building to, so it went up for auction. Some rich fella from Denver bought it for little of nothing. He's gonna build a hotel."

"I wish I could've seen them one last time," I said. "Talked to them. I guess I should've realized they were gettin' older, but, in my mind, they were kinda frozen in time. Like they'd always be the same age and doin' the same things, you know?"

"Maybe, but when I was a kid, I thought they were about one sneeze away from the dirt," Drew said. "I'm impressed they made it as long as they did."

"Since you brought up Tennessee, I was wondering if I could get your opinion on something."

"Sure," Drew said. He sat up on the edge of his seat. Drew loved to give his opinion, but even more than that, he loved being *asked* to give his opinion.

Disregarding my initial hesitation, I told Drew all about the dreams I'd had. He sat quietly and listened intently as I relayed most of the details. His face was somber, and his eyes were pinched tight.

Some were unnerved by Drew's ability to switch from being foolhardy to serious so quickly. I knew him, though. It wasn't always easy for Drew to pay attention when folks were talking. But he'd lock in if it was something he knew was important. He wouldn't miss a word and could recall every detail for days. I swear, when Drew was in that headspace, you could fire off a cannon beside him, and he wouldn't blink.

When I finished, Drew sat quietly contemplating while I waited for him to respond. After a moment, he finally spoke. "It's quite the coincidence you would tell me all this now."

"Coincidence?" I said. "How's that?"

"I thought you would've already heard," Drew said. "But after hearin' your story, I'm not sure you have. See, I wasn't finished tellin' you about what I learned in Jonesborough," he said. "Long story short, the Peabody's aren't the only ones pushin' up daisies."

"What do you mean?"

"I hate to be the one to break it to you," Drew went on, "but Mr. and Mrs. Ashbourne are gone too. Happened about a year ago. It seems there was a fire. The plantation house burned down with them in it."

"Hmm," I said, taking it all in. I wasn't sure whether or not the news should be upsetting, but it wasn't. Maybe I felt a touch of something for Mrs. Ashbourne, but not enough to draw any real emotion from me. "What about Logan?"

"Logan was gone on a month-long huntin' trip," Drew said. "He came home and had to bury his folks, as well as a few house servants. From what I hear, he's in charge of the whole operation now. And what I hear ain't good at all."

"Tell me what you found out."

"Logan took over, and things are bad," Drew said, inching closer. "He's mistreatin' the workers somethin' awful. Neighbors miles away say sometimes they can hear the screams of the ones he lined up for a beatin'. Says it happens on a nightly basis. The bartender at the saloon told me Logan shot three of them tryin' to escape just a month before."

"He shot them? He can't just shoot people," I said, anger rising in me.

"I guess he can if they're his property," Drew said.

"They ain't his property," I snapped. "Slaves were freed a long time ago, in case you haven't heard. Besides, those men and women never were the Ashbourne's property."

"Apologies, Moses," Drew said. "I didn't mean to upset you."

"I know, Drew," I said, sinking back into my chair. "It's not like the sheriff there would do anything about it. If I know Logan, I'm sure he has the law in his pocket by now. Did you hear anything else?"

"Nothin' worth remembering."

I took a deep breath and released it slowly. "What do you think about my dream? What do you make of it all?"

Drew leaned back and rocked a bit. "I don't know much about things of a heavenly nature," Drew began. "But, I figure I know just enough. The way I see it, if the good Lord decides to make Himself as clear as a summer's night to me, I better listen."

I shook my head. "I'm glad all of this seems clear to you," I said. "Because it's kinda muddy to me."

"Nah, it ain't muddy at all; you just don't wanna see it. Those people need you, and you gotta help them. You know it, Moses. You know it's true."

"I don't know any such thing," I said. "Sometimes, a dream is just a dream. Nothin' more."

"That's not the kind of talk I'd expect from you." Drew tried to explain several times before he finally primed the pump enough to find the right words. "Listen, I never claimed to be a wise man, but I sure ain't a scared one."

"What does that mean?"

"It means I think you're actin' yella – respectfully, of course. If you were locked up, held against your will, and whipped on the daily, you better believe I'd come for you. I'd ride in, spit flyin' and guns blazin'. I'd like to think you'd do the same for me."

"You know I would," I said.

"Then why won't you do it for them?"

"Look, I'm not scared," I barked. "I'm just – It's like – I don't know what I am."

"You're scared," Drew said. "You just don't want to admit it. Like I said, a lack of wisdom has caused me no small amount of trouble in my days." He raised a finger. "But being fearless has saved my hide more than once."

"And which is the better virtue, wisdom or fearlessness?"

Drew scratched his jaw and squinted. "I don't know," he said. "Maybe they're both just as important. Maybe the wise and the fearless need each other."

The wise and the fearless. As much as I hated to admit it, Drew was right. I was scared. But hearing Reverend Phillips and Drew say words I'd never shared with either of them gave me pause. "The words of both the wise and the fearless will move you to action," I muttered to myself.

"Okay, I don't know what all that means," Drew said, "but I do know that you're wastin' away out here. You gotta change something. You gotta do something."

"You may have a point," I conceded. "It's not like there's a whole lot keeping me here anymore. I could get rid of all of it."

"It's a fine place," Drew said. "It's just that, right now, it seems like more of a prison than a home. You don't have to get rid of it. Keep it. Just leave it for a while. Have an adventure, and then come back to it. Then maybe you'll see it differently."

"I hate it when you make sense," I said.

"How about this?" Drew began, "You come with me to smooth things over with Jack. He always liked you better than me anyway. If you're with me, I just might have a chance of surviving. We'll celebrate like old times, and then you can make your way down to Tennessee."

"I'll tell you what, Drew," I said. "I'll go with you and keep Smiling Jack from murdering you, and in exchange, you come with me to Tennessee. Help me get those folks out of there alive."

A slow smile stretched across Drew's face, and he gave out a yelp loud enough to rile up the coyotes in the distance. "You got yourself a deal," he said. "This is gonna be just like old times. Moses and Drew on the trail once more. That's a good name for a book, don't you think?"

"I don't know about all that," I said with a grin. "How about we get some sleep tonight and head into town for breakfast tomorrow? We'll figure everything out then."

"Best plan I've heard all day," Drew said. He laughed and shook his head like he couldn't believe a trip was happening. Then he locked eyes with me, and his smile faded. "Moses...I really am sorry about your wife and daughter. I know I'm a shoddy substitute, but I'm here for you.

I'm here to help now. You don't have to have it all figured out just yet. Sometimes, the things we're looking for come when we least expect them."

Chapter 12

Drew and I awoke before sunrise, and he helped with the morning chores. It was quiet and chilly out, and the sky was covered in billowy, gray blankets of clouds. Having an extra pair of hands was helpful, and we made short work of the morning duties. It was still dark out when we finished.

"That is one fine beast you have there," I said as we checked in on Drew's horse. "What do you call him?"

"This here's Stormy," Drew said, patting the stallion like a proud papa. "He's the horse I've wanted my whole life. I bought him off a trader in St. Louis a while back. Never ridden one faster, I can tell you that. What about you? What are you ridin' now?"

"Oh, I've just been hitching up Hurley over there." I pointed to the stubborn mule who stared at us, chewing straw hanging from both sides of his mouth.

"You mean you don't have a horse?" Drew said. "What kind of cowboy are you?"

"I'm not a cowboy. You don't see no cows around here. I'm a rancher – a sheep rancher."

Drew smirked. "A rancher with the finest twelve sheep I've ever laid eyes on."

Drew and I made our way into town at a leisurely pace, which Stormy didn't seem to appreciate. On the other hand, Hurley was quite content with our progress. He was familiar enough with the route and typically made the trip with little to no direction from me. I'd put the shotgun in the buckboard that morning before we left. With all the talk of Sutton, Smiling Jack, and Logan Ashbourne, I felt a little anxious going around unarmed.

Drew and I left Stormy and Hurley at the livery once we were in Virginia City. On any other day, I would have kept Hurley attached to the wagon and out of the way somewhere while I took care of my business. But Drew said he'd pay for it, so I agreed. It was still early enough that there weren't many folks around as we made our way down Main Street toward the Rusty Nail.

Jimmy Tittle greeted us as we entered, and we sat near the back of the saloon. Aside from Skillet, who was propped up at the bar and halfway through his first drink of the day, we were the only ones in the place.

"Quite a lovely establishment you have here," Drew said as Jimmy poured us some coffee.

"Thank you, sir," Jimmy replied, unaware of the sarcasm in Drew's voice. The Rusty Nail was nothing fancy and could've used a bit of cleaning, but the coffee was strong, and the food was hot.

"It'll do," I said to Drew as Jimmy returned to his post at the bar. "These people here are good folks."

Drew nodded toward Skillet. "What about him? What's he all about?" he said in a low voice. "He think there's still a war going on? If so, the government oughta issue him a bigger coat."

"He's alright," I said. "He's just a bit odd, that's all."

Drew finished his breakfast and pushed his plate away before taking a big sip of coffee. "Let's get down to it," he said. "We've got a few things to figure out. First off, I've been thinkin', and I can't figure out how we're going to make this happen."

"Make what happen?"

"Moses, I know you want to help those people at the plantation. Hell, I do, too. But, right now, I don't know how we're gonna get to Bozeman, much less Tennessee. You don't even have a horse."

"I can ride Hurley," I said.

"That's a fine plan until the shootin' starts. If we get into a scrape and have to hotfoot it, that mule of yours ain't gonna put any distance between you and Jack's boys."

"Maybe not," I said. "But I'd rather not have any shootin' to begin with."

"Everybody'd *rather* not get shot at," Drew said. "But sometimes things happen. Don't act like you don't know about that life. We were in it together, remember? You know how things can go bad fast."

"Maybe I can rent a horse from the livery."

Skillet coughed a bit, then squirmed in his seat to face us. "Horse trader's in town today," he said with a grunt. "Got some fine animals from what I've heard."

Drew ignored him and kept talking. "Also, how many people would you say we'll be taking from the Ashbourne's plantation?"

"I don't know how many will come with us," I said, "but altogether, there's probably about a hundred, a hundred-fifty."

"A hundred and fifty?" Drew yelped, slapping his hand on the table. "How are we gonna move that many people? How would we feed them? We'll need wagons, supplies, and a few hired guns for protection. And where are you planning on taking them? We can't just leave them to wander around in the wilderness."

Drew's questions, valid as they were, sucked the wind from me. "I don't know," I said. "I haven't had time to think this through. Maybe I was a fool to think this was possible. It's probably best if we drop the whole thing. I ain't nothing special, and I sure ain't got the means to put this plan into action."

"Don't get all down about it," Drew said. "There ain't nothin' here that can't be figured out. These are all just obstacles to overcome. You seemed pretty sure about it yesterday. Don't start doubtin' your plans now just 'cause I start pokin' holes in 'em."

The words Titus said to me in my dream played in my head, "*The path will open before you. You will not go alone, and you will not be forsaken.*"

"Whether or not I have doubts don't matter much," I said. "If we don't have the money, it ain't happening regardless."

Skillet coughed again, which, at this point, I was sure was intentional. He stood and faced us. "I got money," he said.

"Good for you, old man," Drew answered. "Maybe you can use it to buy yourself another arm."

"Don't you get uppity with me, boy," Skillet said. "You have some respect for your elders. I'm tryin' to help."

I held a hand up to quiet Drew. "He don't mean no harm, Skillet. He's just a loudmouth is all."

"Yeah, well, somebody's gonna' shut it for him one day," Skillet said with a huff.

Drew stood up. "Any day you're ready, old-timer. Name it."

"Sit down, Drew," I said. He did. "Skillet, what's all this about you having money?"

"Shhh," Skillet said, glancing around even though no one else was there. "We can talk, but not here." Then, he shot a glare at Drew. "And not in front of him."

"Don't mind me," Drew said as he stood and headed for the door. "I got some things to take care of. Moses, I'll meet you at the livery when you're done." Drew left, and Skillet motioned for me to follow him outside.

Skillet and I walked down Main Street in the opposite direction of the livery. When we were sufficiently far enough from the saloon, according to Skillet's estimation, he continued. "I got money," he said. "Plenty of it. Enough for whatever we'd need."

"*We?*" I said. "What are you gettin' at?"

"I want in," Skillet said. "I want to help you boys rescue them poor folks you were talkin' about. Tennessee, wasn't it?"

"I don't know, Skillet," I said. "This could be a dangerous trip, and I don't know if I feel good about takin' your money anyway."

Skillet groaned. "Far as I see it, you wouldn't be takin' anything. I'm offerin' to give it up willingly. And, so we're clear, I ain't scared of a little danger. I was a military man, you know?"

"I know," I said. "I didn't mean any disrespect."

"Besides," Skillet went on, "I was a cook for the Union. I had to look after an entire regiment. A couple of hundred on a wagon train don't spook me. I'll handle gettin' the supplies and some folks to help out. And if it should come to it, I'm also good in a fight."

"Is that right?"

"Look, I know I only got one arm, but I can stir a pot and shoot a Winchester good as anybody. Probably better than that greenhorn you've thrown in with."

"It's not a bad idea," I said reluctantly. "But I need to know where this money came from. I thought you were broke. Lord knows you've bummed enough drinks off people. I've never even seen you when you weren't at least half drunk. I appreciate the offer, but I ain't lookin' to finance this thing with stolen money and equipment."

"I ain't stole nothin', Moses," Skillet said, raising his voice. "And just because I enjoy a drink now and then don't make me a drunk. I made money being a soldier. And I made even more for losin' my arm. I get a check every month from the government, and I ain't never spent a nickel of it."

"You keep it all in the bank?"

"The bank?" Skillet said with a sour face. "I don't trust the bank to do nothin' but cash checks. I hide my money away somewhere safe."

"I just...I'm not sure, Skillet," I said.

"Listen," Skillet went on with a touch of sincerity. "You're young enough that you don't think about these things, but I may not have much time left on this earth. I mean, you see how I live. I just want to do somethin' good with the time I've got left. I've got money, and I ain't got no family to leave it to. Let me help. Let me go with you. You're a good man, Moses. If you've set your mind to helpin' these people, then I know you've got your reasons. I may not know your reasons, but I reckon they're likely good."

"And what about Drew?" I said. "You don't seem too keen on him. You gonna be able to get along? It's a long trip, you know?"

"Ah, I ain't worried about the likes of him," Skillet said. "I knew hundreds of hayseeds just like him in the service. All hot air and grandstanding. I just hope the fella can handle his iron as well as he runs his mouth."

"You can trust Drew," I said. "He crows like a rooster sometimes, but he can handle himself. And he won't take off when things get tough."

"Good to know," Skillet said, nodding. "If you trust him, then I'll give him a chance. But I *will* keep an eye on him."

"I sincerely appreciate the help, Skillet, but I still feel ill at ease about takin' your money."

"Then don't," Skillet said. "You won't ever have to lay eyes on a coin of it. As far as you know, God could've dropped it from the sky. I'll take care of everything. You can trust me."

"Thank you, Skillet," I conceded. "I guess this is happening then?"

"Oh, it's happenin'," Skillet said. "But first, you need a proper horse. The man I told you about – the horse trader settin' up behind the livery. He's an old friend of mine. Name's Calhoun. Tell him to put it on my tab and pick out whatever horse you want. But make it a good one. Calhoun won't give you any trouble."

"You sure?"

"I've never been more sure of anything in my life."

CHAPTER 13

"About time you got here," Drew said. He was waiting for me outside the livery. "I thought you might've had a change of heart."

"Sorry to keep you waiting, Your Majesty," I said. "But while you were out here doin' whatever it was you were doin', I was busy securing the funds for this job of ours."

"You serious?" Drew said, wide-eyed. "You mean you got somebody to put up the money? That fast? Just like that?"

"Just like that."

Drew dropped his shoulders and stared at the sky. "Please tell me you didn't tell that old cuss at the bar he could come with us," Drew said. "What was his name? Fryin' Pan?"

"His name is Skillet, and yes, he's coming with us. He's coming because he's willin' to foot the entire bill, and he was a cook for the Union Army. He'll keep our camp well stocked and make sure the men, women, and children are fed. And, since it ain't costing us a nickel, you're gonna make an effort to get along with him. You have to. I'll lose my mind if I have to listen to you two jawin' at each other the whole way."

"Yeah, I hear you," Drew said. He could be hardheaded, but he knew how generous it was for Skillet to agree to pay. "Just no more surprises, okay?"

"I do have one more surprise for you," I said with a grin as Drew groaned. "Well, not exactly. Maybe it's more of a surprise for me."

"As long as you don't tell me Skillet has a wife and six kids comin' with us, I'll be fine," Drew said.

"Oh, just come on."

Drew and I walked around the livery and went downhill to where the horse trader had set up. It was late morning, and people were stirring. A good-sized crowd gathered at the corral as the trader brought out his horses. He had about two dozen in all, beautiful creatures with fresh, clean coats that shined in the morning light. The corral smelled of hay, leather, dirt, and manure. I loved that smell. And so did Drew. I never knew anyone who loved horses more than Drew, and these were impressive, to say the least.

"Wait," Drew said, his mouth hanging open. "You're gonna buy a horse?"

I nodded. "Whichever one I want."

"Skillet?" Drew said with a grin as I nodded. "Okay, but I'm helping you pick. I can't leave this up to you, or you'll end up ridin' outta here on another mule."

"How can I help you gentlemen?" the trader said as he approached. He was a hefty man with a drooping handlebar mustache and a dusty bowler hat. All smiles and handshakes, I imagined I could be looking at Drew thirty years from now.

"Are you Mr. Calhoun?" I said.

"Well, Calhoun's right, but I don't get called 'mister' very often," he said with a hearty chuckle.

"Good to meet you. My name is Moses Colter, and this here's my associate, Drew Harlan."

"Associate?" Drew muttered with an upturned lip. "What kind of business you runnin'?"

"I'm lookin' for a horse, Mr. Calhoun," I said before Drew could interject any further.

"You've certainly come to the right place," Calhoun said. "If I don't have what you need, I can get it for you. All from the finest stock."

"A friend of mine named Skillet told me he knows you," I continued. "He said you two were close."

Drew raised his eyebrows. "So Skillet's a friend, but I'm an *associate*?"

I continued to ignore him.

"Skillet and I go quite a ways back," Calhoun said. "Served together. I've eaten his grub more than I'd care to admit. He's a bit of an unconventional fella but a loyal friend still. I hoped to see him if he still resides around these parts."

"I'm sure you'll see him around," I said. "He don't roam too far from the saloon. Anyway, Skillet said to tell you it was okay for me to put a horse on his tab. Said you'd know he was good for it."

"Absolutely," Calhoun said. "Skillet's credit is certainly good with me, Mr. Colter. And any friend of Skillet's is a friend of mine. Now, what are you in the market for? Something for work? Cattle driving? Transportation?"

"He needs something fast," Drew said. "Strong and fast."

Calhoun looked at me, and I nodded. "I'll pull a few for you to take a look at," he said.

It had been a long time since I'd felt excited about much of anything, but my heart was racing while I waited for Calhoun to show me his horses. The first one he brought out was a sturdy Quarter Horse gelding. A Chestnut. He was a muscular one, and he moved slowly but with purpose.

"I don't like him," Drew said.

"What? Why not?" I said. "He's a fine horse."

"Yeah, but I don't like his eyes," Drew said, turning his head sideways to get a better look. "They're scared eyes. I don't trust scared eyes – not in men or horses. Let's keep lookin'."

The second horse Calhoun showed us was a spirited, young, dappled gray Appaloosa. He moved about playfully and had a little gleam in his eye. I was keen on the creature's disposition. He was lively and a little rowdy.

"No thanks," Drew called out. "This one's too inexperienced. He's a fine animal, but not for what you'll need."

I wondered if the man had any horse Drew would approve of. And then, Calhoun brought out a Palomino mare with a flaxen mane and tail. She was graceful and powerful, a big girl with solid legs and determined movement.

"If you're looking for speed," Calhoun said, "this old gal is faster than a scalded cat. She may not have the most genteel pedigree, but she's healthy, strong, and ain't scared of nothin'. You should know I only carry the best and stand by every horse I sell."

"I like her," Drew said, though I'm not sure he had any legitimate reason to support his opinion. "What do you think, Moses?"

"She got a name?"

"She'd be yours to name as you see fit," Calhoun said. "I've just been calling her Beauty."

Drew and I looked the mare over for the next few minutes. Everything was on the up and up, and she appeared healthy. I made eye contact with a grinning Drew and immediately felt like an excited kid again. "I'll take her," I said.

"Excellent," Calhoun replied. "Are you planning on riding her out of here? Do you have any tack or equipment with you?"

I shook my head. "Nah, but I may need to check with Skillet before spending any more of his money."

Calhoun waved his hand at me. "Not to worry, young man," he said. "I'll ensure you have everything you need, and I'll tell Skillet it was my doing. I don't want to hold you boys up any longer than need be. Besides, Skillet owes me."

"Thank you, Mr. Calhoun," I said. "That's very kind of you."

After a short wait, Mr. Calhoun led the Palomino out. She was saddled and ready to ride. "I think you'll find you have everything you need here," Calhoun said. "Not knowing you and your associate's exact line of work, I took a few liberties. I hope you don't mind. I included the rifle scabbards, saddlebags, and bedroll."

"He doesn't mind at all," Drew interjected. "Thank you for your help."

"Strictly out of curiosity," Calhoun said, smiling, "but did you decide on a name for her?"

I knew immediately. "Her name's Cali," I said.

Calhoun shrugged. "Not the most common name for a horse, but I'm sure it won't make any difference to her. You have a good day, Mr. Colter, and enjoy your new companion." He patted Cali's neck. "And goodbye to you too, old gal. Be good to this man." Mr. Calhoun shook our hands one last time before returning to work the crowd.

Drew and I led my new horse over to the livery as we chatted. "How do you feel about her?" Drew said, nodding to Cali.

"I can't wait to get her out there on the trail," I said. "By the way, thanks for your help."

"Don't mention it," he said. "But wait here, I got something to give you." Drew ducked into the livery and returned with an armful of goods, which he placed on the ground.

"Merry Christmas," he said. "First, take this." He handed me a gun belt with two holsters. "Since it's embarrassing you don't have your own."

"Fair enough," I said.

"And this too," he went on as he tossed me a jacket. It was a brand-new duster.

I'd never owned a duster. As I'd explained to Drew many times, I wasn't a cowboy, nor did I want to dress like one. "It's not really something I'd ever wear, but thanks," I said.

"Oh, yes, you will wear it," Drew said. "I can't have you walking in to see Smiling Jack lookin' like some yokel. It's new, and it's clean. There's a shirt and pants here, too."

"Drew, I don't think Smiling Jack is going to care if –"

"And I got a shaving kit so you can trim that mangy coyote fuzz off your face. You've got to pull yourself together, Moses. Now, go get changed so we can get out of here."

"We can't take off just yet," I said. "I got no one to look after the ranch."

"Taken care of," Drew said. "I met that reverend friend of yours while you and Skillet were having your secret meeting. Nice fella. I explained everything to him. Told him we'd be heading out today and that you needed someone to take care of your place for a few days. He said to take as long as you need – that he'd get the church folk together, and they'd start this afternoon. I thought it strange that he looked so happy to hear you were leaving, but since he offered to help, I didn't ask any questions."

"I appreciate that, Drew," I said. "The reverend is a man of his word. He'll take care of things. I suppose you had a productive morning after all."

"Yeah, just hurry up and go change," he said. "Oh, and one more thing." Drew dug into his bag and pulled out two revolvers. He handed them to me, grip first. "Here, these are for you."

"Drew, where'd all this come from?"

"Let's just say I truly *have* spent all of Smiling Jack's money now," Drew said with a smirk. "We're officially broke."

"Well, you could take one of these back," I said, holding up one of the revolvers. I glanced down at the pearl-handled revolvers on Drew's hips. "You know as well as I do nobody needs two revolvers. The second one's always for show."

"And what's wrong with that?" Drew said. "Trust me, brother, you could stand a little more showmanship in your life."

"Can you believe everything that's happened in just a few short hours?" I said.

"I have to agree, it's pretty amazing. Almost like it was meant to be," Drew said.

"You know I couldn't have made all this happen without you."

"Well, good for you, you don't have to," Drew said.

CHAPTER 14

At twelve years old, I had yet to hit any noticeable growth spurt, but Drew, at fourteen, was all angles and elbows. It was as if someone took the Drew I remembered and stretched him out faster than his frame could keep up. His well-worn shirt was too short to tuck in, and the sleeves were rolled up past his elbows. Drew's pants were full of holes and didn't even cover his ankles. I felt guilty about how well I was dressed. I didn't deserve nice things any more than Drew, and seeing how different our lives had become was painful.

Nonetheless, Drew had managed to sneak onto the plantation, and I couldn't have been happier to see him. I had no genuine friends to speak of. Logan was a horrible excuse for a sibling, and I had to be careful acting too friendly with the workers. I couldn't risk angering Mr. Ashbourne. By the time I made it out of the house to join Drew, it was nearly half past one that morning. We trekked across the plantation grounds, careful to keep off the pathways and out of sight. The last thing either of us needed was to get caught.

Though it was dark, it was still warm out. The cicadas were singing, and their high-pitched trills and ticks gave life to an otherwise quiet, stagnant night. We sneaked across the plantation like a couple of jittery raccoons, making our way to the stables. It was Drew's only request.

"Thanks for showing me," Drew whispered.

"Sure thing," I said. I pointed to the stables. "The horses are just up there, but let's wait a minute and watch. I don't want Gullet to catch us."

"Who's Gullet?" Drew said.

"His name's Harold Gullet, and he's the overseer here. Trust me, Drew, he ain't the friendly type. Let's keep it down until we get to the stables."

Crouched low behind the wagon shed, Drew and I listened intently. Hearing anything over the relentless cicadas was challenging, but we did our best. We were on alert for any sounds or movement nearby, but there was nothing. Everything was still.

"You know, Moses," Drew said. "I'm embarrassed to admit it, but I've never ridden a horse before."

"What? Never? But you love horses. You talk about cowboys and riding all the time."

"Yeah, I talk about it, but I ain't never done it," Drew said. "Do you ever get to ride?"

I didn't want to answer, but he did ask me directly. "Yeah, I get to ride," I said. "Mr. Ashbourne has me workin' all over the plantation. So, I get to ride about two or three times a week."

"You lucky skunk," Drew said. "You wanna trade?"

It wasn't a question I knew how to answer honestly, so I avoided it. "Come on. It looks clear. Let's go take a look."

Drew was on my heels as we made it to the barn without incident. We slid the door open just enough to squeeze through and shut it behind us. It was pitch black inside, so I fumbled around until I found the lantern. It took a few tries before I managed to light it.

"These are our Thoroughbreds," I said. "I know they're your favorite."

The Thoroughbreds stirred a bit. Their ears pricked forward as they watched their unexpected guests, but they were surprisingly calm overall. As Drew and I approached the stables, a few horses extended their muzzles in greeting. Drew reached out and gently rubbed the nose of a dark bay.

"We call him Cisco," I said.

Drew giggled like a little kid. "Hey there, Cisco," he said. "You're a strong boy, aren't you?" Considering how the lantern cast such deep shadows, I wasn't sure, but I thought I saw a tear on Drew's cheek. "Hey, Moses, can I tell you something else?"

"What's that?"

"Remember when I said I'd never ridden a horse before," Drew said as he continued to pat Cisco.

"Do I remember?" I said. "It was only like three minutes ago. Of course, I remember."

"Well, like I said," Drew went on, "it's embarrassing to admit, but...I never really even touched a horse before. Not a real one. I mean, I've patted a donkey and a couple of mules. But nothing like this."

Just then, the barn doors were thrown open, and three men entered with guns drawn. Each carried a lantern in their free hands, which they immediately hung on the wall. "This is a good way to get yourselves shot," one of the men said. "What do you boys think you're doing runnin' around here at this time of night?" It was Harold Gullet.

To Harold's right was Earl, a wiry fella with stringy, black hair that hung to his shoulders and a thin mustache. He was grinning, and I could see his silver teeth. To his left was Carl, a husky man with a long, bushy beard and a straw hat. Carl was strong as an ox and as mean as they came. The only person on the plantation scarier than Carl was Harold Gullet himself.

"He asked you a question," Earl chimed in. "You and your girlfriend here lookin' for a little alone time or something?"

"This is my friend, Drew," I said. "He just wanted to see the horses."

"I told you I saw them come this way," a fourth voice said. It was Logan. He stepped between Gullet and Earl. "I heard them talking right before Moses snuck out. They're probably trying to steal something."

Gullet spoke to Logan. "This Drew kid, is he from the orphanage?" Logan nodded, and Gullet cursed under his breath. "Carl, get 'em outta here."

Carl put his gun away and grabbed Drew and me by the arms. He dragged us past Earl, Logan, and Gullet and shoved us to the ground just outside the stables.

"You ain't gotta be so rough about it," Drew yelled. He jumped to his feet and dusted off his shirt. "We were just lookin' at 'em."

Carl rested his hand on his gun. "You might not wanna' keep runnin' your mouth, boy," he said. Drew stood his ground and glared at Carl as if there wasn't an ounce of fear in him.

"Oh, looks like we got ourselves a tough guy," Earl said with delight. "I like the tough ones."

"He don't look so tough to me," Logan chimed in.

Carl pulled his revolver and pressed it against Drew's face.

"Hold on, Carl," Gullet said. Carl put his weapon away and stepped back. "How'd you get all the way out here from the orphanage?" he asked Drew.

"I walked," Drew replied.

I prayed Drew wouldn't say anything to make things worse, but I knew he was angry. Drew was always unpredictable when he was angry.

"That's a long walk," Gullet said. He stared at Drew like he hadn't entirely decided what to do with him.

"Good observation," Drew said. "You must be a bonafide genius."

I spoke up. "We didn't mean to cause any trouble. Just let us go, and you won't have to worry about us again."

Harold Gullet still hadn't taken his eyes off Drew. "You know what we do with trespassers and orphans that sneak around here at night?"

"I have no idea," Drew said. "But I'm sure you're just dyin' to tell me."

Logan Ashbourne's face flashed with anger. "Don't let him talk to you that way, Gullet."

Earl drew his gun, holding it at his side. "You better show some respect, you loudmouthed milksop." Then to Gullet, "Just give the word, boss."

"Relax, Earl," Gullet said. "Everybody relax." He stepped over to Drew with a cool smile. "The boy's just scared. You heard them. He just wanted to see the horses." Drew glanced from me to Gullet, hoping to get some indication of what was about to happen. I had nothing to offer. "So, you like the dark bay, huh?"

Drew nodded. "It's a fine horse," he said hesitantly.

"Hey, Earl," Gullet said, "Wasn't it Cisco that got that nasty gash on his leg not long ago?"

"I think so, boss," Earl replied.

"And weren't we afraid we might have to put him down?"

Earl smiled a sick grin. "We were. In fact, I don't think that leg's gonna heal proper at all. It's probably best that we put him down now."

"Go get him," Gullet said.

We all stood silently while Earl led Cisco out into the open and tied him to a post. Earl moved aside, slapping Drew on the back of the head as he passed. Logan looked on with what I can only describe as pure delight. I never understood why Logan seemed to enjoy the pain of others. I guess it made him feel powerful.

"Sometimes takin' care of horses means makin' the tough calls," Gullet said to Drew. "Doin' the right thing. Unfortunately, sometimes, you gotta take an animal's life rather than see it suffer. See, old Cisco here is sufferin'. You don't want him to suffer, do you?" Drew stood motionless.

"So, since you seem so interested in our horses and work, I think I'll show you what it's like to be a real cowboy."

Drew looked at me with panic in his eyes.

"You don't have to do this, Harold," I said. "We'll just go."

"Shut up," Gullet said as he removed his revolver and held it out to Drew. "Take it." Drew reluctantly and carefully took the weapon.

Both Carl and Earl drew theirs again. "Boss?" Carl said.

Harold Gullet held up his hand. "It's okay, Carl...Earl. Drew here is gonna show us how to put an animal down."

Drew shook his head. "I ain't doing it."

"You will," Harold said, his voice growing louder. "You will put that gun up to Cisco's head, and you will pull the trigger."

"No," Drew replied. "I won't do it." Then, Drew pointed the gun at Harold. "I'll shoot you first."

Before anyone could react, Harold Gullet grabbed the revolver and backhanded Drew across the face, knocking him down. "Don't you ever point a gun at me, or I'll drop you where you stand," Harold yelled at Drew. Then he composed himself. "Now, you wanna rethink this, or you still tellin' me you ain't gonna do it?"

Drew stood up slowly and glared at Gullet. The side of his face was already red and swollen. "I ain't doing it."

"Earl," Harold called out. "Who was supposed to be watchin' the stables tonight?"

"I'm not sure, boss," Earl said.

"It was Clover's night to be lookout," Logan added.

"Earl, go get Clover," Harold said.

Clover was one of the workers who lived on the plantation and mostly cared for the horses. I liked Clover. He was an older gentleman who was always kind to me. He taught me how to clean the horses' hooves, look for signs of illness or injury, and groom them properly. We had been tending to Cisco's leg for a week, and he had nearly recovered completely. The animal didn't need to be put down.

After a few moments, Earl returned, dragging Clover by the strap of his overalls. Clover took a moment to assess the scene before addressing Harold. "Mr. Gullet," he said. "I'm sorry I stepped away for just a bit. My boy, he real sick with fever, and I was worried. Please forgive me, sir, I promise you –"

"Shut up, Clover," Harold said. Then to Carl, "Take him over there and tie him up beside the horse."

Clover attempted to put up a fight, but he was no match for Carl, who was much younger and stronger. Carl struck Clover a few times, stunning him before tying up his hands and feet and securing him to the post next to the Thoroughbred.

"Let's try this again," Harold said, returning his attention to Drew. He handed him the revolver once more. "Earl, help me out," Harold said.

"Yes, sir," Earl replied, all too happy to be involved. "Whatcha need?"

"Here's what's gonna happen, Earl," Harold continued. "This little bastard is gonna put Cisco here down, or you're gonna put Clover down."

Earl yelped. "Yessiree," he shouted. "There ain't nothin' better than a standoff." Earl pressed the barrel of the gun to Clover's head. Clover was conscious but still dazed and offered no resistance.

Harold shoved Drew over to the horse. "What's it gonna be, boy?" he said. "The horse or Clover?"

Tears began to leak from Drew's eyes, but his face was like stone. "Please don't do this," Drew said.

"I'm not doin' it," Gullet answered, "you are."

"Don't make me," Drew said. "Please."

"Harold, don't," I said. "There ain't no need to –"

"Quiet, Moses," Logan said. "This is all your fault anyway."

Gullet ignored Logan's interruption. "You got five seconds to put that horse down before Earl puts a hole in Clover's head," Gullet said. "And just so we're clear, I don't care which one dies. It costs about the same to feed either one."

Drew looked at Earl. "Don't think I won't do it," Earl said, laughing. "Killin' a darkie ain't nothin' new for me, son. Time to be a man."

Harold began to count. "Five...four..."

Drew was breathing heavily and gently placed the barrel of the gun next to Cisco's head. His hand was shaking. The horse looked at Drew rather calmly. He didn't seem frightened but tried to nuzzle Drew's hand.

"Three...two...You better do it, boy!" Harold screamed. Spit flew from his mouth. "One. Do it!"

Drew made a sound halfway between a cry and a scream before pulling the trigger. Cisco dropped, and Drew fell to his knees, sobbing.

CHAPTER 15

Before Drew and I left Virginia City to face Smiling Jack, we met briefly with Skillet. He said he'd secure everything needed while we were away. Typically, transporting over one hundred people across the country requires weeks of planning – possibly even longer, given my limited expertise. However, there was an urgency to my dream, fueling the notion that we shouldn't wait any longer.

If the weather cooperated and the travel was easy, the ride to Bozeman would take Drew and me around three days. Then, assuming Smiling Jack didn't murder us, we would return to Virginia City, pick up Skillet, and continue to Tennessee. For Skillet, that translated into roughly one week to choose a route, gather supplies, and secure any needed equipment, men, and horses.

I was sick to my stomach thinking of everything left to do. There were so many moving parts, so much we didn't know, and far too little time to prepare. To say I doubted myself would be an understatement. Everything we planned was rooted in pure gut instinct. My gut. Maybe the Lord had a hand in it, but unless He showed up to drive a wagon for us, there was still a chance we were all dead wrong. I knew dwelling too long on such thoughts might make me turn coward and quit. Instead, I set my mind on the task at hand. Get to Bozeman, meet with Jack, avoid getting killed, and return home.

As Drew and I rode along the dusty trail, the sun was directly overhead, and the day was nice and warm. My newly acquired mare, Cali, moved easily and confidently like she'd belonged to me for years. Her soft footfall kept a steady rhythm as her hooves collided with dirt.

Before us, the rolling hills stretched out and eventually surrendered to the mountains beyond. Large swaths of wildflowers swayed in the breeze, their fresh scent mingling with the earthy aroma of pine and grass.

It had been a while since I'd traveled any notable distance from home, and I forgot how much I enjoyed being on the move and seeing new sights. Drew and I used the time to catch up on old times, and I can't remember the last time I was so chatty. It reminded me of when we were young boys back at the orphanage, trying to keep quiet after lights out. We laughed a lot and told stories, but mostly, we enjoyed each other's company. The conversation flowed freely, and it felt like Drew and I had effortlessly slipped back into our old friendship. Our burdens were on hold for the moment, and our souls could rest. The thud of hooves, the rustling of gear, and the creak of our saddles were comforting and familiar.

"Do you remember when Jack had us rob that coach outside Wichita?" Drew said, grinning.

"If I remember correctly, we hit a lot of coaches back then."

"It was the one with the rich couple traveling alone," Drew continued. "Remember, the guy had a white suit on. Biggy Jenkins pulled him out of the coach and threw him in the mud."

"Oh, yeah, I remember," I said, laughing. "We were all mad 'cause we couldn't understand why he was wasting so much time with the man in the first place. We were just tryin' to finish the job before anyone else happened by. Biggy didn't care, though. He said he wasn't leavin' until he saw that white suit covered in mud."

"He never was the brightest fella," Drew said.

"You know what else happened on that job?" I said. "We were hotfootin' it outta there when that storm blew in."

"Oh, here we go again," Drew said. "Go ahead and get it all out. Have yourself a good laugh."

"The way I recall," I continued, laughing despite myself, "the storm got so bad, the three of us had to shelter in an old barn and wait it out."

"Yeah, yeah," Drew said with a chuckle. "Laugh it up about how ole Drew was scared out of his mind."

"Scared is an understatement. We were all scared, but you were terrified. To be fair, it was a monster of a thunderstorm. You were convinced that the wind would bring the barn down on top of us or that lightning was gonna strike us all dead."

Drew scratched his chin. "Well, I ain't never liked thunderstorms. If that's a crime, then call me yella' and lock me up. But I've seen things. Nasty business, storms are. I don't mess around with Mother Nature. I'd rather stare down a pack of outlaws than get caught out in the thunder and lightning."

"Man, you're a brave one, aren't you?" I said, "Smiling Jack doesn't stand a chance."

Drew and I shared a good laugh and kept riding. While there was plenty of conversation, there were moments of quiet reflection. As the miles stretched on, the weight of our undertaking began to sink in. Drew was anxious about facing Jack. He'd go silent for long spells, his face all twisted up and serious. Sometimes, he'd share his concerns, but mostly, he kept things locked up in his head. I didn't press him.

As we followed the trail to Bozeman, a steady breeze whistled through the trees, and the songbirds were putting on a concert. With all I'd seen of the world and the sights and sounds I'd witnessed, nothing brought more contentment to my soul than the quiet countryside.

We stopped for the night and made camp. Skillet had packed some dried venison and biscuits, which we ate while sipping coffee and staring at the campfire.

"You think we can work all of this out with Jack?" Drew said as he poked at the fire with a stick.

"I think we can," I said, my voice steady. "The root of the matter is, you did something stupid, and we're tryin' to make it right. I know Jack can be coldhearted. Lord knows we've seen it plenty of times. But we were together for years. We were family. That's got to count for something." I poured another cup of coffee and grinned. "Besides, it's not the first time you've made a mess of things."

Drew laid back against his saddle and took out his revolvers. He was tracing his finger along the pearl handles, admiring the craftsmanship. "You're right. Family should count for something," he said. Drew paused. "You know, I was thinking about how those folks at the plantation are counting on us. They just don't know it yet."

"I know," I said quietly. "We'll figure out our next move as soon as we're done in Bozeman. One thing at a time."

"I hope you're right," Drew said. "Although, you do have a knack for figurin' things out. Always have."

"Maybe so," I said. "Sometimes you just have to make a choice and hope for the best. If it works out, you look like a genius."

"And if it don't?" Drew said.

"Then it don't matter because you're too busy cleaning up your mess to worry about what people think."

Drew and I continued to talk until the stars were out. We shared stories about the past, hopes for the future, and possible outcomes of our current circumstance. It was a comforting reminder of the friendship we'd managed to cling to since we were young.

"I gotta say, Moses," Drew said. "When we were kids, we'd talk about all the adventures we were gonna have. And, in a way, I guess we did. But this...being out here together. This is much better than anything we ever did with Jack."

"I suppose you're right," I said. "Who'd have ever thought we'd end up here? Like this?"

"Life has a funny way of surprising you," Drew said. "Sometimes in good ways and sometimes not."

We lay there in silence as the fire began to wane and crackle. The familiar quietness of the wilderness enveloped us, and we were nearly asleep. I was happy and at peace, but a small part of me felt guilty for it. I'd been mourning for so long that feeling good made me uneasy. But I knew it was all in my head. Elise was gone, and she wouldn't want me wasting happy moments wrestling with guilt. She'd be pleased that Drew and I were together.

"You know, Moses," Drew said as I drifted off. "Whatever happens from here on out, we'll face it together. Just like old times."

CHAPTER 16

The city of Bozeman had grown since I last came through. It had spread into the Gallatin Valley, becoming a respite for those looking to start a new life in the West. Drew and I rode into town around midday. The streets were bustling with activity, filled with men and women from all walks of life. Ranchers, homesteaders, traders, and businessmen moved about with purpose as a continuous flow of covered wagons and horse-drawn carriages crisscrossed the lively streets. Men loaded and unloaded them, hoping to buy or sell goods and supplies before venturing on. A flourishing market was a necessity for survival in these parts. Montana was a formidable land with more challenges than most, and her people were a rugged bunch. Still, Bozeman had a welcoming beauty that couldn't be denied.

We rode around a bit to get the lay of the city and locate the Bozeman Hotel. Sutton said that's where we'd find him, and we didn't have to search for long. The Bozeman Hotel was difficult to miss. It was an impressive three-story structure with a wrap-around veranda and a large sign out front. Compared to the rustic structures surrounding it, the Bozeman Hotel was a modern gem that demanded attention. Its facade was decorated with ornate wood trim made by men who took pride in their work. It was precisely the kind of place I'd expect to find Smiling Jack and his associates. Jack had a taste for the finer things in life, but he never quite managed to acquire them while I was running with him.

We dismounted and hitched our horses on the east side of the hotel. It had been years since I'd seen Smiling Jack, which wasn't long enough as far as I was concerned. Leaving that world behind was the best decision I ever made. I vowed never to get drawn back into living such a life of depravity. Part of that vow included never again laying eyes on Smiling Jack Davis, but here I was. Memories of those days, both good and bad, came rushing back. There was no denying who we once were. Drew and I were out-laws – part of a gang of degenerates responsible for innumerable acts of cruelty and debauchery. Though I had escaped that life physically, knowing who I had been wasn't as easy to abandon. Shame latched onto my soul like a leach, feeding on my peace.

Drew and I pushed through the doors and walked toward the front desk. "We're looking for a man by the name of Sutton," I said. "He asked us to meet him here."

Sutton called out from behind us. "Then it appears you've found the right place, gentlemen. Come, have a drink with me."

Sutton was heeled, but that came as no surprise. In his line of work, I doubt there was ever a time he wasn't. He was strangely comfortable, which made me all the more nervous, and he didn't strike me as the type to bluff. We followed Sutton into the bar and sat at the nearest table. He ordered the bartender to bring three glasses and a bottle, which came quickly. "I hope you boys had an easy ride," Sutton said as he poured the drinks.

"Easy enough," Drew said. "This place is nice. You been in town long?"

Sutton sipped his drink and ignored the question. "Drew Harlan, you are not an easy man to track down. Hell, boy, you must be half Chippewa. Tested my patience something fierce."

Drew smiled. "I assure you my elusiveness was never intended to try your patience. It was more a matter of self-preservation."

"Understandable," Sutton said. He drank again and gently placed his glass on the table. "Let's get down to it. Do you have the five thousand dollars or not?"

"You see, about that," Drew began. "I'm going to need to –"

"We need to talk to Smiling Jack," I cut in. "I'm sure he'll be willing to see us, and we need to work out an arrangement."

Sutton laughed. "For the life of me, I can't figure you boys out. Is one of you the brain and the other the muscle? You sure don't strike me as hard men, but I could be mistaken. Then again, neither of you looks profoundly intelligent either. It makes me wonder if you ain't nothing but a couple of no-good charlatans. Minus the charm, of course."

"We ain't nothin', mister," I said. "We are who we are."

"You ain't nothin', but you want a meeting with Jack?" he said. "About the five thousand dollars you don't have? Let me guess, you want to convince him you're good for it and ask for more time."

"Something like that," Drew said.

Sutton finished off his drink. "I may get the opportunity to shoot you boys yet," he said, looking genuinely hopeful. "I'll set it up, but you'll have to stay the night. Jack will meet you at his office first thing in the morning."

"His office?" Drew said. "Jack has an office? Here in Bozeman?"

"It's at the end of the main thoroughfare," Sutton said, pointing in the general direction. "Green building with a sign that reads, 'Davis Enterprises.'" He stood up and adjusted his hat. "Don't you turn gutless and try sneakin' off in the middle of the night. Either of you. If you do, there won't be no more talking. Just shooting. I'm tired of chasin' you."

Sutton left, and Drew looked at me and grinned.

"Are you serious right now?" I said. "A man threatens to kill us, and you sit here grinnin' like a mule?"

"Well, yeah," Drew said, smiling even more. "See, first of all, Sutton *didn't* shoot us. That's reason enough to be happy, ain't it? Second, Smiling Jack has apparently opened some place called Davis Enterprises. Hopefully, that means he's looking to go legit, which also means he may not be interested in shootin' folks no more. Also a good thing."

"Maybe you're right," I said.

"And third," Drew went on, "Sutton left half a bottle of whiskey on the table that I intend to finish tonight. What more do you need to put a smile on your face?"

That night, Drew and I camped just outside of town, seeing as neither of us had money to rent a room. The meeting with Sutton worked out, but I wasn't nearly as comfortable with our current situation as Drew. Still, I didn't want to spoil his good mood, so I let him laugh and cut up for a while, keeping my worries to myself. The one thing I did find comfort in was the fact that Sutton had underestimated us. He saw Drew and me as weak, and we were happy to play that role as long as possible. With a bit of luck, we might get out of this mess without things going sideways. We'd reach an agreement and be on our way. Like Drew said, people were counting on us. They just didn't know it yet.

The following morning, we were on our way to Davis Enterprises. If something bad were going to happen, it would be today. Drew took a deep breath as we walked. "Smells nice out today," he said. "Clean and crisp. Good day to die, don't you think?"

"Good as any," I said. "But do me a favor and try to avoid sayin' something stupid that might get us killed."

"Don't doubt me, Moses."

"Oh, I do not doubt your ability to irritate people," I said with a grin. "Just don't do anything dumb. Tell Jack you're sorry, let him scold you if he wants, and pray you don't have to pull those pearl handles."

"You think we should go in there carrying?" Drew said.

"You can do what you want," I replied, "but there's no way I'm going in there without iron."

We stepped into the freshly painted green building and told the receptionist we were there to meet with Jack. She had us take a seat before disappearing into what I assumed was Jack's office. She returned with a smile and said, "Mr. Davis will see you now."

Drew and I stepped into Jack's office, and my gaze was immediately drawn to the bulky man standing behind an oak desk. Smiling Jack hadn't changed much except that he was clean and well-dressed like a banker or businessman. Though he was a large, tall man, he wasn't what most folks would think of as fat. Jack was built like a barrel. Solid and thick. He had grown a full salt and pepper beard, neatly trimmed, and his eyes still had their familiar mysterious glint. When my eyes met his, a torrent of memories flooded my mind. I immediately thought of those I'd once considered family – the desperate, rugged men who made up our gang. I could almost feel the camaraderie, fear, and anger we'd all lived with daily. Most painful was the reminder of all the people I'd hurt throughout the years at Jack's bidding. Maybe they weren't all innocent, but none of them deserved such treatment.

"Well, if it isn't Moses Colter," Smiling Jack said as he stepped around his desk. He grabbed me firmly and hugged me. "My boy. I never thought I'd lay eyes on you again. The Prodigal Son returns."

"Hello, Jack," I said, ignoring his comment. "Looks like you're doing well for yourself."

"Hi, Jack," Drew said, unable to keep quiet. "Glad to see they let you out early."

Jack grabbed and hugged Drew as well. "Are you now?" he said, pulling away and returning to his desk. "I'm willing to bet *you* were especially surprised by the news of my early release." Jack sat down and motioned for us to sit in two cushioned chairs.

"Listen, Jack," Drew began, "I'm sorry about the misunderstanding, but I –"

"No, you listen," Jack said. His voice lost any hint of the pleasant tone it had before. "I'm sure you have a very well-rehearsed speech to give, but I don't think I can stomach it. Talk all you want, as you generally do, but allow me to save us both some time. As a sign of respect for my own intellect, I refuse to believe a word that comes out of your mouth. You stole from me. I found out. I want my money back."

"I understand, Jack," Drew said. "But if you'll just let me explain, I'm sure we can –"

"Sutton," Jack called out. "You and Jesse come in here, please." Sutton and the man I assumed was Jesse entered the room, both carrying shotguns. They situated themselves behind the desk on either side of Jack. "You boys do me a favor," Jack said to them. He pointed at Drew. "If anything comes out of this fool's mouth that sounds like an excuse or some declaration of his innocence, fill him with lead."

"It would be our pleasure," Sutton said.

I believed him.

Jack stared at Drew for what felt like an eternity. "Now, what is it you have to say, Drew? I am rife with anticipation."

If there was ever a time I wished for Drew to be decidedly less Drew than usual, it was then. One wrong comment and Sutton wouldn't hesitate to shoot him. Then I'd draw, and Jesse would shoot me before my iron cleared the holster.

"No excuses," Drew said soberly. "I took the money. I thought I could put it back before you got out of prison. I lost it all, and you got out early. And, here we are."

Jack clapped mockingly. "You see how easy that was," he said. His namesake smile returned to his face. "Now, let's continue our discussion like civilized gentlemen. Like businessmen."

"I'd like that," Drew said.

"I've heard a bit about you boys," Jack said. "Heard you've both gone straight. Lawmen in town told me Drew's been running bounties. I suppose that's not too far-fetched. Who better to catch an outlaw than an outlaw? It was far more surprising to hear that Moses went and got married and purchased a ranch, like a genuine family man."

Neither of us spoke. I refused to share any details of my life with Smiling Jack. He was a manipulator and a user. If there were anything that could give him an advantage over someone, he'd leverage it. The less he knew about us, the better.

Jack chuckled for some unknown reason. "Well, you boys always did make quite the duo. Never a dull moment with the two of you."

"We figured it was time to leave the old life behind," Drew said. "It was time for a change."

"Uh-huh," Jack said with a nod. "Time to walk the straight and narrow." He paused. "*After* you took my money, of course." Jack turned sideways and leaned back in his chair. His thick fingers were drumming on the desk. "What about you, Moses? I admit, I was rather hurt you could move on so quickly. I thought you'd be with me for the long haul. You had a good thing going with me and the boys."

"I appreciate everything you did for me," I said. "You saved my life more than once, and for that, I'm grateful. The truth is, I wanted something different. Something honest."

"Honest?" Jack said, raising an eyebrow. "Honesty is a rare commodity. I haven't found much of it in this life – not outside the family we made. Sure, we were outlaws, but we never pretended to be anything different. That's about as honest a life as a man could hope for, don't you think?"

I pursed my lips. "Maybe honest wasn't the best word," I said. "I suppose I needed to feel like I mattered. Like I had a purpose. Or at least a purpose bigger than myself. I wanted to live clean and be a respectable man."

Smiling Jack squinted. "So, you bought a sheep ranch, married a pampered little church girl, and got to work raising a litter of kids."

"Not too far off," I said.

"We're trying to turn things around," Drew added. "We wanna help people. As a matter of fact, we're plannin' to head down south to free some plantation workers Moses grew up with. We want to give them a chance at a new life."

Jack sat up and leaned forward. "Well, I'll be. Moses Colter, outlaw turned shepherd of men, and his partner Drew Harlan, hired gun turned hero."

"All we're tryin' to do is make amends for the past," I said. "We've caused too much pain and seen too much hurt. It's time we did somethin' good for a change."

81

Jack's lips curled into a phony smile. "I must say, I am impressed, boys. And, as much as I applaud you for moving on from your troubled pasts, let's not forget why we're here." His face turned hard, and he glared at Drew. "You owe me five thousand dollars. I want it now."

"I want to pay you," Drew said, "but I can't come up with that kind of money right now. I need some time."

"How much time?" Jack said.

"We have to go to Tennessee," I said. "Like Drew told you, some folks there need us. It's gonna take a few months, which is why we can't wait. We can't get caught by winter."

"So I'm supposed to sit around and wait for months," Jack said, jabbing a thumb toward Drew, "just hoping that this arrogant jackass is going to show up with a smile on his face and my cash in hand?" We didn't answer. "I'd do better just shooting you both now and calling it even."

The air was instantly electric. Drew's hand fidgeted around his revolver.

"Come on, Jack," I said. "Things may be different now, but we were family once. Give us a chance to make it right."

As the words left my mouth, I noticed Jack's face softened and his eyes twinkled. "You're right," he said. "We were family once, and family deserves a second chance." Drew's hand relaxed. "How about this, Moses? You pass the deed to that ranch of yours over to me, and I'll hold onto it till the end of the year. If Drew comes through with the cash, you get the deed back, and we'll put this behind us. If he doesn't, or if you two get yourselves killed along the way, the ranch is mine."

I sat there silent for a moment, my mind racing. The ranch meant more to me than anything else. It was the last piece of Elise I held on to. But there was no choice to make. Drew's life was worth more than some stolen money or sentimental memories.

"Alright," I said. "It's a deal."

"Moses, you don't have to do this," Drew said. "I'll figure something out."

"No, I'm doing it," I said, "and that's that." Then to Jack, "I'll have the deed in your hand by the end of the week."

"Excellent," Jack said as he reached out his hand. "Shake on it."

I shook on the deal and said to Jack, "But the ranch is mine until the first of the year. I get your money to you before then; you return the deed."

"Deal," Jack said. "Now, both of you, get out of here before I change my mind."

We stood, and I glanced at Sutton and Jesse as they relaxed their grip on the shotguns. Drew and I were nearly out the door when Jack called out. "Hold on a minute, Drew," he said. "Those pearl-handled Colts you have on you – you buy them with my money?"

"I did," Drew said. "Sorry about that."

"No need to be sorry, son," Jack said sternly. "Just leave them on the desk before you go." Drew hesitated. Then, in a move that could've gotten him shot, Drew pulled both guns faster than lightning, flipped them over in his hands, and laid them carefully on Smiling Jack's desk.

Jack smiled as if he was impressed, though I didn't figure it was because of Drew's speed. He was likely more impressed with Drew's pure gall. We tried to leave again.

"And what about that horse of yours?" Jack said to Drew. "Maybe I'll take that too."

Drew turned slowly and faced Jack. "You ain't gettin' the horse," he said flatly. "Now, we're gonna leave. Either of your boys here come after us to collect my horse; I'll kill 'em. Then I'll come back and kill you."

"Hold on now," I said. "Let's all just calm down. Jack, I understand your frustration. Drew owes you, and you're within your rights to take his horse. But we already agreed on a deal. Let's keep it. Besides, how's Drew supposed to make your money back without a horse? Let us be on our way, and we'll get your money."

Jack sat for a moment before flashing a cold smile. "It's been one hell of a reunion, boys," he said. "You take care of yourselves and keep that temper in check, or the next one might not go so well for you."

"Likewise," Drew said as we left Jack's office.

We didn't speak until we were outside and well away from Jack's office. "Well, that went great," Drew said.

"Good enough," I replied. "At least we're both still alive."

Drew stopped in the middle of the road. "Moses," he said, "thank you for what you did back there. I won't let you down."

"You better not," I said with a grin. "Look, you're my brother, and that's what brothers do. They look out for each other." I pulled one of the revolvers Drew had given me and passed it over to him. "Here, take this. Nobody needs two of them anyway."

CHAPTER 17

At fourteen, Mr. Ashbourne decided I should have more freedom around the plantation regarding my coming and going. The unexpected privilege afforded me extra time to spend with the Ivywood workers. I had grown closer to Titus and his twin boys, Fisher and Tate, who had recently turned eleven. Titus treated me like one of his own. He taught me how to shoot a rifle, catch fish, gather and store tobacco, and all sorts of things a young man should know. In return, I taught his family to read. They weren't great at it, but they had made admirable progress. Titus and his wife, Charity, were especially thrilled to begin reading their Bible for the first time. I felt like one of the family, even sharing meals with them occasionally.

It had been nearly two years since I'd last seen Drew, not since that horrible night Harold Gullet forced him to put down the horse. Drew and I had taken to writing each other once a week, but it had been a month since my last letter, and Drew had yet to reply. So when the opportunity came to travel into town with Titus, I jumped at the chance. If I played it right, maybe I'd get to see Drew, even if it was for a short while.

The warm morning worked diligently to become a hot afternoon as the wagon rumbled toward Jonesborough. Fisher and Tate sat in the back, arguing about who was the fastest runner. Titus repeatedly instructed them to sit down whenever the argument escalated, and they tried to leap out of the wagon to resolve it. Titus handled the reins with a practiced ease, and I sat beside him, trying to mimic his peaceful composure as we watched the scenery pass by.

"Titus," I said, breaking the silence. "Do you ever get tired of workin' at the plantation?"

Titus laughed. "I figure a man's gotta work somewhere," he said. "You do somethin' long enough, you tend to get used to it. Ain't nothin' wrong with honest work. Keeps a man busy and his family fed."

"Yeah, but it's nice on days like today, right?" I said. "Going to town is sort of like getting a break, don't you think? It feels that way to me."

"I reckon you right," he said as if it was something he hadn't considered. "I do like gettin' away now and again. It helps remind me there's more to this world than workin' fields and doin' chores."

His words struck a chord with me. The plantation was a fine enough place to live, but I wanted to see more of the country. Even as a boy, I longed for my freedom. I wanted to find a place that felt like mine one day. The plantation was Mr. Ashbourne's dream. I wanted my own dream, and I was naive enough to believe it was possible.

"How did you and Charity end up working for Mr. Ashbourne, anyway?"

Titus stared at the road ahead as if gazing into the past. "Our kin worked these parts for long as folks been here. We was born not too far away. I was wantin' to marry her, but Charity said she wouldn't till I had steady work. So I got to lookin' around and ended up meetin' Mr. Ashbourne. He a hard man, but fair. Said if we worked for him, he'd keep a roof over our heads and food on the table. It's more than a lot of folks like us get."

"Titus," I said carefully, "are you...are you slaves?" I instantly regretted the question. I didn't want to offend Titus, but I wanted to understand how their arrangement worked.

Titus glanced at me as he clicked his tongue and flicked the reins. "No, Moses," he said quietly. "We ain't slaves. But we ain't free neither." He offered no further explanation, and I didn't ask any more questions.

We crossed the Colter River, which was not much more than a trickle. It had been a blistering summer, and there was a severe drought that didn't look like it would end anytime soon. As we entered Jonesborough, we were greeted by the smell of fresh bread from the bakery and the lively chatter of people going about their daily business. We pulled up to the mercantile, and Titus secured the horses. Fisher and Tate jumped out of the wagon and lined up to race one another down the street. "Hey," Titus said to them in a tone that stopped them in their tracks. "You boys stay by me and don't touch a thing. Keep your heads down and only speak if spoken to. Answer 'yessir,' or 'nosir,' nothin' else. Understand?" They nodded and followed Titus into the store.

Once the clerk loaded the supplies onto the wagon, Titus signed for the goods, and we were ready to begin our trek back to the plantation. "Titus," I said, "Do you think it would be okay if we stopped by the orphanage for a minute? It'll be quick. I want to say hello to Drew and the Peabodys."

Titus grimaced. "I ain't sure about that, Moses. Ain't that a little out of our way? You know Mr. Ashbourne don't much like detours."

"Yeah, I know," I said. "I was just hoping to see them is all."

Titus hesitated and then sighed. "Alright, we can run by, but you gotta be quick. No dawdlin' or Mr. Gullet'll come down on the both of us."

My heart raced as we pulled up to the Grace House Orphanage. I heard children laughing and playing outside, and I leaped from the wagon before it stopped. I ran through the front door and nearly collided with Mr. and Mrs. Peabody.

"Well, if it isn't Moses Colter," Mr. Peabody said.

"Good morning, Mr. Peabody. Mrs. Peabody," I replied with a smile.

"Oh, come here, boy," Mrs. Peabody said as she pulled me in for a hug.

"How's plantation life treating you?" Mr. Peabody said.

"It's good. We're just in town to pick up some supplies. We don't have much time to visit, I just wanted to stop by and say hello. Would it be okay if I spoke with Drew?"

Mr. and Mrs. Peabody shared a glance as their smiles faded. "It would be," Mr. Peabody said, "but we don't exactly know where Drew is."

"What do you mean? He's not here anymore?"

Mrs. Peabody placed her hand on my shoulder. "Moses, Drew ran away about a month ago. He snuck out in the middle of the night, and we haven't heard from him since."

The news was like a kick in the gut. I was worried sick and angry as a hornet at the same time. Why would Drew run away? Was he okay? Where did he go? And, most importantly, why didn't he try to take me with him?

"I'm sorry, Moses," Mr. Peabody said. "I know this must come as a shock. I'll tell you what, if he shows up, we'll send word to let you know."

I climbed back into the wagon a few moments later, but my mind was miles away. Titus sensed something was wrong, but he didn't pry. He let me sit in silence. "We should be gettin' back," he finally said, and with a flick of the reins, we were moving again.

The streets of Jonesborough seemed to close in on me as we eased along. Though I rarely saw him, Drew was something like an anchor for me. The world was full of people, but Drew was the only one to which I felt tethered. He was my brother. And he left me.

"Hey, hold on there," a man called out. I looked past Titus to see a skinny fella with a few missing teeth flagging us down. His face was wrinkled up in a sneer as he approached.

"Yessir? Can I help you, sir?" Titus said.

The man pointed at Titus, then to Fisher and Tate. "You boys are on the wrong side of town, ain't ya?" He turned his head, spit, and then wiped the dripping tobacco from his chin. "What business you got outside the mercantile?"

"We just makin' a quick stop, sir," Titus said. "We'll be on our way. We ain't lookin' for no trouble."

"Well, maybe trouble's lookin' for you, darkie," the man said, his voice full of disgust. He glanced at the goods in the back of the wagon. "You must work for some big operation." The wagon was full, but the cargo was nothing particularly impressive. It was mostly flour, cornmeal, and sugar – things of that nature.

"We with the Ashbourne Plantation," Titus said.

"Ohhh, well la-ti-da," the man said. "You must be one of them uppity negros, huh? Bet you think you're somethin' special, don't ya?"

I felt my blood boil. I was about to tell the man to shut up and leave us alone, but Titus raised a hand to silence me.

"We gonna get goin' now, sir," Titus said. "You have a good day."

"Oh, no, you don't, boy," the man said. "It's about time you learned your place." The man grabbed Titus by the arm and pulled him from the wagon.

Titus fell into the street, and the skinny idiot started kicking him and laughing. The horses jerked, and Fisher and Tate yelped with fear, but the man kept on kicking and laughing. Something in me went numb, and I remembered very little of it afterward.

There was a click, and the man froze. He turned to me. I stood at the back of the wagon with a rifle pulled firmly into my shoulder. The man's bravado left his body instantly, and his face went ghostly white.

"Easy there, boy," the man said as he slowly backed away. "Don't do nothin' stupid. I'm familiar with your pa', you know? You don't want him to hear you're out here pullin' guns on folks, do you?"

"He ain't my pa," I said, taking aim. "I don't want to shoot you, but I will. Now, get lost."

I'm sure he wanted to, but the man said nothing. He simply turned and ran like the coward I knew he was. I held the gun on him as he ran away until Titus took it from my shaky hands. We climbed back into the wagon and continued on as I sat there seething.

"You ought not done that, Moses," Titus said. He was scraped up and bleeding, and I could tell by the way he spoke that he was in pain.

"He could have killed you, Titus. Somebody had to stop him."

Titus groaned and held his ribs. "You don't pull a gun on no man less'n you ready to use it."

"I *was* ready to use it."

"Not on no man like that," Titus said. "He ain't worth it. He just wanted to take me down a peg or two. Make hisself feel tough. World's full of men like that."

"Well, it shouldn't be," I replied.

"Yeah, I know. Let's just hope Mr. Ashbourne don't hear 'bout it."

CHAPTER 18

The ride from Bozeman back to Virginia City had been relatively uneventful, which is how I preferred it. As Drew and I rode into town, the familiar sights and sounds of home welcomed us. The sun was setting, and the sky was a brilliant blend of reds and blues, smeared in the waning light across the horizon. We passed the livery and saw Skillet out front loading up a wagon with clattering pots and pans while he grunted and cursed.

He looked up and saw us approaching. "Well, if it ain't the penniless adventurers returning from their latest undertaking." Skillet laughed at his joke. He had removed his Union coat and was sweating through his stained, white button-up.

"Good to see you too, Skillet," I said as I sat my horse.

"Got out of there without dyin', I see," Skillet said to Drew. "You must've let Moses do the talkin'."

"Mostly," Drew answered.

"How'd things go here?" I said. "We finished our business in Bozeman, and we're ready to head out whenever you are."

"Best news I've heard all day," Skillet replied. He had more energy than I'd ever seen. It was a refreshing departure from the near-passed-out state I often found him in. "We ain't got much time to spare if we hope to make it back before winter sets in. What you plan on doin' with these folks when we get 'em here anyway?"

"I've got a few things in mind," I said. "I'm still working it out."

Skillet nodded and rested his one hand on his hip. "I've been busier than a bee in a flower shop since you boys left."

Drew spoke up. "And you're sure you've got everything we need? It's a long trip, you know."

Skillet shook his head. "Am I sure? Boy, I was runnin' wagon trains while you was still spittin' up mama's milk. Don't you worry about me. Chucklehead."

"Hey, I'm just asking," Drew said. "I only see two wagons, and that ain't enough to move all those people."

"Of course it ain't, you dim lunk," Skillet said. "After we get to Jonesborough, I'll get what we need. For now, we gotta travel lean and fast." He looked at me. "I'm hoping most of those farmhands of yours can handle a wagon well enough." I nodded. Skillet motioned to his own wagons. "Both of these are about as loaded down as I'm comfortable with. Gotta conserve where we can."

Drew chuckled. "Hey, if you're worried about haulin' too much weight, we can always chop off your other arm."

"Funny," Skillet said, unimpressed. "I can only imagine the hours of side-splittin' entertainment you're gearin' up to provide on the daily."

"Consider it a perk of the job," Drew said with a nod.

"It's getting late," I said. "I'm guessing you're okay pullin' out first thing tomorrow?"

"Sounds fine to me," Skillet said. "For now, you boys take care of your horses and join me over at the Rusty Nail. I got some people I want you to meet."

"People?" Drew said. "What people?"

"People who ain't annoyin' and don't ask stupid questions," Skillet said. "I told you boys I've been busy. Got us a couple of folks who've joined the cause, so to speak."

Drew and I rubbed down our horses and left them at the livery before walking to the Rusty Nail. "Hey, take it easy on Skillet," I said before we entered. "He's workin' hard for us, and he sure don't owe us anything."

"I can't promise that," Drew said, buzzing with energy. He paused, looking like a thousand possibilities were running through his head. "But I'll do my best."

And he always did his best. I knew the chances were slim that Drew could control his mouth for very long. It was never out of meanness, though. He had a mischievous streak, but he never meant any harm. It was just his way.

We pushed through the doors and saw Skillet seated at a table with an Indian fella on his left and a tall, dark-haired lady to his right. As we stepped inside, Skillet smiled, and they all stood as we walked to the table.

"Moses, Drew," Skillet said, "Let me introduce you boys to a couple of my friends."

"Friends? I didn't know you had friends," Drew said. He immediately caught himself and glanced at me. "Sorry."

Skillet didn't seem to notice. He gestured to the Indian. "This here is Kawit, but everyone calls him Two Feathers."

The Indian looked to be in his mid-forties, but it was hard to know for sure. He was dark-skinned with a stern, heavily lined face, probably from years spent living outdoors. Long, black hair hung past his shoulders, and over his right ear was a braided strand with a few beads and two feathers attached. I assumed that was how he got his nickname. Two Feathers was lean, but he looked strong. He wore a combination of traditional native attire and practical gear. He nodded to us both as we introduced ourselves, but he didn't speak.

"He know English?" Drew said.

"Of course, he knows English," Skillet huffed. "He just don't talk much. Somethin' you could learn from."

"He has a point," I said to Drew.

Skillet continued. "And this lovely lady is Eleanor, although she prefers to be called Nellie." Nellie looked to be about the same age as Skillet but appeared much more agreeable. She was a pretty lady with an oversized smile and a good-natured way about her.

Nellie didn't waste any time getting to know us. She moved around the table with a booming laugh and hugged us. "It's good to see you boys in the flesh finally," she said. "I feel like I'm meetin' two famous figures as much as Skillet has gone on about you the last few days."

That was surprising to hear. "Well, I hope he didn't oversell," I said. "Otherwise, I might have to act more refined than I am." Nellie laughed harder than I expected, and we all took a seat.

Drew and I exchanged pleasantries and tried to get to know Nellie and Two Feathers since we would be spending a lot of time together. Two Feathers hardly spoke, answering 'yes' or 'no' to most of our questions. Nellie, on the other hand, had no problem talking. Her energy seemed boundless, and her joy infectious.

"So, Skillet," Drew said. "What made you pick these two fine folks for the job?" Drew seemed very interested in our new friends.

Skillet downed his drink and said, "I met Two Feathers in the Union. He's a tracker. Reads sign better than anyone I've ever known. He's a hard worker and moves through the woods like a ghost. You never know when skills like his will be handy on the trail.

"And Nellie and I have known each other for years," Skillet went on. "Old family friends, you might say. Nellie's always up for an adventure, and as soon as I sent word, she came running." Nellie laughed in her spirited way and agreed. "Now, Nellie's got a way with folks. Everybody loves Nellie. Always have. Plus, her skills with a Winchester ain't nothin' to sneeze at."

Nellie winked at us. "Don't you forget about my cookin' skills, Skillet. I can give you a run for your money, that's for sure. A trip without good food ain't a trip worth takin' as far as I'm concerned."

"I've got to hand it to you, Skillet," I said, "you've done some good work here and found some fine folks."

"I have to agree," Drew added, "Nice work, old-timer."

"I told you fellas this is all in my wheelhouse," Skillet said. "Makes me feel alive again, like the old days. But listen to me – all of you. Don't expect this job to be some Sunday picnic in the meadow. It's gonna be real work with real danger. It'll take all of us givin' everything we've got." We all nodded in agreement. "The way I see it, the key is to move fast. We'll travel light and pick up what we need along the way. We've gotta get those people out of there and keep 'em safe. It won't be easy, but they need us. So, if any of you have doubts, you'd best back out tonight. After we leave in the morning, there ain't no turnin' back."

CHAPTER 19

We all knew the trip from Virginia City to Jonesborough would be long and grueling. None of us were strangers to travel, but no one besides Skillet had done so with more than a hundred people in tow. Just before sunrise, we all gathered around the wagons. Drew, Skillet, Two Feathers, and Nellie were all there. At least no one had a change of heart overnight. Though I tried to hide my trepidation from the group, the magnitude of this undertaking was setting in, and I was ill at ease. Montana to Tennessee and back sounded reasonable enough when it was simply a conversation around a saloon table. In practice, it felt nearly impossible.

The distance alone was enough to spur my worry. Numerous challenges could arise at any time, and I felt ill-prepared for most of them. You never know what manner of trials the open country can throw your way. Still, the distance was only one of the realities that gave me pause. What if we made the trip to Tennessee, and the plantation workers didn't want to leave? What if they decided they were better off where they were? How I ever thought this was a good idea was beyond me. This harebrained plan had materialized as a result of a dream. I felt like a fool, and my worries were gnawing at my resolve.

"Mr. Colter," a man called out. It was Reverend Phillips, racing toward the livery. "Mr. Colter, I'm so glad I caught you before you all left."

"Good morning, Reverend," I said as I shook his hand. "What brings you out so early? Is everything okay?"

"Oh, yes, Mr. Colter," he said, slightly out of breath. "All is well. I just wanted to inform you of a couple of things. First off, I managed to gather enough volunteers from our congregation to ensure your land is maintained and your animals are cared for while you're away."

"I really appreciate all you've done for me," I said. "I don't know how I can ever repay you."

"Don't concern yourself with that," Reverend Phillips said. "You just worry about helping those poor souls in Tennessee. But there's one more thing." He glanced at the others. "May we speak privately?"

"Sure, Reverend," I said. We stepped away from the group, and it was clear something weighed heavily on his mind. "What's wrong? Tell me."

"It's nothing serious," he said. "It's just...well...I had a dream of my own last night. I can't say I've ever experienced anything like it. It was about you. I woke up and had the strongest feeling that the Lord was telling me to get to the livery quickly – that I had to tell you about my dream before you left."

"Go ahead, Reverend. Speak your mind. Tell me about it."

Reverend Phillips took a deep breath. "It was short, but you were in it. You were sitting with your back against a huge rock, and you were terribly distraught, Moses. I'm not sure how I knew, but I could sense your mind was flooded with...something like...it's hard to put into words because it was only a feeling. But, I suppose I'd call it doubt. You doubted yourself, your friends, me, the Lord, all of it."

"Sounds about right," I said.

"Anyway," he continued, "that's when I heard it. A voice that sounded like a rushing river and howling wind and thunder. I believe it may have been the Lord. The voice said, 'Though he doubts, I will make this man's name great. For now, he is blind, searching but not finding. However, soon he will see me with his own eyes.' Then, I woke up and rushed here to tell you."

I considered his words, though I wasn't sure what to make of them, so I quickly put them away. Talk of having a great name was uncomfortable. I wasn't trying to be great. I just wanted to do the right thing.

"I appreciate you telling me, Reverend. I won't pretend to know what it means, but oddly enough, it does help."

The Reverend smiled. "I'm glad. Please know that while you're away, my congregation and I will pray for you daily. I'm very proud of you, Moses."

I nodded, thanked him, and shook his hand before Reverend Phillips left. It struck me as unusual for him to say he was proud of me. I couldn't recall anyone having said that to me before, and it stirred something within me. Not sure what to make of it, I returned to the group and fixed my mind on the task at hand.

"Everything okay?" Drew said.

"Yeah, everything's good. What's going on here?"

Skillet and Nellie were griping at each other about the practicality of his packing job. Two Feathers had grown bored with their arguing and sat, leaning against the rear wagon wheel, sharpening his knife.

Drew looked at me and shook his head. "What kind of traveling sideshow have we put together here? We're really gonna trust these people with our lives?"

I laughed. "We could do worse."

Finally, Nellie gave up, and Skillet got his way. He gathered us together. "We're gonna take it one step at a time, everybody. A trek like this ain't no sprint, so settle in and take it day by day. Our first stop is Fort Laramie. It's a fine place to rest and restock, but it's gonna take a few weeks to get there. Until then, we camp, hunt, keep an eye out for any danger, and keep movin' forward."

Drew wasn't keen on Skillet acting like he was in charge, but it didn't bother me. His planning and experience were comforting, and he meant well. We mounted our horses, Drew on Stormy, Two Feathers on his Appaloosa gelding he called Denali, and me on Cali. Skillet drove the lead wagon, and Nellie followed in the second. Skillet had also taken the liberty of loading down my mule, Hurley, to help haul goods. Hurley was a little lazy, but he was more than capable. We were on our way.

Our first day on the trail was a combination of excitement and uncertainty. The weather was nice and we made good time. Drew and I mostly stayed with the wagons, but Two Feathers rode ahead to scout a good location for camp. Just before sunset, he returned and informed us there was a nice clearing up ahead near the river. It wasn't long before we were gathered around the fire, sharing a simple meal of dried meat and beans with biscuits.

Skillet walked us through the process of preparing meals for large groups. And though none of us were very interested, it didn't stop Skillet. When he finished, Nellie took over and regaled us with stories of her days on the trail that had us all laughing – even Two Feathers. Not to be outdone, Drew shared a few remarkable stories of his own, some of which might be deemed unsuitable for polite company. We had a good time, and I could tell this crew had the chance of becoming a tight-knit bunch.

We settled in that night under a sky full of stars. The gentle crackle of the fire, the soft breeze, and the muffled conversations lulled me into a peaceful sleep.

We resumed our travel the following morning, and Drew and I found ourselves riding alongside Skillet's wagon in silence. In the distance, great snow-peaked mountains stood like giants, challenging our resolve. We knew, before long, the terrain would become rugged and unforgiving, but the going was easy for now.

Skillet's gravel-like voice broke the silence. "You see those mountains up ahead, fellas? They may look beautiful, but they can be downright treacherous. Our biggest challenge right now is gettin' through 'em safely. The weather can change in a heartbeat, and paths can disappear if we get caught in snow." "Good thing we got Two Feathers," Drew said.

"Yes indeed," Skillet replied. "And we're gonna need him. I'm keepin' a watchful eye on the weather, but Two Feathers don't seem too worried. As long as Two Feathers is unruffled, so am I."

"One thing at a time, though, right?" I said.

Skillet nodded and scratched his graying chin. "That's right. The first step is Fort Laramie. After that, we'll figure out the next."

"Hey, Skillet," Drew said. "How'd you lose that arm anyway?"

"Cannonball," Skillet said matter of factly. "Never saw it comin'. One minute I was takin' aim on some confederate, and the next, I was on my back. I didn't even realize the arm was gone until I tried to get up. Never found it either."

"Never found what?" Drew said.

"The arm. Never found the arm."

"Why'd you want the arm?" Drew said. "It ain't like they could sew it back on."

Skillet's voice dropped, and he stared straight ahead. "Had my wedding ring on that hand," he said.

Neither of us replied. It felt like a subject Skillet would rather drop.

CHAPTER 20

No one could remember a drought as severe as the summer I was fourteen. Creeks dried up, crops withered, and the workers were miserable. The unyielding heat even made Mr. Ashbourne more disagreeable than usual. And though no one admitted it, everyone was grateful when Mrs. Ashbourne talked him into joining her on a trip to visit her sister in Mississippi. She sold it as an opportunity for him to get away from the stress of the plantation. Mr. Ashbourne reluctantly agreed and they left by hired stagecoach on a hot Sunday morning.

Three weeks had passed since I drew my gun on the man who attacked Titus in Jonesborough. While Titus worried about news of the incident reaching Mr. Ashbourne, we were relieved when nothing came of it. The man had kept silent for some reason, and now Mr. Ashbourne would be away for several weeks.

Still, there was little cause for celebration since seventeen-year-old Logan Ashbourne was left in charge of everything. For Logan, it was his first time shouldering such responsibility. He undoubtedly considered himself highly qualified, but the rest of us only felt a growing unease. It was as if the entire plantation held its breath, waiting to see what fresh chaos would be wrought in Mr. Ashbourne's absence.

I sat underneath a shade tree with Titus and his twin boys, Fisher and Tate. We were thoroughly exhausted since Mr. Ashbourne had us hauling water from the river to keep the tobacco plants alive.

"Wonder what they up to?" Titus said. He nodded to Logan, who stood across the yard talking to Harold Gullet and his skinny friend Earl.

"Don't know," I said, "but it probably ain't good."

Logan waved his hands around in aggressive gestures. His voice was loud enough to hear but not loud enough to make out what he said. A frustrated Harold Gullet shook his head and turned to leave, but Logan grabbed him by the shoulder and spun him around. He then jabbed a finger into Harold's chest and pointed directly at us. Harold ultimately relented, dropped his head, and walked toward us with Logan and Earl close behind. My heart twisted into a tight knot. It was no secret that Logan had a mean streak but in the absence of his folks, who knew what he might try?

"I got a job for you, Titus," Logan barked as he stormed up.

Titus stood. "Yessir," he said. "What can I do for you, Mr. Ashbourne?"

"There's a stack of creosote posts behind the wagon barn," he said. "Go grab two of them and put them in that open area there." He pointed to the clearing. "I want them to stick up seven to eight feet out of the ground and placed ten feet apart."

"I can do that, sir," Titus said.

"Then get to it," Logan went on. "And they better be sturdy – strong enough to tie horses to. I want it done before supper. Harold and Earl here are gonna make sure it's done right."

"Fisher…Tate," Titus said. "You boys go on to the house and see if your ma needs help." The boys nodded and ran off.

I'm sure Titus was just as puzzled as I was by Logan's odd request, but he didn't question it. Obedience was a survival skill each of us had learned to practice. So, without further explanation, Titus went to work.

The day wore on, and the heat refused to relent. Titus struggled, drenched in sweat and breathing heavily. I offered to help, but Gullet wouldn't allow it.

"This ain't your business, Moses," he said. "You can stand around and watch, but stay out of it." I didn't have much choice but to comply, so I stood there with a sick feeling in my gut as Titus dug the holes and placed the massive posts.

By the time he finished and the posts were firmly in place, the sunlight was beginning to wane. Titus all but collapsed and desperately downed a jug of water I'd fetched from the house. As he drank, Logan returned to inspect his work.

"This'll do," he said as he shook each pole, testing their strength. "Gullet, you got the rope?"

Harold nodded, and Carl came walking up with a sour face and an armful of rope. "You sure about this, Logan?" Harold said. "Your folks won't be too happy if you kill one of their best."

"Ain't nobody dying," Logan said. "Now, do as you're told and tie him up."

Titus placed a hand on my shoulder and whispered. "It's okay, Moses. Whatever's comin', let it be."

Everything inside of me wanted to step in and put a stop to whatever was about to happen, but I knew better. If I interfered, Logan would only make it worse for Titus.

It happened quickly. Harold and Carl flipped Titus onto his belly and tied a rope around each of his hands and feet. Titus didn't resist – didn't beg or plead. He never made a sound. When they'd bound him up tight, Earl took hold of the ropes tied to Titus's wrists. He wrapped them around the tops of each pole and tied them off. Carl did the same, securing Titus's feet to the bottom of each pole. They pulled all the slack from the ropes, and Titus was left to half stand, half hang there, spread eagle. His eyes were wide, like a trapped animal, and his face contorted with confusion, anger, and pain.

I knew I had to watch my words, but it felt wrong to stand there and say nothing. "Why are you doing this, Logan? What's going on?"

"You know exactly what's going on," he said bitterly. "And you better thank the Lord you aren't getting the same."

I felt my face flush with anger, even in the heat of the early evening. I hated the sound of Logan's voice. His words dripped with sadistic satisfaction.

"I have no idea what you're talking about," I said.

"Then you're even dumber than I thought," he snapped. Earl laughed, showing off his silver teeth. "Did you really think no one would find out? My pa may be too cowardly to set things right, but I'm not." He stepped to Titus, inches from his face. Titus turned his head, averting his gaze. Logan spoke into his ear with a tone that was practically a hiss. "The next time you decide to go into town and backtalk a white man in public, I'll kill you. Then I'll split up your wife and kids and sell them off. Do you understand me, boy?"

Titus nodded, and Earl chuckled again. Harold Gullet spoke. "How do you see this going, Logan? What you want us to do with him?"

"Leave him out here. Give him enough water to keep him alive, but don't let him eat. Whip him three times a day, but be mindful not to kill him."

"How long you plannin' on keeping him here?" Harold said.

Logan shrugged. "He can stay right where he is till I'm satisfied he's learned his lesson. I'll let you know when I've made up my mind."

Earl came over and punched Titus in the gut a few times. Titus groaned and coughed and pulled against the ropes to no avail. "Enjoy your evenin'," Earl said, tipping his hat to Titus. Then, he, Carl, Harold, and Logan all left.

"I'm awful sorry about this, Titus," I said. "I didn't know this would happen."

Titus struggled to catch his breath. "No way you coulda known," he said, gasping for air. "Do somethin' for me. Let Charity know. Tell her and the boys to keep in the house for the night. Tell her not to come out here till ain't nobody around."

"I will, Titus. I'll let her know."

"And tell her them boys don't need to see me like this," he said. "Keep 'em away till they cut me loose."

For three days, Titus hung there, exposed to the elements. The sun came up and baked him during the day, and the moon looked on, offering little respite through the sweltering night. I took care of him as best I could. I'd sneak water to him during the day, but I couldn't chance sneaking him food. Too many eyes were on him, waiting for me to try something. I visited Titus often, but we didn't speak much. There wasn't much to say. Earl performed his daily duty like clockwork and with far more exuberance than necessary. Three times a day, he administered Titus's prescribed beating. It took every ounce of strength Titus had to survive the ordeal. Near the end, he stopped responding to me altogether. He drifted in and out of consciousness, laboring to breathe and fighting to stay alive.

At the end of the third day, Harold showed up and cut the ropes. He watched as Titus collapsed, checked to make sure he was breathing and walked away without concern. Charity rushed out, and I helped her carry Titus to his bed. It wasn't easy. Titus was a large man, and he couldn't offer us any assistance, but we managed. Once we got him settled, Charity thanked me but said I should go – that she would take care of him from here.

I stepped out of Titus's house, and my eyes met the gaze of at least twenty other workers who had gathered to check on him. They stood there silent, anger and helplessness etched on their sweaty faces. "He's alive," I said. No one spoke. "Charity is taking care of him. That's all I know."

One by one, they turned and walked away, returning to their work without further discussion.

Something changed in me that day. No man deserved such treatment, regardless of his station in life or the color of his skin. The faces of Titus, Charity, and those who cared for them haunted me long after the matter was settled and time had repaired what it could. I couldn't shake it. Seeing all that happened had scarred my soul. The hurt and shock would subside, but the mark it left remained. As a result, a silent, fiery rage was ignited within me. I held it inside, nurturing it like a wounded animal until the day came to set it free. Now wasn't the time, but I made a vow to myself. I would never forget what happened, and one day, I would make it right. I wasn't sure how it would all play out, but I knew I could no longer stand by and allow such cruelty to persist.

CHAPTER 21

W e'd been on the trail for weeks and encountered very few people. The occasional trapper or hunter would cross our path, but we kept to ourselves since it was difficult to distinguish friend from foe. We were tired, but Fort Laramie was in our sights. My heart quickened, and my energy returned as the wagons trundled toward the palisades surrounding the fort. Drew let out a whoop at the sight of it, and the rest of us mimicked his call like a dumb flock of birds.

"No offense to any of you," Drew said, "but I can't wait to talk to some new folks. They got a saloon here, Skillet?"

"Course they do," he answered. "There are two things you can count on at Fort Laramie; you'll find plenty of interestin' folks and no shortage of libations."

Drew whooped again, and so did we. "If ya'll don't mind," Drew said, "I think Moses and I are gonna' ride on ahead. You know, get a head start on the evening's festivities."

No one objected, so Drew and I gave our horses a kick and raced ahead. We rode into Fort Laramie, and it was immediately apparent that this was a lively settlement filled with all manner of folks. Far more people than I'd expected filled the streets and shops. We saw soldiers in uniform, traders and travelers, and even families with women and children. A steady buzz of chatter brought the place to life, and the sound was energizing. What had brought all these people to the same place at the same time? It was incredible to think that each of us had our own lives, stories, and circumstances that had led us here.

We rode straight to the livery, where a thick, bald man with a full beard greeted us. "We got more comin' in behind us," Drew said. "Take extra good care of these horses for us, would ya? A fella named Skillet will pay you for everything." The man nodded and led our horses away.

"You enjoy that a little too much," I said as we walked the crowded streets.

"Well, you're gonna have to narrow that down," Drew said with a grin. "I enjoy *what* a little too much?"

"You love tellin' folks that Skillet's handling payment for any and everything."

Drew shrugged. "I make it a point never to refuse a friend's generosity, Moses. You have to learn to enjoy things. The way I see it, I can either feel guilty about takin' Skillet's money, or I can be happy he offered it. Either way, he's still paying."

"I suppose you're right," I said. Drew had an uncanny knack for finding the bright side of almost anything. I admired his unique point of view, and he never failed to challenge my thinking. If I was honest, Drew had a far easier time than any of us when it came to enjoying life.

"Yeah, I'm right," Drew agreed. He slapped me on the shoulder. "Now, let's turn that brain of yours off for a while and have a good time. We're young – well, young enough, and alive, and –"

"Alive enough," I cut in.

"Yes," Drew yelped. "Alive enough to have a good time with a good friend. What do you say we hit the Laramie Saloon and forget about our troubles for one night?"

We pushed through the swinging doors of the Laramie Saloon and were greeted by the warmth of laughter, the clinking of glasses, and the low hum of conversation. The air was thick with tobacco smoke, and the smell reminded me of the plantation. A young fella wearing a striped shirt with a red vest was pounding out tunes on the piano as a few drunks swayed and sang along. The place was packed, but somehow, Drew spotted an open table and waded through the raucous crowd to claim it. A few moments later, we had procured a bottle and some glasses, and we were laughing and having a good time. It was nice being there, being a part of this moment, and sharing it with Drew.

At some point during the evening, a couple pushed through the crowd and asked if they could sit with us. Drew was especially thrilled and even offered to buy them a drink. They were obviously travelers. The man sat down to my right and introduced himself as Nicholas. He removed his large satchel and hung it on the back of his chair. Nicholas was well-weathered, with dark skin and deep creases on his forehead. His hair sat high upon his head, a dark, wavy mass that looked like it might have had bits of leaves and twigs tangled up in it. The woman with him called herself Audrey and shared that she and Nicholas had been married for ten years. Audrey was pretty but just as weathered as her husband. Her blonde hair was tied up in a messy fashion, and her eyes had a mischievous twinkle.

The couple shared stories about their travels around the world. Nicholas told of distant lands and exotic foods, people, and cultures. He conveyed it all so vividly; his memories felt like my own. Audrey picked up when Nicholas trailed off. She told riveting tales of their grand adventures that sounded like something out of a Penny Dreadful. Drew soaked it all in, asking questions and egging them on to tell us more. Listening to their fantastic stories made me wonder what it would be like to have such a life – to strike out and explore a world outside of my own. We stayed there for quite a while, talking, laughing, singing, and sharing our stories.

"You know," I said, "it just occurred to me that my associate and I never asked what you do for a living. Like I said, I'm a rancher, and Drew here is –"

"I'm his associate," Drew said.

Nicholas laughed heartily. "Audrey and I are itinerant photographers," he said. "We travel the world capturing sights that inspire us."

"Is that right?" Drew said, amazed. "And people pay you to do that?"

"Oh, yes," Audrey said. "We sell to newspapers, museums, publishers, and individuals. We're not fussy about who gives us money."

"Hey, Moses," Drew said, placing both hands on the table. "Maybe when we're done with everything, we can get ourselves a camera. We could go to Africa or something."

"Oh, so you're a photographer now?" I said.

"Well, no," he replied. "But I could be one day. So could you."

"Wouldn't that be something," I said. "Drew Harlan, bounty huntin' photo artist."

"Why can't I be both?" Drew said, followed by a booming laugh. "Then maybe folks could have some decent photos for their wanted posters."

"Well, gentlemen," Nicholas said. "It has truly been a pleasure, but Audrey and I are resuming our travels bright and early tomorrow morning. We'd better get some shuteye. How long are you fellas in town?"

"Two nights," I said. "Just long enough to give the horses a good rest. Then we're moving on to Tennessee."

"Hey, sounds like we're headed in the same direction," Audrey said. "Maybe we'll see each other out on the trail."

"That would be nice," I said.

It was getting late, so Drew and I decided to meet with the rest of our crew after bidding farewell to Nicholas and Audrey. We walked along the street, which was far less crowded now, chatting as we strolled.

"Hey, Moses," Drew began. "Have you thought any more about how we're gonna get that five thousand dollars to pay Jack?"

I took a moment to collect my thoughts. Truthfully, I hadn't considered it at all since leaving Bozeman. It was a hefty sum of cash, and I knew the prospect of paying it back weighed heavily on Drew. "If I'm being honest, I'm not sure how we're gonna pay him back," I said. "But look, we've come this far. We'll figure it out. I think we should keep pressing on and give it some time. That, or you could go ahead and spring for that camera now."

Drew chuckled. "Yeah, we'll figure it out," he said. "Or, maybe we'll all catch a bullet first, and it won't matter."

"That's always a possibility," I said jokingly. "Think about this...We just spent the evening with folks whose job it is to travel and take pictures. That's the world we live in now. You and me, we got our strengths too. You're a fast talker with a mind as sharp as anybody. You're quick as a jackrabbit on the draw, too. You always told me I'm good at figuring things out and talkin' folks down when they're riled up. And so we're clear, I ain't too slow on the draw myself. If there are people out there who'll buy pictures from itinerant photographers, then there are people who'll pay for what we can provide. We just need to keep our eyes and ears open."

Drew nodded. I could see the wheels turning in his mind. "You know, I think you're onto something, Moses. We ain't too shoddy. Good enough to get paid for something anyway. Although no offense intended, you might want to reconsider ranching as a profession. That don't seem to suit you too well."

Drew and I laughed. "You have a point," I said. We walked on in silence for a bit.

Drew breathed deeply as if trying to inhale every ounce of the night. All the sights, sounds, and smells were such a change from the open country. "You know, Moses," he said after a moment. "We're doing alright. Not too bad for a couple of Grace House's finest orphans, huh?"

"Not too bad at all, Drew."

Chapter 22

Two months had gone by since our stop at Ft. Laramie. The weeks marched stubbornly on as we pushed toward Tennessee, and life on the trail was just how I remembered it. On its own, any given day could bring any number of challenges – or none at all. Depending on the circumstance, a day could be remarkably dull or frighteningly troublesome. It was as if each day had its own inclination – its own color, and as a collection, those days began to form a mosaic of memories. The rugged terrain we'd traveled left us with a collection of peaceful reflections, daunting tasks, and necessary risks. Each moment was like a shard of tinted glass, a new shade of color to chronicle our journey.

During the day, we moved steadily through the evolving landscape. Each territory displayed its unique temperament. Great, colorful valleys, hulking mountains, open plains, and vast farmlands were alive with their particular beauty. All manner of sunsets marked the end of our daily travels, washing the evening skies in colors poured right out of heaven. At night, stars hung like diamonds in the darkest of skies. The rain came and went. Cold would occasionally catch us by surprise. The sun was a friend one day and an enemy the next. We moved on.

Settlements along the way offered both respite and the threat of peril. Skillet paid for rooms at most stops so we could get a good night's sleep in a real bed. He warned us each time not to get used to it since the return trip would afford no such comforts. In the larger cities and towns, we experienced the full spectrum of the human condition. We were blessed by the warm hospitality of strangers who shared meals and advised us on our travels. Some offered us supplies simply out of kindness. But others challenged us. Leering glances or outright threats came from men who'd faced one too many hardships in life. Hurt had left them trusting few and fearing none. I didn't fault them for their distrust. We all have our pain, and most men tend to cling to their learned perspectives. We have little control over how our life experiences shape us. Each of us has suffered, each of us has loved. Everyone has their own story.

As the weeks slowly unfurled, we grew into a makeshift family of sorts. Drew, Skillet, Nellie, Two Feathers, and I now shared a history. Our individual stories merged and would continue to do so for as long as we remained together. Each of us was like a unique shard of glass in that big, intricate mosaic – removing any one of us would leave the picture incomplete.

Before long, the fresh scent of Tennessee woodlands wafted toward us on the breeze, signaling that we were nearing our destination, possibly just a few days away. I'd be lying if I said I wasn't worried. There were so many variables to consider, so much that could go wrong, and little margin for error. Still, the closer we got, the more I was determined to see things through. I gave my doubts over to faith. Of course, I questioned the wisdom of that, but the alternative was to cling tightly to my worries and possibly infect the rest of our crew with the plague of my insecurities. I would not do that. So, I concluded that if the Lord had spoken to me, He'd have to provide the way. If I was wrong and he was not involved, if I'd made it all up in my head, then I'd figure it out and hope for the best. Regardless, it was clear that any notion of control I had was merely an illusion.

Two Feathers returned to camp just before sunset with three rabbits, which Skillet turned into a stew. We sat around the fire, eating, talking, and laughing as usual. However, the closer we got to Tennessee, the more dispirited our conversations became. Even Drew and Nellie were more reserved than usual. Perhaps they struggled with the same doubts I did. Or worse, maybe they doubted me.

"Skillet," Drew said, breaking the silence, "not to pry, but a while back, you told us about losing your arm. You mentioned something about not finding your wedding ring. Moses and I were talkin', and neither of us recall you ever mentioning a wife. Were you married? Or, *are* you married?"

Skillet shared a glance with Nellie, who nodded slightly. "I was married," Skillet said. "Not for very long, mind you, but I was. Her name was Evette, and she was the prettiest girl I ever laid eyes on." Though he spoke to us, Skillet's gaze was fixed on the fire as if he used it to peer back in time. "Sweeter than Tupelo honey, she was. We met when her bothersome cousin accused me of stealin' a piece of candy from her father's shop."

"You did steal that candy," Nellie cut in. "You know it, and I know it. And it was more like a handful than a piece."

"Wait," Drew said. "Nellie, you were the bothersome cousin?"

Skillet laughed, and Nellie nearly choked on her stew. "Darn right," she said. "But what some call bothersome, I call a beloved, trustworthy relative. I'd advise you to take Skillet's words with a grain of salt. The man can't tell a story straight to save his life. He'd rather climb a tree and lie than stand on the ground and tell the truth."

"Now that's just downright mean," Skillet said with a grin. "If you have a better version of the story, be my guest."

"Gladly," Nellie said. "As I was saying, I was left in charge of the shop alongside Evette while her father went to grab a bite to eat. The man barely made it out the door before Skillet came slinkin' in like a chicken snake. He must've been hidin' out there all day, just waitin' for her pa to leave."

"Untrue," Skillet said. "I just happened to be passin' by when I noticed two lovely young women in Mr. Tucker's establishment, so I decided to drop in and pay them a visit."

"Mmhm," Nellie said in a way that made it seem like they'd had this argument several times before. "Except Evette was in the back of the store when Skillet decided to pay his visit. He came in lookin' all dodgy and shifty. Asked me if we had any flour – as if a young man would be droppin' in to check the status of our flour inventory."

"I can't help that I was a good son," Skillet said. "I was only checkin' so I could let my ma know. That woman loved to bake; God bless her. I feel sorry for you, Nellie. It must be hard livin' such a cynical life."

"Anyway," she went on, "when I turned to the counter, I saw Skillet stuffin' a handful of peppermints in his pocket, and I started hollerin' for Evette."

"Evette came out, and they both took to yappin' at me," Skillet said. "Callin' me a no-good thief and a reprobate. I tried to explain that Nellie was mistaken, but they didn't wanna listen to reason, so I ran."

"You tried to run, but we caught you," Nellie said. "Shifty little weasel."

"Go ahead then, Nellie," Skillet said, "tell 'em what happened when you caught me."

Nellie rolled her eyes. "When we caught up to him, I took a hold of his collar and made him empty his pockets."

"And..." Skillet said.

"*And* there was no candy," Nellie said. "To this day, I don't know what he did with those peppermints, but I know what I saw, you shyster. You took them candies."

Skillet shook his head. "Ain't no judge in the country would convict me based on that testimony."

"A judge wouldn't, but the good Lord knows what you did," Nellie said, grinning. "Now, why don't you finally own up to it and tell us what you did with the peppermints, Skillet?"

Skillet shrugged. "I'm sure I have no idea what you're talkin' about. Never have, never will. More to the point," he said to us, "seein' as how Evette was so embarrassed for falsely accusing me, I asked her if she'd go to the spring dance. You know, to make up for it. She said yes, more out of guilt than attraction, I'm sure. And, long story short, we were married a year later, right before I went off to do my stint in the Mexican-American War."

Nellie lowered her eyes, fixing them on the fire. Her smile slowly faded. "I still miss her," she said. "We were like sisters."

"I know," Skillet added. "I miss her too."

"What happened?" Drew said quietly. "Not to be crass, but...did Evette pass before her time?"

Nellie and Skillet nodded. Finally, Skillet spoke. "She died the first winter I was away at war. Influenza took her and her pa both. I still remember the last thing I ever said to her. I told her that I loved her and that I'd see her again before she even had a chance to miss me. Of course, I didn't know how right I was."

Nellie sniffed quietly before getting up and walking away from the fire. We let her have her space.

"I'm sorry I brought it up, Skillet," Drew said. "I should've let it be."

Skillet shook his head. "No, it's okay. I miss Evette every day. And let me tell you, fellas, it is truly painful to lose your love. Moses knows. But when I think of her and remember who she was, there's joy and comfort in it, too."

I knew all too well what Skillet described. It's strange how some memories can be the happiest and the most painful at the same time. It's as if the heart and mind battle over which one has it right. In the end, both are right. The lens we choose is what alters the view. Different perspectives.

We sat in silence, listening to the popping of the fire. Then, Two Feathers spoke. "Grandmother said spirit lives on. Death not the end.

Death is passage to different world – one where spirits dwell. We die so new journey can begin. Journey not finished without roaming spirit world. Man live. Man die. Spirit is eternal."

"Beautifully said, old friend," Skillet said. "Thank you for sharing." Two Feathers nodded and eased back into his quiet observation.

"Does a fella get a horse for that, Two Feathers?" Drew said with genuine wonder. "You know, for all that spirit world wandering?"

"What did I miss?" Nellie said as she returned and took her seat next to Skillet. Her eyes were puffy and red, but she was smiling.

"Two Feathers is teachin' us about spirits," Drew said. "I'm trying to find out if I can keep my horse. Or, if I get a spirit horse, I suppose."

Nellie didn't seem to hear him. "Well, Moses," she went on. "We're not too far out now. I'd wager all this has to be stirrin' up some things in you. How you feeling?"

I took a deep breath and tossed a couple of twigs in the fire. "Well, after mulling it over, there's something I want to tell you all. I don't feel right draggin' you into this without knowing the whole truth."

CHAPTER 23

B y the time I turned seventeen, I had finally outgrown the constant oversight of Mr. and Mrs. Ashbourne. Having completed my schooling, Logan and I became integral cogs in the running of the plantation. Logan, at twenty-one years old, was managing the day-to-day workings. On the other hand, I was little more than an extra pair of hands for any uncompleted tasks.

Sometimes, I was responsible for making deliveries to town. I was on my third delivery of the day as the loaded-down wagon rattled and creaked along the road toward Jonesborough.

Mr. Ashbourne had been corresponding with his brother in Savannah. They were deliberating whether or not it was advantageous for me to leave Tennessee and join him in Georgia. As I recall, the plan was for me to work at his brother's horse ranch. They were desperate for bodies and extra hands, and Mr. Ashbourne saw an opportunity to rid himself of me. I didn't want to go, but my wants certainly didn't factor into the decision, and the weight of it all hung over me like a storm cloud.

A potential move to Georgia wasn't the only surprise I was dealing with. A week ago, I received a letter from my long-lost friend, Drew. I hadn't heard from him in nearly four years and had started to doubt whether he was still alive. That seemed the only logical reason for his silence. So when the letter arrived, I didn't know whether to be thrilled or angry. All I knew for sure was that I missed my friend.

I remember running to my room, closing the door behind me, and tearing open the envelope. Drew's words practically danced on the page, and my heart raced with excitement.

He began by apologizing for not keeping in touch. He'd joined up with a 'great group of fellas' who'd promised him the things Drew desired most, adventure and freedom. They'd kept him fed, helped him make his own money, and had even given him a horse. He raved about how thrilling his life had become but offered no details. Most notably, Drew wrote that he was coming for me – that he and I would be a part of this crew and live the life of our dreams.

Being a drifter and adventurer was unquestionably Drew's dream, always had been, but I was unsure. Drew would likely be surprised by my hesitation. Cutting all ties and traveling the country was all we ever talked about. Sometimes, it was easier for me to borrow his passion than to find my own. Growing up, Drew was always confident about life and clear about what he wanted. I had tried to adopt his aspirations, much like a man trying on a new shirt, but I wasn't sure it fit. As much as I desired to reunite with Drew, it troubled me that he might turn up one day unexpectedly and pressure me into a decision I wasn't ready to make.

I turned into the plantation drive and pointed the wagon toward the barn, happy to be done for the day. As I pulled up, I noticed some commotion. Something was wrong. Dozens of workers gathered together, with Harold Gullet and Logan Ashborne holding court. I climbed down from the wagon and raced over. Harold's sidekicks, Earl and Carl, were there as well. They both had a hold of one of Titus's boys. It was Fisher. Fisher was fourteen years old then, and he and his twin, Tate, were nearly as tall as their father. Fisher didn't appear scared, but I knew he must be. Fear wasn't far behind when Harold, Earl, Carl, and Logan were together.

I stepped up, hoping I wouldn't draw attention to myself. There was talk of theft. A grave offense when it came to the Ashbournes. Harold Gullet had been instructed to administer punishment swiftly and publicly when it came to thievery.

"Why'd you do it?" Harold said to Fisher.

"I didn't steal nothin'," Fisher said flatly.

Earl slapped him across the cheek. "Watch your tone, boy."

Harold narrowed his eyes at Fisher while Logan looked sternly at him.

"Harold, you know we can't tolerate these people stealing from us," Logan said. "Take care of this."

Harold ignored him. "You went into the house?" he said to Fisher.

"Yessir," Fisher answered.

"You went to the kitchen?"

"Yessir."

"And you took a sweet roll?" Harold said.

"Yessir, but I didn't steal it," Fisher replied.

Harold huffed and shook his head. "If you didn't steal it, then who gave it to you?"

Fisher didn't respond. He simply shook his head. I believed him when he said he didn't steal the sweet roll. Titus and Charity had always been strict about such things. They'd taught their children to do right from the time they were old enough to understand what right was. Fisher wouldn't do something so brazen. Someone gave him that sweet roll, but I knew he wouldn't tell. If he did, whoever gave it to him would suffer the same consequence, if not worse.

Fisher's fellow workers looked on, their heads held low and their faces blank. They'd been submitting to the cruel treatment of Harold Gullet for years, and their wills had been long since broken. They wouldn't protest. They wouldn't fight. They'd allow the beatings and mistreatment to continue because they felt powerless to stop it.

"Last chance," Harold said quietly. "Did you steal from the kitchen? Yes, or no?"

Fisher raised his head, his eyes level with Gullet's. He hesitated momentarily but answered calmly, like a young man accepting his fate: "No."

"That's enough," Logan called out. "We're wasting time. Get the whip. Make a couple of the others hold him, and let's get this over with."

Carl pulled the braided leather whip from his belt and shook it out. Before he could begin, Mr. Ashbourne stepped out of the house and called from the porch. "Logan, I need to see you and Harold up here."

"We'll be there directly," Logan answered.

"Sorry, but it can't wait," Mr. Ashbourne said. "It's an urgent matter. Business. I need you both in here now."

Logan swore and angrily motioned for Gullet to follow him. "Take care of this, fellas," Logan said to Earl and Carl. "And make sure this lyin' dog feels it for a week."

Logan and Gullet walked toward the house as Earl ordered two workers to take Fisher by the arms and hold him. "If he squirms away from you, you're next," he said. "I'll whip the lot of you if I have to."

They held Fisher firmly as Earl backed away, and Carl stepped up with the whip. "I'll count 'em off, Carl," Earl said. "Whatcha say we aim for forty this time?" Carl nodded, and Earl began to count. "One." The whip came down onto Fisher's back with a painful crack. "Two." Another strike. Fisher groaned. There was already blood on the whip. "Three." Another strike.

113

Rage welled within me, and my voice erupted before I realized it. "Stop it," I demanded. All eyes were on me.

Earl's gaze locked onto mine. His eyes were cold. Possessed. "You'd best mind your own business, Moses," he said dismissively.

I turned to Carl, who stood at the ready with his whip. "Carl, stop this. You know it ain't right." I caught a glimpse of hesitancy on his face. It was short-lived.

"Three," Earl yelled out. Carl whipped Fisher again. Fisher cried out in pain, and tears began to streak down his face.

It was at that moment when the world around me went quiet. Time slowed, and I could feel my heart thudding in my chest. Fueled by nothing more than anger and fear, I lunged at Earl. Even now, I'm unsure why I chose Earl instead of Carl since it was Carl who delivered the beating. But there was no reasoning behind any of it. There was only instinct. Earl was shocked when my body collided with his. I wrapped my arms around his waist and slammed him to the ground. There was a heavy thud when his back hit the dirt, and Earl immediately fought back. We rolled around for a bit, neither of us gaining the upper hand. I punched when I could – kicked and grabbed. Unfortunately, I was no match for Earl, and he soon got the better of me. Earl managed to get on top of me and had me all twisted up as he latched on with his arms and legs. He was laughing. Laughing and slapping me in the face as he held me down.

"Oh, I been waitin' for this," he mocked as he kept slapping. "You gonna' cry, Moses? Ain't nobody here to pull me off of you now, is there?"

I struggled and twisted, grunting and writhing, but it was all in vain. Earl repositioned me, flipping me over and pinning me with my rear end in the air. He began spanking me like a child, laughing the entire time as he tried to humiliate me. His laughter grew louder with each swat.

Finally, Earl let up, and I heard him draw his gun. He pressed the barrel against my head. I struggled until I managed to get a hand on the weapon. I pulled the gun free from his grip, and Earl immediately released me. We scrambled away from one another and struggled to our feet. I pulled the hammer back on the revolver, and the click sounded like thunder in the silence.

"Oooooh," Earl said, smiling with his eyebrows raised. His silver teeth were gleaming. "You gonna' shoot me now, boy?" He fake lunged at me a couple of times. "Go ahead, do it," he taunted. "You won't. You ain't got the stones."

I stood there, breathing heavily with a loud ringing in my ears. My face was red and stinging from being slapped so many times. "I'll do it, Earl," I said. "Don't test me."

Earl bent over, cackling. "Don't test me, he says," Earl bellowed. "You believe this kid, Carl?" Then to me, "How about this? I'm gonna walk over and take that gun from you before you do somethin' stupid and get yourself killed."

"Stay away from me, Earl," I said, aiming the revolver at his chest.

Earl looked annoyed, as if I was some nuisance he didn't have time to deal with. He reached out and snapped his fingers. "Give it to me," he said. Neither of us moved. "I said, give it to me," he said louder. When I didn't respond, Earl took two quick steps toward me.

I never even realized I pulled the trigger.

There was a boom and a flash of fire and smoke. I felt the weight of the revolver as it jerked my hand back. I was numb. When the smoke cleared, Earl stood before me with a crazed look.

For an instant, I expected him to take the gun from me and punch me, but he didn't. He coughed, and a spatter of blood shot from his mouth. It got on my face. Earl looked down at the hole in his gut and dropped to his knees. His eyes were open when he collapsed onto the blood-soaked earth. Carl dropped the whip and ran.

I still had the revolver pointed at Earl's lifeless body when I felt hands on my shoulders. Someone took the gun from me. "Moses," a voice said. "Moses, look at me." I turned toward the man's voice and realized it was Titus. He shook me a little. "Moses, tell me you hear me."

"I hear you," I said. "I hear you, Titus."

He continued in a low, urgent whisper, "You gotta go, Moses. You hear me? You gotta go. You gotta run."

I heard the words, but they didn't make sense to me. I was dazed and lost in a fog of shock. "Go where?" I said. "Where am I going?"

"Away from here," Titus said. "Anywhere. They catch you, they'll hang you for this. You can't stay."

"I don't know what to do," I said, panic filling my voice. "I don't know where to go. I'm scared, Titus."

He shook me again. "Listen here, you ain't got no time to be scared. Tate's fetchin' you a horse. It's packed and ready. Keep off the roads, and don't tell folks your real name." Titus took a wad of cash and stuffed it in my pocket. "Take this. We'll do our best to slow 'em down, but they'll be comin' for you. Now, get on the horse, boy. You ride, and don't you look back."

Tate rode up at a gallop, nearly colliding with several folks. Without time to think, I scrambled into the saddle as Tate jumped off. Titus slapped the horse's rear and shouted, causing the animal to bolt forward. I held on for dear life. Once I regained my balance, I leaned low over the horse's neck and urged him on as fast as he would go. As I raced toward the treeline, I looked back and saw the Ashbourne plantation disappear in a cloud of dust. I haven't laid eyes on it since.

CHAPTER 24

It was entirely dark out, and the campfire's soft glow illuminated the concern on my friends' faces. "I should've told you everything before now," I said. "I tried to talk myself into believing it didn't matter. But, of course, it matters. I'm sorry for that. The truth is, I don't know what we're about to walk into."

Drew knew nearly everything about my life, so I reckoned he wasn't caught off guard by anything I'd shared. But it was different for the others. We didn't have the history I had with Drew. I couldn't have held it against them if they decided to pack up and leave.

Skillet spoke first. "Moses, we all knew this wasn't gonna be some Sunday mornin' stroll when we agreed to help. I wish you would've told us the full story, but it don't change nothin' for me. I'm still in." He looked to Nellie.

"I don't feel like we have a choice," Nellie said. "Those folks need us. If we don't help, what's gonna happen to them?"

I shook my head. "I'm not sure, but I'm willing to bet it'll be nothing good. Logan Ashbourne is a cruel man. He's been that way since he was a boy. Barring him having some profound change of heart, I expect things are even worse now. He'll either end up killin' them, or he'll mistreat 'em so bad they'll wish they were dead."

Nellie nodded. "Then there ain't no question. I'm in, too. I can't tolerate folks being mistreated. I may not be a soldier like Skillet or a bounty hunter like Drew, but I can hold my own, and I ain't afraid of trouble. Besides, it's obvious you care about these people, and I care about you."

"You know I'm in," Drew said. "I only hope Harold Gullet is still around. He and I have some unfinished business." Drew hadn't mentioned it, but I knew Harold Gullet had to be on his mind. What happened with the horse when he was a kid – there was no way Drew could let it go.

Instinctually, we turned our eyes to Two Feathers, who simply shrugged his shoulders. "Some men do wrong. Other men made to stop them. This man is bad. We stop him."

"Simple enough," Skillet said. "Well, Moses, it sounds to me like you gotta squad that's willin' to see this through with you. We'll be pullin' into Jonesborough soon, and we have a lot to talk through. We need a plan."

I nodded. "You're right. And thank you, all of you. No more secrets. From here on out, everybody knows everything, and we make decisions together."

We sat there for a moment before Two Feathers stood. "I'm going now," he said, offering no further explanation. "Be back by sunrise."

"Hold on, pal," Drew said. "Where you off to?"

"Bandits close by," Two Feathers said. "Been following us all day. I go watch them. Let you know if they mean trouble."

"Wait," Drew said. "They've been following us all day? How do you know?"

"They not very good at hiding," Two Feathers said. "I go now."

"Go ahead, Two Feathers," Skillet said. With a stiff nod, Two Feathers left to fetch his horse. "He ain't the best conversationalist, but you can trust the man," Skillet said to the rest of us. "One thing about Two Feathers is you gotta let him do things his way. I give him his space, and he's never let me down."

"I believe you," I said. "But just to be safe, let's take turns on lookout tonight. We don't need any surprises."

"I'll take first watch," Drew said. "I ain't tired no way."

I wasn't sure if I'd sleep knowing bandits were nearby, but it wasn't long before I drifted off and slept soundly. It was just before my watch, around two that morning, when I was jarred awake. Gunshots. Two of them.

"You all hear that?" Skillet whispered loudly, rummaging around for his Spencer rifle.

"Sounds like it came from northeast of here," I said, pointing in that direction. "Skillet, what do you think?"

"Same," he said. "Probably a quarter of a mile."

"That's right," Drew said, racing back from his lookout position. "What's the plan, fellas?"

"You and Nellie stay here with the wagons," I told Skillet. "Drew and I will ride out and see if we can locate Two Feathers – find out what the shots were about."

Skillet and Nellie agreed, and Drew and I quickly saddled our horses. We had become adept at packing up and leaving at a moment's notice, a skill honed from our past lives on the run. I grabbed the Schofield Drew had given me and checked that my twelve-gauge was secured in its scabbard before mounting my horse. Drew was already on Stormy, waiting for me. He carried the matching Schofield and had a Winchester resting across his lap.

We set off northeast toward the gunshots. Side by side, we moved slowly, hoping to remain unseen. The night was washed in a silvery glow, and the full moon offered plenty of light to navigate. As we reached the tree line, we began a gradual incline. The horses struggled as the brush thickened and the slope steepened, but the top of the ridge was within sight. We knew once we reached the crest, we'd have a clear view of everything below.

Two more shots rang out. Then several. We were close and clearly headed in the right direction. Trying to keep quiet no longer mattered, and we raced forward up the bluff, pushing our horses as fast as we dared through the dark. Soon, we topped the crest of the hill and found a small opening where we could stop and take a look. In the clearing below, a small campfire of coals glowed eerily with two lifeless bodies sprawled out next to it. A third man, with his back to us, was wildly shooting into the trees opposite us as he moved toward his horse. He mounted up and took off, firing a few more aimless shots.

Two Feathers emerged from the treeline on horseback and gave chase to the man. I don't know how he spotted us from where he was, but he did. He pulled to a stop and called out to us. "Get back to wagons. Now." Two Feathers flicked the reins and yelped as his Appoloosa kicked up dirt and bolted after the other rider.

Drew and I shared a glance before turning our horses and darting back down the incline. Whatever reason Two Feathers had for directing us back to the wagons was not something to stop and question. After all, Skillet told us to trust the man, and I trusted Skillet.

With grim determination, we raced ahead, hooves pounding and hearts racing. The forest was a blur around us, and more gunshots rang out in the distance. When we cleared the woods, we rode like the devil himself was chasing us as we thundered into camp. We flung ourselves from the saddle and scanned the area as we ran up.

What we saw stopped us in our tracks. In the middle of camp, Nellie was held captive by what I assumed was one of the bandits from over the bluff. He had a knife pressed to her neck. Skillet was crouched beside one of the wagons with his rifle resting on the wheel, pointed at them. The man noticed us and took a few steps back, dragging Nellie with him.

"Stop right there," he said. Drew and I both pulled our revolvers and put some space between us. "Drop the guns. All of you." His desperate eyes darted about like a cornered animal. Nellie was doing her best to stay calm and still.

"Come on now, fella," Drew said. "There ain't no need for all of these theatrics. What is it you want? Let's work something out."

The man looked strong and more than capable of handling himself. His face was smeared with sweat, dirt, and blood. He was desperate but steady. I had no doubt he'd kill Nellie if we pushed him. "Where's the Indian?" the man said. "Tell him to show himself."

"He ain't here," I said. "The last we saw, he was chasin' one of your buddies on horseback, headed east. It's just us."

The man was starting to panic. "I said drop the guns," he screamed. Nellie whimpered. "I swear I'll slit her throat. You think I'm afraid to die? Well, I ain't. But if I go, I'm damn sure takin' her with me."

"Alright, we hear you," I said. "Everybody put your weapons down."

"Ah, you sure about that?" Drew said. "Seems like a risky proposition to me."

"Do it," I said. "You too, Skillet."

I dropped my revolver and kicked it in the man's direction. Skillet grumbled something I couldn't understand and tossed his rifle aside. Drew looked at me like he was disappointed but still went along. He flipped the gun around and held onto it by the barrel.

"You," the man said to Drew. "Bring me your gun. Nice and slow. Lay it on the ground in front of me." He pressed the knife forcefully against Nellie's throat to show he meant business. "Hurry up."

Nellie groaned a little but kept quiet. Drew moved slowly and carefully and placed the gun on the ground at the man's feet.

"Now back away," the man said. Drew showed his palms and did as he was told.

When the man saw his opening, he threw Nellie to the ground and snatched up the revolver. "Now, bring me the horse. The black one."

"Oh, come on," Drew said. "How many times is somebody gonna try to take my horse?"

"Do it, Drew," I said.

Drew huffed like a kid being told to finish his chores. Nellie scrambled away from the man but stayed put on the ground.

"You," the man said to me. He gestured to Nellie with the revolver in his hand. "Tie her up."

"Tie her up?" I said. "Why? We'll give you what you want, and you can be on your way."

"I said tie her up," he bellowed as he pulled the hammer. "Make it tight. She's comin' with me. Call it insurance. If I look back and see any of you followin' me, she dies."

Drew returned, leading his horse, just as I began to tie up Nellie. "Don't worry," I whispered. "We'll get you back."

The man snatched the reins from Drew and yelled at him to back away. He pointed the revolver at me. "Hurry up," he hollered.

Those were the last words he ever spoke.

It happened in an instant. A figure emerged from the darkness like a ghost and grabbed the man from behind. The revolver fired, but it was pointed straight up into the air. There was a large knife. The man's throat was slit clean and deep. He made a gargling sound and collapsed, bleeding out on the ground. Standing behind the man's lifeless body was Two Feathers. He had a look on his face like he'd done nothing more than pour himself a cup of coffee.

The rest of us looked on, a bit shell-shocked. Two Feathers didn't say a word. He casually pulled out a piece of cloth and began wiping the blood from the blade of his knife.

"Two Feathers?" Drew said carefully. "Everything okay?" Two Feathers simply nodded and returned his knife to its sheath. "That was a bold play there, don't you think?"

Two Feathers looked at each of us, finally noticing our surprise. "Man needed killin'," he said. "I kill him."

"What about the others?" I said.

"I kill them too," Two Feathers replied. "They won't be back."

"You killed all of 'em?" Skillet said. "How many were there?"

"Four men," Two Feathers said. "I listened to them around the fire. They killed others. Planned to kill us tonight. I kill them first." Two Feathers' horse, Denali, walked up behind him, and Two Feathers retrieved a pack he was hauling. "Here," Two Feathers said. He tossed me the bag, which was stained with blood. "Sorry about your friends."

I opened the pack, and inside was a thick stack of photographs, a notebook, and a camera. The pack belonged to Nicholas and Audrey, the itinerant photographers Drew and I met in Fort Laramie.

"They traveled the entire world only to end up getting killed by a bunch of no-good outlaws in Tennessee," I said, mostly to myself.

CHAPTER 25

We did our best to put the incident with the bandits behind us. As we rattled along the rugged terrain, the wagon creaked steadily beneath Skillet and me. Drew and I decided to give our horses a break, so Cali walked alongside Skillet's wagon. Stormy was tethered to Nellie's wagon, where Drew rode. He'd been keeping an eye on her since the encounter with the bandits.

"Is Nellie doing okay?" I said to Skillet. "She's been quiet lately. You think she's still shook up?"

Skillet kept his gaze fixed on the winding trail in front of us. He held the reins with his only hand but somehow managed to keep his Spencer rifle balanced on his lap. "How could she not be? I'm sure it's still botherin' her, but don't let it worry you. She's tough as nails, that one. It'll take her some time, but she'll come around. Nellie's a hard woman to keep down, Moses."

I nodded. "I have no doubt she is. It has to be weighing on her, though." I could still picture the knife pressed against her throat and the fear in her eyes.

"I've known her most my life," Skillet said. "If I was a bettin' man, I'd wager Nellie's melancholy will turn to hellish fury any day now. You know, woman scorned and all that."

"You concerned about that?" I said.

"Concerned? I'm lookin' forward to it," Skillet said. "We're gonna need her good and hacked off with all the trouble we have coming. Don't let that big smile and sunny disposition fool you. I ain't known many women that can put a man in his place quicker than Nellie Dagget. We're lucky to have her – her and Two Feathers both."

"You know," I said, shifting the conversation, "I couldn't help but notice how easily Two Feathers cut that fool's throat. Don't get me wrong, the man had it coming, but still. It was like...like it wasn't nothin' to him."

Skillet twisted up his face in thought before glancing at me. "Two Feathers, he ain't like you or me. He's a good man, but he lives by a different code. I met him durin' the war. We joined up with the Union at the same time. I was a cook, and he was a guide. We was friends from the start. I was one of the few white men who'd speak to him at all, which wasn't too difficult a prospect for me. I enjoyed talkin' and he rarely said a word, so we got on well. Two Feathers always had a way about him. A calmness that none of the rest of us had. I've always respected that."

"Do you know anything about what he did before the war?" I said.

"Not a lot," Skillet continued. "I know his tribe was murdered by settlers moving west when he was just a boy. Nasty business. They burned their crops, destroyed their homes, and killed all the men, women, and children. All except Two Feathers. One of the men caught him and wanted to spare him. Thought he'd keep him and teach him to be civilized, if you can imagine. Anyway, Two Feathers escaped the settlers after a few months and set out alone. After drifting for a few years, he joined up with the Union Army."

"Why would he want to fight a white man's war?" I said. "His people were wiped out by white men."

"And that's exactly why he joined them," Skillet said. "Two Feathers figured that by helping the Union, he might earn their help in return. He hoped that folks would start seein' Indians as people instead of savages, and that the government would be grateful enough to protect them and their lands. Plus, he hated the idea of slavery, so he joined up."

"So all of this feels familiar to him in a way," I said. "Us going to challenge Logan Ashbourne and free those people."

Skilled nodded. "I'm sure it does. It's an uncomplicated idea, and that appeals to him. Two Feathers views the world simply, without the emotions that regular folks get hung up on. He makes a decision, follows through, and that's that. There is right and wrong. Day and night. One or the other. He weighs things out, acts accordingly, and moves on. I don't know if his is a good way or not. Never been able to decide."

"I suppose it's a good way," I said, "unless the day comes when he reckons he's right and you're wrong."

"That's true," Skillet chuckled. He flicked the reins a bit and stretched his legs. "Two Feathers has saved my hide many times over the years. He ain't one to spin a fancy yarn or crack a joke, but when he speaks, the man means what he says."

I mulled over Skillet's words for a while. It helped to have a better understanding of Two Feathers, and I found myself with a newfound respect for the man. He'd been through no shortage of hell in his life, yet he still believed there was right and wrong. And he aimed to land on the side of right, all while carrying himself with a type of serene resolve. There was undoubtedly more to him than first appeared, and I was thankful to have him on our side.

Still, there were more pressing concerns to ponder. First and foremost, we needed a plan to confront Logan Ashbourne and ensure the release of the plantation workers. We'd kicked around several ideas while traveling but hadn't landed on anything solid yet.

The sun eased down into the arms of the Appalachian Mountains as we rode into the modest town of Greeneville. It was small but busy, just the same. The weathered wooden structures and the gaslit street lamps gave the town a distinctive charm.

Skillet knew the place well. He said he'd stayed here for a spell during the war and always felt welcome. I was also somewhat familiar with the town, having made several delivery runs for the plantation when I was younger. It hadn't changed much.

We wound through Greeneville's narrow streets till Skillet reigned in at the livery and wagon yard. A kind old gentleman named Oscar greeted us before we even climbed out of our seats. After a brief chat, he took our horses, secured our wagons, and assured us he'd keep them safe and sound.

Skillet then led us to a place called The Lane House, a local tavern where we could get a good supper and a solid night's rest. It was a nice tavern with dark wooden floors and a polished oak bar. The smell of freshly baked bread greeted us as we entered, and a smiling lady named Debbie showed us to our table. According to Skillet, The Lane House had been a welcomed respite for Union and Confederate soldiers alike during the war. His face lit up as we took our seats, and he couldn't resist sharing stories of his time in the service.

"Whatcha think, Two Feathers?" Skillet said, scanning the room. "She ain't changed a bit, has she?"

Two Feathers shook his head. "Same," was all he said.

125

The Lane House was bustling with travelers, which was surprising given the town's small size. Their voices blended into a continuous hum of activity, a pleasant sound to most of us, except for Two Feathers. He was rarely at ease in crowded spaces.

"Well, everyone," Skillet said, "this'll likely be our final stop before Jonesborough. Eat, rest up, and say a few prayers tonight. There won't be time for such things when it all breaks loose."

"Since we're here for the night," Drew said, "we might as well ask around a little. See if anybody knows anything about what's happening at the Ashbourne place."

"Just be careful," Nellie said. "We don't need word spreading that a crew passed through here askin' questions about the Ashbourne's Plantation."

"She's right," Skillet said. "The best thing we got goin' for us is that Logan Ashbourne don't know we're here. We need to keep it that way. Don't muck things up."

"Have a little faith, why don't ya?" Drew said to the table. Then, mockingly to me, "Moses, why don't you come with me to the bar? You know, help make sure I don't say something ignorant and ruin everything?"

I agreed, shrugging my shoulders at the others as Drew and I walked over and squeezed into the last empty seats at the bar. I sat at the end with Drew to my right. Next to Drew was a rather portly fella with thin black hair, round spectacles, and an impressive double chin. He was likely considered influential in his circles – a portrait of the modern businessman. A clean white button-up shirt and creased pants with shiny, black shoes completed the look. I figured he was someone whose work was conducted primarily indoors, probably behind a desk.

"Hello, sir," Drew said, extending a hand. "My name's Frank Filmore. How are you this evening?"

The large man wiped his thick hands on his napkin and pulled himself away from his plate of fried fish to shake Drew's...or Frank's hand.

"Pleased to meet you, Mr. Filmore," he said in a deep voice. "I'm Robert Bishop."

I decided to keep quiet and let Drew handle this. Besides, I didn't enjoy pretending to be someone else. At least not as much as Drew. It was like he had a collection of characters filed away in his head, and he could pull one out whenever needed.

"Are you from Greeneville, or are you just passing through?" Drew said.

Robert took a swig of water and wiped his whole face with his napkin. "Oh, I've lived here going on fifteen years now. I moved from Knoxville back in the summer of sixty-one. I take it you're just visiting since I don't believe I've seen you around before."

"Yes, sir, I'm just passin' through," Drew said as he motioned for the barkeep. He was working out some kind of accent, but I wasn't sure what he was going for. "My family's in the horse ranchin' business in the Texas hill country. You ever hear of Tranquility Ranch?" The man shook his head. "Anyway, I was nearby making a delivery and thought I'd drop in for a visit on my way out. Right nice town you've got here, Mr. Robert Bishop."

"Thank you," Robert said with pride. "We believe it's a fine place with fine people. I've known several good folks from Texas as well. I've never been, but I always wanted to. I suppose you and I have something in common, Mr. Filmore. It would appear the family trade keeps us both busy. I'm in the accounting business myself."

"Oh, a numbers man," Drew said. "And please, call me Frank."

"Yes indeed. I took over the business for my father a few years ago. Have you ever heard of Bishop and Warwick? It's a pretty big operation. I have clients from here to Nashville."

"You don't say?" Drew replied, feigning interest. "I was never too keen on the business side of things. I just never took to it. My brother handles the bookkeeping. I do my darndest to keep my feet firmly in the stirrups."

"There's nothing wrong with that," Robert said. "So you say you were nearby making a delivery? Where was that?"

"I hauled a dozen Thoroughbred stallions across the country for some rich fella at the Ivywood Plantation, just outside Jonesborough. For the life of me, I can't remember his name, though."

"The Ivywood Plantation?" Frank said with a grin. "That rich fella would be Logan Ashbourne."

Drew pointed at him and snapped his fingers. "That's it. Ashbourne. Logan Ashbourne. I knew it was something like that."

"Believe it or not, Logan Ashbourne is a client of mine," Robert Bishop said. "We've had an account with his family for years. It's mostly a tobacco operation, but they love their horses."

"Yes, they do," Drew went on. "There was another fella there with Mr. Ashbourne. His name is slippin' my mind as well. Big fella. Kind of rough, you know?"

"Probably Harold Gullet," Robert said. "He's been with the plantation since he was just a boy. And yes," Robert said as he glanced around, "he is a rather tough customer."

"You know," Drew said, leaning in closer to Robert and lowering his voice, "I don't know nothing about this place or how things work here in Tennessee. But something about that whole Ashbourne operation seemed a little off to me. Does that make sense?"

Robert nodded knowingly and raised his eyebrows. "Well, first off, I'd ask that you not judge the great state of Tennessee by what you may have encountered at the Ashbourne residence."

"How's that?" Drew said, urging Robert on.

Robert Bishop drew in a heavy breath and repositioned himself on the barstool. "Well, they've had a bit of trouble lately. The law got involved and everything. About a year ago, two of their workers turned up dead. A couple of hunters found their bodies in a cave about three miles from the plantation. They'd been shot in the head. It was quite the scandal for this county, let me tell you. Anyway, the law investigated and even questioned some of the workers. The story I heard was one of the colored folks ratted on Logan Ashbourne. He told the deputy that Ashbourne had the men killed when they tried to escape."

"You don't say," Drew said before downing his drink. "What did he mean by that? That they tried to escape? Like I said, I don't know how you folks in Tennessee run things, but if a man wants to leave a job in Texas, he just walks away."

Robert nodded enthusiastically. "Absolutely, and that's the way it should be. But some folks...some folks still operate the way they did before the war, if you know what I mean. Now, those men aren't technically slaves, but they sure are treated like it. They work but don't get paid the same way you or I would. They get paid with food on their plates and a roof over their heads."

"I don't know, Robert Bishop," Drew said. "That don't sound much different than slavery to me."

"Nor does it to me," Robert said. "But men like Ashbourne don't like the idea that there's something out there they can't own. That includes people."

"How'd things end up playin' out with the law? Did anybody get arrested?"

Robert shook his head. "No, sir, they didn't. The Sheriff said there wasn't enough evidence to warrant an arrest."

"No evidence? What about the fella that squealed?" Drew said. "Did he testify?"

"He never got the chance," Robert said grimly. "Three days after he talked to the law, the man turned up dead by a fatal blow to the head. Ashbourne claimed he was kicked by a horse while trying to shoe him. Who knows what really happened."

"So, they just dropped the whole thing?" Drew said.

"Far as I know," Robert replied. "I didn't expect much to come of it anyway. The Ashbournes have had the law in their pocket for as long as anyone remembers. Just a few years back, the whole plantation house burned down with Augustus and Josephine Ashbourne inside. Those are Logan's parents. Everyone thought Logan had something to do with that, too, but no one could prove it."

"It sounds to me like folks would do well to steer clear of the Ashbournes," Drew said. Then he laughed and slapped Robert on the shoulder. "Hell, I'll still take their money, though. You know what I mean, don't you, Mr. Bishop?"

"Indeed I do," he said. Robert Bishop then stood up, wiped the crumbs from his shirt, and slicked his thinning hair back. "Well, it has been a pleasure, but I must be on my way. The little woman worries if I don't get home in a timely manner. Good luck with the horse trade, Mr. Filmore." He shook Drew's hand. "Look me up if you ever find yourself in these parts again."

"Will do, Mr. Bishop," Drew said. "And thank you for the rather stimulating conversation. If I'm ever in the market for an accountant, I will surely come to call on you, good sir."

Robert Bishop left the tavern with a smile on his face as Drew turned to me. "Well, that was something, don't you think?" he said. "Sounds like everything we've suspected about Logan could be true after all."

"Unfortunately, it does," I said. "It also sounds like this could be a lot tougher than we thought. Logan won't give up easily. Things could go bad."

"I'm gonna operate under the notion things *will* go bad," Drew said. "It saves time that way."

I nodded. "By the way, nice work there, Mr. Frank Filmore. You played the good Mr. Bishop like a German fiddle."

Drew grinned, tipped his hat, and, in his worst Texas accent, said, "Well, thank you, partner. Much obliged."

CHAPTER 26

I was seventeen, I had shot and killed Earl Weston, and I was running for my life on a stolen horse. It all happened so quickly I didn't have time to think things through. Titus told me I was in danger, to ride and not look back. So that's what I did. Once I'd gathered my wits, my first inclination was to circle back and seek refuge at the Grace House Orphanage. It was the only home I'd ever known aside from the Ashbourne's. The idea passed quickly. Harold Gullet would be hunting me, and Grace House was likely one of the first places he'd look. I'm sure the Peabodys would've tried to help me, but I couldn't burden them with my troubles or put them in danger.

I rode alone through the Tennessee countryside for twelve days. I avoided roads when possible, kept my head on a swivel, and steered clear of any form of civilization. My days were spent navigating dense woodlands, crossing creeks and rivers, and covering my tracks. I hunted small game like rabbit and squirrel with a .22 revolver I'd found tucked away in my saddlebag. It wasn't long before the hardtack and dried beef ran out, and the .22 became my lifeline. During the day, I kept on the move, hunting as I went. When nightfall came, I made camps in secluded areas, using the skills Titus taught me growing up.

All things considered, I was faring quite well until my ammunition began to dwindle. It had been two days since I'd eaten anything other than berries and wild greens. My belly ached with hunger, and I decided that hiding in the wilderness was no longer an option. Unless I planned on starving to death, I'd have to seek out the nearest town, find a little work, and fill my stomach. It was a risk, but I had to make money, buy food and supplies, and keep moving.

The most significant obstacle in my plan was figuring out where I was actually going. With no family or friends to speak of, I mostly wandered aimlessly, hoping for some idea to come to me. It never did. I was as lost as a boy could be, alone in a world that wanted nothing to do with me.

After a few days of searching, I came upon a modest-looking mining town called Copperfield. Small settlements like this could spring up almost overnight, filled with prospectors seeking their fortunes. Word would spread each time someone struck it big, and a town would quickly form with saloons, general stores, and boarding houses. Such was Copperfield, a small, muddy outpost in the middle of nowhere Tennessee, filled with rugged men who carried the scars of hard work and sacrifice.

There wasn't much to the place. It had a few stables, a general store, a rundown hotel, and three shabby saloons where hardworking men could unwind. Oddly enough, the best thing about Copperfield was its lack of a sheriff. With no law around, there wasn't anyone looking to track down a murderous runaway. As long as I kept my head down, I'd be safe.

I rode the dark bay into town and hitched him outside one of the saloons, an establishment called Smitty's Place. Stuffing the .22 into my waistband, I decided to take a look around the sad little town. Desperation gnawed at my gut as I went from business to business, asking for work. I tried the Copperfield Hotel first. When they asked, I told them my name was Drew. Granted, it wasn't the most creative answer, but it was a name I wouldn't forget. One by one, from the hotel to the stables to the saloons, they all turned me away. The business owners made it clear they had little patience for outsiders, and I quickly discovered that Copperfield was by no means a friendly place.

With my hope dwindling and my stomach growling, I returned to where I'd hitched my horse at Smitty's Place. A sign on the wall read, "Today's Special: Bowl of Chili with Cornbread, twenty-five cents." My mouth instantly watered as I shoved my hand into my pocket and pulled out a handful of wadded-up bills. Titus had given me four dollars in all. I didn't want to spend it, but I didn't want to starve either, so I went in and asked for the special. A skinny grump of an old man took my money, slopped a couple of spoons of chili into a bowl, and dropped a piece of cornbread on top. He grunted something that might have been "thank you," and I nodded and carried my meal to the nearest table. I couldn't recall a time I'd ever been so hungry, but I tried to pace myself and not devour the meal too quickly.

The dimly lit saloon was practically empty since most of its usual patrons were still at work in the mines. One fella sat at the table across from me, sipping on a glass of whiskey. He was in his mid-thirties, lean and dirty, with skin darkened by the sun. He watched me closely, but I didn't care. I would finish eating, leave Copperfield, and try my luck in the next town. There had to be someone looking for a hard worker.

Just as I finished wiping the bowl with my last bite of cornbread, the man stood up and ambled toward me. "Morning, son," he said with a slow, southern drawl. "You mind if I chat with you for a minute?"

"I suppose not," I answered. "Can't stay long, though. My pa is waitin' on me."

He smiled at me and shook my hand as he sat. "My name's Mark."

"Drew," I lied.

"You know, I couldn't help but hear you askin' about work earlier," Mark said, leaning back in his chair. "Anything pan out for you yet?"

"Not yet," I said. "Why, you got work?"

He shook his head. "Nah, I'm just passin' through. Is that your bay out front? The gelding?"

"It's my pa's horse," I said. "He let me bring him into town since I was lookin' for work and all."

"Uh-huh," Mark said. He looked me over like he was searching for some clue as to who or what I was. "What kinda work is your pa in?"

"He don't – he ain't working right now," I said, my mind racing. "He got hurt down at the mines. I've gotta find work to help out."

Mark put his elbows on the table and leaned in close. "Your pa's outta work, you say?"

I nodded. "That's right."

"So your pa is outta work, but he's got no problem with his boy ridin' into town and spendin' money on old Smitty's chili special of the day?"

"I gotta eat," I said with a shrug. My voice shook.

"Alright, let's cut to the chase," Mark said. "You ain't got no pa waitin' on you to get home. More than likely, you're a runaway or a grifter, but that ain't no concern of mine. You see, I'm on my way up to Kentucky, but my horse stepped in a hole about ten miles outside of town. I need a horse. You got one."

"I ain't givin' you my horse, mister," I said.

He grinned. "Do I look like some common outlaw to you? You think I'm the kinda' man to just take a fella's horse and leave him stranded?" He stared at me for what felt like minutes. I didn't respond. "Now, I'm gonna forgive you for assuming I am a man of ill intentions, but I'd advise you not to insult me further."

"I don't rightly know what kind of man you are," I said. "But if you ain't tryin' to rob me, how about you just tell me what you want."

Mark slapped the table and laughed. "Now, that's somethin' I can respect – a man who gets right down to business. I'll tell you what I want, Drew. I want to buy that horse from you. I'll give you a fair price. Ten dollars. You can eat a lot of chili with that kind of money. And, just to show there ain't no hard feelings, I'll throw in a box of cartridges for that peashooter you're carrying."

"Sorry, mister, I can't sell the horse," I said. "I'm leaving town myself as soon as I'm done here. Besides, the horse is worth at least fifty dollars."

Mark looked shocked. "Fifty dollars?" he said. "What kind of horses are you all breedin' up here in Tennessee? That gelding better have a golden mane to fetch a price like that."

"Don't matter if it's gold or not," I said, "'cause I ain't selling."

Mark took a settling breath and leaned forward. He reached down and removed a Colt revolver from his holster, and placed it on the table between us. His face hardened, and his voice was barely above a whisper.

"Here's how this is gonna go," Mark said. "I tried to be fair with you, but since you insist on makin' things difficult, the deal has changed. See, I'm gonna stand up, leave this saloon, get on your horse, and ride away. If you step one foot outta this saloon before I'm long gone, I'll put a hole in your chest. Is that clear...Drew?"

I nodded stiffly and stuffed my anger. My jaw was clenched, and my eyes narrowed. "I need that horse," I said, trying to match his tone.

"Tough break," he replied. Mark stood and walked toward the door before stopping and turning to the bar. He tossed a coin to the old man. "Hey, Smitty, get my friend here another bowl of chili, will ya? He's had a helluva day." Mark smiled, nodded at me, and left the saloon.

I scrambled to the window but wasn't dumb enough to go outside. I watched as the stranger approached my horse and gently patted his neck. There was nothing I could do.

"Chili's up," Smitty called out as he dropped the bowl onto the bar.

I wanted to punch something or run outside and stand up to the thief. But I knew better. The man had a way about him that made me believe he was telling the truth. There wasn't any law around to stop him from shooting me and taking off. So, with no horse and no bravado, I sat down and ate my second bowl of chili. I needed time to come up with a plan anyway.

I'd taken no more than two bites when I noticed some commotion outside. Smitty must have heard it, too, since he immediately reacted, clearing the glasses and heading toward the back. "You'd better take cover, boy," he said as he raced to his office and slammed the door. I took Smitty at his word and found a table to turn over and hide behind. It was quiet, and I could make out most of what was said outside.

"I ain't gotta tell you a damn thing," I heard Mark yell.

"Oh, I reckon you do," a gruff voice answered. "My friend asked you a simple question. Where'd you get the horse? Don't make this more than it's got to be."

"Where does anybody get a horse, you moron?" Mark bellowed. "I bought him."

"From who?" another voice said. The voice of a younger man. "Who'd you buy the horse from? And when?"

"I don't know," Mark said. "Some runaway who was lyin' about lookin' for work. Probably just tryin' to find some sucker to rob."

"Listen, mister," the younger man went on. "You need to start searchin' for some better answers real quick like. Otherwise, I'll let my friends here help jog your memory."

I crawled over to the window and peeked outside. Mark stood by my horse with his back to me. Two large, rough-looking characters were facing him. One of them held a shotgun. The younger man was blocked from my view.

"So now you're threatenin' me?" Mark said as his hand drifted to the revolver on his hip. He wasn't planning to draw on them. He moved too slowly for that. He was just readying himself. Mark attempted to carry on with his angry rambling when the big man with the shotgun slammed the stock right into his forehead. He was mid-sentence when the dull crack sounded, dropping him to his knees.

"Get him outta here, fellas," the younger one said. It was then I noticed him. Drew Harlan stood there proudly, dressed like a legitimate gunman, boots to hat. He stepped toward the saloon and strained to look inside. "Moses, you in there?" he called out. "Come on out if you are. It's me, Drew."

I raced out the front door just as Drew walked up. "I'm here," I called out. "And boy, am I glad to see you, Drew."

A wide smile stretched across Drew's face, and he playfully punched my shoulder. "Look at you," he said. "Moses Colter in the flesh. Where have you been hidin' fella? I've searched every pig trail, saloon, and outhouse from here to Jonesborough. It's about time you got sloppy."

"How'd you find me?" I said. "How'd you know I left the plantation? Did you hear about what happened?"

"Woah, slow down," Drew said. "Let's go sit and talk. Everything's gonna be fine. You got nothing to worry about now."

Drew and I returned to Smitty's and sat at one of the tables. Old man Smitty eased out of his office and gazed warily at us. Drew assured him all was well and asked for drinks and two bowls of chili. I had no qualms with it.

"I heard about everything," Drew said. "Titus told me."

"You saw Titus? Is he okay?"

Drew nodded. "He's fine. The day after you left I snuck onto the plantation looking for you. Of course, you weren't there, but I ran into Titus while I was sneaking out. He told me about what happened with you shootin' Earl and how you had to run. He pointed me in your direction and told me about the dark bay you made off with. Me and the fellas have been looking for you going on two weeks now."

"I appreciate you lookin' for me," I said. "And finding me. I was about to lose my horse when you showed up."

"I knew that fella was lyin'," Drew said. "I'm glad Charlie cracked the fool good. At least we got here before he made off with your horse. So, what's the plan now, Moses?"

"I ain't got one," I said. "The last plan I had was...don't starve."

Drew pounded his fist on the table. "Perfect," he said. "There ain't nothing to worry about now. You can ride with me and the boys. I'm telling you, you're gonna love it. Being out in the open country, riding from town to town, doing jobs – there ain't nothin' like it. And look at this..." Drew pulled a thick roll of cash from his pocket and slapped it down on the table. "Believe me, there's a whole lot more where this came from."

"Who are these folks you been running with, Drew?" I said, my face lined with concern. "Those fellas with you looked a little rough."

Drew huffed. "You mean Charlie and Tommy? Don't be fooled by them. They may look tough, but they're softer than a kitten's belly."

"I don't know, Drew," I said. "It seems like you might be mixed up in something dangerous."

"Listen," Drew said. "I get it. You tend to get a little nervous about things. But these ain't some bushwhackers I fell in with. We're legitimate. Now, I will admit that sometimes things go sideways, and we do what we must. But mostly, we're solid. And we could use a stand-up guy like you."

"If you say so."

"Just give it a chance," Drew said. "I got somebody I want you to meet. He's a great man and a real straight shooter." He glanced out the window. "Look, here he is now."

The saloon doors swung open, and a heavyset gentleman stepped inside. He was dressed nicer than most but was covered in road dust. He removed his hat to reveal a slick, bald head and a closely cropped, black beard. Stepping toward us with a huge smile of straight, white teeth and a boisterous laugh, he reached out his hand.

"Hello there, son. You must be Moses Colter. Your friend Drew here speaks very highly of you. Very highly indeed." He paused. "Pardon my manners, my name is Jack Davis. Most folks call me Smiling Jack."

CHAPTER 27

Drew and I huddled behind a cluster of rocks on a ridge over-looking the sprawling Ivywood Plantation. We left our horses picketed among the trees and brush below and climbed to our vantage point just as the day was ending. The sun was low in the sky behind us, shielding us from the view of those below.

Drew lifted his field glasses, and I extended my spyglass to see how much the plantation had changed since we'd last been there and if there were any new threats to contend with. It was our last exercise in secrecy and whispers. After today, there would be no more moving in the shadows. Everyone would soon know who we were and why we were here. So, for now, we gathered as much information as possible until the veil dropped and we were exposed.

The plantation hadn't changed much. However, several new structures had sprung up for equipment and storage, and six manned watchtowers now covered the grounds' perimeter.

"Looks like Gullet's been tightening things up," I said in a low voice.

"Yep," Drew said. "Brought in more guns too. He's got one in each tower."

"Wonder what's got them so spooked? Why would a tobacco farm need so much protection."

"Well, look who we have here," Drew said, tapping me on the shoulder and pointing out a group of men near the tobacco fields.

I lifted my spyglass and focused on Logan Ashbourne, who was barking orders at one of his workers while looking as arrogant as ever. He'd put on some weight since I'd last seen him and looked more like his father than I remembered. Next to him was Harold Gullet, who, besides having a few more miles on him, still looked strong and capable. The hulking, slow-moving Carl was nearby, and I assumed he remained Gullet's right hand.

Workers were toiling away in the waning light, their figures appearing as mere shadows against the backdrop of the fields. Seeing them work while Logan, Gullet, and Carl looked on with smug superiority filled me with anger. But that anger passed quickly. I surveyed the watchtowers, noting the armed men stationed inside, and a deep sense of despair took over. On our best day, we were no match for such firepower.

I lowered the spyglass and turned to Drew. "Counting Gullet, Logan, Carl, and the fellas in the towers makes at least nine armed men. Not good odds if things go poorly."

"We've handled worse," Drew said, putting away his field glasses.

"Yeah, but not without a crew."

"We have a crew," Drew said.

"We don't have a crew," I answered bitterly. "We've got a cold-blooded Indian, a one-armed cook, and a woman who nearly got her throat cut a few days ago." The words came out more harshly than I'd intended.

Drew stared at me. In that moment's silence, doubt began to creep into my heart like a murderous specter, muddying my thoughts and tapping my resolve.

"What's going on with you, Moses?" Drew finally said. "This ain't like you. Since when are you afraid of a few guns and a bunch of loudmouths? I ain't never known you to turn yella."

"I ain't yella," I snapped. "It's just..."

"It's just what?" Drew said, raising his voice. "If you got somethin' to say, go ahead and say it. What's this all about? What's got you turned all inside out?"

"I've been thinking," I said, lowering my voice. "I think maybe we should call this whole thing off. It just ain't worth the risk. What if all we do is make things worse? What if good folks get hurt or killed?"

"What if nobody gets hurt or killed?" Drew's answer came in an instant. "All these good folks you're talking about? What if they've been hoping and praying someone would show up to help them? What if it's worth the risk to *them*? Don't they deserve to choose for themselves?"

"Don't you understand? I let some foolish dreams and Reverend Phillips' naive way of thinking get to me. None of this is real. It can't be. I sold myself a bill of goods, and now, when it's time to cash in, I gotta face the fact that it's all worthless."

"If what you're saying is true, then you must think the rest of us are dumber than rocks. There ain't none of us been duped. We're all grown, and we all knew what we were gettin' into."

"No, this is on me," I said. "This is my fault. I went and made up some tall tale to find somethin' worth living for – somethin' more than feeding sheep. I've hauled you all across the country to find some reason to live, to feel like there's meaning. But it's all for nothing. I'm starting to believe there's no meaning in anything, just the stories we tell ourselves. Now, I'm putting a lot of good people at risk. And for what? Pride? Desperation? To help folks who never even asked for it?"

Drew locked onto my gaze. His eyes were those of a man who had weathered a lifetime of hardship. Drew was a friend, and he knew me better than anyone. He spoke carefully with concern and resolve in his voice. "Moses, I don't mean no disrespect when I say this, but this ain't about you no more. And it ain't about you doubting yourself either."

"I know it ain't about me," I snapped. "But to say it ain't about me doubting myself? That's where you're wrong, friend. This is most certainly about me –"

"No, it ain't," Drew said firmly. "All this moaning and whining ain't got nothin' to do with your doubts. This is about you being scared. You're scared things are gonna go wrong. You're scared folks you care about will get hurt. And you're scared you'll be the one to blame when it all falls apart. You may not like hearing it, and it might make you mad, but the truth is the truth. You're scared, and it just ain't like you. I've seen you face worse than Logan Ashbourne, and doubt never played any part in it."

There was a lump in my throat, and my eyes stung with tears. I made an effort to speak a couple of times before the words finally came out. "When I lost Elise and my – When I lost Elise, I learned what it was to lose the one thing you care about more than anything. You and me, we've had a hard life, but I never felt pain and fear like that before. It did something to me, Drew. It's like it hollowed out my insides, and I haven't found anything to fill it back up. But when all of this came up, something changed. I felt like I had a reason to exist – like I wasn't hollow no more. I was alive, and it felt good. But now..."

"Now, it's all real," Drew said, "and instead of feeling good about it, that hollow ache is creepin' back in." He paused. "I get it. I have it too sometimes."

"What do you do about it?"

Drew grinned. "Usually, I just drink and play cards till it goes away."

"We could try that, I suppose," I said with a laugh.

"Seriously, Moses," Drew went on, "we can't turn back now. You know that. You can't ignore all those dreams and your talks with the reverend. And you sure can't turn your back on all those good folks down there in that Godforsaken place. They need us. And from what you've told me, you need them. We've come too far to give up. So, go ahead and be scared. Be scared and do what you have to do anyway."

Drew didn't realize it, but his words were a lifeline for me. He never struggled to believe in anything or anyone he cared about. Although I didn't always have that kind of confidence, I drew strength from his unwavering convictions. His strength became my own.

"You're right, Drew," I said. "We're gonna do this. We have to."

Drew smiled and slapped my shoulder. "There he is," he said. "Now, what's the plan? I say we go in guns blazing. We can rescue those folks, deal with Ashbourne and his hired guns, and be done with the whole mess."

"We gotta find a way to do this without more bloodshed. Those men and women have gone through too much pain already."

Drew nodded. "I'm with you on this. We'll do it however you see fit. Just let me know when you get it all figured out. But you better have a darn good plan 'cause we got one shot at it."

"The way I see it playin' out," I said, "you and I are gonna walk right in there, tell Logan Ashbourne we're taking those people, and then leave. No guns. No spilled blood."

Drew raised an eyebrow and exhaled slowly. "Alright, Moses. I trust you. I'll be right by your side every step of the way."

As we began the descent from our perch, the distant rumble of thunder echoed across the hills. To the east, the sky was like a black, smoky shroud. Was it an omen? My first thought was that the good Lord was either showing me He approved of my decision or warning me to turn back. I brushed the thought away as quickly as it came to me. I would press on, follow my gut, and do what I thought was right.

Chapter 28

Although it was already mid-morning as Drew and I made our way toward Ivywood Plantation, the day remained dark. Yesterday was clear and bright, with a vast blue sky and wispy white clouds. Now, the sky had become a roiling expanse of smoky gray. Heavy, black clouds billowed on the distant horizon like stormy seas whipped into a furious churn. As expected, the threatening weather made Drew anxious, and he kept a cautious eye on the horizon as we walked.

"You good, Drew?" I said. "You've been awful quiet. What's on your mind?"

Drew kept an eye trained on the skies. "I'm thinkin' it's a good thing we brought our slickers."

"Yeah, and what else?"

Drew turned to me and paused. "I'm just considering things. Is this still how you wanna do this? I told you we'd do it your way, and I meant it. I just want to make sure I'm clear about what's happening. The plan is still the plan, right? No horses? No guns? No...nothing?"

"The plan is still the plan," I said. "We're gonna walk in, state our business, collect our people, and move out."

Drew walked on with me in silence for a few moments. "And you really think it's gonna happen that way? All easy-like?"

I shook my head. "No. But that's still the plan."

"Mmhm," Drew muttered. "So, for the sake of conversation, what if the plan doesn't work? Again, I'm not doubting, just asking. What'll we do then?"

"If it doesn't work like we hope," I said, "then we'll come up with somethin' different – a new plan."

Drew nodded vigorously. "Got it. Good. Sounds good. If the plan don't work, we come up with a new one. Simple enough."

"Relax, Drew," I said, resting my hand on his shoulder. "Ain't nobody gettin' shot today. Just remember to keep a level head. We walk in. We walk out. Nothin' foolish."

Drew nodded, and he and I pressed on with no further discussion.

Not only was it dark that morning, but it was quiet. Still. It was like every living creature for miles around was watching and waiting, captivated by the foolishness of men. The only sounds were those of wind-rustled trees and our boots stomping along the compacted dirt road.

A few uneasy minutes later, our path led us right up to the front gate of Logan Ashbourne's estate. Our entryway was blocked by iron bars and two familiar figures. Gullet and Carl. The two recognized us immediately and stepped onto the road to meet us. Both men were armed. Harold Gullet led the way with narrowed eyes and a bit of amusement and suspicion playing on his face.

I spoke first. "Harold...Carl," I said, keeping my voice steady. "It's been a while."

Harold grunted and shook his head. "Get a look at these two, Carl," he said. "A motherless degenerate and a murderin' fugitive." He looked at me. "I ought to call the sheriff and be done with you, but I gotta say, I am interested why either of you would show your faces here. You plannin' to come back and finish the job, Moses? You gonna try and kill the rest of us like you did Earl?"

"We're here to see Logan Ashbourne," I said, hoping to move the encounter along. Gullet was baiting me into a confrontation, but I refused to oblige. "It's important."

"You're Drew, right?" Harold said with a nod in his direction. He seemed to ignore my comment altogether.

"That's right," Drew said flatly. "You missed me, Gullet?"

Harold laughed mockingly. "You remember this fella, don't you?" Harold said to Carl. Carl's expression didn't change. "He's the one that snuck in here as a boy and killed old man Ashbourne's favorite horse. Now he's got the nerve to show up makin' jokes."

"All we wanna do is speak to Logan," I said. "If you'll kindly show us to him, we'll say our peace and be on our way."

"You know, I'm still confused. What makes you think it's a good idea to stroll in here askin' to see Logan Ashbourne?" Harold Gullet continued. "I mean, look at you. You ain't even heeled. I always knew you boys was a touch funny in the head, but this makes me think you actually *want* to die."

"Are you gonna take us to Logan or not?" I said. "As hard as it might be for you to wrap your head around, we didn't come all this way to reminisce with the likes of you."

Harold glanced at me, then to Carl, and back to me again. He smiled. "Sure thing, Moses Colter." He opened the gate. "Right this way."

As Harold Gullet led us to the plantation house, I could feel the eyes of the workers boring into us. At first glance, I didn't recognize any of them, but it had been several years since I'd walked these grounds. Their hushed whispers and wary glances followed us up the drive. The Ivywood Plantation was smaller than I remembered, but I suppose most things look more imposing when you're a kid. The same could be said of Harold and Carl. I was terribly afraid of them as a boy, and rightfully so. I still considered them formidable, men worth being cautious of, but the fear I once had was no longer there.

I glanced up at the hills on either side of the plantation. Skillet and Nellie were perched atop them, hidden, rifles at the ready. They'd insisted on providing Drew and me cover, but it wouldn't make much difference if shooting started. We were unarmed and outmanned. Still, Skillet and Nellie wanted to help, and I couldn't deny them that.

We reached the front steps, and Harold Gullet turned to us with one final mocking huff. "Stay here," he said, rolling his eyes. "Carl, keep an eye on them. I'll be right back with Mr. Ashbourne."

We watched as Harold ascended the stairs and entered the home. Drew, Carl, and I stood there in silence until Drew decided to speak. "Hey, Carl," he began, "Does Logan make you call him Mr. Ashbourne now?" Carl didn't look at Drew and didn't answer. "I figure that's gotta be a burr in your saddle, don't it? A spoiled, aggravating little twit like that struttin' around like he's the governor. I don't know how you do it."

"Ain't no concern of yours," Carl mumbled.

The sky had grown so dark that it appeared evening had come early, and a roll of thunder rumbled like a primal growl that shook the earth. Drew muttered something about disliking the look of the clouds and urged me to hurry things along.

"Drew," I said, whispering forcefully. "In case you haven't noticed, we're in the middle of a situation here. Forget the weather."

Drew grunted in disagreement.

The door swung open, and Logan Ashbourne stepped onto the porch with Harold Gullet by his side, shotgun in hand. Logan stopped short at the top of the stairs.

"Moses Colter," Logan said slowly and deliberately. I hated the sound of my name coming out of his mouth. I could practically feel his disgust. "You've got some nerve showing up here after what you've done." He looked at Drew. "And with Drew Harlan, no less. I see you're still living in your friend's shadow, huh, Drew?"

"If it's all the same to you, we can cut the chit-chat," Drew said. "I assure you we are no more thrilled to see you than you are us."

"Fair enough," Logan said. "You always were the more direct one. So, exactly why are you here, Moses? Are you planning on turning yourself in for killin' Earl? I can send word of your confession to the sheriff straight away if you'd like. Or did you come here to try your hand at killin' me?"

"I ain't here for nothin' like that," I said. "My hope is that you and I can settle our business like gentlemen. There ain't no need for killin' today. Truth be told, there never was a need for it."

"Well, there's finally something we can agree on," Logan said. "Now out with it. I'm growing bored with this, and I have a lot to do today. What is it you fellas want?"

I turned around and motioned to the workers with a broad sweep of my hand. "I want them," I said. "All of them."

Logan glared at me momentarily as if he was assessing what to make of my words and whether or not our presence was a threat. "You want them?" he said. "Them *what*? Are you talkin' about horses? Tobacco crops? Wagons?"

Thunder boomed again as I shook my head. "No, I'm here for your workers – the ones you hold here against their will. I don't mean to start any trouble, but I aim to take them out of here."

Logan searched our faces like he was waiting for someone to tell him this was all in jest. He released an uneasy laugh. "You're here to take my people? The ones who keep this whole operation running?" He pointed toward the workers who had ceased their chores to watch the scene unfolding. "These people?"

"Yes, these people," I said. "They've endured more than their share of torment at the hands of you and your men. And I'm certain whatever debts they owed you or your pa have been paid several times over. It's time for you to do right by them."

"And doing right by them is letting them go with you? Even though they belong to me?"

"They don't belong to you," I said. "No man belongs to another. Not anymore. They work for you. Nothin' more. You don't pay them, and you shoot them when they try to leave."

"I pay them with a roof over their heads and food in their bellies," Logan said as his face flashed red. "As for shootin' them, sounds like you've been listening to the gossip of old maids and drunk cowboys. We already have the law in these parts, and I doubt they need your assistance. Besides, the only folks around here that get shot are trespassers."

"I'll be fair with you," I went on. "If any of them want to stay here on the plantation, they can. I'll only take the ones that wanna go. A man reserves the right to leave a job anytime he wants."

"I don't know how you think things work," Logan said, "but there are only two kinds of men in the world. Men with power and men without it. They ain't got no power, and they'll stay here as long as I see fit whether they like it or not. This is still the south. And this is still my land. And these..." Logan waved his hand at the onlooking workers, "these people are mine."

"Seems like you and I aren't gonna reach an agreement," I said. "Not yet, anyway." I paused as Logan and I stood there staring at one another. "The way I see it, these folks were always more my kind of people than yours. Now they can decide. I ain't lookin' for a fight, but I'm here to tell you that you gotta let these people go."

Logan Ashbourne laughed, his voice like a whip. He waved a dismissive hand at me and Drew. "Look around you, Moses. I've got half a dozen armed men just waiting for me to say the word. And let me tell you, they are killers, the best gunmen in the state.

"Now, since I'm feeling somewhat generous today, I'm gonna give you and your friend a chance to turn around and scurry back to whatever rock you've been hidin' under. Or you can stay, and I'll have these workers you love so much dig a couple of holes for the two of you."

I shook my head. "There's no need for that. We'll go. But you're making a mistake."

"My only mistake is being kind enough to let you walk away," Logan said. "I could have the law here before you reach the front gate."

"You could," I said. "But I don't think you will."

"It's time for you to go," Logan said, seething. "And just so there's no confusion, if you come back, I'll have my men shoot you on sight."

I nodded and turned to leave, but Drew stayed put.

"Logan, you can try your best to puff yourself up and intimidate us," Drew said, "but it just don't work no more. One way or another, these folks are comin' with us. We'll be back soon enough."

Carl trailed behind us as we left the property. Drew and I said nothing as we walked away and passed through the front gate. As soon as our boots hit the road, the clouds opened up, and rain began to pour. It felt as if the Lord Himself was mourning the struggle to come.

CHAPTER 29

The rain fell with relentless determination as we met up with Skillet and Nellie and walked back to camp. Fortunately, Nellie had the forethought to pack everyone's slickers, making the long walk a bit less miserable than it might have been otherwise. We moved along, hunched over, side by side, none of us talking. There would be plenty of time to discuss things when we were safe and dry. Two Feathers had stayed behind to wage his own war against the elements and set up camp. As we returned from the Ivywood Plantation, we couldn't help but marvel at the quality work Two Feathers had accomplished.

Our camp had been transformed into a covered haven. Two Feathers had dug a series of intricate ditches to divert the standing rainwater, ensuring we wouldn't be up to our knees in mud. He'd stretched rain covers between the surrounding trees, creating a spider web of shelter to protect our belongings. He even fashioned a covered fire pit for cooking supper and amassed a hearty pile of firewood to keep us warm throughout the night. Skillet and Nellie, tired from our slog through the rain, lavished praise upon Two Feathers for his quality work and the time and effort he'd saved us all.

Supper was prepared quickly. It consisted of a humble fair of beans and bacon with biscuits and a handful of greens Nellie had gathered. We ate heartily and enjoyed the dry warmth Two Feathers had provided.

With little else on our minds, the conversation soon turned to the pressing matters of Logan Ashbourne and the workers of the Ivywood Plantation. We each had our own opinion on the issue but fully agreed on the part that mattered most. We would complete our mission.

Drew was never one to mince words or hide his thoughts, and he kicked off our conversation with his disdain for Logan. "I'd love to rip that silver spoon out of his mouth and choke him with it," he muttered. "I can't stand the look of his smug face. I'd just as soon shut him and Harold Gullet up for good."

I leaned in closer to the fire. "Logan is certainly spoiled, but he's more than that, Drew. Logan's dangerous, cruel, and easy to set off. We have to treat him like a powder keg so he don't blow and take everyone with him. One thing is clear, though. He won't let those folks go without a fight. That's why we gotta be smart about this."

"What that fella needs is somebody to rough him up good and proper," Skillet said as he stoked the fire. "Probably never had the boot put to him in his life. He's like a slice of fine-cooked beef shank. It looks tough enough, but it's softer than butter when you put the knife to it."

Nellie had been listening intently to each of us. "Logan Ashbourne is a mama's boy with a chip on his shoulder. He thinks he can do whatever he pleases, 'cause he's never been taught no different. But Moses is right. He is dangerous. With enough money and power, any man can be dangerous."

Drew nodded and tossed a stick in the fire. "Money has built him a nice, safe world where he's the king. I'll give it to him, though. He's smart enough to surround himself with muscle. The man has never seen a gunfight in his life, but he's loaded for bear."

"And seein' how he was so willing to involve the Sheriff," I added, "means he ain't worried about the law either."

Skillet grunted. "It's likely they're on the payroll too."

Two Feathers had been quiet. His eyes darted from one of us to the other as we spoke, eyes as strong as steel and sharp as a hawk.

"I sneak onto plantation?" Two Feathers said with an eerie calmness. "I go in quiet and kill Logan Ashbourne in his sleep. Cut his throat. Sneak away. Hired guns will leave. We take people and go."

A hushed silence fell over our circle, broken only by the pattering of rain upon the tarps and the crackle and hiss of the fire. It was a tempting offer – a violent yet swift resolution to our problems.

Without a doubt, we all considered it, but it was Drew who finally spoke. "No, Two Feathers. As much as I'd love to see that, we can't let ourselves become what we despise. Killin' Ashbourne ain't the right thing to do if we can keep from it. We gotta get those people out, and we gotta do it the right way."

"Drew's right," I said. "If everything works out, we'll leave here with no blood on our hands. But if Logan Ashbourne decides to fight, we'll do what we must."

"What's the plan now, Moses?" Drew said. "You know...the new one?"

I ran a hand through my matted, wet hair. "Well, while I don't aim to kill Logan in his sleep tonight, I could use your help, Two Feathers."

Two Feathers nodded. "Should I saddle horses?"

"Yeah, I think so," I said. "I want you to help me sneak onto the property tonight. I need to talk to Titus and see what he and his people make of all this. We need to know we have their backing. If so, and if they want to be freed, we'll do everything in our power to make it happen."

Two Feathers didn't reply. He simply ran off into the dark, rainy night and began to saddle our horses.

Skillet placed his hand on my shoulder. "We support you, Moses. Always will. We'll do things the way you see fit. But please be careful. This rain might give you some cover, but it won't hide you from everything. They got a lot of eyes around that place. And a lot of guns."

"You want me to go with you, Moses?" Drew said. "I can back you up."

I shook my head. "I think we can move faster with just us two, and there's less chance of being spotted."

Drew reluctantly agreed as Two Feathers returned, soaking wet. "Horses ready," he said. "We go now?"

"Sure thing," I said. "And I'm sorry you haven't had a chance to properly case the grounds yet, Two Feathers. I guess I didn't think that through."

"I know the plantation," Two Feathers said.

"You do?" Drew answered. "How's that?"

"I was there today," Two Feathers said. "Watched everything. Heard everything."

"Wait, you were there the same time we were?" Nellie said. "And you got close enough to hear everything?"

Two Feathers nodded but did not explain.

"That can't be," Skillet said. "When did you find time to get the camp ready? And how could you do all of this and still get back before us?"

"When you leave, I make camp," Two Feathers said, "then sneak on plantation. I listen and ride horse back while you walk."

"Well, I'll be," Drew said. "Two Feathers, you are a genuine man of intrigue."

CHAPTER 30

The rain continued, pelting us with fat, heavy drops as Two Feathers and I tethered our horses and crept toward the plantation. Mud squelched beneath my boots and pulled at my legs as I walked. My bulky slicker kept me dry but made scratching sounds as we moved through the brush. I worried I might be making too much noise, but my main focus was keeping up. In contrast, Two Feathers moved with the grace of a shadow. He wore no rain gear, and his moccasin-clad feet barely left a trace in the mud.

At the treeline, Two Feathers stopped and looked to me for direction. I gestured toward the workers' living quarters and pointed out the small wooden structure that once belonged to Titus.

It was late, and the plantation slumbered beneath the weight of the storm. Two guards were making rounds, their bundled-up forms barely discernible through the murky downpour. Fortunately, that meant the guards would also have difficulty spotting us.

Watching Two Feathers move so skillfully across the grounds was indeed a marvel. He slipped through the shadows with silent precision, keeping us out of sight of the gunmen in the watchtowers. My heart raced as we neared the workers' quarters. I hadn't realized how much I'd missed Titus, Charity, and their boys, Fisher and Tate. It would be good to see them again, even under such troubling circumstances.

When we finally reached their humble living quarters, Two Feathers motioned for me to continue inside while he kept watch. Using only his hands and eyes, he communicated more clearly than ever. If there was trouble or anyone approached, he would warn me with two knocks.

I nodded and stepped to the front door as Two Feathers faded into the night. A coal oil lamp faintly flickered through the window, meaning someone was awake. I knocked softly and held my breath as I heard shuffling.

With a loud creak, the door swung open, and in the entryway stood my old friend Titus. It only took one breathless moment for recognition to dawn in his eyes. A broad grin spread across his lips as he pulled me inside and quickly shut the door behind us. My feet immediately left the floor as Titus grabbed me in a bear hug that nearly squeezed the breath out of me. Some may have thought it a rather undignified greeting, but I appreciated it nonetheless. Titus dropped me to my feet and called for Charity while looking at me like I was a prodigal returned. We stood in the dimly lit room, water dripping from my hat and slicker, when Charity stepped into the light with a smile bright enough to chase away any storm.

"Moses Colter," Titus said in an excited whisper. "Alive and well and standin' right in front of me. I told you, Charity. I told you it was him. It sho' is good to see you, Moses."

The sound of his voice was comforting. Since I'd last seen him, Titus had certainly aged. He was almost entirely gray, with just a patch of dark hair above his forehead. The soft, golden light from the lamp called attention to the deep lines crisscrossing his weathered face, much like the trenches of the tobacco fields where Titus had spent most of his years. Still, he remained Titus. Large and imposing but gentle and peaceful.

"It's good to see you too, old friend," I said as Titus finally gave space for Charity to hug me as well. She handed me a towel to dry my face, but I didn't have time to do much more. It felt nice, and as the warmth began to seep back into my bones, we sat in the rough-hewn chairs adorning their modest home.

"I seen you when you and the other fella came up," Titus said, "but I thought it best to keep away."

"That was probably a smart move," I said. "There's no need to get Logan Ashbourne any more riled up than he already is. By the way, that fella with me was Drew Harlan."

Titus' eyes grew large. "Drew Harlan? Your friend from the orphanage? You don't say."

The three of us spoke quickly, and the conversation flowed naturally as if the time that separated us had never existed. We had shared years of memories, days of both joy and pain, and those experiences bound our spirits. It was a connection more powerful than time. Titus and Charity told me of their struggles and how things had changed since I left. Logan

Ashbourne and Harold Gullet had grown even more cruel after Logan's parents died.

Had the situation been different, I could have sat and talked for hours, but unfortunately, I had not returned that evening to sit and reminisce. The rain drummed even harder on the roof, and I thought of Two Feathers hiding out in it. I needed to hurry the conversation along.

"Titus, Charity," I said, "I know you're surprised to see me, and I'm sure you're wondering why I'm here." They both nodded and watched me intently. "The truth is, I've come here to take you away from this place. I have land in Montana, where you can build a new life far away from this plantation and Logan Ashbourne. It won't be like it is here. My home will be yours. You can work the land, raise livestock, or do whatever you want. It'll be up to you. Whatever money you make, you can keep, and you'll be free to come and go as you please."

I don't know what I expected, but the silence that followed was nearly unbearable. Titus looked to Charity, then to me. His eyes held a mixture of hope and sadness, and only then did I realize the weight of the decision I was asking them to make. Whether or not my offer appealed to them didn't change the fact that this plantation had been their home for decades. Giving them mere moments to make such a life-altering decision wasn't entirely fair.

Charity began to speak, but Titus placed a hand on her knee, and she dropped her eyes and fell silent. "Moses," Titus began, "thank you for wanting to help, but Charity and I can't leave all these good folks behind. I don't mean no disrespect, but we got friends and family to think of. They done suffered this place right along with us. Sometimes these folks...well, sometimes they need a body to help. They need protectin'. My boys, Fisher and Tate, they here too. They both grown now with wives and youngins of their own." He smiled, and his eyes watered up. "My grandbabies. I can't just leave 'em."

I nodded, suddenly feeling the gravity of his conviction. "I understand, Titus. I'm sure I'd feel the same in your shoes, but I don't know if I was clear. You see, I've planned for this. We're not just here for you and Charity. We're here for everybody. Any of your friends and family willing to take a chance on a better life are free to come along. That's why I came here to see you tonight. I want you to find out who all is willing to join us. If no one wants to, we'll pack up and head home. But if even one of you wants to go, we'll get you outta here."

Titus leaned forward, resting his elbows on his knees. He looked to Charity, and they shared a hopeful smile. His gaze was intent and unwavering. "Montana? That's a long way, ain't it?"

"It is," I replied. "And it won't be easy. It's likely to be downright miserable at times. We can count on trouble along the way, and there's no shortage of things that can go wrong. But being free out there in dangerous territory has to be better than stayin' here, don't you think?"

Titus nodded and looked to Charity, who smiled and nodded as well. "I'll talk to 'em, Moses," he said. "I'll tell 'em everything you just said and find out what they wanna do. See how many are willin' to go. Then I'll send word."

"I know this is a lot to throw at you, Titus," I said. "But I promise, I'll do right by you. I'll do right by all of you."

"What about Logan Ashbourne?" Charity said gently. "He ain't about to let us just pack up and leave. How you plan on handlin' him?"

"I'll take care of Logan," I said. "And I'll keep us safe. I didn't come all this way to get folks killed. Just be ready to move when the time comes. Trust me. If we just walk, the path will open up for us."

Two Feathers knocked twice on the door before pushing it open and peering inside. "It's okay," I said to Titus and Charity, who were startled at the sight of an Indian easing into their home. "This is Two Feathers. He's a friend."

"Moses," Two Feathers said quietly. "We go now. Weather getting worse. We should move."

"Go," Titus said. "I'll send word as soon as I'm able."

"We'll be waiting," I said as I approached the door.

"And, Moses," Titus called out, "it sho' does my soul good to see you. Thank you for not forgettin' about us."

CHAPTER 31

Two Feathers and I rode side by side toward camp, keeping our heads down through the unyielding rain. My hat was pulled low to shield my eyes while the raindrops beat against my slicker. The wind had picked up, whipping around pine needles and debris while the trees swayed around us. Most ominous were the clouds rolling overhead. They were practically boiling, igniting the horizon with orange flashes like fire riding on the wind.

We returned to camp, where Drew, Skillet, and Nellie huddled around the flickering campfire. Once we'd secured the horses, Two Feathers and I joined them and filled them in on my talk with Titus. Drew was consumed with the severity of the weather and could hardly concentrate on the conversation unfolding around the fire. He jumped at every flash of lightning and clap of thunder. The shelter Two Feathers had put together was holding for the moment, but I had my doubts it would survive the night.

My words had little effect on improving the group's mood, mostly because I had no new information to offer. Nothing about our situation would change until Titus sent word of the workers' decision.

With a heavy sigh, Skillet posed the question I most dreaded. "What's our next move, Moses? We can't stay here long if we plan on beatin' the winter. Plus, we have a more pressing problem."

"What's wrong, Skillet?" I said. "Are we running low on supplies? Is it a money problem?"

Skillet shook his head. "It ain't a money problem. It's a supply problem. I'm gettin' worried, friends. I went into town to ask around about buying some wagons, but nobody wants to sell to us. They've heard about us and what we're plannin', and they're all scared of Logan Ashbourne." Skillet removed his hat and ran a hand through his stringy, gray hair.

"Without more equipment, we can't move all those people. We've got two wagons and a mule, and that ain't near enough."

I nodded. "Don't worry about the wagons," I said. "Somethin' will come through for us. We can check the towns nearby if we have to. As for beating the winter, I don't suspect we'll be here much longer. I figure we should be headin' out in the next day or two."

"No offense," Skillet said, his face etched with concern, "but how do you figure all that? How are you so sure we'll get the wagons we need and get on the trail in the next two days? It's like you know somethin' we don't."

I didn't know any more than anyone else in our crew, but I had a gut feeling stronger than my doubt. I couldn't explain where my assurance came from because it didn't even make sense to me. But I believed the Lord would make a way for us, or at least I hoped He would. I tried to share my thoughts as best as possible, but I knew my words offered little comfort.

Drew spoke up in the silence that followed, turning the conversation back to the weather. "How much worse you reckon this storm's gonna get?" Drew said. "Can we even travel in this?"

"Storm is strange," Two Feathers said. His eyes followed the clouds, west to east. "Never seen storm like this. It's unnatural. It's living and breathing. Watching us."

Drew gawked at Two Feathers like he'd just turned into a ghost before his eyes. "That is downright terrifying," he said. "Moses, please remind me to never talk to Two Feathers about the weather."

Nellie didn't seem to hear Drew or Two Feathers at all. And, if she did, she certainly thought there were more important things to discuss than the weather. "If the townsfolk know about us, you can bet Logan Ashbourne knows where we're camped," Nellie said. Her eyes, typically warm and filled with laughter, were shadowed by doubt and worry. "What do we do if Ashbourne sends his men after us? We're sittin' ducks out here."

"He won't," Drew said, his eyes scanning the sky. "Logan's had enough heat on him with the plantation house burning down and the workers they found dead. He may be above the law, but there ain't nobody *that* much above the law. There's no way he wants more attention right now."

I considered Drew's words for a moment. Something about what he said rang true to me. No one is so above the law that they can get away with anything they please. There are limits to everything, including power and influence. Maybe we should find out how far those limits stretched. It was then I noticed the circle of concerned faces turned to me, waiting for answers. Their worries and expectations pressed down on me, but I had faith we were doing the right thing.

"Listen, I know we got problems," I said forcefully. "But I still believe the Lord is in control of all this." My voice was steady with a conviction I hoped wouldn't be short-lived. "I believe it's time for Logan Ashbourne to learn he has limitations just like the rest of us."

"Sounds nice," Skillet said, "but how you plan on doin' that?"

"Tomorrow, I'm going into Jonesborough," I said flatly. "I'm gonna find the Sheriff and explain what's happening. And I'm gonna turn myself in for killing Earl. I'll tell them it was self-defense."

Drew finally took his eyes off the black horizon and looked at me. His apprehension was clear, and his voice strained with worry. "Moses, you can't do that. You can't trust the law. Especially not here."

The others anxiously agreed, hoping to change my mind, but I was determined. I knew it was the right thing to do. It echoed through my bones.

"I can't allow Logan Ashbourne to use the law to threaten me, Drew. It's time the law worked for the people it was meant to protect."

As if in response to my declaration, a deafening crash echoed through the heavens. The trees around us shook and creaked, sounding like they might snap in two. Then, the hailstorm hit. Hail the size of plums fell from the sky, thudding against the earth and pounding against the covering. Two Feathers raced off to release the horses as we scrambled for shelter beneath the wagons. He soon returned, and we all huddled close together as the storm raged around us. I'd seen hail before, but never like this. Icy stones plunged toward the earth for what felt like an hour. It was deafening under that wagon, with hail slamming against the sides and top.

When it finally eased up, well into the early morning hours, we crawled from our hiding place to assess the damage. The camp was wrecked, the wagon covers and stretched canvases shredded, and the horses were nowhere to be found. I was beginning to think Two Feathers was right. This storm might actually be alive and angry. My prayer was that we'd endured the worst of it. Still, the rain continued to fall.

CHAPTER 32

B y the time I turned nineteen, Drew and I had been running with Smiling Jack for nearly two years. I don't know if it was a life I willingly chose or if I was little more than a casualty of happenstance. Still, life with the gang settled into a peculiar kind of normalcy over time, and I felt safer than ever before. Jack kept us fed and well-armed, and we always had a secure place to lay our heads at night. It was the life of adventure we'd always dreamed about. However, as Drew and I soon discovered, our sense of security was a double-edged blade.

Jack's gang was a ragtag collection of young men with complicated pasts – a dozen troubled souls with a dozen different stories of pain and regret. Drew and I were the youngest of the bunch. At times, if the night was still and quiet or if the drinks had been flowing freely, we'd all sit around and revisit tales of our not-too-distant pasts.

Jack's boys told their stories differently than most folks. Customarily, a man would recount painful experiences with a melancholy spirit or insightful reflection. But those young men spoke of pain and loss with thinly veiled anger, like they believed life had wronged them and wanted someone to pay for it. More often than not, that someone turned out to be a stranger carrying something the boys wanted or an unfortunate individual who happened to cross their path on a bad day. Back then, I didn't understand the rage they carried or why they were so consumed by it. I only knew I didn't share their view, and my story didn't sound like theirs at all. So, I kept my past to myself. Still, I liked the boys well enough, and we all managed to find comfort and camaraderie to help ease our troubled circumstances.

Smiling Jack had shown himself to be a generous man as far as Drew and I were concerned, and he always ensured we had a bit of coin in our pockets. Mostly, we kept busy running deliveries. We were paid fairly for work that required little beyond our loyalty. Early on, we learned not to ask questions about our cargo. Some days, we knew exactly what we were hauling – basic supplies, equipment, and the like. At other times, it was a more mysterious endeavor with sealed envelopes and locked boxes that hinted at the workings of a world beyond our station.

It wasn't lost on Drew and me that the other members of our gang often undertook more dangerous tasks. They'd spin thrilling yarns about their close calls with bullets and death, and they spoke of killing as casually as recalling their morning chores. I often wondered if their indifference toward matters of life and death was merely a show of bravado or if the gravity of taking a man's life held no weight for them.

"Come on in, Moses, Drew," Smiling Jack said as we entered his makeshift office. No matter where we set up, Jack always had an office. Sometimes, it was little more than a tent with a desk and a few chairs inside. "We need to discuss some things, so why don't you have a seat." My heart pounded as we sat facing Jack. "First off, I want you boys to know that I appreciate what you do for this outfit. You've shown yourselves to be worthy of trust, which is worth far more than gold as far as I'm concerned." He leaned back in his creaky old chair, his typical smile strangely absent.

"Thank you," Drew said. "We've enjoyed runnin' with you, Jack." Only a moment of silence followed, but I could tell every tick of the second hand tried Drew's patience. "Is everything okay?"

"I hope so," Jack said, tapping on the desk with his thick fingers. "You see, boys, up until now, you've both reaped the benefits of this gang without takin' on the same risks as the others. Now, that's not to say you're at fault in any way. I've taken my time with you because I needed you to prove yourselves. I wanted to see what you fellas were made of before you started workin' the high-paying jobs. But now, I need you. Your tab's been runnin' long enough. It's time to pony up."

"We'll do whatever you need, Jack," Drew said. "Moses and I have been chompin' at the bit to get out there and earn our way."

Smiling Jack fixed his gaze on me. "How about you? Do you agree, Moses? You ready to show what you're made of?"

"I wanna do whatever I can to help the gang," I said, hoping my voice wasn't as shaky as it felt. I'd heard what the other fella's jobs were like, and I wanted no part of it. Luckily, my dodgy answer seemed to suffice. Jack didn't press further, and I offered no more than necessary.

Jack smiled, showing his straight, white teeth, and nodded. "Very good, boys," he said. "That's exactly what I wanted to hear. I'm proud of you both. I really am. Now, how 'bout we get down to business."

Smiling Jack's pride in us felt nice, but it was a fleeting comfort. He proceeded to outline the new job he had for us. And based on the intensity with which he delivered the details, we knew it was one we had to get right. Drew and I were to deliver rifles, pistols, and ammunition to a place called "The Last Chance Saloon," just outside the dusty little town of Carsonville.

"I'm not gonna lie to you boys," Jack said. "This ain't like the jobs I've sent you on before. The man you're meeting is named Brett Turner, and he's one mean bastard. He's likely to have at least a couple of his men with him, who I suspect will be mean bastards as well. Don't go lookin' for a warm welcome. He's expecting me to make the delivery personally, and I'm sure he won't be happy to see you two pullin' up. Just do your job and don't talk too much. All you need to do is make the drop, collect the money, and get out of there. Don't hang around or answer any questions about me or the gang." Jack paused, glancing at Drew. "And don't do anything to rile him up."

"You can count on us," Drew said as he stood and adjusted his gun belt. "We'll take care of it for you."

"You just keep your hands off that iron while you're there," Jack said. "Unless old Turner don't leave you any other choice, that is. Am I clear?" Drew and I nodded and quickly left Jack's office to collect the wagon. It was already loaded and ready.

We set out on our trip, but my apprehension overshadowed my optimism. Drew, on the other hand, was excited to prove himself. He saw this job as our first step to becoming bonafide members of Jack's gang. As the wagon bumbled along the trail, I must have checked my revolver half a dozen times to make sure it was still loaded.

The Last Chance Saloon absolutely lived up to its name. Standing alone in a clearing by the side of the road in the middle of nowhere, it was indeed the last chance any traveler might have to patronize a saloon for quite some time. Nothing but open country spread out for miles in every direction. The saloon itself was little more than a wooden shack of splintered planks. It had a sagging roof and a hand-painted sign created by an unskilled artist. We stopped just off the side of the road. It was quiet.

A single horse was tied off in front of the saloon, but there was no sign of anyone waiting on a delivery.

"You ready?" Drew said, climbing out of the wagon.

"Hang on, Drew," I said. "Somethin' don't sit right about this. It's too quiet. And it feels like eyes are on us."

"You worry too much, Moses," Drew said as he went about inspecting the crates of guns and ammo. "It's a good thing it's quiet. Why do you think they chose this place? It ain't like we can meet these fellas in the middle of town with the law watchin' our every move. Just relax. Everything's gonna be fine."

I climbed down from the wagon. "Maybe you're right," I said. "I just hope this Brett Turner fella shows up soon so we can be done with this."

Brett Turner never showed up.

"Let me see your hands," a voice called out, followed by no less than eight men who rushed out from behind and within the saloon. They ran toward us with guns drawn. Drew and I threw our hands up, and in an instant, the deputies had us on the ground and cuffed.

One of the lawmen stepped up to us. "Get 'em on their feet," he said. He was a tall man in his mid-fifties with a wiry, black mustache growing past his chin. He had just started working on a fresh wad of tobacco. "I'm Sheriff Mac Daley of Carsonville County, and you boys are under arrest for possession of stolen firearms with intent to sell those firearms to known fugitives."

"What? We don't know no fugitives," Drew said. "And we didn't steal anything. We're just doin' a job."

Sheriff Daley turned and walked to Drew. He stopped inches from his face. "And who you doin' a job for?" he said. "Who hired you?"

"He never told us his name," Drew lied. "He was a nervous little fella. Said he had delivery work if we were interested. He offered us a hundred dollars. Even paid us half up front and said he'd give us the rest when we got back."

"Uh-huh," Sheriff Daley grunted. He looked at me. "I suppose this is the story you're goin' with too?" I nodded as I held his gaze. Sheriff Daley turned his head and spit, then directed his men. "Get 'em in the wagon and on into town. Lock 'em up, and I'll be in after a while. Maybe they'll be more willin' to tell the truth after they spend a little time behind bars."

Drew and I took a humiliating ride into Carsonville in the back of a prisoner wagon. We didn't speak, but we both knew what the other was thinking. We'd failed. We let Smiling Jack down and likely lost a ton of money. There was little doubt he'd be furious. I only hoped he wouldn't be angry enough to send us on our way or leave us to rot in jail.

After a long ride through the heat, the deputies pulled to a stop in front of the jailhouse. They unloaded us, walked us to our cells, shoved us inside, removed our cuffs, and told us to sit there and keep our mouths shut. That's exactly what we did. Smooth talking wasn't enough to wriggle our way out of this, and we didn't want to say anything that might accidentally put heat on Smiling Jack. So we kept quiet.

I lay on my cot for the next four hours, watching the daylight fade into night through the bars of the small window at the top of my cell. There were two deputies on duty. They sat at a small desk, playing cards and chatting about everyday life – things like work, family, and how bad the coming winter might be. I listened to their prattle and wondered which was the better life, the dangerous life of an outlaw or the safe life of normal folks. I never fully reached a conclusion, but the fact remained that Drew and I were locked in a cell, and they weren't. Suddenly, the front door opened, and Sheriff Daley entered, stomping the dirt from his boots.

"Don't tell him nothin'," Drew whispered. "Right now, we're just a couple of delivery boys who got mixed up with a bad fella. What we don't tell 'em, they can't know. They'll probably let us go tonight if we don't say anything foolish and get ourselves in deeper than we already are."

"Hello, young men," Sheriff Daley said. "How we doin' this evening?" He pulled a stool up in the hallway between our cells and took a seat. He was still working on a cheek full of tobacco. "Let's get right to it. I'll shoot straight with you. First off, I believe you when you say you're just the delivery boys. You may or may not have known what you were haulin', but that don't matter much to me. I don't, for one second, believe you boys are the brains of whatever operation this is, but I know damn well there's more to it than you've let on."

"It's like my friend here said," I spoke up. "We were in Bellerive the day before yesterday, and this odd fella offered us a job. Paid us half up front. We agreed, rode all the way out here, and nearly got ourselves shot. That's all there is to it. We don't know who he is or who he's working with."

"Yeah, I got that much," Sheriff Daley said. "Seems awfully strange that somebody tryin' to move a wagon full of stolen guns would hire two young men he didn't know. There's a lotta money in that wagon."

Drew shrugged. "What can I say? We must have the kind of faces people trust."

Sheriff Daley cleared his throat and spat right onto the floor. "Uh-huh," he said. "And tell me, boys, how is Smiling Jack doin' these days?"

"Who?" Drew said, blank-faced.

"Oh, I'm sorry," Sheriff Daley went on, "his God-given name is Andrew Jackson Davis, but most folks know him as Smiling Jack. He runs with a gang of rough customers and a few greenhorns lookin' to make names for themselves."

"Never heard of him," Drew said, staring at the Sheriff.

The Sheriff looked to me, and I shook my head.

"Well, that's a shame," Sheriff Daley said. "I thought we finally had him on something this time."

"Is this Smiling Jack a wanted man?" I said.

"No," the Sheriff replied, "but only 'cause he's slipperier than a greased copperhead. If I could find somethin' that'd stick to that fool, I'd die a happy man. You boys listen to me when I tell you he's no good. Young fellas like yourselves don't need to get tangled up with the likes of Smiling Jack."

"We'll keep our eyes open for him," Drew said. "We're honest folks, Sheriff. We don't wanna accidentally get mixed up with no lowlife degenerate."

Sheriff Daley stood up and slid the stool back across the room. "No, you surely do not," he said. "Deputy Barnes," he called out to one of the guards. "These young men are free to go."

Drew and I looked at each other with grins on our faces. Drew mouthed the words, "I told you."

"So that's it?" I said. "We can just leave?"

"I don't have anything on you boys," Sheriff Daley said. "Like I said, you don't strike me as the type to be makin' decisions. It's more likely you were considered the most expendable of the group by whoever sent you on this fool's run. But the fact is you were caught with stolen firearms in your possession, and I can't just ignore that. So as soon as you fellas pay your five hundred dollar fine, you're free to leave." He tipped his hat. "Good evenin'."

"Wait, Sheriff," Drew said. "We ain't got five hundred dollars. Can't we work somethin' out?"

"Of course," Sheriff Daley said. "If you can't afford to pay the five hundred dollars, you can always serve the time. Considerin' you were already locked up all day, I could probably get you out of here in, say...a month or so."

"A month?" Drew said with a yelp. "A month for makin' a delivery?"

"Yes, sir," Sheriff Daley said. "A month for makin' a delivery of stolen weapons. It's a fair offer. Of course, you could take your chances with the judge. But, things tend to get complicated if we have to bring the judge in."

Drew and I dropped into our bunks, defeated. "Guess we might as well get comfortable, Moses," Drew said. "Looks like we're gonna be here a while."

"You know how this works," the Sheriff said. "You help me get what I want, and I'll work with you. You give me somethin' that'll stick on Smiling Jack, and you can walk out of here tonight."

"I wish I could help you," Drew mumbled.

"Alright then," Sheriff Daley said as he put on his coat and stepped outside. "Keep an eye on 'em, will you, Barnes?"

Sheriff Daley left, and Drew and I spent a restless night in the Carsonville County Jail. Our minds were consumed with the fear of what might happen next. We were either facing the wrath of Smiling Jack or the prospect of spending a month in jail. Neither was a particularly appealing option, but I couldn't see Drew or myself working with Sheriff Daley to bring trouble down on Jack.

It felt like I had only just fallen asleep when the morning light spilled in through the tiny window. I had no more than sat up and stretched when I was startled by the booming voice of Smiling Jack Davis. "Hello, Deputy," he said forcefully to Deputy Barnes. "I'm here to bail out a couple of prisoners if you don't mind."

"Yes sir," Deputy Barnes said, "can I ask your name?"

"Certainly. My name is Andrew Jackson Davis, but most folks know me as Smiling Jack." Jack flashed a beaming smile at Deputy Barnes to show how he came about the nickname.

The good deputy reacted like someone had just drawn a weapon on him. He jumped up from behind his desk and nearly knocked over his chair. "Just a moment, sir," he said, stumbling toward the front door. "Let me get the Sheriff." Deputy Barnes raced from the jailhouse and sprinted off down the street as Smiling Jack walked back to our cells, his smile slowly fading.

"Did you talk?" he said. "Either of you spill anything about me or the gang?"

Drew and I exchanged glances, our loyalty holding steadfast. "No, Jack, we didn't say a word," I replied.

"The Sheriff asked about you, though," Drew added. "We told them we had no idea who you were. Said some anxious fella in Bellerive hired us. They don't know nothin', but they sure seem to want you bad."

Jack's smile returned. "They always do," he said. Just then, the door opened, and Deputy Barnes entered, followed by Sheriff Daley.

"Good mornin'," the Sheriff began. "My name is –"

"Oh, I know who you are, Sheriff Daley," Smiling Jack said. "From what these young men told me, you know quite a bit about me as well."

Sheriff Daley grunted and glared at Jack. "Not as much as I wish."

Smiling Jack pulled a roll of cash from his pocket. "I believe this will cover it," he said. "Five hundred dollars, right?" He dropped the money on the desk.

"That's right," Sheriff Daley said. "I thought you boys said you didn't know Andrew Jackson Davis."

"They don't," Smiling Jack said. "We just met. I heard a couple of young men were locked up and in need of assistance. You know how much I long to provide stability, care, and guidance for underprivileged young men such as these two. I figure I might even take 'em under my wing for a while."

We walked out of the jail as free men, and Jack led us to our horses. As soon as we were far enough away, he finally spoke, though not in the angry or disappointed way we feared. Jack seemed pleased with how things turned out.

"You boys okay?" he said as we climbed into the saddle. "They didn't mistreat you, did they?"

"We're fine," Drew said. "And we're both real sorry about how things played out."

"I'm sure you did all you could," Jack said. "And you did right by not talkin'. I'm proud of you both."

We expressed our thanks as we eased out of town and back toward camp. "You know, boys, this was a good lesson for you," Smiling Jack went on. "It might go against what most people believe, but you can't trust the law. The law ain't here to protect folks like us. We look out for each other and make our own law."

As we left Carsonville, our freedom left a bittersweet taste on my tongue. I was grateful to be alive and out of jail, but the unsettling reality of our situation was a burden of its own. Jack was right. Our world wasn't governed by law or the consensus of men. We were soldiers, and Smiling Jack was our general. Our world was one where trust was rare, morality was a weakness, and loyalty was the most treasured commodity.

CHAPTER 33

Morning broke on a somber scene as Skillet and Nellie worked tirelessly to repair the damage wrought by the previous night's hailstorm. They worked quickly, with unwavering determination, which was heartening to see. The storm had been unforgiving, a cruel twist of nature that left all of us shaken. I had barely pulled on my boots when Drew and Two Feathers rode back into camp with smiles and a glimmer of hope that our luck might be changing.

Two Feathers, atop his Appaloosa, Denali, and Drew, astride his Thoroughbred, Stormy, were returning with our missing horses. My Palomino, Cali, and my mule, Hurley, followed them into camp. According to Drew, he found the horses at an abandoned shack in the middle of the woods. It was a feeble shelter from the relentless hailstorm, half-collapsed as it was, but it offered them enough shelter to survive the night. As soon as the horses were tended to, Drew and I wasted little time downing our coffee and heading into town. Drew still thought it a foolhardy plan to trust the local Sheriff, but he supported me nonetheless.

The storm had passed, but the rain fell steadily as Drew and I rode into Jonesborough. It was a slow, slogging ride, and as we neared our destination, the Colter River came into view. My thoughts were pulled back to when I was a boy, the night Deputy Wesley pulled me from its waters and delivered me to the Grace House Orphanage. I considered what might have become of me had he just rode on by and left me there. However, that was a puzzle with far too many missing pieces, and as we approached the banks of the Colter, I was jarred from my contemplation.

"Would you look at that," Drew said in awe as the tumultuous waters rumbled past. "I ain't never seen it like this before." Usually, the Colter River was little more than a placid, winding stream, but now it surged with unrestrained fury. It had breached its banks, raging fiercely enough to prove deadly to anyone caught in its current. Most concerning was the fact that the rising waters nearly covered the only bridge for miles. I could feel Drew's uneasiness as we approached the crossing, the sturdy, wooden frame bridge creaking beneath the force of the churning river. I reassured him the best I could and crossed ahead of him, hoping to prove the bridge would hold. Although he clearly had his doubts, Drew silently crossed the river without protest.

We rode into Jonesborough with a gray, gloomy haze hanging over the waterlogged town. Stopping outside the Sheriff's office, we tied up our horses and climbed the front porch steps. A sign on the door read, "Jonesborough Sheriff's Department: Office and Jail, Sheriff Jacob Stringer."

"You still sure this is a good idea?" Drew said. "There's bound to be another way."

I smiled at him. "Just come on and don't say anything dumb."

Drew grinned. "Can't promise that."

Sheriff Stringer welcomed us as we stepped inside. He was friendly enough, but he greeted us with a list of questions that didn't seem to require an answer. "Good morning, I'm Sheriff Stringer," he said. "I don't believe I've seen you men around here before, have I? You fellas new in town or just passing through? How can I help you?"

I wasted no time with pleasantries. "Sheriff, my name is Moses Colter, and I'm here to confess to killing a man."

Drew groaned a little under his breath.

The sheriff raised an eyebrow and took a step back. Stringer was a heavyset man, probably in his forties, with large mutton chops and a thick mustache. He motioned to the chairs in front of his desk. "Come on over here. Sit down, and we'll have a talk." Then he called out to the back room, "Deryl, can you come out here, please?"

We took our seats, Sheriff Stringer behind his desk and Drew and I in the chairs before him. Deryl came from the back, finishing off a biscuit and wiping his face. He was a painfully skinny fella, wearing a collared shirt and vest, both too large for him. "Yes, sir, whatcha need?"

Stringer nudged his head toward me. "This man here is Moses Colter. He said he's coming in to confess to killing a man. I wanted you here to take notes while we talk."

"Sure thing," Deryl said, scrambling to find a pencil and paper. He was coughing from the hunk of biscuit he'd attempted to polish off.

I relayed the whole story to Sheriff Stringer. I told him exactly how Earl and I ended up in an altercation when I was only seventeen in the summer of '58. I told him about the cruelty that Earl, Carl, Harold Gullet, and Logan Ashbourne had inflicted on the workers at the Ivywood Plantation and how I was standing up for them. Stringer and Deryl glanced blankly at one another upon my mentioning Logan Ashbourne, but I continued. I told him how the cowards had strung up Titus for three days and how Earl was responsible for making sure Titus remained as miserable as possible. Then, I told him about how I stood up to Earl, how there was a fight of sorts, and how I unintentionally shot him. When I'd finished recounting the facts, Sheriff Stringer lifted his eyebrows and scratched the back of his neck.

"And you say this happened in the summer of '58?" Sheriff Stringer said.

"That's right," I replied.

"What's that, fourteen years ago now?"

"Fifteen," I said. "Still, killin' is killin', and I figured I should get this off my conscience and confess."

Sheriff Stringer nodded. "Logan Ashbourne and Harold Gullet, I know. They're still at the Ivywood. Another fella there is named Carl Bancroft. It's my understanding he's been working for Ashbourne a while."

"I'm sure it's the same Carl," I said. "I can't see there bein' more than one of them."

"I've never heard of this Earl fella, though," Stringer said. "Do you know his last name?"

I shook my head. "Earl was all I ever called him."

"Hmm," Sheriff Stringer said. "Deryl, go pull up the files from the summer of '58. See if you can find anything about a killing that happened or anything at all on a fella named Earl." Deryl dropped his pencil, nodded, and raced off to the back.

We sat there for a moment; Sheriff Stringer looked at Drew. "And exactly who are you?"

Drew rose from his seat to shake the Sheriff's hand. "Good morning, sir. My name is Drew Harlan. Pleased to meet you."

"Likewise," the Sheriff said blankly. "You here for support, or are you a witness?"

Drew smiled. "I'm just here as a friend. I was told not to say anything ignorant or offensive, so I just kept quiet."

Before Stringer could reply, his deputy, Deryl, returned with a thick file folder that he placed on the Sheriff's desk. "Found something," he said. "I didn't expect it would be so easy, but it was right on top of the stack."

Sheriff Stringer opened the file and leaned back to read it, mainly because Drew was trying his best to get a look. He scanned a few documents and then closed the file. "Why are you doing this now?" Sheriff Stringer said. "Why after so long?"

"This has been eating at me for years," I said. "I was tired of it hangin' over my head."

"I can respect that," the Sheriff said, "but, Mr. Colter, it appears there's nothing here to confess. The man you shot was named Earl Weston. From the looks of things, he was a bad egg from the start. He had a rap sheet longer than the Old Testament, but he always managed to weasel his way out of any real trouble. Anyway, according to our files, a witness came forward not long after Earl was killed. The statement claims his killing was in self-defense and that Earl instigated the whole altercation."

I blinked in disbelief when a weight I hadn't even realized I was carrying suddenly lifted. I shared a glance with Drew, who simply shrugged. "So, who was the witness?" I said.

Sheriff Stringer shook his head. "The record doesn't say. Apparently, the witness asked to remain anonymous. They must have been believable, though, for it all to be dropped the way it was. Unfortunately, all of that happened years before I came to Jonesborough, so I'm afraid I won't be much help outside of what's in this file."

"All those years looking over my shoulder for the law," I muttered more to myself than to the Sheriff, "only to find out no one was even lookin' for me."

"Listen," Sheriff Stringer continued, "I never knew the man outside of what I just read about him, but I've known several like him over the years. I can promise you, there wasn't nobody crying over the death of Earl Weston. I know it's not an easy thing to live with, taking a man's life, but hopefully, that can offer you some consolation."

The news was comforting, but I didn't have the luxury of celebrating. There were more pressing concerns to deal with. "There is one more thing I could use your help with, Sheriff." He nodded, and I continued, telling him about the workers at the Ivywood Plantation who wanted to be free of Logan Ashbourne and Harold Gullet. I explained the cruelty they'd endured and how they had longed to leave but were trapped by fear and a lack of options. Sheriff Stringer shifted in his seat, squinted his eyes, and rubbed his forehead as he listened. Sensing the Sheriff's discomfort, Drew added that we were also aware of the more recent troubles at Ivywood Plantation. He mentioned the workers who'd been found shot and killed and the unusual circumstances surrounding the death of Logan's parents.

"So, what are you asking me to do exactly?" Sheriff Stringer said.

"I ain't here to steal another man's workers," I said, "but if they want to go, I aim to take them with me. All I ask is that you come along with us. Help mediate the situation and keep the peace."

Sheriff Stringer looked at his skinny deputy, who offered a quick head shake. Then he looked to us. "Are you fellas sure you want to do this? Logan Ashbourne is a powerful man with enough money and influence to make your lives miserable if he feels threatened."

I leaned forward and locked eyes with the Sheriff. "There ain't no man deserves to be treated like a slave. We're following through with this, Sheriff. All I'm asking is that you help us keep things from getting out of hand. You're the law. Those people need you."

Sheriff Stringer exhaled a troubled breath. "Listen here, fellas, I don't think this is a good idea, but I can see you're hellbent on it. I'll tell you what, give me a couple of days to let this weather clear up and for things to dry out a bit, and I'll ride out –"

"That's not gonna work, Sheriff," I said. "We're planning on heading outta town . Two days at the most. We need to meet with Logan Ashbourne, and it needs to happen this afternoon."

Reluctantly, Sheriff Stringer agreed to join us. He asked us to give him a few hours to round up some help, which was fine with us. We still hadn't secured any wagons, and we didn't know how many workers were planning to come with us. Our collective unease hung over the Sheriff's Office like a heavy cloud. Still, the prospect of freeing Titus, his family, and the rest of the workers at the Ivywood Plantation felt like a hopeful ray of sunlight peeking through the haze.

CHAPTER 34

"If we have to, we'll leave on foot," I told Skillet. "We'll find a place somewhere that'll sell us wagons and mules. We'll go through Memphis or Louisville if need be. Logan Ashbourne may be a powerful man, but he don't control every town between here and Montana."

Our camp, once an impressive haven, had devolved into a much more temporary structure following the hailstorm. Nellie and Two Feathers had worked all morning, rigging a patchwork canopy of ragged tarps to protect from the continuing downpour. Afterward, Two Feathers went hunting while we did our best to stay dry at camp.

The rain took its toll on each of us. Tempers flared hotter than usual, especially Skillet's. He was a man who needed instructions to follow or orders to carry out – probably a holdover from years of military service. Still, the fact that I didn't have a solid, straightforward plan to offer was a particular matter of contention.

"All I'm tryin' to say," Skillet continued, "is that I don't believe we're doin' enough to find the wagons we need. We gotta figure this out, and pretty dang quick. It just don't sit right that we ain't prepared for the trip that's comin'."

"Skillet, I haven't forgotten about the wagons," I said, trying to manage my mounting frustration. "It's just a matter of finding the right opportunity to act. We're in a tough spot here. You know as well as I do that Logan Ashbourne's grip on this place is tighter than a hangman's noose. We have to be patient and we have to be careful. The most important thing right now is getting those workers out of Ivywood. The rest we're gonna have to figure out as it comes. First things first."

Skillet huffed and grunted as he went about adding wood to the fire. "I reckon you and I just disagree on what 'first things first' actually means."

"I guess we do, Skillet," I said, my voice finding an edge. "But the thing you have to understand is –"

"Oh, just stop it. Both of you," Nellie cut in. She was typically the group mediator and voice of reason whenever our arguments got us stuck, going in circles. "We're all here, safe and together, ain't we? I know this blasted rain has us all on edge, but it won't last forever. Soon enough, we'll take on those workers, have our wagons, and be on our way. Now, when and how it all plays out is somethin' I don't know. Truth is, none of us do. But I'm tired of hearin' about it, and I'm damn sure tired of listenin' to the two of you fussin' like a couple of guinea hens. So we're gonna stop it now. Take a break. Got it?"

Skillet and I grumbled our agreement like two kids yelled at by their ma. It seemed a temporary fix at best, for despite Nellie putting an end to our disagreement, a thick fog of uneasiness and irritability still loomed over the camp.

I turned my attention to Drew, hoping to distract from my sour mood. Drew, however, was deeply enthralled with his own curious project. He sat leaning against the rear wagon wheel, inspecting the contents of the pack left behind by the photographers we met in Fort Laramie. They were good-natured folks who'd met their unfortunate end at the hands of bandits. Nicholas and Audrey. Drew fiddled with the camera, intrigued by the machinery and marveling over how such a device actually managed to capture images.

"You got that thing figured out yet?" I said, snapping Drew from his intense study.

"I got no clue how this thing works," Drew said. "But, it sure is something. Look at this, Moses." Drew held up one of the photographs. "Can you believe this? A lion on the hunt. Probably about to nab himself an impala. And they saw it. They actually laid eyes on this old boy in the wild. And even more impressive, they managed to snap a picture without gettin' themselves eaten. Amazing."

I sat down beside Drew and cycled through the stack of photographs. Several images showed exotic animals such as lions, zebras, giraffes, wildebeests, and even elephants. In addition, there were images of awe-inspiring landscapes that we assumed were the African savannas. "These are really good, don't you think?" I said to Drew.

Drew nodded. "They were professionals, after all. What a life. I'd love to go to Africa one day, wouldn't you?" I shrugged. "It just seems a shame how big this world is and how little of it most folks get to see. I don't know about you, but I don't wanna miss any of it. I wanna see the whole thing."

"You want to see all of it?" I said. "The whole world?"

"Well, why not?" Drew went on. "Seems to me, if I'm gonna go through the trouble of seeing some of it, I might as well go on and see it all. I am a firm believer in what I call the Yes/And Philosophy."

"Oh, I can't wait to hear this."

"It's like this... why settle for a simple 'yes' when I can have a 'yes, and'? Take dessert, for example. Most fellas finish their meal at a restaurant and then debate which sweet to order for dessert. But why choose? If you asked me whether I wanted a piece of chocolate cake or cherry pie, I'd say, 'Yes, please.' The Yes/And Philosophy."

Our conversation was interrupted by Nellie, who had been watching for anything unusual since we first made camp. She pointed out a couple of approaching riders, and each of us rose to our feet, our hands instinctively reaching for our weapons. We watched as the riders moved slowly yet deliberately through the falling rain. They were undoubtedly headed in our direction, riding like men doing their best to appear unthreatening.

"What do you think?" Drew said, his forehead wrinkled. "Friendly or no?"

"Can't tell yet," I said.

"How do you wanna handle this?" Drew said as they continued their slow progress toward us.

"Everyone, take a seat," I said. "We'll be real friendly-like. Just go on with whatever you were doing, but be ready in case they ain't interested in bein' friends."

Drew, Skillet, and Nellie sat as the men drew near, and I got a better look at them. They were two rather large, tough-looking black men. Both traveled atop massive, gray workhorses. Their hats were pulled low over their faces, and there weren't any weapons on them, as far as I could tell. Still, I couldn't dismiss the possibility they may have a pistol tucked away beneath their rain-soaked coats.

"You Moses?" one of them called out as they approached, his voice cut through the pattering rain. I nodded, my hand staying close to my revolver. They dismounted, continuing their slow, deliberate movements and being careful not to cause any unnecessary alarm. Their boots touched down on the muddy earth, but the men didn't approach us. Instead, they stood firm beside their horses.

"My name is Tate, and this my brother, Fisher. We Titus' boys."

I recognized the twins as soon as he said their names. When I left, they were not much more than boys, but their faces still possessed some of those boyish features I remembered. I smiled and moved toward them, glad to see smiles stretching across their own faces. "Fisher and Tate," I said. "Do you fellas remember me?"

"'Course we remember you," Fisher said. "We always knew you'd come back one day."

"It's good to see you," I said.

"You too," Tate replied. "How long ya'll been here?"

"Just a couple of days now," I said. "Come on over and have a seat." I introduced them to everyone, and Nellie offered them a cup of coffee, which they cautiously accepted. After a few moments of polite conversation, Fisher and Tate got to the heart of their visit. They were delivering a message on behalf of the Ivywood Plantation workers.

"Everyone wants to leave, Moses," Fisher said, earnestly. As soon as the words spilled from his lips, it felt like a gust of hope blew through the camp. His eyes watered up a bit. "They all scared, but they wanna go. We got a hundred sixty-eight total countin' the kids. You really plannin' on followin' through with this?"

I nodded and locked eyes with him. "I'm set on it. We all are."

"I sure hope so," Tate said. "These folks been waitin' a long time for a chance like this."

For the first time in days, my heart swelled with joy and a newly revived determination. After all we'd been through, it appeared to be truly happening. I leaned forward as I gathered my thoughts. "Tell the others to pack up their belongings but not to make a show of it. Get it done real quiet like. Tell them to go on livin' their lives like they always do, like it's just another day at the Ivywood. The last thing we need is Logan Ahsbourne feelin' like he needs to flex his muscle. When the time is right, we'll give the word and lead you all out. Just be ready."

Tate and Fisher nodded and finished up their coffee before saying their goodbyes and mounting their horses. I watched them as they rode away, throwing their hands up and giving one last wave before disappearing into the murky, gray horizon. There was still a load of details to work out, but one of my greatest concerns had been alleviated. The Ivywood workers had made their choice. They wanted their freedom, and soon they'd get it. We'd leave Tennessee together and help them start their new lives with us in Montana.

CHAPTER 35

I t was a quarter till four, and our meeting with Sheriff Stringer and the impending confrontation with Logan Ashbourne loomed over us much like the merciless weather. The rain had let up some, but still fell. Two Feathers continued to insist that the rain was unnatural, but that assessment, true or not, didn't have much bearing on the job at hand. Flooding was becoming a legitimate concern for the town of Jonesborough and areas nearby. The Ivywood Plantation was no exception. Drew and I rode our horses up to the front gate which was wide open with no guard in sight. As evidenced by the collection of muddy tracks, several riders had already passed through.

"Should we wait here?" Drew said. "Or just go on in?"

"Yeah, let's do it," I said. "It looks like the Sheriff and his men may already be here anyway. And if he's in there talking to Logan, I want to hear what's said."

We rode through the gate and followed the drive up through the heart of the plantation. Dense, placid clouds lolled overhead. They blanketed the sky and gave everything a sort of colorless pallor, as if the rain had washed away all the pigment from the land. The tobacco fields were in a dismal state. The hailstorm from last night had ravaged the precious plants, leaving them in tatters. A large number of workers, all soaked to the bone, labored desperately to salvage whatever leaves or plants they could. I was pleased to observe their willingness to carry on with their work like always. They purposefully ignored Drew and I as we passed, which meant Fisher and Tate had done their jobs well, convincing everyone to continue with business as usual.

We made our way toward the plantation house until we were met with a sight that fueled my growing sense of unease. There was a gathering of armed men. As we suspected by the tracks, Sheriff Stringer had already arrived. He was flanked by no less than half a dozen of his own men, each clutching rifles, shotguns, and carrying pistols. A group of Logan's men sat on the front porch of the plantation house, keeping out of the rain. The only exception being Harold Gullet and Carl Bancroft who planted themselves on either side of Logan, facing the Sheriff and his men.

As we got closer, it was Harold Gullet that first caught my attention. His cold stare was fixed on Drew and me, his squinted eyes filled with venomous hatred. It was the type of look I'd seen on men's faces just before they decided to draw iron. I didn't return his gaze. My business was not with Harold Gullet today. Drew, however, stared right back at Harold. He didn't talk about it much, but I knew Drew and Harold had unfinished business. Drew was simply waiting for an opportunity to settle things once and for all. Carl Bancroft remained still, eyes straight ahead as if he didn't notice us at all, like an emotionless sentinel. Still, he had a firm grip on his Winchester, and I knew he wouldn't hesitate to use it if the need were to arise.

"I ain't ordering you to do anything," Sheriff Stringer said to Logan as we climbed out of our saddles. "And I ain't tryin' to make you give up your workers. I'm only here to make sure things stay civil."

Logan pointed at the Sheriff, red faced and antsy. "I know you say you ain't here to tell me what to do, but you damn sure made me pull my men from the watchtowers, didn't you? Sounded like an order to me, Sheriff Stringer."

"I told you," Sheriff Stringer went on, keeping his voice steady, "that was simply for the protection of my men and yours. It's only a precaution, nothing more."

It was then Logan realized Drew and I had arrived. His furious gaze landed on me as I walked up beside the Sheriff. "I'll tell you one thing, Moses Colter. You ain't taking one damn worker from this plantation so you might as well get that outta your head." He paused. "I'll kill you first. And I don't care if the law's here with you or not."

"Now, let's not resort to threats," Sheriff Stringer broke in. "That won't lead to anything good. I'm sure we can work this out. There's no need for violence."

Logan's words were hateful but his intentions were clear. I wouldn't have been surprised had he chosen to make good on his threat right then, but I refused to let his bluster unnerve me. "Logan," I replied with a calm insistence, "we want to resolve this peacefully. These men and women have made their wishes known. They don't want to be here. They want to leave. I'm only asking you to stop treating them like your property and let them go."

Logan turned his spiteful, fury-filled eyes to Sheriff Stringer. "I can't believe you're siding with these two. I thought you and I had an understanding, Sheriff. Have for years anyway, but now I'm not so sure. You better watch your step. This is a fine line you're walkin' here."

It was shocking to hear Logan speak to a lawman in such a manner, but Sheriff Stringer brushed off his insinuations. "We can get through this without bloodshed," he urged Logan. "Just take a breath, trust the process, and let's find a solution that works for everyone."

"Fine, Sheriff," Logan conceded grudgingly. "Go ahead and handle things your way. But mark my words, these folks ain't leaving. Good old Moses here just wants to steal my workers and drive me out of business. First my tobacco crops were destroyed and now this. If I didn't know better, I'd swear that hailstorm was somehow his doing."

"Could be," Drew spoke up. "Then again, it might just be a sign that even the good Lord Himself is dog-tired of Logan Ashbourne and the way he treats folks."

"That's enough," Sheriff Stringer said, raising his voice for the first time. "I want all of you to pipe down and let me do my job." We all complied, albeit reluctantly, Logan included. "Now, Moses," Sheriff Stringer went on, "it's your contention that these workers, regardless of their particular reasons, all want to leave? With you? Is that correct?"

"Yes, sir," I said. "They all want to leave, but their reasons are all the same. They're tired of being mistreated and abused."

"And, Logan," the Sheriff went on, disregarding my claim, "if I heard correctly, you don't think this was the workers idea at all. You are under the impression that this is nothing more than Moses tryin' to steal away your help. Did I get that right?"

"That's right," Logan said blankly as he crossed his arms. "Now, can we move this along? As you can see, Sheriff, we have a lot of work left to do here."

"Seems to me we can solve this matter rather quickly," Sheriff Stringer said. "All we need to do is hear from the workers. Let's find out what it is they really want." He looked at Drew and me. "I'm tellin' you now, you boys keep your traps shut. You interfere with my questioning and this is over."

Drew pointed at Logan. "Same goes for him too, right, Sheriff?"

Sheriff Stringer sighed. "Yes, Drew. The same goes for Mr. Ashbourne." Then Stringer called to his deputy. "Deryl, walk out there to the field and grab a couple of men at random. Tell them I need to ask them some questions."

Deryl jumped into action and raced out into the field as we all looked on, wondering where this was headed. It only took a moment for Deryl to return with two workers following closely behind. One was a thin man, younger, his skin as dark as coal, and bucked teeth protruding from his mouth. The other was an elderly gentleman with silver hair and a hunched posture. He walked with a slight limp, his body bearing the weight of years spent in the tobacco fields.

Stringer summoned them forward, urging the men to move quickly. "Come on now," he said. "We need to get this all sorted out."

I glanced at Logan who stood there, his arms still crossed and a cocksure grin on his face. Drew's eyes darted back and forth from Logan to the Sheriff. I'd known Drew my whole life, and I knew his anger was simmering just beneath the surface. No one I knew had a stronger sense of justice. Drew hated the thought of anyone being taken advantage of. Unfortunately, this situation was turning into something that was anything but fair.

"Now hold on, Sheriff," Drew said, his neck flashing red. "You can't ask them what they want with Logan and his goons standing right here. That's like asking a bird if he wants out of his cage while the cat's sittin' there waitin' on supper."

"That's enough out of you," Sheriff Stringer said, sticking a finger in Drew's face. "Another word and I'll have you locked up. You understand what I'm tellin' you?"

"Oh, it's clear as crystal, Sheriff," Drew said as he stepped back beside me.

Logan Ashbourne and Harold Gullet exchanged triumphant glances. They both looked at us, their smiles like a hundred tiny daggers ripping through our resolve.

Sheriff Stringer spoke to the younger man with the bucked teeth first. "I'm trying to figure some things out here, and I need to ask you some questions. What's your name, boy?"

"They call me Clem," he said, his voice trembling. "Can I help you?"

"I just need to know a couple of things," Sheriff Stringer said. "First off, how do you like it here? Does Mr. Ashbourne treat you well?"

Clem couldn't keep his eyes from cutting to Logan Ashbourne as he spoke. "Mr. Ashbourne treats us real good. Keeps food on the table and a roof over our heads."

"Good to hear," the Sheriff said. "One more thing. Do you want to leave the Ivywood Plantation? Are you or any of your friends plannin' on going with these two fellas?"

Clem looked at Drew and me for what felt like an eternity, as his eyes welled with tears. He swallowed hard and answered in a shaky voice. "I got no plans for leavin'," he said. A single tear rolled down his face, and he fervently wiped it from his cheek. Logan couldn't contain his sickening glee. I grabbed Drew by his shirt and pulled him back a bit, reminding him to keep quiet.

"Thank you, Clem," the Sheriff went on. "And what's your name?" he said to the older gentleman.

"Name's Russell," he said. "Been here goin' on thirty years now."

"How about you, Russell? Do you share Clem's opinion on Mr. Ashbourne? He treat you well?"

Russell grunted. "He ain't nothin' like his daddy, but..." Russell caught my eye and shook his head. "...but he do take care of us. In his way. And 'fore you ask...no. I ain't leavin' either. Matter fact, ain't none of us gonna leave. Musta been some nasty gossip said otherwise." Russell then glared at Logan in a way that made it seem like he had more to say. "Was that answer to yo' likin', sir?" he said with a counterfeit smile. Logan didn't answer – didn't react at all. He simply locked eyes with Russell, breathing heavily with a blank stare until Sheriff Stringer spoke up and dismissed the workers.

It was disheartening to watch such a loathsome charade, and as the men returned to the field, I couldn't help but feel like I had failed them. Their sense of powerlessness resonated with me in a way that made me feel like I was a kid again, lost and scared.

"There you have it, Sheriff," Logan said, his voice dripping with triumph. "My workers are loyal. They know they got a good thing here. They ain't going anywhere."

Sheriff Stringer cast a glance at Drew and me before addressing Logan. "Very well, Mr. Ashbourne. It appears that your workers are indeed content. I don't think there's anything more to be done here."

Drew attempted to protest, but I stopped him. This was a battle that didn't go our way, but there was still a war to consider. Sheriff Stringer told us it was time to go, so Drew and I accepted our defeat and climbed into our saddles.

"This don't end here, Logan," Drew said as a deep peal of thunder rumbled in the distance.

"You best be on your way now, boys," Logan called out to us. "There ain't nothin' but trouble here for you."

We rode away from Ivywood Plantation, yet again, with nothing to show for our efforts. Only this time, we were escorted off the property by Sheriff Stringer and his men. It had been a discouraging endeavor to say the least. The day had not been ours, and it seemed fitting at that moment that the rain began to fall harder than it had all day.

"What do you want to do now, Moses?" Drew said as he patted Stormy.

"I've got an idea," I said. "Let's go update the others, then I want to go back to the Sheriff's office. Stringer may have some information in that file of his that'll help us."

"I don't know, Moses," Drew said. "Sheriff Stringer seems like a dead end to me."

"You may be right, but we won't know for sure until we try."

CHAPTER 36

After leaving the Ivywood Plantation, Drew and I stopped by camp to fill everyone in on our fruitless meeting with Sheriff Stringer and Logan Ashbourne. We lingered long enough to answer their questions before mounting up and heading back into Jonesborough. The rain was lighter than before, but the wind took charge while the rain took a break. It met us head-on, howling through the towering pines that swayed and creaked in protest. We leaned forward and pulled our hats down as stinging droplets were driven into our faces, slicing through the air sideways like tiny daggers.

Our horses, on guard with their ears pinned back, were no less affected by the unruly weather. Strong gusts of wind and the occasional snapping branches kept both animals fearful and tense. Cali's muscles were taut, and her eyes darted nervously at the slightest rustle or movement in the brush. It was the most skittish I'd ever seen her, and Stormy wasn't handling his unease any better.

Drew was fretting over the brutish conditions as well. I couldn't blame him. We'd had a rough go with the storms the last few days. I was concerned Drew's anxiousness would eventually get the best of him, but he pressed on. His hands gripped the reins tightly, and he kept a wary eye on the swaying branches and darkened woods bordering the road. Drew had seen his fair share of perilous situations and dangerous places, but something about the thunder, lightning, and wind unnerved him to the core. Still, Drew crossed the bridge into Jonesborough much quicker than he had the first time, which was surprising. It looked to me like the bridge was hanging on by a thread and could give way at any moment. I decided it best to keep that thought to myself.

We arrived in Jonesborough just after dark, and the town looked nearly deserted. By now, the streets were little more than narrow, muddy creek beds, which is likely why so few people were moving about. Despite the challenges brought on by the weather, the buildings and businesses lining Main Street were beginning to come to life. Light spilled from their windows, reflected in golden, watery puddles, inviting patrons looking for food, drink, and a dry resting place.

We hitched our horses outside the Sheriff's office and climbed the slick, wooden steps. Upon entering, we were greeted by the skinny deputy, Deryl, who sat behind his cluttered desk, engrossed in a game of solitaire. He glanced up, saw us, and nearly fell out of his chair. He leaped to his feet as fast as if he'd seen a rattlesnake.

"Sheriff ain't here, fellas," Deryl said in a shaky voice. "He said he didn't wanna see you anyhow. Said he'd had enough of you two for one day." Deryl was on edge as if something he'd dreaded was now happening. "You might as well head on out. Try again tomorrow."

"Hey, it's alright, Deryl," Drew said, doing his best to put the man at ease. "We just stopped by to thank you for keepin' everything calm and orderly today. That's all."

"Oh," Deryl said, his shoulders relaxing a bit. "Well...in that case...come on in." He paused. "You boys have a seat, and I'll pour some coffee."

"No need to trouble yourself," I said as Drew and Deryl sat. "We don't have long. Like my associate said, we just wanted to thank you properly. By the way, you wouldn't happen to have an outhouse nearby, would you? It was a long ride, and I have a pressing matter to attend to if you catch my meaning."

Deryl turned and pointed to the back of the office. "Sure, just head through the entryway into the back and keep going straight. You'll see a door leading outside, and the outhouse will be on your left."

"Thank you very much, Deryl," I said with a smile.

"Just please don't touch anything back there," Deryl added.

"You don't have to worry about me," I told Deryl. "Just give me a few minutes, and Drew and I will let you get back to your duties."

"Take your time," Drew said with a laugh, waving me on. "My good pal, Deryl, and I will shoot the breeze till you're done."

As I stepped away, Drew asked Deryl if the coffee offer was still on the table. Then he asked if Deryl had any objections to making it Irish.

Moving as quickly and quietly as possible, I went into the back room of the Sheriff's office and walked straight through to the back door. I made a show of opening and closing it, hopefully creating the illusion that I'd stepped outside. I stopped and listened for a moment. Drew kept Deryl occupied, laughing, chatting, and being his wonderfully loud self. When I was satisfied it was safe, I rifled through the box of files stacked neatly near the back door. Most of the pages were filled with mundane details of the Sheriff's daily affairs, but I had a specific document in mind. Luckily, it didn't take long to find the file concerning the death of Earl Weston. I carefully removed the first few pages, folded them, and stashed them in my pocket. Once more, I opened and closed the back door a bit louder than needed and returned from completing my business.

Drew and Deryl had clearly hit it off in the brief time I was away. As I walked in, Drew was pouring more whiskey into their cups while he and Deryl laughed and cut up like they were long-lost friends.

"Thank you, Deputy," I said. "I think we should probably be on our way now."

"What?" Deryl said as his laughter faded. He was undoubtedly feeling the effects of the Irish coffee. "There ain't no need to take off now, is there? Me and my new friend here were just gettin' into some interesting conversation. Sit. Stay for a bit. The weather's terrible out there anyway."

"I wish we could, Deryl," I said, glancing at Drew. "But we still have a couple of matters to attend to this evening. You ready, Drew?"

"Sorry, Deryl," Drew said as he rose to his feet. "Moses is right. He's about as fun as a muddy opossum sometimes, but he *is* right. We need to get moving."

"Well, darn it," Deryl said, genuinely disappointed. "You fellas be careful out there, and know you're welcome here any time."

"Thank you, Deryl," Drew said. He even bowed a little. "It certainly has been a pleasure. You, sir, are a true gentleman and a wonderful conversationalist."

Deryl laughed and returned the bow. "As are you, my good man." He straightened up and was still chuckling to himself as we left the office.

Once outside, I pointed to the closest saloon down the road and motioned for Drew to follow. We trudged across the flooded street as the wind and rain ripped through the town. Two shops down, along the boardwalk, was a place called Doreen's Saloon and Eatery. It had been in Jonesborough since Drew and I were kids, but neither of us had ever been inside. We could hear the hoopla before we even got close and were surprised by the number of people present as we pushed through the doors. The interior was a stark contrast to the gloomy dusk beyond its walls. It was a lively place. Drinks flowed, music rang out, and the working girls made their rounds. At least four separate card games were in progress, and the clinking of glasses and lively chatter filled the room.

Drew and I found an empty table and began skimming through the pages of information I'd taken from the sheriff's office. Truthfully, we didn't even know what we were looking for. All we knew to do was scan the text and search for any clues that might offer direction.

Several statements were given about what happened the day Earl died, but there was nothing I hadn't already heard. I found the account offered by the anonymous witness, but the name had been blacked out and was impossible to decipher.

Ultimately, it was Drew who hit paydirt. While the witness's name was illegible, the file included the name of the Sheriff who'd taken his statement: Sheriff Cameron Wesley. The name struck a chord with me, but I couldn't quite place where I'd heard it.

Just then, a cheerful woman with rather large hair approached our table. She was all smiles as she wiped her hands on her checkered towel. "Good evening, fellas. My name's Doreen, and I run the place. Can I get you boys anything to eat or drink tonight?"

"That depends," Drew said. "What's good here?"

"Oh, we got a mean stew," she said, "and some of the finest Tennessee Whiskey you'll find anywhere."

"Yes, please," Drew said with a grin. "Sounds perfect." He looked at me, and I nodded. "Go ahead and bring us some of that mean stew and fine whiskey."

"Comin' right up," she said.

"One more thing, ma'am," Drew said. "My name is Drew, and this is Moses. We're only in town for a few days, and we're looking for Sheriff Cameron Wesley. Would you happen to know his whereabouts?"

Doreen laughed heartily. "You boys are about ten years too late," she said. "Sheriff Wesley married a good southern woman and moved to Elizabethton."

"Elizabethton?" I said, "That's not too far from here, right?"

"It's about a day's ride," she said. "If you're gonna find him, that's where he'll be."

"Did Wesley give up on being a lawman?" Drew said. "Or is he the Sheriff over in Elizabethton now?"

She laughed again. "No, he didn't give up on bein' a lawman," Doreen said. "In fact, he's a U.S. Marshal now. Has been for the last few years."

Drew and I ate our stew and finished our drinks, the whole time fixated on where I'd heard the name Wesley before. We put off going out in the weather for as long as possible but eventually decided to report to our crew and let them know we'd be heading out to Elizabethton first thing in the morning.

Once outside, the wind and rain greeted us like an insufferable visitor who'd overstayed his welcome. We stepped into our saddles and rode until we reached the Colter River. Drew took a few minutes to watch and inspect the bridge while I sat there staring at the tumultuous waters. Then, something about that murky water jogged my memory. I did know Cameron Wesley, but he wasn't a U.S. Marshal when I knew him. He wasn't even a Sheriff. Deputy Cameron Wesley was the man who pulled me from the Colter River when I was seven years old.

CHAPTER 37

After a brief sleep, Drew and I hit the road for Elizabethton the following morning. It was still dark when we left, and Skillet had packed some hardtack and dried beef for our trip. We no longer questioned whether or not the rain would continue, for it seemed to have taken up permanent residence. Drew suggested we embrace our situation and consider building an ark to float the Ivywood workers back to Montana. Interestingly enough, he and Skillet had a full-on argument over why such an endeavor would never work out. Skillet provided sound points to back his claims, while Drew argued for his own entertainment.

The trail to Elizabethton was clear and well-traveled but seemed to stretch endlessly as we pushed through the wind and driving rain. The rhythmic drumming of raindrops on my weathered hat and slicker, combined with the gentle rocking of the horse, lulled me into a sort of trance. When the breeze occasionally let up, the scent of wet leather and musky horsehide hung in the air. It reminded me how tough the last few weeks had been on our animals. Their manes were matted, and their coats glistened with rain, but they pressed on, loyal and true.

Mostly, we rode in silence, but occasionally, Drew would recall some detail of our journey that he wanted to discuss. "How 'bout old Clem?" he said, referring to the hunched-over old man who worked the fields for Logan Ashbourne. "He seems tough as whiteleather, don't you think?"

"Sure does," I agreed. "Clem didn't seem too intimidated by Sheriff Stringer's questions either."

"I was honestly impressed," Drew said. "I mean, Clem said all the things he was supposed to, but he did it in a way that made it clear how much he can't stand Logan Ashbourne."

"Logan knew it, too," I added. "He didn't say nothin' about it because things were playing out in his favor. But he sure stared the old man down. Clem still has some fight in him. I just hope the others do, too."

"I suppose we'll find out soon enough," Drew said.

It was nearly half past three in the afternoon when we finally rode into Elizabethton. We were wet, tired, and hungry, and the quaint little town was a welcomed sight. Elizabethton wasn't as large as Jonesborough, but it was clean and friendly-looking, nestled against the backdrop of the Appalachian Mountains.

The main street was lined with small shops, their wooden signs creaking in the wind as they swayed above the entrances. The roads were mostly cobblestone, which I usually don't care for, but riding on something other than mud for a change was nice. The townsfolk were active despite the nasty weather, moving about under the covered boardwalk.

Drew pointed out a spot ahead of us called the Appalachian Inn. It was a prominent, two-story structure that looked warm and inviting, so we stopped in to get a good meal and dry out a bit. We tied off our horses and entered through the front door. Inside, the inn was clean and smelled like freshly brewed coffee. The floor and bar were made of dark, polished oak, and an oversized chandelier fashioned from elk antlers hung prominently in the center of the room. Behind the bar, a mirror ran the entire length of the wall, and the shelves contained more varieties of alcohol than I'd ever seen in one place.

Only a handful of folks were relaxing at the inn that afternoon, all of whom exuded a certain air of refinement. Still, several of them greeted us politely as we entered, making us feel welcome despite our haggard appearance. They engaged in quiet conversations over glasses of various colored drinks while they watched the rainfall through the impressive plate-glass window.

"Good afternoon, gentlemen," the barkeep said as he went about wiping down the bar with a gleaming white cloth. It was already the cleanest bar we'd ever seen, so I wasn't sure why he wiped it so diligently. He was a handsome man, clean-shaven and tall, with a warm smile. "Please, sit wherever you'd like, and someone will be with you in a moment."

We chose a table near the bar when Drew pointed out the surly lookout perched on a stool at the back of the room. It seemed odd for a nice place like The Appalachian Inn to need someone on guard. With such amiable and affluent clientele, I couldn't understand why they would require the services of a hired gun. He was a rugged man with strong features and grim-looking scars that marred the right side of his face. Leaning against the stool beside him was a double-barreled shotgun. He scanned the room, sizing up everyone, especially Drew and me. Neither of us took offense to his attention. We didn't exactly appear to hold the same social standing as the typical patrons of their establishment. After a while, he lost interest, and Drew and I settled in for a hearty meal of fried chicken and greens.

Just as we finished up, the lookout left his post and visited the bar. He spoke to the barkeep with little emotion or expression, solidifying my impression that he was a practical, no-nonsense sort of fella. I listened in on their conversation, but it was of little substance. As far as I could tell, the lookout wasn't necessarily the friendly sort. Most aren't. But I figured it was likely difficult to be approachable, having such an imposing nature and intimidating scars. Overall, he posed no threat to us, but I concluded it was probably best to mind our own business and leave him be. It shouldn't have surprised me that such a thought hadn't occurred to Drew.

"How you doing, partner?" Drew said to the man.

"Afternoon," he replied blankly with a single nod.

"Nice place you got here," Drew continued. "You been here long?"

Looking slightly annoyed, the imposing fella stepped over to our table. "I've been here about a year," he said. "Name's Roy."

"I'm Drew, and this is my friend, Moses. We're just passin' through." Drew paused. "Tell me, Roy, what's a place like this need with a capable fella such as yourself?"

"Ah, I don't reckon there's much of a need," Roy said with a grunt. "I think they keep me around to look mean, hold a big gun, and help nice folks feel safe."

"Makes sense," I said. "Seems like a plum job."

Roy chuckled a little, which was odd to hear from such a stoic individual. "Yeah, I suppose it is. Most days."

"Hey, Roy, let me ask you something," Drew continued. "We're lookin' for Marshal Cameron Wesley. Any idea where we might find him?"

Roy paused for a moment as if trying to decide whether or not he should trust us, but ultimately, he must have decided we meant no harm. "Marshal Wesley lives west of here," he said, pointing outside. "Keep followin' the road there until you get to the livery, and you should see his place. Wesley's got a little white house with green shutters. There's usually some chickens out front. If you go now, you might catch him at home."

"Thank you, Roy," Drew said. "It was good to meet you. You're doin' fine work here. This place is lucky to have you."

Roy mumbled something that sounded like a "thank you," and Drew and I were again out in the elements, climbing into the saddle. As usual, Drew managed to find a way to stumble into something helpful. I shouldn't have doubted him.

We followed Roy's directions and soon were in front of the livery. About a quarter of a mile off the road was a neat white house with green shutters, just as Roy described. Considering how hard we'd been pushing our horses, we decided to leave them at the livery to dry out and be pampered a bit while we continued on foot.

A grizzled old man named Pete ran the livery. We explained to him that we'd only be a short while, so he immediately set to work rubbing down the tired animals while feeding them a couple of apples for good measure. When Drew was satisfied the horses were in good hands, we left the livery and trudged toward the marshal's house.

As we stepped onto the front porch, I had a moment of doubt as to whether or not this was a good idea. It was a long shot to think Marshal Wesley would care enough about our situation to help us. For all we knew, he was in cahoots with Logan Ashbourne like everyone else within a hundred miles of Jonesborough. I forced my doubt aside and knocked on the door. After a moment, it swung open to reveal a middle-aged man with a gray goatee and closely cropped hair. His eyes held a glimmer of recognition, and a crooked smile graced his face.

"Hello, Marshal," I began, "My name is –"

"You don't need to introduce yourself to me, son," Marshal Wesley said, holding onto his grin. "There's no way in hell I'd ever forget Moses Colter. Look at you. You've grown up well, I see. Nice and strong. Although you look about as waterlogged now as you did the day I pulled you out of the river."

I laughed and shook Marshal Wesley's hand. He invited us in and had us sit in the chairs arranged near his fireplace. "You boys will have to forgive me, but I don't have a thing to offer you. My wife is away, and she's the hospitable one in this household."

"I appreciate it, but we don't need anything, Marshal," I said. "It's more than kind of you to agree to talk to us for a few minutes."

"Sure," Wesley said with a furrowed brow. "You seem upset, Moses. Is there something I can help you with?"

We shared the story of Logan Ashbourne and the workers we were attempting to liberate, about their terrible treatment and how Logan was holding them against their will. Marshal Wesley listened intently as Drew and I took turns recounting what we believed to be the most pertinent details. I also explained how we were able to locate him here in Elizabethton, including how I stole the files from the Sheriff's office.

When we'd finished, Marshal Wesley looked at me with a reaction I didn't expect. He was shaking his head and laughing. And just when I thought he was done, he laughed some more.

"I'm sorry, fellas," Marshal Wesley said. "It's just...I've been waiting for something like this for years."

"How do you mean, Marshal?" Drew asked, glancing at me.

"You see, boys," he began, "everyone in Tennessee knows that Logan Ashbourne is as crooked as a bucket of fish hooks. Problem is, no one's been able to make anything stick to him. But I think that might have just changed."

"So you think you can help us?" I said.

"Moses Colter," he replied, "not only can I help you, but it will be my greatest pleasure to shut that spoiled bastard up once and for all. Hell, boys, you don't realize it, but you've given me a gift. It's like Christmas mornin' around here. I'd offer you a whiskey to celebrate, but I don't touch the stuff. Never agreed with me."

"Your help is enough, Marshal," I said. "How do you think we should go about this?"

"We can leave right now if you want," Marshal Wesley said. "I'll have to put together a posse, but that won't take long. We can be there by sunrise if we get on the trail within the next hour or two."

"I don't think we can do that," Drew said. "We rode our horses pretty hard to get here. They're at the livery now, but they'll need some rest first."

Wesley nodded. "Not to worry, fellas. I'll get you some horses, and then I'll have old Pete get someone to deliver them back to your camp as soon as they're rested. I don't wanna waste time on this. Let's get those workers out of there and get you all on your way to Montana."

I felt as if I'd exhaled for the first time in months. "Thank you, Marshal," I said. "I don't know what we would do without your help."

"Well, let's don't go celebrating just yet," Marshal Wesley said as he stood up and shook our hands. "Let's take care of business first."

There was a knock at the door, which seemed to surprise Marshal Wesley. "I can't tell you boys the last time I had two unexpected visitors in the same afternoon," he said. He crossed the room and opened the door to reveal none other than Titus' sons, Fisher and Tate, along with Two Feathers. They were an unsightly lot to behold, standing there soaked to the bone and huffing like they'd just finished running a race. I was genuinely concerned Marshal Wesley might shoot them on site, seeing as how they weren't the most upstanding group of fellas to find lingering on your front porch.

"What do you boys need?" Marshal Wesley said hesitantly. There was a bit of edge to his voice.

"They're friends of ours," I said. "We didn't know they were coming, but they're okay, Marshal." Trusting my word, Marshal Wesley ushered them inside and let them warm up by the fire.

"We sorry to bother y'all," Fisher said, still breathing heavily. "We didn't know where else to go."

"What's wrong?" I said. "Did something happen?"

"It's old Clem," Tate said. "They killed him, Moses."

"Who killed him?" I said.

"Mr. Ashbourne and his boys," Fisher said.

"Logan Ashbourne?" Marshal Wesley cut in. "You saw this happen?" Fisher and Tate shook their heads as their chests continued rising and falling. "Listen, you boys sit down here, take a few breaths, and tell me exactly what happened."

"We was workin' in the fields till late last night," Fisher began. "Mr. Ashbourne was pushin' us hard. Said nobody was gonna sleep till them fields was clean."

Tate picked up the story. "It was early on in the mornin' when we heard a ruckus at the stables. We ran over and seen old Clem layin' in the mud, dead. There was blood everywhere, and the side of his head was bashed in."

"Mr. Carl, Mr. Harold, and Mr. Ashbourne was all standin' there," Tate said. "Which was funny seein' as how it was so late. Anyway, they was all there, like I said, pokin' old Clem and nudgin' him with their boots. I reckon they was tryin' to see if he was dead enough for their likin'."

"Did they say what happened to him?" Drew said.

Fisher nodded. "They said one of the horses started actin' up. Said Clem tried to take hold of him, but the horse reared up and kicked him in the head."

"Not to doubt you fellas," I said carefully. "But that sounds like something that could've happened, don't you think?"

They both shook their heads again. "No, sir, Moses," Tate said. "Clem didn't work with horses. Never did. He was scared of 'em. He shoulda' been in the fields with us, but Mr. Harold called for him. Clem left and didn't never come back."

"You think anyone saw it happen?" Marshal Wesley said. "Were there any witnesses?"

"Don't know," Fisher said. "While we was all standin' there lookin' at Clem's body, Mr. Ashbourne told us Clem got what he deserved. He was mad as a hornet – said the good Lord was gonna' punish all of us if we disrespected him the way Clem did. That's when Tate…" he looked at his brother.

"That's when I hollered at Mr. Ashbourne," Tate said, dropping his eyes. "I told him that he was gonna get what was comin' to him – that the Lord wasn't gonna sit by and watch him keep hurtin' folks. Then I told the others to get their stuff together and be ready to move when you got back." He paused, looked at me, then dropped his eyes again. "I'm sorry, Moses. I know you told us to keep our heads down and not make things worse. It just struck me wrong when Mr. Ashbourne blamed the good Lord for what he did to Clem. I felt like I couldn't hold it back no more."

"It's alright, Tate," I said. "I don't blame you. I might've done the same. But I know Logan didn't just take that from you. What happened next?"

Fisher took over the story as if he was saving Tate from having to relive the confrontation. "Mr. Ashbourne stood there all quiet for a minute. We thought he mighta' lost his mind or somethin'. But then, all calm-like, he pointed at Tate and me and told Mr. Harold and Mr. Carl, 'Take care of those two.' We ran and lost 'em in the woods. We didn't have no place to go so we went to your camp. Two Feathers got us some horses, and we took off after you."

Two Feathers looked at me and nodded.

"I'm sorry you fellas had to go through all that," I said. "But we're gonna' make this right. Marshal Wesley here is gonna' help us."

"Damn right I am," Marshal Wesley said as he grabbed his hat and coat. "Let's go catch us a snake, boys."

CHAPTER 38

In under an hour, Marshal Wesley worked his magic, gathering a posse of fourteen determined, well-armed men. He also arranged for Pete, the livery owner, to lend Drew and me two dark bay geldings. Drew, who loved his horse more than he loved most people, was uneasy about leaving Stormy behind. Marshal Wesley, however, assured him that Stormy would be well cared for and safely returned to Drew the following day. Something about the way the marshal spoke was reassuring. He was authoritative and confident, unwavering in his conviction that his men would follow his orders. It put us at ease, and Drew ultimately decided that Stormy was in good hands.

We mounted the horses as nightfall was almost upon us. The world was quiet, still, and wet. While not falling steadily as before, the rain had transformed into a thick mist that hung in the cool evening air like a soggy fog. It was still wet and miserable outside, but I was oddly thankful to have a different variety of misery to contend with.

Before long, we were on the move. The trail before us was barely visible through the haunting mist. It felt unreal, more dream-like than physical – an illusionary landscape that blurred the boundaries between reality and the ethereal. The clouds above, the trail below, and the wilderness surrounding us had been thoroughly soaked and brushed onto the night's canvas like a living watercolor. Equally as unsettling was the silence. Aside from the hollow, muffled thump of hooves striking mud, we heard nothing. No wind. No rain. No chirping crickets or crying tree frogs. Nothing.

Despite the treacherous and unsettling conditions, we were a determined bunch. We rode on, insistent upon reaching our destination by morning. We made only two stops throughout the night to rest the horses and grab a quick nap. When we were a few miles from camp, I sent Two

Feathers, Fisher, and Tate ahead to warn Skillet and Nellie of our arrival. The last thing I wanted was to frighten them by showing up with a posse they weren't expecting. As Two Feathers and the twins rode away, their dark silhouettes were swallowed up by the night, eventually becoming one with the somber mist.

The rest of us continued ahead at a steady pace. After a few hours, the pre-dawn light began to peek through the soupy mess around us, and the sky brightened a bit. It was close to five o'clock that morning when Drew, Marshal Wesley, his men, and I rode into camp.

The sight of Skillet and Nellie greeted us like a warm beacon shining through the haze. Their excitement was palpable, and even Skillet was in a pleasant mood. The smell of fresh coffee wafted through the stale, murky morning, rejuvenating our spirits with its tempting aroma. Skillet and Nellie prepared breakfast with a generous spread of biscuits, ham, and gravy. As I watched Marshal Wesley and his men smile, chat, and eat, it occurred to me that Skillet and Nellie were far more than mere stewards of our camp. They were our lifeline, working diligently to keep our spirits high and our bellies full.

Marshal Wesley gathered us all together as soon as we'd finished our meal. There was no doubt that he was the commanding presence of this endeavor. Marshal Wesley spoke with confidence and authority. He outlined his plan without doubt or hesitation, his words heavy with purpose. It was evident that the marshal had dealt with his fair share of tight spots and dangerous men. Drew and I were no strangers to trouble, although we usually found ourselves on the opposite side of the law.

Assignments were dolled out and tailored to the strengths and capabilities of each individual. Drew and one of Wesley's men were assigned a dangerous but crucial task. They were to position themselves on either side of Marshal Wesley, spreading out and keeping a clear line of sight on Harold Gullet. In the event Gullet made any sudden, hostile moves, the command was clear. Take him out before he could hurt anyone. Drew was especially pleased with this assignment. He'd been waiting for a chance at payback since he was a boy. The night Harold Gullet forced Drew to kill that horse, he made an enemy for life. Marshal Wesley picked the right man for the job. I only prayed Drew could carry out his assignment without losing his cool.

I was told to stay by Marshal Wesley's side, ready to lend my voice to the discussion should the situation require it.

To their disappointment, the twins, Fisher and Tate, were given a far less inspiring duty. They were instructed to pack up camp with Skillet and Nellie, then travel into Jonesborough and await further instruction. I could tell by the glances they shared that it wasn't what Fisher and Tate had in mind, but they accepted their assignment without question. I couldn't blame them. If I were in their shoes, I'd want to face Logan Ashbourne right alongside my friends and family. The marshal assured the twins he would see to it that their wives and children were kept safe and that they'd be reunited as quickly as possible.

When all was said and done, there were a few men with no specific duties. Wesley told them to be prepared for anything and to keep a keen eye and a loaded rifle. The camp grew more tense with each passing moment. We all understood the gravity of the situation. There was a strong possibility bullets would fly. Still, our resolve was steadfast, and we were ready for whatever transpired.

Thunder rumbled, distant and mournful, as we set out on horseback toward Ivywood Plantation. No one spoke. By then, it was light out, and the previous night's fog had surrendered to the returning rainfall. As we approached the front gate of the plantation, a lone figure stood guard. Harold Gullet. His face was as hard as stone, and he clutched his shotgun firmly.

Marshal Wesley rode out in front of the posse. His voice rang with all the weight of his position. "I am U.S. Marshal Cameron Wesley, and these men are with me. I'm here to meet with Logan Ashbourne." His words hung there in the silence, both a challenge and a demand.

Harold Gullet had never been a man of many words, but now he offered no response whatsoever. His very stature was brimming with defiance, and he fixed his eyes on the marshal with a spiteful glare. If he was attempting to increase the tension, he'd succeeded. As the moment dragged on, our nerves became more and more frayed. Drew had his hand on his revolver; his eyes locked onto Gullet. I held the opinion that Harold Gullet would have stood there all day, just glaring at us in silence. It was an interesting tactic but ultimately ineffective.

Marshal Wesley, undeterred by Gullet's stoicism, took matters into his own hands. With no further words and no show of fear or anger, he pushed through the front gate and rode onto the plantation grounds. "Let's go, boys," he called back as he cut his eyes toward Gullet. We all followed, riding through the front gate as Harold Gullet stood by, simply watching.

The die was cast. And now, the fate of many lives was hanging in the balance. After all we'd been through, this was the point of no return, and I was more than ready to embrace it.

"Two Feathers," Marshal Wesley called. Two Feathers immediately rushed to the front of the posse. "You good at sneaking? Hiding?"

"Yes, sir," Two Feathers said.

Marshal Wesley nodded. "Can you shoot?"

"Yes, sir."

"Killing folks bother you?" Wesley said.

"Man needs killin', I kill him," Two Feathers answered flatly.

"Good." Marshal Wesley removed a Sharps rifle from his horse and pointed a finger straight ahead, toward a ridge just beyond the plantation. "Take this rifle. I want you to head up there, nice and quiet like. Find a good vantage point and keep a bead on Logan Ashbourne. If any fightin' breaks out, put a hole in him."

"Yes, sir," Two Feathers said, strapping the Sharps to his back.

Marshal Wesley looked him dead in the eye. "I'm trusting you. Don't let that slippery bastard out of your sight. As far as you're concerned, nothing else matters. Things go south, and your only job is to make sure he's dead."

Two Feathers nodded and raced away.

CHAPTER 39

To our surprise, Logan Ashbourne was working – something I had never seen in all my years living at the plantation. But there he was, with half a dozen workers, salvaging material from a collapsed stable. By the looks of it, one of the massive oak trees had fallen, nearly destroying the horse barn. Only a third of the structure remained standing; the rest had been reduced to little more than splinters and firewood. The rain had subsided for the first time in days, but no one had any confidence it was over. Ominous, black clouds churned overhead, spurring Logan to work quickly before the storms returned.

Logan's back was to us as we rode up with the marshal and his posse. The sleeves of Logan's sweat-stained dress shirt were rolled up past his elbows, and his fine alligator skin boots were caked with mud. Logan was filthy, and his thinning hair stuck out in all directions. He panted and huffed as he struggled to clear away the fallen debris. Yes, Logan Ashbourne was working, but he did so with the graceless movements of a man who'd never had to pull his own weight.

"Looks like bad business," Marshal Wesley called out as we approached. "Having a little trouble, Mr. Ashbourne?"

Sweating and breathless, Logan turned to find himself face to face with a U.S. Marshal and fourteen armed men. "Oh, good God," he said, groaning as he tossed a splintered board aside. "I would love to go one damn day of my life without either the law or Moses Colter keeping me from my work."

"What happened here?" Marshal Wesley said.

"What happened?" Logan Ashbourne snapped back mockingly. "A big ass tree blew over on my barn and killed seven of my finest Thoroughbreds. That's what happened. For a lawman, you ain't too keen regarding powers of observation, are you?"

"Sorry about your horses," the marshal said in a tone that made it seem like he wasn't.

"Who the hell *are* you?" Logan said, still red-faced and annoyed. "And why are you on my property? I see you have a badge, but Stringer didn't say anything about taking on more deputies."

Wesley paused. "Does Stringer generally run things like that by you, Mr. Ashbourne? Hiring practices and the like?" Logan didn't reply, but I could see his mind reeling. Though his ill-tempered disposition was still firmly intact, he was also concerned. "Logan Ashbourne, I am U.S. Marshal Cameron Wesley. We need to talk. But first, if you have any men in those watchtowers, you need to call them down now."

As customary, Logan's arrogance knew no bounds, and he was beginning to recover from his initial shock. "There ain't no men in the towers, Marshal," Logan said. "As you can plainly see, every man I got is working his ass off today. It might do you some good to climb off that gelding and put in an honest day's work yourself."

For a moment, Marshal Wesley smiled as if Logan's hubris amused him. I wondered how long he'd allow Logan to show such disrespect. "Mr. Ashbourne, you and I *will* have a conversation this morning, and I suggest you choose your words wisely moving forward."

Logan stood up straight and saluted like a soldier. "Yes, sir, Marshal Wesley, sir," he answered in a booming voice before addressing the men working around him. "You boys, stop what you're doing and get outta here," he snapped. "Go find something else to do. Lord knows there's plenty to be done." The workers cleared out quickly, with the exception of Harold Gullet and Carl Bancroft. They walked up beside Logan, planting themselves on either side. Rarely had I ever witnessed Drew as locked in and focused as he was at that moment. The only thing in his world was the revolver on his hip and Harold Gullet.

"U.S. Marshal Cameron Wesley," Logan said, nodding. "I knew I recognized you. You weren't quite so puffed up back when we all called you *Sheriff* Cameron Wesley. So tell me, Marshal, what brings a bigshot lawman like yourself all the way down to the Ivywood Plantation? If you're lookin' to purchase some tobacco, it might be a while."

Marshal Wesley dismounted, and the rest of us followed his lead. He took a few steps toward Logan before addressing him. "I'll pass on the tobacco, Mr. Ashbourne. I'd rather we get right to it if it's all the same to you. I'm here because it appears your questionable business practices

201

have brought some serious accusations upon you. Specifically, allegations of slavery and murder."

"Slavery and murder?" Logan replied, his eyebrows raised. "I'm not sure if I should be offended or concerned, Marshal. First off, the men you see here are workers, not slaves. Slavery has been long since abolished, thanks to the unwavering humanitarian efforts of this great nation. The men and women who work for me get fed and sheltered, just like any other workers you'll find in these parts."

Logan's gaze shifted to me, and I noticed the familiar hateful glint dancing in his eyes. "You feelin' good about this, Moses? I bet you are. But, I gotta tell you, I'm a little disappointed in you. What kind of man runs off to find the law instead of handling his own problems? I suppose living with all those sheep in Montana has gone and made you soft."

Everything in me wanted to race forward and punch Logan Ashbourne in his smug face, but I kept my head clear and calm. This moment was more significant than any petty revenge. Today was about liberating these plantation workers – an endeavor that required patience and restraint.

Logan continued with his insults, turning his attention to Drew. "And you...Drew Harlan, the prize orphan idiot and horse killer. I can't believe, after all these years, you're still following Moses Colter around like some two-bit huntin' dog." Logan paused to laugh at his comment. "It must be awfully damn humbling to be partnered up with Moses Colter and still not be the brains of the operation."

Marshal Wesley didn't allow Drew to respond before breaking in. "That's enough of that, Logan. All of your bravado and insults aren't going to help you today. I'll find out about the slavery claims soon. And, to be clear, Clem Jackson's death is also under investigation."

"Sheriff Stringer already did an investigation," Logan answered firmly.

Marshal Wesley nodded. "I am aware of that, and I have found the Sheriff's cursory examination of the matter to be lacking. Let's just say I'm here to dig a little deeper."

Logan's eyes flashed with anger, and his voice grew strained. "Clem's death was hard on all of us, but it was an accident. The Sheriff took statements himself and he agreed. That's the end of it."

"That's very good to hear, Logan," Marshal Wesley said. "For the record, I have no reason to doubt Sheriff Stringer. And, if what you say is true, I don't suppose a few more questions should trouble you much. Will they?"

Logan nodded stiffly. "Fine. Just get on with it."

"You know," Marshal Wesley said, shaking his head, "I think I've changed my mind. I believe it's better if you and I talk tomorrow in town. You can meet me at the Sheriff's office bright and early." He pointed to Harold and Carl. "You might as well bring them too."

Marshal Wesley paused and looked around the plantation. "As for your workers," he continued, "I'm gonna go ahead and take them with me now. We'll head into Jonesborough for questioning and to ensure everything here is on the up and up. I'm sure it's nothing for you to worry about."

Logan's irritation was boiling over. "I know what's happening here. They've already been asked, and none of them want to leave. Dammit, Marshal, this is my livelihood, and I won't sit by and watch you destroy it."

"It seems to me you're doing a right fine job of that yourself," Marshal Wesley said. "After we finish our questioning, your workers will have a choice to make, Logan. They can return here and continue working for you or leave with Moses and Drew. Or, hell, they can strike out on their own if they want to. The point is, it'll be their choice."

"This ain't right, Marshal, and you know it," Logan said, lowering his voice. "I've already lost my tobacco fields and my Thoroughbreds. I can't afford to lose my workers too. You can't just ruin a man's life because you want to play Jesus to a field full of negros."

With a sense of calm finality, Marshal Wesley said, "I wish you luck, Mr. Ashbourne." Then he turned to one of his men. "Jeb, ride ahead and tell Sheriff Stringer we're on the way. Tell him we'll need a place to set up – something bigger than his office."

Jeb raced to his horse, mounted, and spurred the animal on, galloping off toward Jonesborough. Things were fully in motion now, and Marshal Wesley was intent on following through with his promise to help.

The marshal's next order cut through the remaining tension like a razor. He lifted his head and called out to all the workers scattered throughout the fields, the plantation house, and the barns and corrals. They gathered quickly, all of them wide-eyed, their nerves stretched tight like a drawn bow. From the crowd, Titus caught my eye, and I nodded stiffly to him, hoping to communicate that his sons were safe.

"Workers of the Ivywood Plantation," Marshal Wesley announced, "all of you are leaving here with me now. I'm taking you to Jonesborough to ask you some questions. Afterward, you're all free to do as you see fit. You can return here to the Ivywood, you can leave with Moses and Drew, or you can set out on your own. But for now, gather any belongings you don't want left behind, but only what you can carry. My men and I will lead the way, and you will follow on foot. Do you all understand?"

A swift current of nods and murmurs of consent rippled through the swarm of workers. They fully understood the opportunity that lay before them and the choices they'd soon face. Marshal Wesley barked at them to move it, and the workers scattered in all directions, frantically grabbing everything they could carry.

As I watched them scramble to gather their meager possessions, I couldn't help but be moved. These men, women, and children had toiled under the Ashbourne's oppression for years and were now taking their first steps toward freedom. Once desperate and helpless, their faces now had a glimmer of hope. Some were even smiling as they took their loved ones by the hand and rushed off to their homes.

When the crowd had fully dispersed, Titus was left in its void. He stood there for a moment, looking at me with tears in his eyes before racing forward and hugging me. "Thank you, Moses," he said quietly as he held onto me. "Thank you for not forgettin' us. The Lord used you to bless us. The Lord's plan is always greater than our struggle."

Titus released me and raced away to join Charity as she packed their essentials. I stepped into the saddle and caught Drew's gaze. He simply grinned and nodded before jumping on the dark bay and riding off.

Tears welled in my own eyes as I watched those workers pass through the front gate of the Ivywood Plantation. Their shuffling steps echoed with the promise of a better life. A future. We had set out on this mission seeking justice, and though the path ahead was long, the first steps had been taken. It was comforting to know that the Ivywood Plantation might no longer be a symbol of despair. Now, it might stand for something altogether different. Eventually, it might become a monument of resilience and freedom for all those who've been oppressed.

"Let's head out," Marshal Wesley called as his men mounted up. He made for the front gate before stopping and turning back. "Logan Ashbourne," he called. Logan turned toward him, dejected and fuming mad. "I expect you to turn yourself in for questioning first thing tomorrow morning. If you fail to show up, I will issue a warrant for your arrest. You have yourself a fine day, Mr. Ashbourne."

Chapter 40

Apprehensive but hopeful, the workers from the Ivywood crossed the worn wooden bridge into Jonesborough as free men and women. The Lord had granted us a reprieve from the rain on our journey from the plantation, but as soon as we entered the town, the heavens welled up and wept in earnest once more. Still, the workers' smiles never faltered, undeterred by the downpour. It was a good day. Their optimism remained strong despite plenty of uncertainty about stepping into the unknown. Fear of the unknown wasn't as powerful as the hope of a better life.

Marshal Wesley led the procession up Main Street as the townsfolk spilled out of their homes and businesses, lining either side of the muddy thoroughfare. They scrambled about, jockeying for position to ensure a clear view of the spectacle unfurling before them. I felt like we were part of a traveling circus, passing through town to advertise our big show. Most onlookers remained sheltered under the covered boardwalks, while others stepped right out into the rain to get a good look.

Needless to say, the whole affair was rather unnerving. Until then, I hadn't considered that anyone from Jonesborough knew or even cared who we were or what we'd been doing. Maybe they still didn't know. Perhaps the mere sight of such a desperate lot was enough to capture the entire town's attention. Unsure of what was about to occur, Marshal Wesley pulled to a stop, whirled his horse around, and ordered his men to spread out.

"What do you make of all this?" Drew said, riding up next to me. "You don't reckon they mean us any harm, do you? What if Logan got to them?"

I shook my head. "I don't think so. I figure they're just curious."

The workers grew noticeably leery of the gathering crowd. Their wide eyes darted from one side of the road to the other as the rain poured. Their stained and dirty clothes were drenched and clung to their weary bodies, but their spirits were unbroken. Then, as if it had all been arranged beforehand, the good people of Jonesborough began to clap and cheer for the freed Ivywood Plantation workers. Men, women, and children trumpeted their support with a victorious welcome. The show of support moved several workers to tears, while others laughed and grinned and embraced one another. And for the first time that day, I noticed a thin smile crack Marshal Wesley's stony face.

As the celebration continued, Marshal Wesley was met by Sheriff Stringer and his lanky deputy, Deryl. Stringer stepped up to the marshal and nodded weakly as drops of rain bounced off his broad-brimmed hat. "Marshal Wesley," he began, "I've arranged accommodations at Doreen's as you requested." He pointed to the saloon. "She's got a couple of offices you can use. I figured you could carry on with your questioning there if you'd like."

In return, the marshal offered Stringer a nod and said, "Thank you, Sheriff. That'll be fine." In short order, Marshal Wesley ushered the drenched workers into the warmth of Doreen's Saloon and Eatery. It was a little tight once everyone was inside, but it would only be necessary for one night, and it was warm and safe. Doreen had cleared most of the tables, and the space felt much larger. In their place, she'd spread out pallets and blankets on which they could rest.

"Come on in, everyone," Doreen called out. "Quickly now. Let's get you all warmed up. You can drop your things wherever you'd like and have a seat until we figure out how we're gonna take care of you folks."

"That's right," Marshal Wesley added. "Just find a spot and hold tight for now. My men will divide you into groups, and we'll get on with our questioning. Hopefully, it won't take too long and you fine folks can be on your way."

I thanked Doreen for allowing everyone to stay in her place. She smiled and said she was glad to help, but I could see the concern on her face. Having the saloon packed full of frightened families awaiting instruction was overwhelming. Still, it felt as if something important was about to happen within those walls. This place wasn't simply a refuge from the storm; it was a place where voices would be heard, some for the first time, and truth would finally be revealed.

"Ms. Doreen," the marshal said, "can you make sure we get these folks a good meal? Supper tonight and then breakfast in the morning should be enough."

Doreen quickly crossed the room and whispered to Marshal Wesley as she eyed the crowd of men and women. "I'll make sure they all get fed and have a place to sleep tonight, but I'm runnin' a business here too, Marshal." She raised an eyebrow and leaned in closer to him. "Who's responsible for payin' for everything? Their meals and lodging?" It was a fair question. Doreen's apprehension had nothing to do with her desire to help the poor souls and everything to do with protecting her livelihood.

Marshal Wesley placed a hand on Doreen's shoulder. "Don't you worry, ma'am. The state of Tennessee will cover any expenses you incur. I'll personally ensure you're fairly compensated for your services and time." It must have been the only issue troubling Doreen, for upon hearing those words, she leaped into action, chatting with her new guests and calling for her cooks to fire up the ovens.

Doreen soon disappeared into the kitchen to help prepare supper, and Marshal Wesley quickly divided the workers into ten groups. Each of Wesley's men was assigned a group and spread out around the saloon to offer everyone as much privacy as possible. Within a few minutes, the room was abuzz with hushed voices recounting stories of cruelty, fear, and perseverance. There was no denying the weariness and trepidation of the abused workers, but despite their worries, they continued to share the truth of their lives. Each soul had a tale to tell, and the room was filled with the murmuring of collective experiences. The long-suppressed truth spilled as freely and powerfully as the rain.

During their earnest confessions, Deputy Deryl entered and asked if he could speak with me privately. We pushed through the doors and sat in two wooden chairs lined up against the outer wall of the saloon. The covered boardwalk shielded us from the elements, and the clatter of rain on the tin roof helped muffle our voices. A steady downpour cascaded from the overhang, forming a watery curtain separating us from the street.

"What can I do for you, Deryl?" I said. "Is everything okay?"

Deryl nodded. "Everything's fine, Moses. And I must say, it's a wonderful thing you're doin' for these folks. Lots of us think so. In fact, quite a few of our townsfolk have been stoppin' by the office to ask if there's anything they can do to help. I told them I'd check with you."

I stared out at the thin waterfall rolling off the roof, my mind racing with thoughts of everything we needed for our trip. "The people of Jonesborough really want to help us?" I said.

Deryl nodded. "They do. Like I said, lots of them. It surprised me, too. I figure they all bought in once they heard what you fellas was doin' here." He lowered his voice. "And truth be told, I don't think they care for Logan Ashbourne. Maybe they see this as their way of stickin' it to him, you know?"

"Well, it works for us," I said. "Of course, supplies for the road would be appreciated. But if anybody's feeling especially generous, we could use some wagons, mules, and maybe horses. I know it's a lot to ask, but that's what we need most. Logan Ashbourne has every trader around here in a chokehold. Nobody will sell to us. We can make it on foot for a ways, but I'd rather move quicker if possible. Montana's a long way off, and winter will be on us before we know it. Even one or two wagons would be better than nothing."

Deryl nodded and stood. "I can't make no promises, but I'll see what I can do, Moses. Those are good people you got in there, and they deserve whatever help we can pull together." With a brisk nod, Deryl pulled his hat down low on his eyes and darted to the Sheriff's Office across the street.

I sat there, staring out at the rain and listening to the muffled voices of the workers inside. Soon, I was joined by Drew, Skillet, Nellie, and Two Feathers. They raced for the shelter of the boardwalk, everyone getting a good laugh at Drew, who nearly slipped when his muddy boots landed on the wet duckboards. They sat in the empty chairs along the wall next to me, and we huddled together to recount what had happened in the last few days.

"You boys findin' that marshal was a fine stroke of luck," Nellie said. "And what a coincidence that you knew him, Moses. And that he remembered you. The Lord works in mysterious ways."

Drew nodded. "He sure does, and that wasn't no coincidence. I don't know what to call it, but I feel like there should be a better word for everything that's happened so far."

Two Feathers responded in his native language, Shoshone, which none of us understood. When Drew asked what his words meant, he took a moment to gather his thoughts in English. "Luck is not fortune; it is blessing. Like being carried by wind." He paused. "My people have a saying – a prayer. 'Grant me the strength of eagle's wings, the faith and courage to fly to new heights, and the wisdom to rely on his spirit to carry me there.' The spirit...it carries us."

"That's a great way to put it," Drew added. "Like I said, it sure don't feel like we're doin' this alone." He nodded to Two Feathers. "We're being carried, like you said. And I'll be honest. I had my doubts at first, but it turns out Moses was right all along."

"Agreed," Skillet added, but his twisted face betrayed him. "There ain't no doubt we've been looked after every step of the way." He paused. "And I ain't one to pour cold water on everybody's good mood, but I'm still worried about us not havin' enough wagons and supplies. The road ahead ain't gonna be easy."

"We've faced tough times before, Skillet," Nellie said. "We'll figure it out. We always do. I believe Two Feathers is right. Look how far we've come." She smiled and patted Skillet's knee. "Don't start doubtin' now."

Two Feathers simply nodded in agreement, his eyes reflecting an understanding beyond our own. He saw this entire campaign as our destiny. I envied his resolve and wished it was my own. My doubts lingered and somehow managed to hang on, but my experiences were slowly changing me. It felt like I had jumped off a cliff and was careening toward the rocky earth. The more I let go and trusted the fall, the more faith I had that I'd find a soft place to land.

The door of Doreen's Saloon and Eatery swung open, and Titus emerged. We immediately greeted him and asked him to join us.

"How are things goin' in there?" Drew said.

"Good," Titus answered. His voice was tired, but his smile stayed strong. "I wanted to thank you all again – proper like. My people in there, they tellin' the truth about the Ashbournes and how they run things. They scared, but they talkin'. You gave us hope. We feelin' like things can change."

"They can change," I said. "And they will, Titus. It won't be perfect in Montana, but you'll have your say about how you and your family live. There won't be nobody telling you what to do or how to do it, and we'll all work together to build something we can be proud of."

"I hope so," Titus said with a somber grin. "I am a little scared of that trip, though. A lot of us are."

"There ain't nothin' to worry about, Titus," Drew added. "Don't get me wrong, it's a bully of a trip, but you and your people are strong. It won't be easy, but we'll make it."

Titus nodded. "And we'll do our share. These folk ain't scared of work. It's all they know. We'll work all the way to Montana."

"We have no doubt," Skillet said. "Just make sure everybody gets some sleep tonight. Don't go celebratin' too much. It's lookin' like we'll have to start out on foot, and we need you all well-rested and ready to move."

CHAPTER 41

I awoke to the shuffling of feet, the clatter of activity, and the low murmur of voices. The restless medley of sounds drifted up the staircase and into the small room where I'd spent the night in Doreen's Saloon and Eatery. I slept well – perhaps a bit too soundly, as pale sunlight managed to peek through my window despite the rain and thick cloud cover outside.

I rose quickly from my makeshift bed of horse blankets, stretched, pulled up my boots, and strapped on my gun belt. Pushing through the doorway, I sniffed desperately, hoping someone had made coffee. There was a peculiar energy in the air, an electric sense of anticipation that seeped through the floorboards and into my consciousness. Everyone was up and stirring, their movements filled with purpose and intensity.

Outside, a long roll of thunder caught my attention as Lisi, one of the Ivywood house servants, met me on the stairway and placed a cup of coffee into my hands. "I got this for you, sir," Lisi said with a proud smile before rushing off.

I descended the creaky staircase to a flurry of activity. It was comforting to see the men and women rushing in and out of the saloon, smiles on their faces and laughter in their bellies. They'd been waiting on this day for a long time, and a collective determination bound us together. Today, we would leave the long, dark shadow of the Ivywood Plantation far behind.

Skillet spotted me as I stepped from the staircase onto the saloon floor. His grin was infectious, and his voice carried the buoyant spirit of a much younger man. "Well, good mornin' princess," he greeted me with a grin. He was oddly giddy. "Hurry up and finish your coffee. It's time to get some dust on them boots. But first, you have to come outside and see this, Moses. It's a miracle. A genuine miracle."

Without awaiting my response, Skillet raced outside, and I followed. As I pushed through the saloon doors, I witnessed a sight more beautiful than I thought possible. Stretching the entire length of Main Street was a line of sturdy covered wagons. Their canvas tops gleamed despite the soggy, gray morning light. Altogether, I counted twenty-six wagons, each hitched to fresh mules. Half of the wagons were already filled with supplies. I peeked inside the closest one and saw barrels of flour, crates of canned goods, and bundles of cloth. The goods had been tied down, packed neatly, and carefully stowed.

I glanced at Skillet, who smiled knowingly and nodded. "The folks of Jonesborough did this," he said, pride beaming in his eyes. "I shoulda' trusted you, Moses. It's just like you said from the very start. All we gotta do is walk the path in front of us." He continued to nod and stare at the wagons. "Hell, forget walkin'. Now, we can ride."

In addition to the wagons, fifteen saddle horses were tethered nearby. The marshal had been true to his word, for included among the horses was my Palomino, Cali, and Stormy, Drew's black stallion. They looked clean, strong, and ready for the trip ahead. The generosity of the people of Jonesborough was extraordinary. They owed us nothing but still chose to help. I often wondered what drove the townsfolk to such charity. It was an unfamiliar notion in my experience. The struggles of the last few months had opened me up to the fact that good people still existed in this world. I'd seen it with my own eyes. Several of those good people walked among me and had become my family. Skillet, Nellie, Two Feathers, and Drew – they all chose to support me even though I had nothing to offer in return. I'd be forever in their debt and wouldn't hesitate to return the same trust and support they'd shown me.

"I've never seen anything quite like it," Sheriff Stringer said aloud as he crossed the street. Marshal Wesley was at his side. "The wagons and goods just kept comin' in. I always knew we had good folks in these parts, but they really outdid themselves."

Marshal Wesley nodded. "I've gotta agree with the sheriff. This beats all I've ever seen. You boys must've crossed paths with a lucky star somewhere along the way."

"Sheriff, can you make sure everyone is properly thanked on our behalf," I said. "I wish I had more time to do it myself."

Sheriff Stringer acknowledged my request with a nod before his gaze shifted toward the front of town. "Well, look who decided to join the party," he said. "I didn't expect him to show, Marshal."

My eyes followed his gesture, and I saw Logan Ashbourne, Harold Gullet, and Carl Bancroft riding toward us. Their dark figures were etched into the stone-like backdrop of that gray morning. Logan sat tall, riding with a confidence that didn't match his current predicament. As usual, Harold and Carl followed closely behind with menacing faces and angry demeanors.

"I wasn't so sure myself," Marshal Wesley said. He paused and watched them ride slowly into town. "Well, it's time to prove yourself, Sheriff. I'm gonna offer you a means to repair my damaged faith in you." He nodded toward Logan. "It's time to take this old boy down a peg. I'll let you and your men do the honors, but I want him in cuffs."

Sheriff Stringer took a deep breath, his shoulders slumping momentarily before he rallied his resolve. He called for Deryl, who raced from the Sheriff's Office, wiping crumbs from his shirt. Deputy Deryl quickly assessed the scene, gawking at Logan and then back at Wesley before composing himself, adjusting his gun belt, and joining the sheriff. Logan watched with a smug grin as Sheriff Stringer and Deputy Deryl approached him.

"Logan Ashbourne," the sheriff called out loud enough to draw the attention of anyone nearby. "You are under arrest for the murder of Clem Jackson as well as the abuse and unlawful detainment of the workers of the Ivywood Plantation."

Logan climbed out of the saddle and stepped right up to Sheriff Stringer, the pompous smile still clinging to his face. "There's no need to make a big show of it, Sheriff," he said, offering his hands. "I'm a peaceful man. Do whatever you need to; just mind your manners."

"Cuff him, Deryl," Sheriff Stringer said, holding Logan's gaze.

Logan Ashbourne didn't utter another word. Deryl secured the handcuffs, took him by the arm, and walked him into the Sheriff's Office. Logan watched me for the entirety of his short walk to the jailhouse, all the while grinning hatefully like a man who knew something the rest of us didn't. I assumed it was nothing more than his attempt to preserve what little pride he had left. Regardless, Logan's glaring and posturing didn't impact me in the slightest. Any trouble he had coming was of his own making, and I was glad to be rid of him.

"Harold Gullet and Carl Bancroft," the sheriff continued. "I'm gonna need you to hand over your guns, and the marshal's men will walk you over to Doreen's. I'm sure he has some questions for you. You both understand?"

Neither of them answered. They dismounted, handed over their guns to Wesley's men, and walked to Doreen's with cold, spiteful looks on their faces. As the men passed by the marshal and me, Harold Gullet took the opportunity to spit on the ground near my feet. He kept walking. Part of me wanted to pistol whip him right there in the street, but I didn't. It was over. We'd won, and there was no need to risk any further trouble.

For the first time that morning, Drew appeared, hopping down from the boardwalk, strutting, and wearing a confident, toothy grin. "Looks like old Gullet don't care for you one bit, Moses Colter," he said. "But, who cares, right? Let the marshal worry about Logan and his riff-raff now. We gotta get moving."

Before I could reply, a sudden, thunderous, cracking boom resonated throughout Main Street, rattling the windows of the stores and shops. The mules snorted and stomped as their ears twitched. We all turned as one; our eyes instinctively locked onto the weakened bridge as it buckled under the pressure of the current. After days, the relentless onslaught of rain and time had finally claimed victory over the structure. The bridge splintered into large chunks that were instantly swept away by the raging Colter River. It happened quickly, and not a single board or nail was left behind.

Skillet was the first to voice what we all feared. "That ain't no good at all," he said with a groan. "We can't cross the river fast as that water's movin'."

It took a moment for his words to sink in. "What does that mean for us gettin' out of here today?" I said.

"I don't know what you fellas are thinking," Drew began, "but we can't be stuck here waiting for this rain to stop. Judgin' how things have played out, we might be here till Christmas."

Marshal Wesley interjected. "You definitely won't be crossing anywhere close by, that's for sure. This rain has been a damn menace. In fact, there's only one spot I'd be willin' to risk it if I was in your shoes. That's the Colter River Dam."

"The Colter River Dam," Drew recited absently. "Can't say I'm familiar with it. I didn't even know the Colter had a dam. How far away are we talking?"

"The army constructed the dam about ten years ago," Marshal Wesley said. "Unless a fella has reason to ride out that far, there isn't much sense in it. There's nothing out there but open territory. With the crew you got with you, you're looking at a three day ride at best. I know it's out of your way, but it's the safest place to cross. And the ground is rocky enough that the mud shouldn't slow you down too much. Or, you decide to wait it out."

I was anything but confident, but my decision was swift and absolute. I refused to face those plantation workers with the news that we weren't leaving today. We needed to put as much time and space between us and Logan Ashbourne as possible. "Let's do it," I said to Skillet and Drew. "What's three more days when we already have so far to go?"

Skillet was thrilled with the decision and wasted no time seizing his opportunity to act. "I'll find Nellie and tell her we're pullin' out in half an hour." He raced away, probably hoping to avoid any further conversation that might change my mind.

I looked at Drew, but his attention was fixed on the seething river. "I told you that bridge wasn't safe," Drew said blankly.

CHAPTER 42

A cool, steady drizzle fell as we left Jonesborough. With overwhelming gratitude, I waved back to Sheriff Stringer, Deputy Deryl, and Marshal Wesley. I watched as their figures blurred and faded into the misty backdrop of the town. I owed those men more than I could ever repay.

As the wagon train began its slow, soggy procession, I couldn't help but consider how much had changed in such a short time. Our arrival had been met with fear and doubt, but our departure was marked by hope and determination. Still, not everyone had chosen to join us that day. Some of the Ivywood workers had families scattered across other towns and states. They decided to strike out on their own, eager to be reunited with loved ones. Others had a yearning for independence with their newfound freedom. They chose to break away from the group and carve out their own destiny. As we told them from the start, there were no hard feelings. Each family's journey belonged to them, and we all respected their decisions. For years, all of their choices had been made for them. It was good to see those men and women taking control of their futures.

Our ragtag assembly left Jonesborough that day with a company of one hundred and thirty-six men, women, and children. Families huddled in small groups, taking charge of wagons they would share on the journey. We'd left quickly that morning with limited possessions and a strong desire to get moving. I'd never laid eyes on a more determined group.

Our path led us alongside the winding Colter River, which writhed through the Tennessee wilderness like an angry serpent. Still, for all its fury, its beauty and strength were inspiring.

Two Feathers, Fisher, and Tate, took the lead, serving as scouts and trackers for our party. The twins had taken to Two Feathers and asked him to teach them how to be proper scouts. They eagerly absorbed Two Feathers' wisdom, learning to read sign and navigate rugged terrain.

Skillet and Nellie rode in the chuckwagon at the forefront of the procession. They were the most seasoned travelers, and Skillet could sense trouble like most folks smelled coffee brewing. Titus and Charity followed closely along with Fisher and Tate's wives and children. I was worried about how the children would handle such an arduous trip. But having youngins reminded us of the future we were attempting to forge. These children would hopefully never know the oppression of power-hungry men – at least not to the extent of their elders.

We all fell into our roles relatively quickly. Some men had spent years working in the plantation stables, and their skills with horses were evident. A few approached Drew and me, offering to take responsibility for the horses and mules, which we thankfully accepted. A small band of men wanted to use their talents as hunters and volunteer scouts, watching for potential threats while keeping us supplied with meat. A large group of women and some men inquired about helping with food prep or cooking. Skillet gladly accepted their help, knowing that their skills would serve us well on the trail.

Our first night was one of the most enjoyable nights I'd ever spent on the road. The rain let up and became a persistent sprinkle. We made camp in a clearing nestled beneath a canopy of towering cedars. There was no talk of pain or hurt or suffering that night. Instead, the camp was charged with exuberant energy.

Music filled the darkened countryside as instruments found the hands of surprisingly talented musicians. Guitars, fiddles, jaw harps, and harmonicas blended in warm, joyful harmony, accentuated by the rhythmic pounding of dancing feet. Laughter and song bathed us in peace as the men and women celebrated late into the night.

Initially, Skillet was concerned with our revelry, afraid it might attract trouble, but Drew was quick to reassure him. The likelihood of danger in the form of outlaws or natives was minimal at best. Given the size and camaraderie of our group, we were, for the moment, safe. The people deserved a night of celebration.

We chatted, sang, and played cards for hours. When the festivities began to wane, and the campfire flames were not much more than glowing embers, Two Feathers found Drew and me leaning against a hay bale, fighting sleep.

"Someone's following us," he said, his voice cutting through the silence. "Single rider, along the ridgeline."

Drew's brow furrowed as he shook himself awake and pondered Two Feather's report. "He's alone? What do you make of it, Two Feathers? Indian? Scout, maybe?"

Two Feather's eyes gleamed with the wisdom of experience. "It's a white man. Hasn't been close enough for me to see his face. I will find his camp tonight."

He was undoubtedly the right man for the job. "That's good, Two Feathers," I said. "But don't let him know you're there. For now, let's just keep an eye on him. See if we can find out what he's up to."

Two Feathers nodded and turned to leave. Before disappearing into the night, he added, "I take twins with me. Teach them how to move quiet. They learn fast. Will help us later."

I agreed, and Two Feathers dissolved into the shadows. Drew turned his gaze to me. "Why is there always someone lookin' to take what someone else has?"

I shrugged. "Greed, I suppose. There's lots of greedy folks in the world."

"Yeah, but they ain't all bushwhackers like the ones we have to deal with," Drew said. "Some folks just seem to wander around lookin' to take what ain't theirs."

"Bushwhackers," I said. Drew nodded. "You know, it wasn't too long ago that you and I were lowdown bushwhackers ourselves. We took a lot of stuff that wasn't ours."

Drew laughed. "Yeah, well, that's different."

"Different? How so?"

"See, you and I weren't your average, run-of-the-mill bushwhackers. We were handsome, charismatic ne'er-do-wells with style and pleasant dispositions. I like to think the folks we robbed went home talking about the lovely young men who liberated them from the burden of their worldly possessions." Drew pointed up to the ridgeline. "These folks, the ones we have to deal with, are nothing more than dimwits. It's sad, really."

"I suppose I'll pay closer attention next time somebody tries to rob me," I said. "Maybe I can encourage them to class up their act a little."

Drew shook his head. "Don't bother. Our good manners and charming personalities aren't something you can teach. A fella either has it, or he don't."

Skillet, having overheard us, approached with a relaxed grin. "I'm off for my beauty rest, fellas," he said. "Breakfast ain't gonna cook itself."

"You want me to cook in the morning, Skillet?" Drew said.

"You? Cook?" Skillet replied with a look of disgust. "I'd just as soon chew on a skunk's tail than eat anything you'd serve up." Skillet laughed at his own joke. "But I am mighty pleased with our travelers so far. They work hard and move fast. If they keep it up, I reckon we'll make better time than we thought."

"Here's hoping," I said. "Let's take it one day at a time, though. For now, my biggest concern is making sure we all get across the Colter River Dam."

As we settled in for the night, the rain fell softly once more. Before sleep overtook me, I lay there considering the dreams that started this whole matter and how I was right to follow my gut. I'd heard it said that the Lord moves in mysterious ways, but until recently, I didn't give it much thought. Somehow, I'd found peace amid uncertainty, and I was sure it came from somewhere beyond myself.

CHAPTER 43

By the time the wagons were packed, and the mules were hitched, the rain returned, intent on soaking the already waterlogged ground even more. Despite the morning's challenges, we were well on our way as the sky shifted from black to pale gray.

Drew and I rode together near the front of the wagon train, looking on as our crew plodded ahead. The mules dutifully sloshed through the muck, pulling our well-stocked wagons and keeping a respectable pace. As far as I was concerned, we couldn't reach the dam soon enough. Still, for reasons I couldn't explain, the idea of crossing the Colter River Dam loomed threateningly. It was the final obstacle we'd face before we were truly free of Jonesborough and the Ivywood Plantation. For me, the journey to Montana wouldn't officially begin until the Colter River was behind us.

Drew and I were soon joined by Two Feathers, Fisher, and Tate, each riding fresh horses they'd switched out earlier. They rode alongside us with troubled lines on their faces.

"We found the camp," Two Feathers began. "Last night." His voice was low and steady, like wind whispering through rainswept trees. "We came quietly. Left quietly. He never knew."

I nodded, my eyes scanning the road ahead. "What did you find out? Is there anything we need to worry about?"

Fisher answered first, his eyes squinted with determination. "It sure ain't nothin' to ignore. The rider was alone, but he ain't a man to take lightly. It's Carl Bancroft."

"Bushwhacker," Drew muttered under his breath. He narrowed his eyes and stared off toward the treeline.

"I was hoping the marshal would keep the Ivywood boys busy for a while," I said. "You sure he's alone?"

Tate chimed in, his voice steady but uneasy. "Wasn't no sign of any others. Banks was up bright and early, just waitin' on us. You can't see him, but he's followin' us right now."

My grip tightened on the reins at the thought of Carl Bancroft tailing us. He was a large, quiet man with a shadowy reputation and a mean streak a mile wide. But Carl was a mystery of sorts. He'd appeared at the plantation one day, seemingly out of nowhere, like a bitter weed. I never knew whether or not Harold Gullet was an old friend or an acquaintance of Carl's. Regardless, Gullet offered him a job on the spot, and Carl had been at the Ivywood ever since. Carl's past was unknown to me, but I assumed he'd grown up a rough and ready sort. I'd personally witnessed the cruelty he'd served up so easily over the years, and I'd always done my best to stay clear of him. Whether or not Carl Bancroft meant us harm didn't change the fact that he was not a man to be underestimated.

"What's the play here, Two Feathers?" I said to our seasoned scout. "Do we deal with him now, or do we wait?"

Two Feathers considered my words, his gaze locked onto the distant horizon. "Let him follow for now," he said. "We know where he is. We watch. Right now, he is a snake hiding in grass. Snakes not as dangerous when you know where they are."

I nodded, trusting Two Feathers' judgment. "Alright, but you fellas keep an eye on him. I don't want Carl gettin' too close. If he does anything that might bring us harm, then end him."

Two Feathers nodded blankly as he, Fisher, and Tate spurred their horses and raced away. The decision to bring Two Feathers along was likely the best decision we'd made, thanks to Skillet. If Two Feathers could teach Fisher and Tate an ounce of what he knew about tracking and reading sign, they'd benefit their people many times over.

With Carl Bancroft claiming territory in the back of my mind, Drew and I rode on, our thoughts heavy with uncertainty. The steady patter of rain on my hat and slicker filled the silence of the next few minutes while I brought my attention back to the men and women in my care. For now, the matter of Carl Bancroft could wait.

Drew and I approached the wagon ahead, where Titus and Charity traveled with their grandchildren and daughters-in-law. Upon spotting us, Titus smiled broadly and motioned for us to ride closer.

"What do you need, Titus?" I called out above the drumming of the rain. "Everything okay?"

"Never better," he replied. He and Charity were more at ease than I ever remembered seeing them. "Charity and I wanted to see if you fellas wanna eat with us tonight. Give us all a chance to catch up a bit. Talk about old times. Whatcha think?"

I exchanged glances with Drew in silent agreement. "You're pulling my leg, right?" I said. "Of course, we'll join you. Done deal. In fact, we ought to get Two Feathers to show us how he hangs tarps. Even in a full-on storm, he knows how to keep your belongings nice and dry."

Charity's eyes lit up with enthusiasm. "Now that's somethin' I wouldn't mind learnin'," she said. "See you boys tonight."

As we rode on, I thought about the bonds already forming among our eclectic group. Soon, we'd cease being mere companions on a journey. We were forging connections that would last far beyond the days of this adventure. These people would become my family. With that in mind, I figured it would be wise to use this lengthy trip across the country to learn more about the men and women with whom I'd be sharing life.

Drew and I continued riding up and down the length of the wagon train, engaging in conversations with each group of travelers. Mostly, we exchanged pleasantries and moved on, but some were more talkative than others. They told us stories about their lives and all they'd endured, and we shared our own stories. Somewhere along the way, it struck me that these individuals were not simply joining us on a trek to Montana. They were heading into the unknown with people they hardly knew, operating solely on faith – faith in me and faith in their Lord. I experienced a renewed determination to deliver them safely to their new home.

Drew, however, had other concerns on his mind. Out of the blue, he looked at me and said, "I've gotta get that five thousand dollars, Moses." His voice was steeled with conviction. "I have to. Otherwise, there won't be no ranch for us to get back to. You know as well as I do, Smiling Jack won't hesitate to take your land from you if I don't pay him."

I'd always had respect for Drew's honesty and candor. He said what he meant and wasn't afraid of what others might think of him. I knew the weight he felt because I felt it as well. The future of the ranch, our dream, and the livelihood of these men and women depended on us repaying Jack and securing the deed to my ranch. Still, I was learning to trust in things I couldn't see, and I wasn't about to stop now. We all had our strengths, and my calm, steady demeanor seemed to comfort Drew.

"Don't get lost in your head over this," I said. "We still have a long road ahead of us. We'll get where we're headed with exactly what we need. I believe that. So, we're gonna walk this path and find out what happens. Regardless, we'll be in it together."

Drew nodded. "You know, I like this new Moses," he said, a sly smile tugging at the corners of his lips. "Out here in the wild, shootin' from the hip, figurin' it out as you go. I've gotta say, this suits you well, friend."

I chuckled a bit, recognizing there was truth in his words. "Who knew all it would take to reveal my life's calling was the pressure of a hundred-plus mouths to feed and a spoiled plantation owner wantin' me dead?"

Drew grinned, and his eyes regained their usual spark. "When you put it like that, it sounds like the making of some Greek tragedy." He laughed. "That ain't us, though. We are lucky men, Moses Colter. Always have been."

CHAPTER 44

Rain drummed restlessly on the taut canvas stretched above us. I always loved the sound. It was soothing and never failed to make me drowsy, especially after a good meal. Two Feathers taught Titus and Charity how to position the tarps to keep them and their belongings dry in almost any weather. Evening eased into nightfall as Drew, Titus, Charity, and I lounged near their wagon. We were comfortable and well-fed, thanks to our camp cooks and the cleverly angled tarps.

Drew slid a little closer to the fire, the glow of the flames dancing in his eyes, and said to Titus and Charity, "It's good to get to know you folks better. Moses told me a lot about you, and like I always say, 'you can't know too many good people.'"

"I've never heard you say that before in my life," I said, poking fun at Drew.

"Well, I'm sure I've said those words at some point," Drew replied as we all laughed. "I am curious, though, how'd you both end up workin' for the Ashbournes?"

The flickering firelight illuminated Titus' face as he shared a knowing look with Charity. It was as if they were trying to decide who should speak first.

"Me and Charity, we know'd each other since we was kids," Titus began, staring at the campfire with a soft smile. "Lived in Tennessee our whole lives. Wasn't neither one of us slaves, though – our folks neither. But both our grandfolks was, and since we was all poor, me and Charity had to work to help out our families. We never went to no schools. But you know that, Moses. It was you what taught us to read."

"That's right," I said. "And you both took to it real quick."

Charity smiled and continued the story. "Titus' daddy worked for the railroad," she said, "and my mama and me worked cleanin' house for some rich white folks after my daddy died in the mines."

"I was always sweet on Charity," Titus said. "Thought she was the prettiest thing I'd ever seen, but we didn't have no time for things like courtin' back then. We worked just as hard as the grown folks, but we did sneak off now and then. We'd act like we was goin' to pick berries so our folks wouldn't know what we was up to. Shoot, we even acted like that with each other. Pretendin' like it was some great mystery how we'd end up at the same patch of berry bushes three or four times a week."

"It wasn't long before we was talkin' about gettin' married," Charity went on, "but we was just kids, and our folks didn't wanna hear such foolishness. So we kept meetin' up, pickin' berries, and thinkin' we had the whole world fooled. But I knew one day we'd be married. I felt it in my bones."

"Things went on like that for a while," Titus said. "Then, one spring, we had a spell of cholera that killed a whole bunch of people. Nasty business. It took both my folks and Charity's mama. Things was bad for us cause didn't neither of us have no other family. Charity got kicked out of the rich lady's place, and the bank came along a few weeks later and took the house my daddy had built."

"We didn't know what to do," Charity said, "so I says, why don't we go ahead and get married? I figured at least we'd be together that way and good Lord willin' we'd figure out how to survive. I knew Titus was a good man, young and strong. He'd find work somewhere. And I had been cookin' and cleanin' since I was old enough to hold a broom. Trouble was, the cholera had everybody real scared, and wasn't nobody lookin' to hire new folks."

"We made a camp and lived out in the woods near Jonesborough," Titus said. "Times was hard, but we was able to scrape by. We'd go into town beggin' for any work we could find to keep from starvin'."

"Then, like some two-bit snake oil salesman, Augustus Ashbourne showed up in town one day," Charity said. "He talked a good game. Told us we could make good money and live a good life if we worked for him at the plantation."

Titus chuckled. "And being young and foolish, we swallowed that snake oil and bought the lot. We showed up at the Ivywood thinkin' we'd finally found a better life. Things started off good, but it all went bad soon enough. I think you fellas know how the rest turned out."

"When we found out you was back in town," Charity said, "we was excited. We knew things was gonna be set right."

"How'd you know that though?" I said. "What made you think I was here to help you?"

"We know'd you was here for us," Titus said. His face took on a hard, weathered look in the campfire's light. "We know'd 'cause we'd been prayin' about it. Prayin' for you, too. Never missed a single day. We prayed that the Lord would keep you safe and watch over you. And 'cause we figured you was the only person in the world that know'd what life was like for us, we prayed that God would send you back to get us. So when you showed up that day, I told Charity the good Lord done heard us, and she should pack her bags."

"You prayed for that?" I said. "All those years? That I'd come back and get you away from the Ashbournes?"

"Yes, sir," Charity said, nodding her head. "We prayed hard too. Asked the good Lord to send you dreams or visions or whatever else it took to get you here."

I glanced at Drew in our shorthand way of communicating. It was just a look, but Drew nodded in agreement, so I told Titus and Charity about my dreams. I explained everything as well as I could and shared all of the unexplained happenings that took place over the past few months. We all knew they weren't merely coincidences. As Two Feathers described it, we were carried from Montana to Jonesborough. Titus was awestruck by my account, but Charity nodded as if everything I explained made perfect sense. As far as she was concerned, we could call it whatever we wanted, but she knew it was the Lord's doing.

"We sure are excited to get to Montana," Titus said. "We've heard stories 'bout land out West. We been told hardworkin' folks can make a life there. That's all we want, Moses. A piece of land, a home, and somethin' to pass on to our kids and grandbabies."

Carrying a steaming cup of coffee, Nellie raced through the rain and into our dry circle beneath the tarps. "Can I please sit with you good folks for a few minutes? Just until it slacks up a bit?"

"Well, I ain't sure it's gonna slack up," Titus said, "but you welcome to join us."

Nellie's arrival, while certainly welcomed, triggered a brief lull in the conversation. The tarp overhead played a lively tune of dancing raindrops, and the fire burned easily on a bed of nice, big, glowing coals.

In the brief silence that followed, I could sense Charity gazing at me across the fire. We made eye contact, and she simply smiled before saying what was on her mind. "Moses," she began, "Titus and I been wonderin' 'bout you the last few years. You know, what you been up to and what your life is like and such."

"Now that's a story I'd love to hear," Nellie said, making herself comfortable and sipping her coffee.

"I am afraid that's a rather boring tale," I said. "I live a quiet life and mostly keep to myself. I got a few sheep and a little home in some beautiful country. But, my life ain't nothin' special. Certainly nothing folks would find interesting, I'm afraid."

Charity shook her head. "I don't believe that one bit. You a handsome young man, Moses. Don't you got nobody waitin' for you back home? A girl you're courtin', or a wife maybe?"

"Now, Charity, we don't need to go nosin' around in the boy's business," Titus said, eyeing me as if he hoped I wasn't offended.

Her question stirred up memories that I had purposefully kept locked away. Still, I knew Charity meant no harm. "It's okay, Titus," I said. "I was married. Her name was Elise."

Titus scratched the back of his neck, and when he spoke, his voice was quiet and careful. "How long were you married, Moses? Do you have any children?"

"Elise and I were married for four years," I answered as the others listened intently. My attention was lost in the coals of the fire for a moment as bittersweet memories flooded my consciousness. "Elise died giving birth. The baby didn't make it either. They've been gone two years now."

A solemn hush fell over the group as they absorbed the information and considered how best to respond. Nellie was the first to speak, gently breaking the silence. "I'm so sorry, Moses," she said. "We didn't mean to pry."

"I know you didn't," I said. "It's okay. Really. There ain't no harm done. It's just not always easy to talk about."

"I imagine so," Nellie said. "Losin' the ones we love can leave a hurt that never goes away. Not fully, anyhow." She paused for a moment. "I hope you don't mind me askin', but the baby...was it a boy or a girl?"

I took a breath. "It was a girl," I replied. My voice shook, betraying my peaceful demeanor, but I kept myself together. "Elise and I, we never had the chance to name her. We talked about it plenty but never settled on a name that fit. Of course, we didn't know it was gonna be a girl at the time.

"Elise never knew anything was wrong right up until she went in with the midwife. We had the doc there, too. After a while, the doctor came out and told me there were complications. He said he would do all he could, but I should prepare myself for the worst." Charity and Nellie wiped their eyes. Titus stared at the fire, and Drew gave me a quick pat on the back. "I buried them together back in Virginia City. I had a gravestone made but didn't know what I should put for the baby, so I just put Elise's name on it."

"Did you have a name you called your daughter?" Drew said. "Like a nickname or something?"

I nodded, my gaze returning to the faces of my friends. "I did. It's a little silly, but Elise was a bit of a dreamer. She always wanted to visit new places and talk to interesting people. She would have loved this. One place she always talked about seein' was California. San Francisco, to be specific. I always meant to take her but never got around to it. I sure wish I had. So, when the baby was born, and I was told neither of them made it, I started calling the baby Cali. I didn't know what else to call her, and leaving her with no name at all felt wrong."

Charity's eyes filled with tears as she reached out and placed a comforting hand atop mine. "I think Cali is a beautiful name, Moses."

We heard heavy footsteps running through the muddy camp toward us. Two Feathers emerged from the rain and darkness, hurrying right into our covering. "Moses," he said, breathing heavily, "you come with me? We need you. Someone in camp wants to talk."

"What's wrong, Two Feathers?" I said, rising. He glanced at the others. "It's okay; you can talk in front of them."

"Carl Bancroft," he said flatly. "He's here. Says he needs you. Says it's urgent."

Drew and I immediately raced away with Two Feathers. "He's at lookout," Two Feathers said as we ran through the rain. "Came up the road on horseback." He pointed. "Right there. Twins watching him. Man say he talk only to you."

The lookout spot, a shallow cave on a rocky hillside overlooking the road, had a small fire burning within. As we got closer, I saw Fisher and

Tate sitting on either side of the fire, holding rifles. Both were pointed at Carl Bancroft, who was seated as well. Drew and I entered the cave, and the twins stood to greet us.

"I don't mean you no harm, Moses," Carl said. "I just want to talk."

"So talk then," Drew said.

Carl kept his seat, but he eyeballed the others. "Can we talk in private?" he said. "Or at least tell them not to point their guns at me?"

"Fisher, Tate," I said, "thank you for keepin' an eye on our visitor. You fellas go with Two Feathers and make sure there ain't no one else sneakin' around. Drew and I will talk to Carl."

It was evident neither of the twins trusted Carl Bancroft enough to leave us there with him. Still, they respected me enough to reluctantly agree. They lowered their weapons and nodded before exiting the cave.

"What do you want, Carl?" I said. "I figured you'd be locked up by now."

"You and me both," the large man grumbled.

Drew and I sat by the fire across from Carl, Drew holding his pistol in his lap. "What's this about, Carl?" Drew said. "Your boss ain't arrested for five minutes before you cut ties and run?"

"That ain't how it is," Carl said. "Besides, Logan Ashbourne ain't in jail no more. Soon as the marshal left, Ashbourne had a lawyer at the Sheriff's Office. The man came up with a slew of witnesses and alibis to prove Logan didn't do nothin' wrong. With all that and a large sack of cash, he got outta there quick enough."

"That still don't explain why you're here?" I said. "Shouldn't you be at the Ivywood helping Logan and Harold figure out how to keep the business goin'?"

"I ain't with Logan Ashbourne no more," Carl said. "I left 'cause...well 'cause he and I don't see eye to eye."

"Makes sense to me," Drew said. "Logan prefers to kill folks, while you're more partial to beating and torture. That about right?"

"You don't know what you're talkin' about," Carl said, shaking his head. "I'm tryin' to help you out if you'll just listen."

"How you plan on helping us, Carl?" I said, eyeing him warily. "And if I ain't convinced I believe you by the time those fellas get back, I'm gonna hand you over to Two Feathers and let him deal with you."

"Logan Ashbourne sent me to tail you," Carl said. "He's puttin' a crew together to come after you. Fifteen, twenty men altogether. Hard men. Killers and seasoned trackers. He means to catch you before you cross the dam. He told his men to kill you boys, destroy the wagons, and march those workers back to the plantation. Says if any of 'em puts up a fight, we're to kill them too."

"But we'll be crossing the Colter River Dam tomorrow," I said.

"Maybe," Carl muttered. "If the army don't come through and shut the road down. Word is there's a helluva storm brewin', and they're worried it ain't safe for folks to cross."

"Another storm?" Drew said, shaking his head. "I didn't know the first one ended. I swear to the good Lord above, if I make it outta Tennessee without getting killed by this weather, I ain't ever coming back."

"How close is Logan and his crew?" I said.

"I don't know for sure," Carl said, "but I know he means to stop you. Ashbourne knows you got that Indian fella with you too, and he knows how good he is at spottin' folks and readin' sign. He'll probably be comin' in from a different direction. And I'm sure Logan and his boys are pushin' hard. I figure they'll likely be at the dam waitin' on you. That's why I'm here. I came to tell you to pack up camp and leave now. Tonight. Don't wait for morning. You might get lucky and beat him to the dam."

"And we're just supposed to believe you had a change of heart?" I said. "How do we know this isn't all planned? Logan sends you in; you get us all worked up till we're ragged and tired. We stay up all night; then you lead us into a trap."

"It ain't a trap," Carl said. "It's more like the only chance you got. You don't wanna believe me? Fine. Do it your way."

"You gotta give us something more, Carl," Drew added. "How do we know you're shootin' straight with us?"

Carl grunted and wiped his hands on his trousers. "Look, fellas, it's not like Ashbourne and I just had a fallin' out and I took off. This is somethin' that's been buildin' for years."

Drew and I nodded, waiting for something that might give teeth to Carl's claims.

"Back when you was a boy, Moses," Carl went on, "that day you killed Earl. I knew right then things had gone too far. It weren't your fault Earl died. It was his own damn doing. Everybody knew it. So after you left, I went into Jonesborough and told the sheriff it was self-defense and that you did nothing wrong. I knew if Logan Ashbourne found out what I had done, I'd be the next unfortunate accident. The sheriff agreed to keep it quiet, but nothin' ever came back on Logan."

"So you were the witness," I said, glancing at Drew.

"We got so caught up in everything goin' on," Drew said, "that we forgot to ask Marshall Wesley about it."

"I believe you, Carl," I said. "So now you've warned us. Probably because you feel bad about what you've done over the years, but I ain't one to judge a man for that. What do you plan to do now?"

"If you'll let me, I'd like to come with you," Carl said. "Start over in Montana. Maybe try to be somebody respectable."

I nodded. "Let me see how all this plays out first," I said. "We'll get the camp packed up and ride through the night. With any luck, we'll avoid Logan's men and the storm that's apparently on the way. You can stick with us until all of this is behind us, then we'll figure out what comes next. But we hold on to your guns, and you ride in the wagon with Skillet and Nellie."

"That's fair," Carl said. "Thank you, Moses."

Chapter 45

Violent winds swept through, ushering in dense clouds that shrouded the sky in ghastly darkness. There was no moon or stars. The billowing gloom choked out all light. Upon our return to camp, I shared the unsettling news about Carl Bancroft, who would now be coming on as our new traveling companion. As expected, the message was met with skepticism and concern. None of us trusted Carl, but if what he said was true, there was no time for hesitation. We had to rouse the men and women and make a break for the Colter River Dam.

"And just where is the backstabbin' snake?" Skillet said.

"He's with Two Feathers, for now," I said, "When we get loaded up, he'll ride in the wagon with you and Nellie so you can keep an eye on him.

"And if something happens?" Skillet said. "If he catches sight of his old friend Logan and decides to be a hero?"

"Then you know what to do," I replied. "I made it clear to Carl that if he tries to double-cross us and lead us into a shootout, the first bullet has his name on it."

"Waste of a good bullet if you ask me," Nellie said.

"Look, I know you don't trust him," I told Skillet and Nellie. "Lord knows I don't either, but my gut tells me we should heed this warning. If Carl's tellin' the truth and there really is a crew looking to keep us from crossing that dam, we need to be long gone by the time they show up."

"I'm with Moses," Drew said. "Even if we're walkin' into a trap, we ain't in no worse fix. The way I figure, we'll likely be facing Logan's hired guns sooner or later. It could be tonight, tomorrow, or even a week from now. I'd just as soon take the fight right to 'em and get on with it."

"These folks with us ain't killers, Drew," Skillet said. "Most of them don't even have guns. If things go bad, they'll be sittin' ducks."

233

"You may be right," I went on. "And if you are, and I lead these folks into trouble, I'll have to live with that. But I can't live with knowing I had a way out of this mess and didn't take it because I was scared. So if it falls on me to make the call, I say we ride. Tonight."

Skillet and Nellie hesitantly agreed, and just after two o'clock that morning, we began to wake our companions. Nellie marched through camp banging on a pot with a stew ladle while the rest of us followed, causing enough ruckus to spook the mules and horses. Folks immediately began to awake, peeking from their wagons with wide eyes as the camp stirred to life. Before long, we'd gathered the entire group, and I shared the troubling news. I was truthful but offered only a vague warning, telling them that bad men were headed our way and we had to run for it. Perhaps it was because the workers were accustomed to men barking orders at them, but I was surprised that no one even asked a question. They wasted no time and offered no resistance. We were all exhausted, but we sprang to action with grim determination. Clearly, folks were afraid, and the threat of impending danger lit a fire under them.

"What do you need from me and my brother?" Fisher said as he and Tate stepped away from the others.

"What I need you boys to do is stay with your family," I said. "Keep your rifles loaded and ready. Hopefully, it won't come to a gunfight, but your family needs to be your priority."

"You sure?" Tate said. "We can help. We can both shoot, and we ain't scared."

"I have no doubt," I said. "But I came here to see you folks out safely, and that's what I aim to do."

Fisher and Tate nodded and hurried off to help pack up camp. It took a bit longer than I'd hoped, but the wagons eventually rumbled along the pitch-black trail. Unfortunately, it appeared as if the heavens had conspired against us, for in that moment, the storms that had dogged our every step returned with a vengeance. The wind roared like a restless beast, bending the large eastern pines and sweetgums and threatening to tear the white canvas tops from our wagons. Rain fell in solid sheets of fury, meeting us head-on and lashing at our faces. Our slickers and gear offered little protection from the wrath of that brutal night, but we were still moving.

Drew and I were on horseback, flanking the wagon train and scanning for any sign of trouble. But we both knew there was little chance of us seeing anything in such conditions. It was painfully clear that, on this fateful night, the storm was our most formidable adversary. Thunder bellowed like cannon fire, and lightning ripped the sky with blinding streaks that lit up the countryside. The cries of the children mingled with the clamor of the storm and the anxious braying and snorting of the mules. The women hid in the wagons, cradling their young ones and trying to ease their fears.

"Hey, Moses," Drew called out as we pushed ahead.

"Yeah, I'm here," I said. It was raining so hard that I could barely see Drew, even though he was only a few feet away. "Everything okay?"

"I was just wonderin'," he continued to yell. "Have I ever told you how much I hate storms?"

I laughed to myself. "I think I've heard somethin' like that. I heard it turns you yella."

"Well, yeah," he bellowed as if such a thing was entirely reasonable. "I ain't ashamed to admit it. When that thunder and lightning start up, I turn yella as a snake's belly." Drew shrugged and nudged his horse on, continuing his patrol.

The whole ordeal played out agonizingly slow, as if the wagons were pushing through a pool of molasses. Every inch of progress was hard-fought. Still, we pressed on through the night, step by laborious step. When the first feeble sign of light graced the horizon, the colossal structure known as the Colter River Dam appeared before us. The good news was that we were nearly half a day ahead of schedule and several hours ahead of our pursuers. The bad news was that the massive dam, which should have promised us safety, now loomed as yet another foreboding obstacle.

Drew and I rode to the front of the wagon train to better see the dam and the road across it. It was a towering testament to human engineering, soaring nearly fifty feet above the raging river to the south. However, on the north side, the waters churned with agitated power and looked like they might breach the wall at any moment. Waves rose from the depths like watery serpents, striking at the dam's wall, spilling over the edge, and swallowing the road. It was a frightful sight, to say the least, one that threatened to crush our hopes of reaching the safety of the other side.

The wagons pulled to a halt, and I could feel the anxious eyes of our travelers fixed on me, waiting for answers. I had none to offer.

"Look," Drew gasped, pointing off to the northwest. In the distance, at least three tornados danced ominously on the horizon. The black, twisting funnels tore across the enraged sky, snapping trees like brittle twigs and hurling gusts of wind across the swollen river.

"It's okay, Drew," I yelled. "Looks like they're movin' away from us." I don't imagine it brought him any comfort.

"We can't cross, Moses," Skillet cried out. "It ain't safe. We gotta' wait for this storm to pass."

As I sat my horse, listening to the train-like roar of the tornadoes, the water slapping against the dam wall, and seeing waves crest the barrier, I was caught in a daze. I knew we had to act. The people were waiting for direction, but my mind was blank. Skillet continued talking, but I had no idea what he was saying. Drew stared at the tornadoes writhing in the distance, doing his best to calm his frazzled horse.

Amid this turmoil, I heard a voice call out further down the wagon train. I spun Cali around and saw Two Feathers riding hard and shouting a warning. It wasn't until he was nearly upon us that I finally understood.

"Men are coming," he cried out. "Ashbourne's men. Almost on us." He pointed down the road to the east. "Thirty. Maybe more, all armed."

Time slowed to a crawl, and the chaos surrounding me began to fade. Though the storm raged, my mind suddenly cleared. All doubt washed away in the rainfall, replaced with a stubborn yet settling peace. There was only one choice. "We have to cross now," I shouted to Skillet.

He shook his head, and I could see the fear in his eyes. "We can't, Moses. We'll be swept right over the edge. If you send us out there, folks are gonna die."

"In about two minutes, thirty armed killers will be on top of us," I responded, desperation in my voice. "If we're meant to die today, I'd rather it be by God's hand than Logan Ashbourne's."

My words seemed to strengthen Skillet's resolve, and he nodded. "Alright then, we'll cross," he called out. "And, Moses, if we don't make it, I want you to know it has been an honor to stand beside you."

Tears glistened in Nellie's eyes as she said, "Same goes for me. And so we're clear, I'd do it all again. Now, let's get these people out of here and stop actin' like we're all gonna die."

"No goodbyes," I said. "This ain't the end. Just keep ridin' and don't stop for anything. Drew and I will hold off Logan's men and try to buy you some time."

Carl Bancroft leaped from the back of Skillet's wagon, his boots sinking deep into the mud. "I can help, Moses," he said. "Give me my horse and gun, and I'll help you hold 'em off."

"I'll take all the help I can get," I said.

Nellie tossed Carl her Winchester, and I pointed him toward the closest available horse. Carl moved quickly, mounted, checked the rifle, and nodded.

"Let's go," Skillet barked at the mules as he snapped the reins. They snorted and stomped, wanting nothing to do with the path ahead of them, but Skillet pushed them ahead.

A strange thing happened as the wagons began slowly moving toward the dam. The raging storm that had pummeled us for the last few hours suddenly stilled. The winds died, the rain ebbed, and even the surging waters began to recede. The sky turned a sickly, pale green, bathing everything in its frightful pallor, and the air felt electric. Instantly, the world was still and quiet.

Then, a gunshot rang out from behind us.

Drew's voice cut through the stillness. "Go now!" he yelled at men and horses alike. "Ya! Ya! Go...go...go..."

Skillet sprang into action and yelled at the mules. They were off, moving faster than they had all night. Those behind Skillet didn't hesitate but followed his lead, driving their mules and horses like their lives depended on it. And unfortunately, they did.

"Come on, fellas," Drew called to Carl and me. "Let's show these boys we ain't scared to mix it up." He spurred his mighty stallion, Stormy, who reared up and whinnied before tearing down the muddy road toward Logan's approaching men.

CHAPTER 46

D rew, Carl Bancroft, and I galloped eastward, our horses' hooves pounding the soaked ground. While welcomed, our momentary respite from the storm provided no comfort. The silence left in its absence was even more unnerving than the thunder, lightning, and howling winds. As menacing as the storm had been, it was a devil we knew, something we could wrap our minds around. But this unnatural hush and ghostly green pallor that settled over the countryside was an enigma. Nothing about it felt familiar or safe. It was as if the world had stopped, the clocks stood still, and all of heaven waited anxiously to see how this confrontation would play out.

Two Feathers, atop his Appaloosa, joined us, riding up alongside Drew. He pointed ahead. "Shots from there," he called out with a calm firmness. "Just up road."

We were moving pretty good when we rounded a tight corner to find the road filled with nearly thirty men on horseback. Fortunately, we saw them just in time to stop, pulling our horses to a skidding halt a few feet shy of crashing into Logan Ashbourne's hired gunmen. Instinctively, Drew and Two Feathers drew their iron, an action mirrored by Logan's well-armed men.

His would-be militia certainly looked the part of experienced killers. They were a hardened bunch, exuding a confident, gritty demeanor formed through a lifetime of hardship and conflict. We'd ridden right into a tense and potentially deadly standoff for which we were sorely outgunned.

"Everybody, relax," I said, my voice cutting through the charged atmosphere. Then to Drew and Two Feathers, "Put your guns away. Nice and slow. Let's figure out what's happenin' before bullets start flying."

Drew and Two Feathers complied, slowly easing their revolvers back into their holsters, keeping their eyes fixed on the hired guns.

"Alright, boys," Drew said to the men. "What do you say we all try to get out of this without bloodying up the road?"

For a moment, there was only silence. Logan's men maintained their hard, unwavering stillness, mimicking the ungodly hush in the air. All was still. Not a single leaf on a single tree fluttered. Without a word, the men spread apart, forming a path through which Logan Ashbourne and his remaining ally, Harold Gullet, rode toward us. They moved forward, side by side, and stopped, positioning themselves between us and the gunmen.

"I'm afraid it's too late for workin' out a deal, fellas," Logan remarked, a self-satisfied smirk on his face. To his right, Harold cradled a shotgun in his lap, his eyes shifting to each of us – watching and waiting. "Well, if it isn't Carl Bancroft," Logan said. "You remember Carl, don't you, Harold?"

Harold glared at Carl. "Nope," he said with a grunt. "All I recall is a cowardly traitor that ran off when things got tough."

Logan laughed. "Oh yeah, that's right. I almost forgot. The Carl we knew is dead – at least to me."

"We can all still walk away from this, Logan," I said. "I know we got you seein' red, but stop and think this through. Do you really want this? Do you want all this blood on your hands?"

Logan's response was cold and measured. "What I want is justice," he said, raising his voice. Then, to his hired guns, "How about you, boys? You fellas want to help me find a little justice this morning?" Their collective response was a chorus of snickering nods and stupid affirmations. "See, Moses, the problem is you never were too smart. Dumb as a stump is what the old man used to say. Lord knows what your folks were like." He paused. "Then again, maybe your folks were smarter than I give them credit for. The fact is, they had brains enough to get rid of you. Hell, now that I think about it, they might have been bonafide geniuses. I'll bet they were *so* smart they couldn't stand the thought of having such a stupid child. Anyway, the fact remains you've never been capable of seeing two feet in front of your own face. You can't steal a man's livelihood and expect him to roll over and smile about it. Not where I come from."

"We didn't take anything from you," Drew barked. "If you're lookin' to be sore at somebody, be sore at yourself. If you had just listened to reason instead of your foolish pride, none of this would be happening."

Logan was undeterred. "That's an awful lot of big talk coming from someone in your boots, Drew Harlan," he said. "One more word outta you, and I'll have my men fill you so full of lead they'll have to drag the bottom of the Colter to find you."

"What are we doing then, Logan?" I said. "If you figure on killing us, then you might as well get on with it. Either way, we ain't lettin' you cross that dam."

Harold Gullet lifted his shotgun, but Logan stopped him with a raised hand. "You know," Logan began, "maybe I'm feeling generous, or maybe you're actually making sense for once in your pathetic life, Moses. Hell, I'm a fair man. Let's make a deal."

"I'm listening," I said warily.

Logan scratched his chin. I noticed a few leaves flutter as a gentle breeze passed by. "The deal is, you boys leave right now, run off to your wagon train, and bring those workers straight back to me. We'll escort them to Ivywood, and I'll let you continue on your way. No blood will spill, and our hands will be kept clean."

I considered his proposition momentarily, weighing it against my sorely limited options. "And if we refuse?"

Logan's hesitation spoke louder than the words that followed. "I'll give you half an hour," he said. "If I don't see wagons headed this way, I'll let these men earn their pay. They'll chase you down, and they won't stop firing until every last one of you lies dead. Men, women, and children. That's my offer. It's the best I can do."

The tension was like an icy block in my stomach as I met Logan's gaze. I'd hoped Logan might have a momentary spark of reason, but that was a rose-colored notion. I took a settling breath. "You've got a deal."

Drew protested immediately. "Moses, we can't do that."

I responded with unwavering conviction as I turned my horse toward the dam. "Drew, Two Feathers, Carl, let's go get them."

Regrettably, Logan had one more card he'd been waiting to play. "Hold on a minute," he said before we could ride away. "On second thought, this doesn't seem like a fair trade just yet. You've cost me time and money, and I reckon we can do a little more to balance the scales." He paused. "Go ahead, Harold."

Harold Gullet raised his shotgun, and a deafening blast tore through the still morning. Carl Bancroft was struck square in the chest, his body crumpling to the ground as he fell from his horse.

We spurred our horses without hesitation, thundering away from Logan and his killers. I'd bought us some time but wasn't sure it would matter. Logan held all the power, just as he'd planned. Still, I had to take every opportunity to keep our people alive.

"Why'd you do that, Moses?" Drew called out angrily. "Why'd you make a deal with that rat?"

"I don't plan on bringin' those folks back to Logan," I said. "I bought us some time to see what we can come up with."

Drew, Two Feathers, and I crossed over the Colter River Dam, which was still passable thanks to the lull in the storm. We stopped just on the other side.

"I can't believe Gullet just shot him like that," Drew said. "I thought they were friends."

"The man is lost," Two Feathers added. "Darkness is in him. Has no light in his eyes."

"If Gullet will do that to Carl," I said, "he won't hesitate to give us worse."

Drew had turned his attention to the road beyond the dam. "Good news is it looks like everybody made it across," Drew said. "And they must be moving pretty good. They're already out of sight."

"Not fast enough," Two Feathers said.

"Well, fellas," I began, "I'm open to ideas. We've got thirty minutes to figure out how to deal with these cutthroats."

Two Feathers spoke up first. "Hillside near the road," he said, pointing back toward Logan's men. "I get into place, kill Logan Ashbourne with bow. Then kill Gullet. The rest will run."

I nodded, willing to entertain any idea. "Drew, what do you think? Should we send Two Feathers to deal with Logan? Far as I'm concerned, it's him or us."

"I don't like it," Drew said, staring at the dam. "We don't know for sure the rest of them will run. They may try to kill us first and then run." He continued staring straight ahead, his mind reeling. "Besides, that's not how we do things."

"Maybe it should be," I said. "At least this time."

Drew chewed on his lip and turned his eyes to me. "I'll do it however you want, Moses," he said, "but it don't feel right. If it comes to shootin', I'll shoot, but hiding in the bushes and picking a man off. I don't know about that. No offense, Two Feathers." Two Feathers shook his head as if Drew had done nothing more than refuse a cup of coffee.

"I understand," I said. "Any other ideas?"

Two Feathers reached into his saddlebag. "We could blow up bridge," he said as he removed three sticks of dynamite from his bag. They were tied together and wrapped in oilskin to keep them dry. "Might work."

"Two Feathers," Drew said, stunned, "where did you find dynamite?"

"Stole from plantation," he said. "First night. Thought it useful."

"Is it enough to do the job?" I said, inspecting the sticks.

Two Feathers shrugged.

"It may not be, but it's worth a try," Drew said, a newfound optimism in his voice. "Let me do it. You boys catch up to the wagons."

"No way," I said. "We do this together."

Drew shook his head. "I've got this, Moses. Trust me. Get to the wagons, and I'll look for a weak spot on the dam. If I can't blow the whole thing, I might make a hole big enough to keep them on the other side. Go ahead. I'll catch up to you."

It was a solid plan that was thwarted as quickly as it was devised when gunshots rang out from across the river. Logan's gunmen raced toward us, firing into the air. Logan Ashbourne and Harold Gullet led the charge.

"It's only been ten minutes," Drew yelped, snatching up the dynamite.

"We should've known the snake would lie," I said. "We'll make a stand here. We can fire from behind these rocks and try to pick them off as they cross."

"That won't work," Drew said, a strange calm settling over him. "Let me do this. You have to stay with the wagons, Moses. Those folks don't need me like they need you. If you die out here, they'll give up. They won't make it."

A loud bang of thunder broke the quietness.

"I can't just leave you here," I said.

"You ain't leaving me, brother," Drew said. "I'm stayin' here to finish the job." He pointed down the trail toward the wagon train. "You got your own job to finish."

Lighting struck nearby in the woods off to our left, and a massive pine tree was engulfed in flames. The horses nearly threw us as we fought to regain control. Drew was steady. Calm. Unflinching. It was as if the deadly storm was little more than background noise to him. Drew's mind was fixed on his task. The approaching riders had nearly reached the dam, still yelling out and firing pistols into the air.

"You have to go now," Drew said. He rode up close and grabbed my shoulder. "It's okay," he said. "It's okay, Moses. Go."

I nodded and motioned for Two Feathers to follow, and we raced down the trail toward the wagons. As we galloped away, it was as if someone had ripped my heart from my chest. I glanced back to see Drew, his back to us, holding the dynamite and sitting on his horse as still as a statue. The gunmen were bearing down on him and would be in shooting range soon. I looked away and pushed Cali ahead.

"There," Two Feathers called to me, pointing at the ridge to our right. "I go to wagons. You ride up ridge. Watch. See what happens. You tell us."

"Thank you, friend," I said to Two Feathers. I veered off the trail, and Cali and I began to climb the hillside.

CHAPTER 47

I sat my horse, perched high above the scene unfolding on the dam below. It was a convergence of sorts – a clashing of nature's fury, the desperation of human will, and divine intervention. I could have never guessed how it played out, but regardless, I had to see for myself. The storm was savagely brutal, returning with the most force we'd seen yet. Winds howled like locomotives, and rain lashed at us like thin whips. Thunder crashed in deafening crescendos, and lightning streaked the sky in flashes of rage. I focused on Drew, alone atop his horse on this side of the dam. Everything hinged on his success. He was our last flicker of hope in our darkest hour.

Having halted their advance at the opposite end of the dam's edge, Logan Ashbourne's men took aim at Drew and awaited instruction. Drew sat motionless with dozens of weapons pointed in his direction, but he showed no sign of retreat. Even from a distance, I could see the resolve in his posture. Drew was willing to die to keep us safe.

Rain and sweat mingled on my brow as the downpour obscured my vision, but I could still discern Logan's sinister cry above the roaring gale. "It's over, Drew. I'm taking them back."

Drew, a man consumed with conviction, didn't utter a word. Instead, he removed a handful of matches and struggled to strike them while shielding them from the rain. Once he finally sparked a flame, he lit the long fuse attached to the dynamite. As thunder rumbled overhead, Drew spurred his horse into a full charge toward Logan and his men.

"Kill him," Logan bellowed, and his men surged ahead, flame and gunsmoke filling the space between. Horses hooves rumbled upon the wooden slats of the dam.

"Come on, Drew," I whispered as if my encouragement might give him the advantage he needed to get out of this alive.

As Drew raced forward, he pulled back his arm, preparing to throw the lit dynamite in one final act of defiance. But before he could release it, a blinding bolt of lightning split the sky, striking the dam just yards in front of him. In that blistering moment, Stormy lost his footing and collapsed, throwing Drew to the ground. He tumbled head over heels, his grip on the dynamite slipping. The explosive flew out of his hands, soaring over the dam's edge and disappearing into the raging waters of the Colter River.

Logan's gunmen pulled to a sudden halt, their horses spooked and scrambling to retreat. One rider was thrown from his saddle and tumbled over the railing, falling fifty feet with a loud thud into the churning waters below.

Despite being scorched and partially ablaze, the dam remained surprisingly intact. The lightning had blasted a large section of the wall away. Water began to spill through, but the structure held firm. Undeterred by the chaos around him, Drew scrambled to his feet and hurried toward the fallen Stormy, who was also regaining his footing. Drew leaped into the saddle, firing blindly over his shoulder as he raced away from his pursuers.

"Kill them all," Logan Ashbourne cried out over the pandemonium. His words ignited a surge of violence in his men, and they charged forward with shouts of rage.

Never before had I seen a horse move with such unearthly speed. No other horse could have covered so much ground so quickly. Then again, Stormy was no ordinary horse. Stormy was the horse Drew had dreamed of since he was only a boy. Drew chose him for his speed, strength, and beauty. He chose him for this very moment.

Lightning tore the darkened sky, and thunder groaned. Rain fell, and the wind howled through bent trees. Stormy galloped forward with an onslaught of bullets, smoke, and deadly men giving chase.

Only then did I realize the inevitable. Drew wasn't going to make it. Stormy was fast, but he couldn't run forever. None of us could. These men would eventually catch Drew, even if it was with a bullet. Then they'd come for the rest of us.

My heart sank, and everything around me slowed to a near halt. My mind cleared, and suddenly, everything was sharp and focused. I took in every detail at once. If I had looked closely enough, I might have seen each individual drop of rain hanging in the air that morning.

Stormy's ears were pinned back, and smoke billowed from his nostrils. His muscles strained to draw every ounce of speed from his tense body.

Bullets tore through the rain toward Drew, pushing the thick, humid air aside in rolling coils of smoke. Logan pumped his fist and screamed inaudible commands to his killers. Their faces were twisted in anger and fear as their eyes darted from Drew to the raging waters threatening to swallow them whole.

With Drew urging Stormy forward, he quickly put a significant distance between himself and their pursuers. By the time Logan's men reached the center of the dam, Drew had exited the other end. The dam was marred by the scorched remains of the earlier lightning strike, leaving a charred, gaping chasm of glowing embers and steam. The turbulent waters poured through, spilling over the road and down the other side.

Logan's men pressed on despite their horses' protests, blindly firing at Drew. Suddenly, a deafening clap of thunder rang out, so powerful it felt as though the sky had split in two. The ground shook beneath us, and it seemed as if my teeth might rattle loose. Every horse in sight, including Cali and those chasing Drew, recoiled in sheer terror. The air was filled with panicked whinnies as horses leaped, kicked, and reared in fear.

An eerie stillness suddenly settled over the scene as the earth trembled and lightning sliced through the morning sky. The air was thick with electricity, and the hair on my arms stood on end. A strange buzzing noise filled the air, followed by an arcing crack. A bolt of white-hot lightning struck the dam again. Blinding tendrils of energy shot across the entire span of the roadway, leaping from man to beast before surging back into the sky above.

Drew spun Stormy around, watching in disbelief as the dam erupted into flames, engulfing the gunmen and their horses. The terrified horses reared and bucked, throwing off their riders as they scrambled to escape. The animals bolted just as a massive wall of boiling water surged upward, rising nearly fifteen feet above the dam in a furious swell. A solid, churning wave of water. Most of the horses had already cleared the dam, but the men left behind had little time to do anything but brace for the coming impact. The churning wall of water crashed down onto the roadway with such force that the entire dam buckled under the pressure. Support beams snapped and splintered as massive chunks of the structure tumbled into the river below. In an instant, all of Logan's men were swept away, along with their belongings, several horses, and any hope of reclaiming his workers. On one side of the chasm stood Drew, and on the other, Logan and Gullet—separated by nothing but a violent, impassable waterfall.

The realization hit Drew at the exact moment it hit me: it was done. We had made it. It would be days before Logan could cross the Colter, and even if he did, he'd already lost twenty hired guns. I couldn't imagine anyone being willing to join a man with a reputation like Logan's. It seemed we were finally free of Logan Ashbourne. Drew released a triumphant yell, flashed a wide, toothy grin, tipped his hat to Logan and Gullet, and rode off.

CHAPTER 48

Drew rode hard, putting as much distance as possible between himself and the gaping chasm where the dam once stood. His face lit up with exhilaration as he urged Stormy forward. Cali and I raced down the slick hillside and met Drew in the roadway.

"Moses, please tell me you saw that," Drew called out. His voice was dry, and a wild joy danced in his eyes.

I rode up to meet him, my heart pounding with fear and relief. "I think so," I said. "I don't know exactly what I saw, but I sure saw it."

Drew yelped with excitement as he removed his hat and ran a trembling hand through his wet hair. "We did it, Moses. We made it."

"We did," I said with a grin I couldn't hide. "But what about you? An awful lot of bullets were flying around. Are you sure you're good? You hit anywhere?"

Drew began to inspect himself, his fingers gently probing around his right shoulder. "I think one of 'em might have grazed me," he said, wincing at his own touch. "But other than that, I'm good."

Nevertheless, as I examined the wound more closely, it was immediately evident that it wasn't a graze. "Hold on, Drew," I said. "That's a little more than a scratch you got there." There was deep gash in his shoulder, and blood soaked through his shirt. "Looks like the bullet took a chunk out of you but it should be okay." I paused, getting a better look. "Yep, it's clean. So that's good, I guess."

"Dangit," Drew muttered, pulling his bloodied hand from his shoulder. "That's gonna hurt like hell when I calm down."

"Yeah, well, it's gonna hurt me too," I said with a crooked smile. "I'm the one that's gonna have to listen to you milk that injury for the next few months."

Drew laughed. "I'm gonna give it all I have."

Before we rode on, I set about tending to Drew's wound as best I could. I stemmed the bleeding and fashioned a makeshift sling using an extra shirt I had stowed on my horse. Drew grunted as I worked on his shoulder, but he sat still until I finished.

Finally, with Drew tended to, we were ready to get to the wagon train. We moved slowly, taking care not to jostle too much until we could get Drew's wound properly inspected.

As we rode, the wind died down, the sky mysteriously cleared, and the menacing clouds parted for the first time in days. The rain that had assailed us stopped altogether. The sun returned, floating in a pale blue sky. It covered the countryside in its golden embrace, and the sweet melody of songbirds danced on the warm air.

"I don't think anyone's gonna believe what happened back there," Drew said with a grunt. "I mean...there was the spooky green sky, Gullet killed Carl, I was gonna blow up the bridge, but I dropped the dynamite. Lightning struck the dam – twice! Logan lied about givin' us thirty minutes, somebody shot me, and the whole dam came down. The whole damn thing. It killed all of those men. Well, except for Ashbourne and Gullet. Seriously, who's gonna believe that story."

"Well, we both know it happened. We saw it with our own eyes. The good Lord took care of us, Drew. He took care of all of us." We rode on silently for a moment as I pondered everything. Drew was right. This tale would be mighty hard to believe if I didn't know the truth. Still, it did happen. And not just the business with the dam, but all of it – from the beginning. Every twist and turn we endured had led us precisely to this point. Free.

"Not to get all soft on you or anything," I said, "but I'm proud of you, Drew." It wasn't the sort of thing we ever spoke about. Truthfully, the words felt odd leaving my mouth, but I thought it was important for Drew to hear them. He didn't answer immediately; instead, he looked at me and nodded. "I mean it. That was a brave thing you did back there, takin' on all of Logan's men like that. And gettin' the job done in the middle of the worst storm I've ever seen." I paused. "Thank you, Drew. Thank you for being my brother."

"I wouldn't have it any other way," Drew said. "And I know you'd do the same for me." Drew grinned. "You're not gonna break down and cry now, are ya?"

I laughed. "You know, I think I might. Just knowin' I'm gonna have to listen to you brag the whole way to Montana is enough to get the tears flowing."

As we drew nearer to the wagon train, a curious sight met our eyes. The entire procession had veered off the road and stopped in an open meadow. Everyone, men, women, and children alike, stood along the roadside, their eyes fixed on the horizon. For a moment, a ripple of fear passed through me. Had some new misfortune fallen upon them? Why would they stop?

Two riders approached, and we immediately recognized them as Fisher and Tate. The morning sun was at our backs, and they came up hesitantly, still unsure who they were about to encounter.

"Hello, riders," Tate called out. He raised a hand to us.

We waved in reply. Drew attempted to yell a greeting, his elation momentarily causing him to forget the searing pain in his shoulder.

"It's Moses and Drew," Tate cried out to the others, his voice carried away on the breeze. "They made it. They did it."

When we closed the remaining distance, Fisher and Tate jumped from their horses to help Drew out of the saddle. The Ivywood workers raced toward us, along with Skillet, Nellie, and Two Feathers, everyone smiling and cheering our arrival. Nellie wasted no time taking charge of Drew, pulling him away to clean and dress his wounds. Drew reluctantly went with her, victoriously pumping his good arm above his head and shouting some nonsense about having a party later. "You fellas are not gonna *believe* what happened," Drew exclaimed as he was led away. The hugs, handshakes, and pats on the back underneath the warm summer sun were a balm for my weary soul.

For hours, we did nothing but enjoy one another's company and share the unbelievable tale of how we managed to escape with our lives. Together, we had emerged as victors from our ridiculously perilous encounter. It was a testimony to the strength of our commitment and the goodness of the Lord. Eventually, we continued down the trail and found the perfect spot to spend the night resting and celebrating. Our journey was far from over, but we would face it together. We'd get right back to work tomorrow, but tonight was a night to eat, drink, and enjoy our success.

CHAPTER 49

We'd been on the trail from Tennessee to Montana for over a month. It was a trek that tested our mettle and strengthened our bonds. The plantation workers were a hardy, resilient lot. Their tireless work ethic had propelled us forward at a far swifter pace than any of us had anticipated, which was fortunate since the days were rapidly growing cooler. I doubted any of our travelers from Tennessee had ever faced a winter as harsh as the one ahead. If we were hit by ice, snow, or frigid temperatures, folks would suffer, and some might not make it, especially our older members. So, despite the fact we were making good time, we continued to ride hard and discover just how much fortitude these good people possessed. They had yet to disappoint.

We continued on as the ever-changing landscape marked our progression. Since departing the time-worn streets of Jonesborough, Tennessee, we had navigated rugged terrain, forged tricky waterways, and traversed hazy mountain passages. Drew's shoulder had finally healed enough that he could ride, scout, and hunt without issue, and I was happy to have him by my side again.

It wasn't long before the rolling green hills of the South gave way to the vast open expanse of the Midwest. We rode through small towns, mining settlements, growing cities, and endless stretches of untamed wilderness.

To our surprise, after a few short weeks, we were already close to St. Louis. The weather had been kind, and we were blessed with a string of warm days and cool, dry nights. Since crossing the Colter River Dam, we hadn't seen so much as a dark cloud or a spit of rain. I certainly didn't mind. Good weather made for high spirits and afforded us more time to appreciate the beauty of our great country.

One day in particular, we passed by an open range of grassy fields, full to bursting with vibrant wildflowers stretching as far as the eye could see. Their fragile petals swayed gently in the breeze, and their wild, sweet scent was finer than the most expensive perfume.

On the trail, the days seemed to run together. A man can quickly lose track of how long he'd been stirring up dust. It felt like time folded in on itself, and the never-ending routines of trail life rendered each day nearly indistinguishable from the next. The sun accompanied us throughout the day. The moon and stars watched over us at night.

Mostly, we rode from sunup to sundown, but sometimes we carried on into the evening. Out on the plains, the nights belonged to the coyotes; their mournful cries echoed across the prairie. At times, we'd catch glimpses of white-tails at night. Their eyes shone like pale lanterns in the dark. We ate, we packed, we unpacked, and we cooked over the fire. Some days, Drew and I made supply runs when our stock was getting low or Skillet needed a particular tool or part for the chuckwagon.

We encountered several cowboys along the way, rugged men with weathered faces, driving cattle into or out of St. Louis. In addition, we met traders, trappers, and families of pioneers moving westward. Most folks were friendly, sharing tales of their adventures and offering encouragement or a cup of coffee. But, there were also those whose eyes held a glint of suspicion, and their greeting was more of a threat than a welcome. Their watchful gazes served as a reminder that the trail was a world where misplaced trust could be deadly.

Despite our daily rigors, we still found moments of respite and camaraderie. Huddling around campfires, we played cards and laughed. The plantation workers sang hymns, their voices ringing with pain and hope. It was beautiful, and I am sure no man has ever heard a more joyful sound. We joked and spun tall tales of questionable origin while the bonds of our friendship linked our spirits.

Smiling Jack used to say that trail dust was thicker than blood. At the time, I didn't understand the sentiment. I didn't have any blood relatives to speak of, so I was in no position to challenge his theory. I was clearly loyal to Drew, but many of the other young men in our crew came and went as often as the changing weather. I had little trust or respect for any of them, aside from the fear of their impulsive natures. That caution worked in my favor, keeping me quiet, compliant, and, most importantly, free of bullet holes.

Yet now, as I rode alongside Drew and our fellow travelers, I began to understand the nugget of truth hiding in Smiling Jack's words. Our misfit band of companions consisted of men and women who were becoming more than friends. It was something akin to family. We took care of each other, shared everything, and were unified by a cause more significant than our individual desires.

The evening before we passed through St. Louis, Fisher, Tate, and Two Feathers came looking for Drew and me. We were seated around a small campfire, chatting away. They stepped softly into the circle of light, their faces bearing unusual expressions.

"Evenin', Moses...Drew," Fisher began tentatively. "You mind if we sit? Chat a while?"

Drew gestured for them to join us with a welcoming smile. He'd been fiddling with the camera recovered from Nicholas and Audrey after they'd met their unfortunate demise at the hands of outlaws. It was a device that fascinated all of us, even though we had yet to figure out how to operate the gadget. Still, its intricate mahogany construction and polished brass accents were fine enough to hold our attention for a spell.

"Have a seat, fellas," Drew said as he passed the camera over to Fisher and Tate. They studied it wide-eyed before absently handing it back. They were quiet. Nervous even. There was no doubt they had something on their minds.

"There's a rumor been goin' around camp," Tate said, getting right to it. His voice was a little shaky. "It's about the both of you."

Drew and I exchanged glances, our curiosity piqued. "Rumors?" I said, raising an eyebrow. "What kind of rumors?"

Fisher glanced at Tate before speaking. "We heard talk that you fellas used to run with a sho 'nuff gang. They sayin' that's where you learned to shoot and ride like you do. They sayin' that's how you was able to handle all Ashbourne's men like you did. On your own."

Drew leaned back, his face twisted with concern. "So, you're sayin' that the good folks here think Moses and I are outlaws?"

"Oh, no, sir," Fisher replied quickly, shaking his head. "Don't nobody think ya'll are outlaws *now*. Only maybe that...well...that you used to be."

Drew chuckled, and the tension eased a bit. "Yeah, well, don't get too worked up about it," he said, keeping his tone light. "Turns out the outlaw life was somethin' we weren't very good at anyhow."

I grinned as well. "And as for what happened at the Colter River Dam," I added, "none of it was any of our doing. You can call it dumb luck, being in the right place at the right time, or the Lord's handiwork. Whichever way you look at it, it wasn't us that made it play out like it did. We could live that day over a thousand times and never see it happen that way again."

"Question, though," Drew said. "Exactly who is spreadin' these rumors you've heard?"

"Oh, nobody, Drew," Tate said. "It's just folks bein' folks. That's all. They don't mean nothin' by it. Fact is, most of 'em feel better thinkin' it's true."

"Well, I don't want to disappoint anybody, but there ain't nothin' about us worth boasting about," I said. "Besides, any man who'll sit around and shoot off at the mouth about being an outlaw is either lying or sick in the head. Either way, you'd do well to steer clear of him."

"I hope you don't take no offense," Fisher said. "We just wanted to know if the rumors was true."

"They are true," I said. "We used to run with a group of outlaws who still manage to give us trouble. We were young and dumb with limited options. We ain't proud of what all we did, but we *are* proud we ain't still doing it."

Chapter 50

B y the time I was twenty-two years old, Drew and I were fully entrenched in the outlaw life. It wasn't as if we had actively pursued lawlessness, but we didn't exactly shy away from it either. I suppose we were considered followers of Smiling Jack Davis, but it was much more than that. He wasn't simply our leader; he was the closest thing to a father either one of us had ever known. He looked out for us, taught us how to live on the run, protected us, and kept us well-fed. Looking back, I still wasn't sure if the care Smiling Jack showed us was genuine. Maybe it was, or perhaps we were merely tools that helped his outfit run smoothly. Regardless, we had become two of his most trusted confidants and, according to Jack, the sons he'd never fathered.

We moved a lot in those days, seldom staying anywhere long enough to draw attention from the law. Or so we thought. Still, Smiling Jack had big plans and spoke of them often, always taking advantage of the opportunity for showmanship. "They call this great country the land of opportunity, boys," he'd say, "and for many, it is. But, as we all have been made painfully aware, a man without means has little hope of getting a fair shake. Yes, a man can always drive cattle or spend years saving his hard-earned money to purchase a mercantile or a saloon – all noble pursuits and sensible occupations. Still, the simple life of a working man is not a reasonable option for men such as us. I'm looking for real money, the kind of money made by bankers, industrialists, and politicians. Unfortunately, such civilized folks tend to put more stock in book learning and ass-kissing than business savvy and grit.

"The way I see it, we can't sit around waiting for the promise of America to shine favor down on us. We have to make our own way. And we will. I'll get us there – all of us. I just need everyone to play their role, keep the faith, and stick with me. As soon as we have the capital, we'll go legit.

That's my promise to you boys. One day soon, we'll be honest-to-goodness businessmen. We just have to be patient."

We'd been camping near a silver mining town in central Colorado called St. Elmo. Jack had allowed us a few excursions into town to let off steam and to watch for any soft targets. After a couple of weeks, Jack decided we needed to rob the bank in the heart of St. Elmo. He assured us that he was acquainted with the bank manager, Jerry Clemens, and spent days telling us how much of a lowdown scoundrel the man was. He laid it on thick, and we lapped up his words like thirsty dogs. To hear Jack tell it, Jerry Clemens was nothing more than a rattlesnake in human skin – a man who reveled in the misfortune of others and used the struggle of poor folks to line his deep pockets. He deserved to have his bank robbed. At least, that's what Jack led us to believe.

Smiling Jack wanted to hit the bank quickly with a small crew, and he trusted Drew and me to lead the operation. Determined not to disappoint him, we took our time, carefully studying the job from every angle until we were fully prepared. After several days of planning, everything was set. We had assembled the crew, coordinated the timing, planned the distraction, and mapped out the getaway. We also identified the best escape routes and contingency plans if things went wrong. Given the amount of preparation and Smiling Jack's unwavering confidence in us, we were convinced the job would go off without a hitch.

Drew would enter the bank first, followed by me. Another member of our crew, a tough-as-nails old buzzard we called Slim, would watch the door. Slim was a wiry, shriveled-up fella who didn't look like much at first glance. But Slim was mean as a coyote with a toothache and could shoot the wings off a gnat at a hundred yards. Two brothers from our gang, Hess and Jim, were posted at the opposite edge of town. It was a small enough town that we could spot them easily from the bank's front steps. The brothers were slippery devils and could lose a posse in the middle of a desert. Their task was to create a distraction, draw the attention of any lawmen or busybodies nearby, and hopefully get them to chase after them. We'd make our move once they took off and were out of sight. In and out. Quick and clean.

We decided to hit the bank just before closing time on Tuesday. We'd secure the money, head out of town in the opposite direction of Hess and Jim, and ride through the night. Jack had a safe house outside San Luis, about a week's ride south of St. Elmo. If everything went as planned, we'd all meet up there as soon as possible.

At just past four-thirty on Tuesday, the brothers opened fire, throwing the town into chaos. With a quick nod to Slim, Drew and I covered our faces and charged into the bank. We were loud, brimming with youthful vigor, and waving our guns around like we meant business. And we did, though we had no intention of taking anyone's life. Armed robbery was one thing, but a murder charge was a whole other matter. Our goal was simple. Get in fast, grab the money, and surprise old Jerry Clemens by emptying his safes for him.

Drew shouted, his voice full of menace, "Everybody, get down on the floor and keep quiet!" The people complied, dropping to the ground as Drew paced around, shouting at them. Meanwhile, I moved through the room, collecting any weapons or valuables they had on them. Drew continued, his tone dripping with arrogance, "My buddy and I are here to rob this bank, and you're all going to get a front-row seat to the show.

"If you have any wild notions of playing the hero, do not. I promise, if you do, I will shoot you. Furthermore, if you try to run, I will shoot you. If you scream, I will shoot you. And if you do anything to annoy either my friend or myself, I will most assuredly shoot you. Are we clear?"

Three men and two women were in the bank that day, not counting the teller and whoever might be in the back. The women mostly whimpered and hid their faces while the men reluctantly handed over their guns and diverted their eyes – all but one of them. A thin, dark, dust-covered fella, who I assumed was a farmer or rancher, was seated closest to the door. He glared at Drew with hate in his eyes as if Drew was a cockroach that needed stomping.

Drew noticed him about the same time I did. "And what are you looking at?" Drew said to the thin man. "Either you was born with that sour, ugly face, or you're just plain dumb enough to toss dirty looks at a man who's holding a gun to your head. I don't know if I should shoot you for being ugly or being dumb."

"You can say what you want," the man answered, "but you wouldn't talk so tough without that gun in your hand."

Drew didn't say any more to him; he just cracked the man across the side of his face with the butt of his revolver. He slid away from Drew, covering his face.

"You broke my jaw, you bastard," he yelled at Drew.

"Well, you're right on two counts," Drew said. "I *am* a bastard, and I guess I *am* tougher with this gun in my hand."

I turned my attention to the nicely dressed man behind the counter. "What's your name?" I said.

"Name's Richard," he replied shakily. "Richard Wilcox."

"Very good, Richard Wilcox," I went on. "I'm gonna need you to go into the back and tell Mr. Clemens there are a couple of bank robbers out here dyin' to talk to him."

Richard wanted to protest, but his desire to keep my gun out of his face was stronger than his duty to the bank. He nodded and nearly tripped over his own feet as he backed out of the room. A moment later, he returned with Jerry Clemens, and I was surprised that old Jerry had walked right out into the lobby to confront us.

"What's the meaning of this?" Clemens said. I could tell he was scared, but he tried not to look it. He was a heavy-set man, neat and clean, with nice clothes and spectacles. His gray hair was thinning and neatly combed, and there was a smudge of food on the side of his clean-shaven face.

"The meaning is rather simple, Jerry," Drew said, turning his gun on him. "We're takin' your money. Now hurry up and fill those bags."

Jerry glanced at his teller. "Richard, do as they say. Hurry now, son. We don't want anyone getting shot today. And please, make sure Connor stays put."

"Connor?" I said. "I don't see any reason Conner should miss the party. Richard, go on and send him out here so I can get a good look at him. For future reference, of course."

Jerry Clemens smiled a big, phony smile. "There's no need for that, sir. Connor won't cause any trouble. He's only a –"

"I'm sorry, Mr. Clemens," Richard called out from the back room. Into the lobby raced a boy I assumed to be Connor. He was no more than six years old, and he ran right up to his pa and latched onto his leg.

Drew and I glanced at one other as Jerry Clemens pushed his son behind him and continued to flash his desperate smile. "Connor is my son," he said as sweat trickled down his face. "Please, gentlemen, take the money. It's all yours. Just please don't hurt anyone."

Richard returned with the cash, and I snatched the bags from his grip. I checked them quickly and then nodded to Drew.

"Whether or not any of you gets hurt," Drew called out, "is entirely up to you. My pal and I are gonna ride out of here, and you all are gonna wait at least thirty minutes before you stick your heads out of this building. Should you feel brave and decide otherwise...well, you know how the story ends."

"Thank you," Jerry Clemens said with tears in his eyes. Standing there like he was, looking all scared and sweaty, Jerry Clemens didn't strike me as the no-good snake in the grass Smiling Jack had made him out to be. He looked like a father, scared to death for his son.

I went out the door first with Drew behind me. But as Drew stepped to the doorway, the thin man he'd pistol-whipped reached out with his right hand and grabbed Drew's leg. With his left hand, he pulled a derringer from his waistband and pointed it at Drew. He was shaky and slow, likely caused by the aforementioned blow to the head. Nonetheless, that split second of hesitation was enough for Drew to react. He kicked the farmer's hand just before the man pulled the trigger. Unfortunately, the bullet meant for Drew struck Mr. Clemens directly in the chest.

Jerry Clemens dropped to his knees as a big red spot soaked through his clean, white shirt. He glanced down at the wound, touched a shaking hand to the blood, and fell over dead. The place erupted into chaos as Drew attacked the skinny farmer, nearly kicking him to death right there on the floor of St. Elmo's Bank. My eyes were fixed on Jerry Clemens and the weeping boy, trying to wake his father as if he had fallen asleep. It was an accident, but it didn't change the grim reality that because of our actions, there was a lifeless man on the floor and a young boy who would grow up without a father.

As we fled, my heart was heavy with remorse. Those people didn't deserve to witness such atrocity. Connor Clemens didn't deserve to lose his father. That farmer didn't deserve to be beaten half to death. And I was pretty sure Jerry Clemens didn't deserve to lose his life, even if what Smiling Jack had told us about him was true.

We rode until dark, stopping to make camp in a shallow cave. Drew and I rested and counted our ill-gotten spoils by the light of a dim fire. We were quiet. Ashamed of ourselves. Regardless of how or why it happened, we had forever scarred the lives of innocent people, and no amount of money could soothe such guilt.

It was that very night, in our silent, shadowy hideout, that I made a decision. I knew I couldn't continue down such a treacherous path. Some of the men in our crew were hardened killers, leaving behind a trail of dead men and ruined lives. That wasn't me. It wasn't Drew either, but every man has to make his own choices in life. For me, my conscience could no longer bear the weight of innocent blood on my hands. I wasn't sure how long it would take or if I'd manage to get out alive, but I vowed to myself that my time with Smiling Jack was coming to an end.

"Drew?" I began. My voice sounded weak. "Drew, you still awake?"

"Yeah," Drew muttered. "Can't sleep."

"We can't keep goin' this way," I said soberly. "We can't keep doin' things to hurt innocent people. I think it's time for us to move on. Make a clean break."

Drew sat up and looked at me. The dying fire gave off just enough light to reveal the worried lines on his face. "Moses, I've trusted you since we were kids, and I trust you now. But where would we go? What kind of life could we make out there on our own?"

"We'll find a way," I said. "We'll find a way to make amends for our pasts. At least we can live a life where we don't have to look over our shoulders constantly. We can do it, Drew. We can be better than this."

Drew laid back down and rolled over with his back to me. "Maybe so," he said with very little conviction. "It's a nice dream anyway."

CHAPTER 51

W hat had started as a thrilling flight to freedom over two months ago
had become an arduous slog toward the ever-distant promised land
of Montana.

We moved steadily through Nebraska's Platte River Valley, a beautifully untamed wilderness. Golden prairie grass swayed in the breeze,
and towering cottonwoods lined the riverbanks. The Platte River was a
twisting ribbon that wound its way through the heart of the state and
brought the land to life. Its wide, sandy banks bore the marks of countless
wagon trains that had etched their stories in the soft earth.

There was far less chatter, singing, and laughter among our group
than in previous weeks. The initial excitement had faded, replaced by a
quiet melancholy for the homes and lives left behind. Even for the most
experienced travelers, the trail can be grueling and unforgiving, and ours
was no exception. The trip took its toll on everyone's spirit.

Arguments popped up like prairie fires, sparked by the constant tension of life on the move. These families yearned for a place to call home,
and many of them were beginning to look back at the Ivywood Plantation
with trail-weary eyes and sentimental memories. I was worried they would
forget how bad things had been for them there. Some did. We'd already
lost a few along the way. Much to our surprise, some families left us. They
willingly returned to a life of servitude to Logan Ashbourne, trading their
freedom for security. I didn't shame them, nor did I attempt to stop them.
To do so would make me no different than the Ashbournes. So I gave them
my blessing, ensured they were well-stocked for the trip, and sent them
on their way. As much as I wanted them to see things my way, it had to
be their choice. I had no right to infringe upon their newfound freedom.
They weren't the only ones. Others left us in a much less conspicuous
manner. They'd departed quietly, gathering only what they could carry and

slipping away in the night. The thought of those families out there alone was troubling, but my loyalties were to those in my care. I had a job to do, and it required my complete attention.

Amidst the growing disharmony, food became a point of contention. Skillet and Nellie relied on our hunters to secure fresh meat for camp. Typically, this presented no great challenge since the land provided an abundance of wild game. But, oddly enough, all we'd managed to kill for nearly two weeks was rabbit. They were everywhere – more rabbits than I'd ever seen. Truth be told, we hardly had to hunt at all. Some mornings, we'd wake up and kill half a dozen of the vermin without stepping foot out of camp. The good Lord provided. That much was clear, but the monotony of our diet had our people on edge.

It was a welcomed sight when we finally caught a glimpse of the large American Flag waving proudly over Fort Kearny. Red and white stripes waved against a crisp, blue sky. It was a reminder that there was still a bastion of law and order even within this wild expanse. The military had decommissioned the post two years earlier, so it wasn't the lively hub it once was. Last I heard, only around fifty men were posted there, and soon, the fort would be abandoned altogether. Still, it was only a few miles away from the city of Kearney. The place was booming with the arrival of homesteaders and the recent railroad expansion. We set up camp nearby, joining several other wagon trains that had stopped to allow men and beasts a well-deserved rest.

We had learned to be careful in unfamiliar territory. People were generally friendly, if not downright curious about our misfit bunch. But most were unaccustomed to seeing a large group of black folks moving across the country. A few were hostile toward us, but considering our numbers, they didn't pose much threat. More often than not, folks gave us a wide berth and avoided us altogether. However, due to several unfavorable encounters, we now entered settlements in small groups, spaced at intervals, to avoid attention. It pained me that such safeguards were necessary, but our world could be harsh, unforgiving, and was unlikely to change anytime soon.

The city of Kearney sat confidently on the windswept plains of Nebraska, a thriving community and trading hub just off the Oregon Trail. Wooden storefronts, saloons, and hotels lined Kearney's dusty streets. Many merchants, both inside and outside the city, set up shops to sell ammunition, leatherwork, weapons, and all manner of equipment. A man could trade for nearly anything he needed, seeing as how most merchants and travelers headed west would likely spend some time in Kearney.

As was our custom, Drew and I ventured into town, and our first stop was the telegraph office. We hadn't received a single message so far, which was fine with me. I'd heard that no news was good news, and I had little interest in debating the matter in my head.

"Good morning, gentlemen." the operator said. She was a petite lady in a pale blue dress, all smiles and good cheer. "Is there something I can help you with today?"

"Yes, ma'am," I replied. "Have you received any messages for Moses Colter or Drew Harlan?"

She wasted no time shuffling through the stack of telegraphs on her desk. After a moment, she smiled and held up two messages. "Looks like you have one from Virginia City, Montana, and another from Jonesborough, Tennessee."

She handed them over, and I hesitantly took them. For some reason, the unease I felt was immediate. We sat on a wooden bench outside the telegraph office, the bustle of the city carrying on around us. I glanced at Drew, who just shook his head and shrugged, so I went ahead and opened the messages.

The first hailed from Jonesborough and was from our friend, Marshal Wesley. I read it aloud while Drew looked on. "Heard you are setting a brisk pace. Wired ahead to lawmen along your route. Asked them to keep your path clear. All is well here. Keep your eyes open. Haven't seen Ashbourne and Gullet since you left."

"Sounds like the marshal's worried," Drew said. "Do you think Logan and Harold would come after us? That's a lot of ground to cover just for revenge."

"I don't think so," I said, "but I wouldn't put anything past those two. Logan is full of poison, and that much hate is hard to keep reigned in. As far as Gullet, he'll do as he's told if it means he gets paid or gets to hurt someone."

"What do you wanna do about it?" Drew said.

I took a breath and thought for a moment. "Nothin' for now. I don't think there's anything we can do. Wesley is a cautious man, and he's just lookin' out for us. Logan and Gullet have bigger problems than us, and they've already lost a ton of men. But, to be safe, we'll have Two Feathers watch our backtrail for a while."

The second message, from Virginia City, bore the name of Reverend Joseph Phillips. It read, "Hope this finds you well. Land has been well cared for. Possible trouble. Jack Davis snooping around. Quiet so far. Hope to see you soon."

Drew let out a huge sigh. "What is *possible trouble* supposed to mean? Seems to me like our lives have been filled with possible trouble for years now."

I folded and pocketed the letters. "We'll keep moving and stay on guard. There's no need to fret over things that *might* happen. I'll tell Skillet, Nellie, and Two Feathers about the telegraphs, but I don't think we need to worry everyone else."

Drew dropped his gaze, and I could tell something else was bothering him. I didn't want to pry, so I waited for him to think it through.

"Moses, I'm still worried about the money I owe Smiling Jack. What are we gonna do? We're runnin' out of time."

"First of all, *we* owe Smiling Jack money. We're doing this together, all the way. I know it's been eatin' at you, so let's put our minds to it til we figure something out."

I'm not sure how much my words helped, but Drew nodded, and we moved on. As we strolled the streets of Kearney, I couldn't help but be impressed with the ambition and optimism that seemed to permeate the air. It made a man feel like anything was possible. The world was changing, and it seemed like we had a good chance at making a real home for us and our people.

We must have walked in silence for a while, just taking in the sights, because it caught me by surprise when Drew pointed and called out. "Look, Moses."

I followed his gaze to a modest shop across the street with a sign hanging out front that read, "Johnston's Photographic Emporium."

"What if we try to sell that camera?" Drew said. "The pictures, too. It might fetch us a decent price if we find the right folks. You know, the kind of folks who like pictures and such."

"It's worth a shot," I said. "Let's go grab the camera and see how much of an appreciation for photography the good people of Kearney have."

CHAPTER 52

Johnston's Photographic Emporium was a small, cluttered curiosity shop of sorts. Our eyes scanned the various cameras, photographs, and strange equipment that filled nearly every inch of space. We didn't understand what we were looking at, but it was interesting nonetheless. The shop owner was a small, hunched-over old man with a shock of wild hair protruding from beneath his cap. He approached us with keen interest. As he welcomed us, Drew took out the camera and placed it on the counter.

"That's a fine-looking field camera you have there," the man remarked, donning a pair of tiny, thick spectacles. "May I?" Drew slid the camera to the old man, who examined it with nimble, experienced fingers, revealing small compartments and hinges we didn't even know existed.

After a moment, he looked up from the camera and removed his spectacles. "What you fellows have here is a Beck field camera – and a nice one at that," he began, demonstrating his expertise. "No doubt it's the tool of a professional." He paused for a moment. "May I ask where you came across this?"

Drew's expression grew somber. "It belonged to some friends of ours. They ran up on some bad men on their way to Tennessee. They didn't make it."

The old man nodded. "I'm sorry to hear that," he murmured as he shook his head. "It's a dangerous country out there."

"Do you think it's worth anything?" I chimed in. "We don't have much need for it, so we were hoping you might be interested in taking it off our hands."

The shop owner winced and sucked in a deep breath through clenched teeth as if grappling with its worth. "I'd say...brand new, it'd be worth around three or four hundred dollars. Of course, I can't offer you that much." He peered at the camera once more before continuing. "I can go as high as a hundred. That's about all I can do."

Drew, never one to settle for less, proposed, "What if I throw in these?" He pulled a stack of photographs from his bag and carefully placed them on the shop counter. The owner gingerly flipped through the collection.

"These are very nice," he commented blankly. "One fifty, but that's really as much as I can do."

Drew wasted no time collecting the photographs and nodding appreciatively. "Well, thank you, sir, but I think I'll hang onto them for now."

Still polite and patient, the old man replied, "I understand. It is an excellent piece of equipment, though. With a fine camera like this, you could take up photography yourself."

Drew chuckled a little. "Now there's a thought," he said, "but I don't think so. I'd hate to sully the life's work of Nicholas and Audrey by running around taking terrible pictures with their camera. They'd never forgive me."

Something about Drew's words piqued the old man's interest. "Excuse me, did you say this camera belonged to Nicholas and Audrey? As in Nicholas and Audrey Ballard? The famous photographers?"

Drew blinked in surprise. "To be honest, I never caught their last name," he admitted. "And I certainly didn't ask if they were famous."

The shop owner's eyes gleamed with newfound interest. He began to pepper us with questions about the couple's appearance, how we knew them, and any details we knew about their travels and work. With our own interest aroused, Drew and I shared everything we knew about our departed friends.

Once the man had heard all we could tell him about Nicholas and Audrey, he looked Drew squarely in the eye and said, "I'll give you a thousand dollars for the camera and three hundred for the photographs."

Now, Drew and I weren't much more than orphaned country boys, but we weren't greenhorns. Bargaining, negotiating, and surviving had been as much a part of our lives as the moon and stars at night. Drew flashed a grin, and tested the waters, and said, "Make it five, and you got yourself a deal."

"Five thousand?" The old man shook his head. "You clearly have something special there, but that's a bit beyond my means." We stood there for a moment, each of us waiting for the other to speak.

Finally, the shop owner broke the silence. "I'll tell you what," he said, leaning in as though sharing a secret. "I'm gonna help you boys out. A man named Lawrence Philburn passed through here not more than a few days ago. He's a wealthy fellow out of Denver – some kind of art collector. He showed up on a fine-looking stage with his wife and four armed men. Anyway, he came by the shop and mentioned that he was an admirer and collector of Nicholas and Audrey Ballard's work. He said he was thrilled to finally meet them and purchase some photographs. The only problem is that the Ballards never showed. Of course, after what you've shared, it's evident why. Mr. Philburn waited in town a few days before finally giving up and returning to Denver. If you can catch up to him, I bet he'd be willing to buy that camera and those photographs from you. I don't know about five thousand dollars, but he'd likely offer you more than I can."

Drew's face lit up like a young boy's at Christmas. "What do you say, Moses? You wanna come with me to chase down a rich fella that loves pictures?"

I nodded thoughtfully. "I suppose we could leave the wagons for a while. Ride toward Denver, find Mr. Philburn, and hopefully make some money. It shouldn't take more than a few days to catch up to the wagon train afterward."

"Just a minute, young men," the old shop owner said. He took out a blank sales receipt and scribbled a message. "When you find Mr. Philburn, give him this. It's a note from me stating the authenticity of your claims. I don't know if it'll help, but it can't hurt."

CHAPTER 53

The wagon train wouldn't pull out of Kearney until Thursday, but Drew and I left on Tuesday afternoon. Our plan was simple. We would track down Mr. Lawrence Philburn, sell him the camera and photographs for as much as possible, and then rendezvous with the wagons. Barring any unforeseen circumstances, we'd rejoin our group before most of them even noticed we were away.

It felt like the old days being out on the trail together. Drew and I knew this territory like the backs of our hands, having traveled it often during our days with Smiling Jack.

As we rode, my mind drifted back to the wagon train and the men and women in our care. Were they safe? Was everyone getting along? Could Skillet and Nellie handle any trouble that might arise? Those questions swirled in my head, but the countryside was quiet and serene. It was sunny and cool with a gentle breeze, and soon, I was lulled into a more peaceful state of mind. It was nice to push my concerns aside for a while.

Drew and I rode well into the night before stopping to make camp by a shallow creek. Our horses grazed on a large patch of bluegrass and drank their fill of cool water. Over a small fire, I made coffee and fried bacon to go along with our hardtack. Settling in under the stars, we used our saddles as headrests before drifting off.

Before sunrise, we were back on the trail, hoping to catch up to Mr. Philburn. The sun peeked over the horizon on a clear and beautiful morning. We rode hard for a while, then slowed to let the horses walk. "You know, Moses," Drew said, breaking the quiet stillness, "I've been thinking about things lately."

"Is that right?" I replied with a smile. "Don't fool around and strain that noggin of yours. As far as I can tell, it wasn't built for heavy lifting."

Drew smiled to himself. "Always the jester, ain't you? But seriously, I owe you an apology. Back when Jack went to prison and you left the gang, I was happy for you. I really was. Heck, I wanted to go with you, but I didn't. Greenbacks blinded me, I suppose. But if I'm being honest, you had it right all along. I shoulda' left with you and never looked back."

"There ain't no need for apologies," I said. "We weren't much more than kids back then. We had our own ideas and did what we thought we should."

"Yeah, but you're my best friend," Drew said. "I let five years go by without settin' eyes on you. You got married, had a child, and lost both of them. I didn't even know. I wasn't there for you. You went through all of that alone. You needed a friend to stand by you. I guess what I'm trying to say is...that was wrong of me, and I'm sorry."

I thought for a moment as the saddles creaked beneath us. "It's not all on you," I finally said. "It's not like I was out there trackin' you down either. I could've done more. I could've come looking for you. I'm sure there were times when you needed me too."

Drew shook his head. "I appreciate you tryin' to make me feel better, but you had responsibilities – a wife and a ranch. You couldn't just up and run off whenever you wanted. It was different for me. I was only livin' for myself." He rode on, silent for a bit. "Anyway, like I said, I'm sorry. It's been eatin' at me, and I had to say it. I should've been a better friend."

"Well, you're here now," I said. "You've risked your neck and saved my skin more times than I can count. Not to mention you've done it all with nothin' but a 'thank you' to show for it. It seems to me that we both could've done more. So why don't we just call it even?"

Drew nodded. "You've got a deal," he said. "We can call it even, but not until I get Jack's money."

"I can agree to that if it helps ease your mind," I said. "But *we* will get Jack's money. We do this together."

We rode on, enjoying the quiet for a while. The sun was warm, and the rhythm of the horses' hooves against the earth was soothing. I thought about how lucky I was to have Drew as a friend all these years. He was wild and unpredictable but was as loyal as a compass to true north. "You know," I said after a while, "I've been thinking about things lately, too."

"Is that right?" Drew said with a grin. "And all this time, I thought that smoke I smelled was from a prairie fire."

"I guess I earned that," I said, laughing. "I was thinking you might want to move onto the ranch with us when we get back to Montana. We could build you a house and look for some honest work. We're close enough to Virginia City, so you could always find somethin' to get into. Who knows, you might even find a good woman and settle down."

"I'll think on that," Drew said. "It sounds real nice, though."

We continued riding, engrossed in our thoughts when a Prairie Schooner appeared around the bend ahead of us. The driver, an older fella, was clearly hauling a heavy load. As he neared, we saw a homemade sign with bright red lettering on his wagon.

"Good mornin'," he called out cheerfully as he pulled to a stop. "Beautiful day, don't you think?"

We introduced ourselves and chatted a bit. Come to find out, his name was Dan, and he had a rather unique business. The words "Dan the Wagon Wheel Man" were painted on his schooner. And that was his business. Dan collected and repaired discarded wagon wheels to sell to travelers along the trail. "You can never be too careful," he advised. "There are some dangerous stretches of countryside out here. The last thing you want is to be stranded with a busted wheel and no spare."

"That's a mighty specialized business you have, Dan," Drew remarked.

"Maybe so," Dan replied. "Especially if I was settled in town. But out here, I'm a hard worker and a skilled wheelwright. It might seem strange to you, but if you were in a bind and needed a wheel, you'd be glad to see me comin'. Yes, sir, I believe I am an asset to the good men and women braving these lonely trails."

"I suppose we can't argue with you there," I told Dan. "Unfortunately...or fortunately, we don't need any wagon wheels right now."

"I understand," Dan said with a shake of his head. "But I better keep movin'. If you need anything, I'll be traveling the stretch between here and Kearney for the next few days. You kids stay safe."

We thanked Dan and continued on our way. The day wore on, and the sun climbed higher as we scanned the road for any sign of Lawrence Philburn's stage. Overall, this side trip was a welcomed distraction from the trail's constant uncertainties. We'd be riding into Fort Laramie and then Virginia City in a few weeks. We just needed to hold everything together until we arrived. Little did we know that, though our journey would soon end, our troubles were far from over.

Chapter 54

It was shortly after noon when Drew and I spotted the stagecoach about a quarter of a mile up the trail. The shop owner in Kearney hadn't exaggerated since it was by far the finest stage I'd ever seen. It was the type you'd expect in a big city and was out of place on the prairie. Still, despite its beauty and craftsmanship, the coach was broken down. Three men, one of whom I assumed to be Mr. Lawrence Philburn, stood around looking lost. We rode up slowly, careful not to startle them.

"You fellas havin' trouble?" Drew called out. The one who was likely Philburn scrambled into the stage quicker than a rabbit's shadow and slammed the door behind him. The remaining two, hired guns by the look of them, approached us cautiously. We sat our horses but kept a respectful distance since the shop owner from Kearney said he'd counted four hired guns. We only saw the two.

"There ain't no need to stop," the first gunman said flatly. He was a rugged sort with a face like a weathered saddle. He had a firm grip on a Henry rifle. His partner lagged behind, his hand resting on his pistol. "We don't need any help, and we sure ain't in the mood for chit-chat. You can keep on moving."

"We don't mean no harm, sir," I replied, sounding as friendly as possible. "And we don't want no trouble either. In fact, we were hoping to talk some business with Mr. Philburn. I assume that's him in the stage."

The gunman squinted at me, his eyes like narrow slits underneath the brim of his hat. "Maybe it is Philburn...maybe it ain't," he grumbled. "Either way, the man in that stage ain't lookin' to do business with the likes of you."

It was then I noticed the busted wagon wheel on the back right of the coach. A second wheel, equally broken and useless, lay discarded in the dust nearby.

"You sure you don't need any help?" Drew asked, nodding toward the broken wagon wheels. "Fine coaches like this don't always hold up too good on the trail."

"We're gettin' along fine," the gunman said dismissively. "We got friends on the way."

His partner, a thin, jittery-looking fella, huffed before piping up. "Yeah, we got friends, alright," he said sarcastically. "More likely than not, they're halfway through a bottle somewhere."

"Shut up," the first man snapped.

Drew always had a way of getting folks to talk. I'd seen him in situations like this many times. He aimed to push these fellas a bit to see if he could win them over. "Look here, now," he began. "You fellas need some help. We need to speak to Mr. Philburn. You help us, we help you. Sounds reasonable, don't it?"

Before the man could reply, Drew decided to call out to the stage. "Mr. Philburn, you in there? Come on out, and we –"

The familiar click of a pistol hammer cut him off. The surly gunman had his weapon trained on Drew. My hand instinctively went to my own revolver, but I didn't draw. I'd come to learn that people who keep their guns holstered tend to live longer. I had no desire to turn a tense situation into a shooting match.

"I don't want to kill you," the man said. "But if you don't ride away now, I damn sure will." His voice was as steady as his aim, and I knew he meant what he said.

Drew raised his hands in a show of peace. "No need for threats now, boys," he said, backing up his horse. "We'll be on our way. I have some photographs for Mr. Philburn and his lovely wife, but I suppose I can keep them myself. You men have a good day."

We were turning our horses to leave when the stage door flew open. "Hold on," Mr. Philburn said, stepping out. His wife gasped from inside. "Excuse me, sir, did you say you had photographs? For me?"

"Why, yes, I do," Drew said as he retrieved an envelope from his saddlebag. "Photographs taken by Nicholas and Audrey Ballard, to be delivered upon payment to a Mr. Lawrence Philburn."

Lawrence Philburn was an older gentleman, tall and thin, with frosty hair and a matching mustache. The change in his demeanor was like night turning into day. He removed his bowler and dipped his head. "I am Lawrence Philburn. Please excuse the curtness of my associates. They are paid well to ensure my wife and I are protected while traveling through this rugged land. I'm afraid they can get a bit overzealous in their duties. But come, let's talk." Then, to his hired guns, he said, "Go ahead and set up camp, gentlemen. It looks as if we'll be here for a while."

Philburn invited us into his coach as his gunmen shuffled away, giving us dirty looks. The stagecoach was nicer than any I'd ever seen, and I felt uncomfortable sitting in the clean seat. We met Mr. Philburn's wife, Margaret, and began to discuss our friends, Nicholas and Audrey Ballard. Drew and I had learned a bit about their fame, but not the extent. It seems they were big names in the photography business, having won medals, received honors, and sold their photographs worldwide.

When the Philburns learned of their demise, they were terribly disheartened. Margaret dabbed at her eyes with a handkerchief while Lawrence comforted her. Even so, the mood soon shifted to excitement at the mention of the camera and the salvaged photographs.

Drew laid it on thick, claiming his were the last photographs ever taken by the famous duo. He was angling for the right moment to talk price, but he was being careful. As generous as Mr. Philburn seemed, most rich folks I knew didn't get rich by making bad deals. Still, Drew handled the interaction like a pro, never mentioning a price. He just kept chatting away, like he, Nicholas, and Audrey had been friends for years.

Finally, Mr. Philburn bit first. "Well, let's not mince words, Mr. Harlan," he said, sitting up straight. "Tell me what you want for the camera and the photographs."

Drew raised his eyebrows and took a deep breath. "Goodness, Mr. Philburn," he began, as he picked up the camera, "how do you put a price on somethin' like this? I mean, we're talking about Nicholas and Audrey Ballard here. I'll sell you the photographs, of course, since they were intended for you. I'm nothing if not honorable. But, honestly, I thought it might be best if I held onto the camera. There's simply no telling what it might be worth someday."

"Oh, come now," Mr. Philburn said with a smile that was all business. "Surely we can work something out. I am a man of means, and I'm sure I can make it worthwhile for you. Give me a try. Name your price."

Drew hemmed and hawed like he didn't know exactly how much money he wanted. I kept quiet. I trusted Drew in these circumstances. Given enough time, Drew could talk a fish out of a lake. Drew shook his head. "I don't believe I could take less than sixty-five hundred in good conscience," he said. Then he just sat there and waited.

Mr. Philburn winced and shifted around like he hadn't expected such a figure to come out of the mouth of such a trailworn country boy. It only took a moment before he flat-out rejected the offer as if he was insulted. Drew didn't seem to mind. He simply thanked the couple for their time and began gathering his things. Mr. Philburn then offered fifteen hundred dollars, to which Drew responded with a shake of his head. It was evident that Mr. Philburn was accustomed to getting what he wanted, and he wanted that camera.

After a display of theatrics and some back-and-forth banter, a deal was finally struck. Mr. Philburn, true to his word, paid generously, even if it wasn't as much as we'd hoped for. Still, in the end, twenty-five hundred dollars was the price we agreed upon. It was more money than a lot of folks have ever seen. And it gave us a good start on what we owed Smiling Jack.

"You know," Drew added as we all stepped out of the stage, "it ain't too safe out here stranded like you are."

"Yes, I am aware," Mr. Philburn said. "We are most upset about it. Unfortunately, it appears our driver is ill-suited when it comes to repairing wagon wheels."

Drew nodded. "Maybe we could help you out – get your stage patched up so you can at least find a safer place to camp for the night."

"If you can get us back on the road," Mr. Philburn said, "I would certainly be in your debt."

"Drew, why don't you stay here?" I said. "Help look after these fine folks in case any trouble comes along. I'll ride out and find old Dan the Wagon Wheel Man. It shouldn't take long."

It took no time at all to locate Dan. When I came upon him, he was in the middle of making a sale to another weary traveler looking for spares. Dan sold me a wheel for four dollars. For an extra two dollars, he said he'd make sure it was secured and balanced. I agreed to his terms and rode alongside his schooner back to Drew and the Philburns.

Dan rambled on about how he only used the finest materials and guaranteed his work. If I'm being honest, I didn't hear half of what he said until he said something that shocked me.

"It's really somethin' how I came to meet you fellas today," he said. "Can I ask you a question? It may sound odd, but are you boys travelin' with a black fella? A big, sturdy sort? A little older than you?"

I was hesitant to answer, but now I was curious. "Well, Dan, we are indeed travelin' with a big, black fella. Several of them, in fact. Why do you ask?"

"Don't think I'm funny in the head or anything, but I had a dream last night. Your large buddy came to me and told me his friends needed help. He said I should head toward Kearney today and that I'd know you when I met you. That's why I stopped and talked to you boys this mornin'. I was plannin' on headin' west, but seeing as my dream felt so real, I decided to do as he said."

"That's quite a tale," I replied, trying to bridle my interest. "Sounds like somethin' right out of the good book."

"Dang sure was," Dan went on. "Spooked me somethin' fierce. Especially with the fire and all."

"Fire? What do you mean? What fire?"

"Oh, sorry," Dan said. "I thought I mentioned it. The big fella that came to me was completely on fire. Just standin' there burnin' and talking as calmly as if it was the most natural thing in the world." He paused. "But that's enough crazy ramblin' from an old man. Let's get this wheel on and get you kids on your way."

My thoughts wandered through all the unexplainable events over the last few months. Each unexpected encounter, every fortuitous turn, and all the dangerous goings-on, it was all too much to be happenstance. There was the dream that started it all, along with the wisdom of Reverend Phillips. The team of Skillet, Nellie, Two Feathers, and Drew fell into my lap when I needed them most. There was the connection I shared to Marshal Wesley, and the fact that he was willing to help us. The wagons, mules, and horses gifted to us by people I'd never met were like nothing I'd ever experienced. Of course, there was the terrible weather and our daring escape from Jonesborough. Not to mention how we crossed the Colter River Dam just before it collapsed. Mr. Philburn, Nicholas and Audrey, Dan the Wagon Wheel Man, the camera and photographs – all of it aligned so perfectly. It was as if we were all pieces being moved around a chessboard, guided by a loving, unseen hand.

We arrived back at Mr. Philburn's stage within an hour. Drew, along with Mr. and Mrs. Philburn, sat on trunks stacked beside the stagecoach. They were laughing and carrying on like family at Christmas dinner. It wasn't surprising. That was Drew's way.

"Hey, I know this wagon," Dan said. "I tried to sell them a few spares not long ago, but they weren't interested. Funny how things change, ain't it?"

Dan took very little time to change the wheel and be on his way. Seeing as it only cost four dollars, I also sprung for a spare wheel. Wealthy old Mr. Philburn was so impressed by our willingness to help that he offered us one hundred extra dollars. It was an obscene amount of money for what we actually did. And as Mr. Philburn began to count it out, Drew shook his head and patted him on the arm. "I'm just glad we could help," Drew said as he glanced at the gunmen with a smile and a nod. Mr. Philburn wrote a bill of sale for the camera and photographs and promised to wire the twenty-five hundred dollars to Fort Laramie for us to collect when we passed through.

Knowing there was a stack of cash waiting on us, Drew and I rode away, grinning like a couple of loons. There was still plenty of ground to cover between here and Montana, but we couldn't help but be encouraged. We were well on our way to making the five thousand we needed to pay off Smiling Jack, and in a few weeks, we'd be back in Virginia City.

CHAPTER 55

Several weeks passed as we rumbled along the trail from Kearney to Fort Laramie. The days grew cooler, which worried me some, but it was comfortable for now. Sometimes, I forgot what a sight our crew must have been crossing the prairie – a few ragged white folks, an Indian, a one-armed cook, and a weary company of black travelers. It had been the toughest on them. They were scared but hopeful, and so far, our trip had been smooth, at least by my estimation. Still, most of our travelers weren't used to life on the move. Over the course of many arduous weeks, their patience had waned, and their nerves were frayed. I wasn't sure what held us all together, but I assumed it was primarily raw determination. We were a motley procession formed of hard work, dreams, and desperation.

Rabbits continued to practically throw themselves into our pots, but the novelty had long been lost. Shooting them offered no challenge, and the familiar flavor became a bland reminder of our monotonous existence. We moved from water source to water source and settlement to settlement. Not a day passed without someone asking how much further it was to the next stop or town. Finding a proper place to make camp was a daily challenge, and the fear of illness hovered over us like a circling vulture.

There was also the threat of Indians. Though most tribes had moved on or resigned to settling on the reservations, it would be foolish for us to carry on as if it wasn't a legitimate concern. A few pockets of resistance existed, and among them, the Sioux were especially troublesome. They were skilled horsemen, as proficient with rifles as they were with bows. Precise and deadly warriors, the Souix would lay in ambush to attack unsuspecting travelers. We all felt better having Two-Feathers, Fisher, and Tate, who diligently scouted the path ahead and kept an eye on our backtrail. We figured it would be unusual for a group of Souix to attack a wagon train as large as ours, but I felt more comfortable being on guard. So far, there had been no sign of trouble, whether from Indians or outlaws.

Despite the monotony and the ever-present threat of danger, occasional moments of levity kept us sane. Our spirits were fastened together by the stories and jokes told around the campfire, the unexpected discovery of a patch of wild berries, or the rare sighting of a prairie dog that sent the children racing off in excitement. The dangers were numerous, but our shared purpose and care for one another united us.

Upon reaching the outskirts of Fort Laramie, Drew and I helped set up camp before venturing into the fort to check on the wire from Mr. Philburn. The promise of a twenty-five hundred dollar payment made even the most challenging stretches of our journey more bearable. Everyone, including the horses and mules, was bone tired. Still, with only one final push to endure after Fort Laramie, everyone pulled together with obstinate resilience. We were clearly the last of the season's travelers pushing westward before winter. As a result, the fort was as sparsely populated as I'd ever seen.

Two messages waited for us at the telegraph office. The first, from Marshal Wesley, offered words of encouragement but no further news of Logan Ashbourne. The second, from Lawrence Philburn, contained all the details necessary for the bank to release our payment. I had my doubts as to whether or not Mr. Philburn would follow through on his promise. Most of my life had felt like one long lesson on the importance of trusting no one. But old Philburn came through for us. Drew still had hesitations, but paying back the five thousand dollars before the first of the year was entirely possible, in my estimation. For once, it seemed as if everything was coming together, and soon, I'd be relaxing in my own home.

The teller at the bank studied the telegraph we brought in, comparing it to one of his own. After a moment, the young man looked up, smiled, and said, "It looks like everything is in order here. I'll get your payment, and we can get you gentlemen on your way." I found it humorous that having taken possession of a few thousand dollars suddenly turned Drew and me into *gentlemen*. "Here you are," the teller said, returning with a stack of cash. "Five thousand dollars."

Drew and I shared a hesitant glance. "I'm sorry, sir," I said, "but I think there's some mix-up. Not that I don't want to take your money, but we were only expecting to pick up twenty-five hundred dollars."

After a moment of confusion, the bank teller returned to his telegraph. His finger traced the lines as he read, and then realization dawned on him. "Oh, yes," he said, "there's a message here for you. It's from Mr. Philburn."

He passed the telegraph over, and I read it aloud. "Moses and Drew," it began, "I can't thank you enough for your help and your willingness to part with the camera and photographs. It seems the death of Nicholas and Audrey Ballard has caused quite a stir among those in the business of photography. As a result, their final works, paired with their personal camera, triggered a bidding war among collectors. A museum in London offered me an obscene amount of money to part with them. I have always considered myself a fair man, and I believe we are blessed so we can be a blessing to others. Please accept this gift and use it to start a new life for yourselves."

Leaving the bank with a sack full of cash, Drew and I were dumbfounded by this twist of fate. We mounted our horses and walked them out of the fort toward our camp, chatting as we rode. We spoke of the providential nature of our journey and how such unforeseen good fortune had traveled with us every step of the way. I don't typically use the word, and certainly not lightly, but the last few months' events had been nothing short of miraculous. While indeed a godsend, the extra money from Mr. Philburn was only one of several miracles that helped us complete our mission and fulfill our dream. What was to come next was a mystery yet to unfold, but our focus remained fixed on Montana for now. We would return to my ranch and start a new chapter without so many threats. Drew and I would ride into Bozeman, clear our debt, and finally be free of Smiling Jack Davis.

Up ahead of us, a lone rider approached. He was pushing his pony hard and coming up quickly. Drew and I instinctively pulled to a stop and checked our sidearms. We couldn't be too careful with the amount of cash we carried. The rider rode up just short of us, and I immediately recognized him. It was Reverend Phillips. He was red-faced, dirty, and looked like he hadn't slept in days.

"Moses," he called out, "I am so glad I found you."

"Good afternoon, Reverend," I answered. "It's good to see you. Is everything alright?"

"It's good to see you too," Reverend Phillips said, "but I'm afraid I must be the bearer of bad news. I rode out, hoping to run into you before you got home. Things are bad back at your ranch, and you're likely riding into danger."

"Tell me what's wrong, Reverend," I said. "Whatever it is, we'll handle it."

"It's Jack Davis," Reverend Phillips went on. "He and his crew have moved onto your land. They sold your sheep and have already built three homes on the property. A group of us from the church went out to confront him, but he said the land belonged to him now. He even had the deed and told us it was all legal. Then he threatened to shoot us if we didn't leave."

Drew glanced at me. "What a snake," he said. "We should've known he was workin' some con on us."

"Thank you for comin' out to find us, Reverend," I said. "At least now we have a few weeks to figure out our next move."

Reverend Phillips nodded. "There's more. Someone else showed up in town just yesterday – a well-dressed man with a mean-looking fella traveling with him. They went directly to your ranch and spent all day with Jack Davis."

"Was it a yellow-haired fella?" Drew asked. "Struttin' around like a peacock? Something of a dandy, traveling with an ugly brute carrying a shotgun?"

"I can't be certain, but it sure sounds like them," the reverend replied.

Drew and I met eyes again. "Logan Ashbourne," I muttered. "This changes things."

CHAPTER 56

I left Smiling Jack's gang when I was twenty-seven years old. In hindsight, my leaving took far too long, but sometimes, a man grows accustomed to a life, even if it isn't one he wants. Five years had passed since Drew and I had robbed the bank in St. Elmo, Colorado. Things didn't go according to plan. Some fella tried to play the hero, and the bank manager took a bullet for it. The bullet belonged to Drew, but the killing was accidental. Drew took it hard, as I imagined he would. Though we were outlaws, we never thought of ourselves as killers. But that's precisely what we'd become in some folks' eyes.

Since the bank job, Drew had gained a bit of a reputation among the others in our crew. The men had always liked him. He kept everyone laughing and the camp in good spirits. But since the shooting, Drew's clout with the younger fellas had increased. Each of the young bucks was itching to make a name for himself, and they envied the attention Drew got from the robbery. They studied him with loyal eyes and held him in high esteem. Still, Drew and I both knew there was no glory in killing. All it does is leave a trail of regret and shattered hopes. We learned early on that a man who lives by the gun will eventually die by it.

I was still searching for an opportunity to leave the gang, but the proper time had yet to present itself. Either that or I was too cowardly to pack up my things and go. It wasn't an easy thing to leave the only life I knew. And if he chose not to come with me, it also meant leaving Drew. We didn't talk about it much. Drew hated change as much as I did. Even talking about leaving made him antsy. Regardless, my mind had long been made up.

I wanted a normal life, one with a wife and kids and a ranch of my own. I'd nearly saved enough to pull it off, but I wasn't sure I could pull the trigger. For one thing, no respectable woman would entertain the thought of marrying a man such as myself. I was nothing more than a second-rate degenerate – an outlaw. I'd known a few women over the years, but I certainly didn't understand what it meant to be a husband or a father. It seemed foolish to expect a woman to stick around while I figured it out. So, while I was ready to cut ties and run, I had yet to devise a workable plan. It felt more like a pleasant dream to focus on during the long nights.

One sunny afternoon, Smiling Jack came to Drew and me and asked us to take a ride. It took most of the day for the three of us to reach the top of a rocky canyon east of camp. We followed the narrow, twisting path of the dry riverbed below, speaking very little as we went. It was hot, and our horses stirred up clouds of dust that swirled around us before getting carried away by the wind.

Finally, Jack reined in at a ledge overlooking a lush valley. A group of men toiled in the fields below while others tended to horses. Their figures were small and distant against the backdrop of the mountains, prettier than any picture a man could hope to see. With the distance between us and the sun to our backs, they never knew we were there.

"What do you think, boys?" Jack's dry voice broke the silence. His eyes were fixed on the fertile valley before us. "Beautiful, ain't she?"

"Sure is, Jack," Drew said. "Don't know if I've ever seen better."

"And what about you, Moses?" Jack said, turning his eyes to me. "It may not be as fancy as that southern plantation where you grew up, but it's nice, right?"

"It sure is," I admitted. "One day, I hope to have a place like this."

A smile played across Jack's weathered face. He removed his hat and wiped the sweat from his brow with a worn bandana. "I'm glad to hear you say that," he said, his tone tinged with pride. "I've decided this here is where we're gonna settle. It's good land, close enough to town for supplies but far enough away to keep to ourselves. It's perfect for us."

"For all of us?" Drew said, his brow furrowed.

Jack nodded. "All of us. Running an operation like the one I have in mind will take a lot of hands. I dream big, boys."

My mind raced with questions, but I tried to play it cool. "You plannin' on buying them out, Jack? How much would a stretch of land like that cost?"

Jack's expression darkened as he recounted his failed attempts to negotiate with the landowner. "An Irishman by the name of Patrick Higgins owns this stretch of land," he explained. "I've made him several offers, all of them fair. But the man has simply refused to listen to reason."

"That's too bad," Drew said, the disappointment evident in his voice. "It would've been a nice place to call home."

Jack's gaze softened. "You two are my best men – loyal and true," he said. "I know you both have struggled with what happened back in St. Elmo, and I'm sorry for that. None of us wanted things to turn out like they did. But I believe in you both, and I need you. I've decided to entrust you with a task of great importance."

I braced myself for what was to come. There was a sinking feeling in the pit of my stomach. "What's that, Jack?" I said. "You want us to scare him? Run him off the land?"

"No," Jack replied. "That won't work, not with Higgins. He's a strong man who lost his entire family moving west. He won't scare easily. The good news is there's no family left to claim the land after he's gone."

"What are you sayin'?" I said, though I feared I already knew the answer.

"We're gonna have to kill him," Jack said softly. "I know...I know...and I don't like it any more than you. But that's how it has to be. It needs to happen, and it needs to look like the work of Indians." He paused for a moment while his words spilled out into the canyon. "If folks think it was Indians, they'll think twice about buying this land after he's gone. I'll wait a respectable amount of time; then, I'll make an offer to the bank. They'll be happy to be rid of it, and we can finally have our own place."

Drew spoke next. "So, are you sayin' you want us to...to murder him?"

I was glad Drew asked the question so directly. Jack had always taught us there was a difference between killing and murdering. According to Jack, we killed when we had to, but we didn't murder.

Jack's eyes were flooded with steely determination as he nodded. "Yes," he said firmly. "And you both know I don't take this sort of thing lightly. I know it's asking a lot of you, but if there were any other option, I'd take it. It has to be this way. And you two are the only ones I can trust with a job like this."

My mind reeled with the weight of Jack's request. "We don't need this land, Jack," I protested. "Plenty of land out there has yet to be claimed – land we don't have to kill for. All we have to do is go find it."

Jack turned his gaze to me, hard and unfeeling. "No," he said. "This is the land. This is our claim. We do this job, and when it's done, I promise you, we will all go legit. We'll be real businessmen. No more thieving or strong-arming."

"I don't feel good about this," I confessed. "It just ain't how – This goes against everything you've taught us. You always said we weren't like other outlaws, that we don't kill needlessly. And we sure never set out to hurt innocent people."

Jack's face softened, and his eyes showed a trace of regret. "You're right, Moses," he said. "We aren't like other outlaws. But sometimes, the world forces our hand. You're a good man. But good men can't always be good because this country is designed to keep us down. We'll never get ahead playing by their rules. The deck is stacked against us. So we gotta do whatever it takes to level the playing field."

"And you want us to do that by killin' a man who hasn't wronged us?" I said. "Whatever rules are holdin' us back, they weren't made by him."

Jack was quiet for a moment. We all were. His eyes shifted from Drew to me. When he finally spoke, his voice was emotionless, almost defiant. "One more job," he said. "That's all I'm asking of you. I understand if you boys can't find it in your heart to help this gang. If you want to ride away, you can go with my blessing. But the fact is, I *will* take this land. It will be mine, and I will become an honest, respected man. I'd love to have you both by my side."

His words stirred all manner of uneasiness inside of me. Essentially, he'd burdened us with a challenge to prove our loyalty. However, he'd also given me the opportunity I'd been searching for. The ties that bound us to Smiling Jack were like cords of steel, but they had weakened over time. I knew good and well I wouldn't kill anyone for Jack Davis. I also knew that the time had come, and I had to go tonight. I'd ridden this path as far as I could, and there would be no other opportunity to turn back. If I followed through with this job, I'd be in the gang for life.

Later that evening, Drew and I stood at the edge of camp, looking out across the peaceful landscape. Jack had given us a day to decide whether or not to help him. The choice was clear. We could help, or we could leave.

"I can't do this, Drew," I said somberly. "It just ain't right. An accident is one thing, but killin' a man who –"

"I know," Drew said. He nodded, his eyes dropping to his boots. "I can't do it either, but I ain't ready to leave Jack yet."

I knew Drew loved Jack. I did, too, though perhaps not as much as Drew. He was a mentor and a father to us. "What's your plan then?" I said. "Once Jack makes up his mind, you know there ain't no changing it."

"I've been thinkin' about that," Drew said. "Tonight, after everyone's turned in or half drunk, I'm gonna sneak down to Patrick Higgins' place and warn him that Jack's comin' for him. I'll slip back into camp before morning, and no one will be the wiser. With any luck, by the time Jack is ready to move on him, Higgins will have gathered enough men to make him reconsider."

"That's not a bad plan," I said, "but why don't you let me do it? I'm not stayin' here anymore, Drew, and you don't want to leave. Let the risk fall on me. I'll warn Mr. Higgins tonight, sneak back into camp, and then tell Jack I'm leaving tomorrow morning over coffee. That way, even if I get caught, it won't come back on you."

Drew nodded and wiped at his eyes. "Thank you, Moses," he said. "I'm gonna miss you, friend. And if you ever change your mind and want to come back, I'll vouch for you."

"I'm gonna miss you too," I said. "And I appreciate you tryin' to leave the door open for me, but we both know I can't come back. Listen, if you ever need anything, you find me. And don't forget who you are. I'm talkin' about the real person you are. The one inside. Don't let Jack change what's good about you."

Drew and I rejoined the others at camp and tried to carry on like nothing was wrong. I did my best to soak up the good things about being in Jack's crew since, in a few hours, I'd be no more than a memory to them. We were a band of broken men and boys who yearned for purpose in life. Jack had offered us a reason to live, and we were all quick to accept. Soon, I'd be on my own without the friendship and protection of our crew. I was terrified, but a nagging in my spirit told me I was doing the right thing.

CHAPTER 57

It wasn't difficult to sneak away from Jack's camp that evening. Back then, we were coming and going at all times of the day and night, so my leaving didn't raise much suspicion. It was a bit of a ride back to Higgins' ranch, and a full moon was perched high above as I stood outside his home. As always, it was a peculiar type of fear, approaching a man's dwelling after nightfall in these parts. Folks who made a home for themselves in the wilderness would likely shoot first and assess the situation afterward. I couldn't blame them for it. Still, there I stood, hoping for a moment of grace before any shots were fired.

I stopped a good thirty yards from the ranch house, my voice cutting through the silence like a rusty knife. "Hello, the house," I called out. I raised my hands in peace. "Is anyone home?" The stillness of the night rang in my ears, and the distant whine of a coyote was the only answer.

After a moment that seemed to stretch far too long, the door creaked open, and the business end of a double-barreled shotgun emerged. A stern-faced Irishman wearing long johns and muddy boots was on the other end of the weapon. He said nothing, letting his shotgun reveal what was on his mind.

"Are you Patrick Higgins?" I said, striving to keep my voice steady. I kept my hands up.

"I might be," came his gruff reply in a thick Irish accent. "Who's askin'?"

"My name is Moses Colter, sir," I said. "I don't mean you no harm. I just came to warn you about some bad business comin' your way."

He grunted. "And you thought sneakin' around a man's home in the middle of the night's the way to go about it?"

I didn't move, and my palms were still showing. "No, sir, I don't. But I didn't have much choice. The folks I'm talking about – the ones who mean you harm, I'm camped nearby with them. But I aim to leave them tomorrow cause I don't agree with their ways no more. They don't know I'm here, and I didn't want to risk them finding out I came to warn you."

With the shotgun still aimed at my chest, Higgins walked down the steps and approached me. "Take the gun belt off," he said, "then toss it over to me. Nice and slow. You should know I got no problem killin'."

I believed him, so I did as he said. Higgins collected my gunbelt and, with a slight nod, lowered his shotgun. "I'll hear you out," he said. "Come on inside, and we'll talk. But if you try anything or have grand ideas about robbing me, I won't hesitate to paint these walls red."

Once inside, we settled into two surprisingly comfortable padded chairs. We sat facing each other in front of a dwindling fire. "Patrick Higgins," he introduced himself, offering his hand. I shook it and felt a wave of relief as he propped his shotgun against the wall.

"You said you're with the fellas camped at the mouth of the canyon?" he said.

I nodded, confirming his suspicion. "That's them. I believe you may have had dealings over this land with Jack Davis. He's the one leading the crew."

Higgins looked confused as he shook his head. "I don't know any Jack Davis," he said. "And it's been six months since I've talked to another soul besides the ones who live on this ranch."

So Jack had lied to Drew and me about Higgins. It was a revelation that twisted in my gut but wasn't surprising. The crux of the issue was that Jack came upon this stretch of land, wanted it, and was using us to get it for him. He'd never offered to buy it from Higgins. Jack never even met Higgins.

Over the next few minutes, I relayed the grim details of Jack's plan to overrun the ranch under the guise of an Indian attack. Higgins listened intently, trying to grasp the full measure of the threat.

"Why warn me about this?" Higgins finally asked. His gaze was sharp, and his mind focused. "You could've just ridden away without worrying about catchin' a bullet."

"I could've," I admitted, "but I don't believe in senseless killing. And I don't think any man deserves to have his land taken from him."

Higgins studied me for a moment, squinting with concentration. "Are you a good man, Moses Colter?"

The question caught me off guard. I paused, genuinely considering his inquiry. "I believe I am," I finally said. "I'm a good man, but I've made a lot of mistakes and have a load of regrets. I've done plenty I'm not proud of, but leaving Jack is my way of making amends. At least it's a start. I'm tryin' to break away and leave my old ways behind me."

Based on the subtle shift in his posture, Higgins seemed to relax a bit. "I believe you," he said, his voice softening. "And I appreciate the warning. I'll be ready for Jack Davis and his boys, should they show up, but I've got a favor to ask."

I nodded and sat up in my chair. Higgins hesitated, then spoke with a voice filled with concern. "I ain't afraid to swap lead with Davis or anyone else, but I don't want my daughter here when it all goes to hell. She's my youngest, and I can't risk her being involved. I was supposed to leave for Cheyenne with her in a few days. I'm takin' her to stay with her aunt so she can be around more civilized folks. My hope is that she'll find a proper gentleman to marry and settle down with." He paused and scratched at his chin. "I want you to take her instead. Get her to Cheyenne safely, and I'll handle Jack Davis. I can pay you a little, and I sure would appreciate your help."

A whirlwind of thoughts assailed me, not the least of which was the knowledge that Higgins had a daughter. Again, Jack had lied when he told us Higgins had lost his whole family moving west. Regardless, I didn't consider myself the right man for the job. I couldn't imagine hauling some rancher's daughter across the country while I tried to put some distance between me and Smiling Jack.

"I don't know if that's such a good idea," I began. "You hardly know me, and the territory we'd be traveling through can be dangerous. Don't you think sendin' one of your men with her would be better?"

Higgins snorted. "There ain't a man in this outfit I'd trust to guard a pile of rocks, let alone my daughter. But you're different. You're a man who knows trouble and, better yet, knows how to sidestep it. I know we don't know each other, but I trust my gut. I believe you *are* a good man, and I think you know how to use that revolver.

"Listen, you ain't got to coddle her. She knows how to ride, and she ain't afraid to work. And God as my witness; she shoots better than any man I got. Get her out of here and make sure she gets to Cheyenne safely. I ain't got much, but I'd owe you for your help."

Against my better judgment, I found myself nodding. Higgins gave a slight smile and called out for his daughter. "Elise, get in here. I got somebody I want you to meet."

From the dark, creaky hallway, Elise Higgins stepped into the warm light of the flickering fire. With light brown hair and pale blue eyes, she was a vision of strength and beauty. She smiled politely, and it nearly took my breath away. As our eyes met, my heart raced, and I quickly stood, removing my hat. I became acutely aware of how dirty and trail-worn I must look at that moment. Little did I know then that this captivating young woman would one day become my wife.

"You sure about this one, Pa?" Elise said. I could see the skepticism in her gaze. "You sure this fella can handle himself? He don't look like much." The mischievous glint in her eyes told me her comment was possibly made in jest rather than contempt. I wasn't entirely sure.

Despite the sting of her words, I couldn't help but admire her spirit. And it was the truth – I didn't look like much.

CHAPTER 58

Patrick Higgins had one of his men take Elise half a day's ride down river from the canyon. I was to speak with Smiling Jack, leave the crew that day, and make my way to Elise. As promised, I'd deliver her to her aunt's home in Cheyenne. The more I thought it through, the more foolish I felt for agreeing to such an arrangement. It wasn't safe. Not only were there general threats the trail offered, but there was also Jack to consider. I couldn't put it past him to send someone after me. He'd made it clear he had no problem eliminating anyone he considered a threat. I had resigned myself to taking such a risk, but involving an innocent young woman seemed reckless. Still, I couldn't leave her behind with the threat of an all-out gunfight brewing.

I pushed those thoughts aside. What was done was done, and I had a battle of my own to face with Jack. I had to confront Jack man to man and let him know I was leaving. The thought made me sick to my stomach. Jack had saved my life more than a few times, including when he found me lost and alone at seventeen. Jack brought me into his makeshift family, and that wasn't something I took lightly.

The morning was warm, and I was up just before sunrise. I found Jack sitting alone by the fire, holding a cup of coffee in one hand and stoking the flames with the other. The scent of sagebrush was heavy, and the distant murmur of the nearby river echoed faintly in the distance. I sat down, and Jack poured me a cup of coffee, passing it over without a word. We sat silently, and I knew Jack was waiting for me to speak. I took a deep breath and steeled myself for the dreaded conversation.

"Jack," I began, my voice strong and sure despite the turmoil inside me. "There's something I need to talk to you about."

Jack turned to me, his eyes narrowing. "I figured as much," he said as he sipped his coffee. Neither his face nor the tone of his voice revealed his thoughts. "Tell me what's on your mind, Moses."

I paused momentarily, gathering my thoughts and searching for the right words. "I've been thinkin' a lot lately about my future and what I want out of life – at least whatever's left of it."

Jack's forehead was heavily lined, and his voice was low and guarded when he spoke. "And what is it you're wantin' out of life, Moses? What is it that's gonna make life all clear skies and whiskey for you?"

"I want out, Jack," I said. The words spilled out. "I want to leave the gang and start fresh somewhere else. I don't want this life no more."

There was silence between us for a moment, with only the soft rustle of wind through the brush. To my surprise, Jack released a low, rumbling laugh. Unforeseen as it was, the sound of his laughter sent a chill down my spine. "You can't be serious, Moses," he said, his voice tinged with disbelief. "You've been with me for years – since you were only a boy. I thought we were family."

I nodded, hardening my resolve with each passing moment. "I know, Jack," I said. "And I'm almighty grateful for everything you've ever done for me. But I can't keep livin' like this. I want something different. I need more out of life than robbing folks and running from the law."

"Listen," Jack said, "if this is about what I asked you to do yesterday, forget about it. I'll find another way to take care of Higgins, or I'll have one of the other men take care of it. You don't have to leave us over it."

"It ain't about that," I said. "Well, it *is* about that, but there's more to it. Things have changed, Jack. You've changed. The fact you'd even think about killin' a man for his land is something I can't live with."

Jack's gaze narrowed again, and a flash of anger filled his eyes. "So you think you're better than us, is that it? You believe you're different than any other lost soul here? Different than me?" He shook his head. "You ain't no different. You're an outlaw like the rest of us. As much as you might dream otherwise, you can't change who you are. You're one of us, but now you think you can just walk away and leave us all behind."

"You're making this something it don't have to be," I said. "I ain't better than any man here, but it's time to find my own way. I'm leavin', but I'd rather not go with bad blood between us."

I'm not sure Jack heard me; his anger grew with each word I spoke. "You're making a mistake, Moses," he said, his voice rising with each word.

"Mark my words, one day you'll regret this. You've been like a – hell, you *are* a son to me. I've protected you, taught you how to shoot and ride, and how to survive. I am not so delusional to think that I've been the best role model a boy could have, but I kept you safe. I kept you alive, and I kept you fed and out of jail. And this is how you choose to repay me? You wanna leave me right when things are about to change for the better? Right when I need you the most, you're abandoning me? Abandoning all of us?"

Jack's words cut me to the core, but I stood my ground. My mind was made up, and his slippery words wouldn't change my decision. "I'm going, Jack," I said. "I know what you've done for me, and in return, I've been nothin' but loyal to you. I think you know that. But it's time for me to go, and I ain't changing my mind."

Jack sat there unbearably quiet, staring out across the terrain as the morning sun cracked the horizon. He glanced at me and held my gaze for a moment. Then, his expression softened, and I saw his anger give way to resignation. Smiling Jack Davis was accustomed to pushing for what he wanted, and he usually got it. But he was also savvy enough to know when he was fighting a losing battle.

"If that's how you feel, Moses," he said, his voice heavy with disappointment, "I suppose there's nothing more for us to say. You can go. I won't stop you, but you sure as hell ain't leaving with my blessing. So, know this – if you walk away now, don't bother coming back. As soon as you leave this camp, you might as well be dead to me. And don't expect your pal Drew to come looking for you, either. At least one of you is still loyal."

Despite my newfound freedom, I felt a pang of sadness at Jack's words. I didn't want to hurt him or anger him. I only wanted out of the life he offered. "I understand, Jack," I said, barely above a whisper. "And, for what it's worth, I'm sorry."

With that, I stood up, nodded to Jack, and walked away, leaving behind the closest thing to a real family I'd ever had. As I rode out of camp, I couldn't help but feel a mix of relief and sorrow. It's one thing to understand what's best for you, it's another thing to do it.

One of the other fellas was on guard, and as I passed him, I asked if he knew where I could find Drew. He told me Jack had sent Drew off long before sunrise to take care of some business, but his words didn't register with me. My only thought was that I had to leave without saying goodbye. I knew Drew would understand, but it still didn't feel right. And regardless of what Jack said, I firmly believed Drew and I would see each other again. But for now, a young woman named Elise was waiting for me to escort her to Wyoming. There'd be time enough later for reminiscing and feeling sorry for myself. Now, there was a job to be done. And, for my own sake and the safety of that pretty young woman, I needed to keep a sharp mind, free from distractions.

CHAPTER 59

The trek back to my modest stretch of Montana land was nearly over. A week's travel was all that separated us from the place I called home. A washed-out canvas of gray, billowy clouds loomed overhead. Their weight pressed down on us with the threat of impending winter. The landscape, typically alive with beauty, now bore the muted tones of the changing season.

It was comforting to be back in familiar territory, but my heart was heavy despite the closeness of home. Word had reached us that Smiling Jack had taken over my ranch, likely with the aid of Harold Gullet and Logan Ashbourne. The prospect of reclaiming my property from such stubborn, cunning men was dispiriting. Not to mention the creeping chill in the air signaling that the first storm of the season would soon be upon us. Time was not on our side.

In the last few days, a recent development had emerged – a lone rider had been tracking our progress from a distance. Spotted first by Two Feathers, the man had been a constant shadow on the horizon, following at a safe distance and keeping out of sight. His intentions remained a mystery, but he'd made no threatening move against us. He only watched. I decided to leave him be for now, but I asked Two Feathers, Fisher, and Tate to keep a constant watch. Sooner or later, he'd make himself known.

As evening fell, our camp began to take shape. Despite our exhaustion, there was a palpable sense of tense hopefulness. Around the fire, Drew, Titus, Charity, and I exchanged the same stories we had told countless times over the past few months – tales that offered us a brief escape from our worries.

As was her way, Charity was as curious as ever about my past with Elise – how we met, our courtship, the dreams we shared. Speaking of Elise brought a sweet ache to my chest, reminding me of the void her passing had left behind. Yet, in those moments, sharing the memories of our lives, I felt her presence. Those brief instances of closeness brought me joy as well as pain, but I found that talking about Elise had become easier as the trail stretched on. Charity was to thank for that. Or, perhaps Charity was to blame for that. My stance changed daily, depending on how high or low my spirits were at the time.

That particular evening, Two Feathers interrupted our reminiscing, letting us know that the lone rider he'd been watching was approaching. As soon as the man's horse was in sight, I knew it was Gregory Sutton. He was bold and unflinching, seated atop his sturdy blue roan. I first met Sutton in Virginia City when he tracked down Drew for Smiling Jack. He was as handsome and confident as I remembered, with the same deadly air of simmering violence. He pulled up and greeted us with a grin, his demeanor calm yet assured. His weapons, a tied-down revolver and a brand new Sharps rifle, spoke to his readiness for whatever may happen next.

"Hello, Mr. Colter," he said as he climbed from his horse. "It's good to see you again."

Drew spoke before I did, remarking on the rifle. It was a piece that hadn't escaped our notice. An 1874 Sharps was a weapon made for long-range shooting. "Nice rifle you got there," Drew said. "You ain't been pointin' that thing at us, have you?" Drew wanted Sutton to know we were aware he'd been following us.

Sutton's chuckle was easy, and his response friendly-like. "Nah," he replied, glancing back at the rifle on his horse. "Contrary to what you may have heard about me, I don't enjoy shootin' folks. Personally, I'd rather risk talkin' things out than drawin' iron. Most folks tend to keep breathing that way."

"I'm glad we agree," I said. "But I'm sure you didn't come all this way to share your philosophy on how to help folks live longer. What can we do for you, Sutton?"

Sutton smiled and nodded. "I forgot you was a smart one, Mr. Colter," he said. "I'm here on behalf of Smiling Jack. He wants to...engage in dialogue with you to see if we can all come to some sort of agreement."

It sounded like Jack wanted to handle this without anybody getting hurt. Either some small part of him still cared for Drew and me, or he was leery of facing us. We did have over fifty able-bodied men. That fact alone would intimidate most folks. However, the men with us weren't fighters.

They were willing to defend themselves, but not men to be feared. Maybe Jack wasn't aware of that.

Regardless, my stance was firm, and my demands were simple. "The only agreement I'm interested in is Jack Davis keeping his word," I said. "If he's not willing to be a man, take the payment we owe him, and leave my land, then there ain't much talkin' needs to be done."

Sutton's demeanor shifted. His smile faded, and his gaze turned ice cold. "Well, I certainly hope you'll reconsider," Sutton said. "Jack wants to meet with you at Ruby River first thing tomorrow. He said you'd know the place. I believe he referred to it as the gathering ground."

"We know it, alright," Drew said, his voice laced with bitterness. "The gathering ground is where we'd meet to figure out how to cheat folks out of their belongings. Seems fittin', don't it?"

Sutton apparently wasn't interested in talking any longer. He climbed back onto his horse, and his parting words were more of a warning than anything else. "If I were you, I'd show up. Let's keep this thing from gettin' messy. None of us wants any more trouble." With that, Sutton nudged his horse and vanished into the fading light of the evening.

Drew and I relayed Sutton's message to the others, and the camp was divided on how to approach this so-called negotiation. "It's a trap," Skillet said, his words echoing the sentiments of many of us. "You can't expect to walk in there and talk sense to a hungry serpent. It just won't work. I say we go in with a smile, shoot 'em all, and take your land back."

Two Feathers nodded, and I was confident he'd be the first to volunteer for such a mission. Drew eagerly agreed as well, but I knew he was more caught up in the moment than wanting a fight. Nellie didn't offer a say either way, and her face didn't betray her desire to stay neutral. Nellie was smart. She was probably thinking through all the angles, looking for one that gave us some type of advantage.

Titus offered a different perspective that resonated with the part of me still clinging to the possibility of peace. "You should meet with him," he said. "Go talk it out, but be smart. Don't go alone. Mr. Skillet's right. It could be a trap. But if we can get outta this without folks dyin', we should try."

When all was said and done, we decided that Drew, Two Feathers, and I would face Smiling Jack at the gathering grounds. It still wasn't clear how Logan Ashbourne and Harold Gullet played into all of this, but I expected they'd likely be there as well. I was scared, but mostly, I was grieved by the whole matter. I never wanted things to come to this, and I surely didn't want to get into a shootout with Smiling Jack.

That night, as I lay beneath the vast Montana sky, my thoughts were not of the impending confrontation, but of Elise. I wondered about her resting place in the city, hoping it had been properly tended to in my absence. I wondered what advice she might offer were she here. I knew she'd love what Drew and I had done, moving all these folks across the country and tryin' to make them a home. And I wondered about the possibility of her looking down on us now. If God saw fit that I shouldn't get through this, I took comfort in the thought that she and I would soon be reunited. I longed to talk to her about all these things and hear her say she was proud of me. And though my mind should have been fixed on tomorrow's dangers, my thoughts of Elise soothed me to sleep.

CHAPTER 60

As the first light of dawn washed over the banks of the Ruby River, Drew, Two Feathers, and I approached the so-called gathering ground. It was a quiet spot, free from prying eyes. Many of our past schemes had been hashed out here, but now it was the backdrop for a confrontation that had been brewing for years. Waiting for us, as if they were part of the landscape itself, was Jack Davis, flanked by Harold Gullet and Logan Ashbourne. Sutton wasn't there, but I knew he was close. I'd be willing to bet he was hidden up in the hills with me in the crosshairs of that Sharps rifle.

We dismounted, and I led our small group forward. Harold Gullet's face was hard and unreadable, his eyes cold and distant. Logan Ashbourne, however, wore a grin full of contempt. And then there was Jack, who greeted us with a smile that seemed far too genuine for the man I knew him to be.

"I'm thrilled you boys decided to come talk things out," Jack began, his voice as smooth as satin on polished glass. "You may feel different, but regardless, I'm happy to see you both. Let's not forget, we were all close once."

"Indeed we were," I replied, unable to conceal the bitterness in my voice. "But it looks like you've found some new friends."

Logan couldn't resist adding his poisonous words to the conversation. "Oh, come now, Moses," he said. "I have to say, I'm a little hurt. Aren't you happy to see your big brother?"

"Why are you even here, Ashbourne," Drew said. "Didn't you get enough of a whippin' back in Tennessee? You here lookin' for a second helping?"

Ashbourne sneered at Drew. "I could ask you the same thing, you motherless piece of –"

"Alright, fellas," Jack intervened. "We all have pasts we'd rather not revisit. Now's not the time anyway. Now is the time for startin' fresh. We're all respectable men here. I'm sure we can reach an agreement."

I decided to cut to the chase. "Here's the agreement," I said firmly. "Give me the deed to my land back and clear out, and I'll give you the money we owe you." I glared at Logan and Gullet. "Then you and your pals can go find someone else to cheat."

For an instant, Jack's mask of civility slipped, and I saw the man beneath – a mean, vindictive scoundrel. "I'm afraid that's not going to happen," he said, regaining his composure. "You see, my new friend here, Mr. Ashbourne, has opened my mind to the underutilized power of our American justice system. I have learned that, with enough cash and persuasion, you can uncover a variety of loopholes and ambiguities in your typical land deeds. And if a man is fortunate enough to have possession of the original deed, as I do, well...anything's possible." He paused. "The bottom line is it's all legal, boys. The land is mine."

Drew's anger spilled out. "You never planned on keepin' your word, did you? This was your angle all along. You wanted Moses' land."

"That's mostly right," he admitted. "I did intend to break my word all along, but the land was a pleasant surprise. When Moses stepped up for you and handed over the deed, I knew the Lord had placed a blessing in my lap. And who am I to refuse a gift from above?"

"Why are you doing this, Jack?" I said, my voice tight with concern. "We have history. We rode together for a long time. I have your money. Just take it, and let's all move on. We don't have to do this."

Jack's response was cold and filled with hurt. "We do have history," he said in a low voice. "That's something I've never forgotten. It's the only reason you're both still breathing. Even when you left, I let you go. I didn't come after you. I didn't go out of my way to hurt you or make your life hell. Unfortunately, you can't say the same."

"You're gonna have to be more specific, Jack," I said. "I haven't even laid eyes on you but twice now in nearly ten years."

"And why is that, Moses?" he snapped.

"Because you told me I wasn't welcome back," I said. "And besides, you've been locked up."

Jack's next words were like a punch to the gut. "You sold me out, Moses. Don't insult me by acting like nothing happened. You know what you did. You went and told Patrick Higgins I was plannin' on killing him and taking his land. Then, you took off with his daughter, leaving us all high and dry. A couple of days later, I went down to talk to Higgins – to make him another offer. He opened fire on me, and I shot back. The bullet had no sooner struck him when the law showed up. I ran and managed to get away, but they hunted me for six months. Finally, they caught up to me, and I went to prison. I never sold any of you boys out. I could have, but I didn't. I took all the blame. I went to prison because of your betrayal."

"We all make our own decisions in life, Jack," I said. "You went to prison because you spent your whole life robbin' and killin' innocent folks. And for years, you tricked us into helping you. I wised up and took off, and you got what you deserved."

"Maybe so," Jack conceded, "but that don't give you the right to stand here and act like you haven't done the same. Let's not forget that's why I took you in to begin with. You killed a man at seventeen years old. And to be clear, no one ever tricked Moses Colter into anything. You've always found a way to get what you wanted, regardless of who you had to hurt to do so."

"It ain't like that, Jack," I said. "You know that. I was lookin' out for folks, that's all. And you sure can't blame me for what happened to you."

Smiling Jack laughed with exasperation as he glanced at Logan and Harold. "It just seems to me that trouble follows you wherever you go," he said, refusing to yield. "It wasn't enough for you to ruin my life. A few years later, you decided to wreck Ashbourne's as well. You stole his workers, destroyed his livelihood, and nearly killed him when he gave chase. You're a selfish man, Moses. And it's time someone taught you a lesson."

"And you think you're the man for the job?" I said.

Jack nodded. "Me and Ashbourne both," he said. "We both took you in when you were at your lowest. We provided for you – gave you a chance in life. And how did you repay us? You tried to ruin us. So now we're gonna ruin you."

"Good luck with that, Jack," I said. "That kind of talk don't scare me much. I was ruined a long time ago."

There was a brief pause; then Logan chimed in. "You tried your best, Jack," he said flatly. "There's just no reasoning with such lowlifes. We've tried for years, and they both keep showing up like stray dogs, begging for scraps. And when you feed them, they bite you. No matter how many times you kick 'em away, they always come back. The only thing to do with dogs like that is put them down."

"I think we've all heard enough," I said, my gaze locked on Jack. "You've made your intentions clear, so allow me to do the same. We will take the land back. And it appears it can't happen peacefully, so we'll just be on our way now. We'll see you soon enough."

Drew, ever the optimist, made one last appeal. "Come on, Jack," he pleaded. "You were a father to me. I know you don't want this."

Jack seemed torn, but Gullet interrupted before he could reply. "I can't wait to get on with this and finally shut that mouth of yours for good."

"You might want to reconsider that plan," Drew shot back. "You ain't what you used to be, Gullet. Seems to me you'd do better to turn tail and run. Take Ashbourne with you. Leave the fightin' to the younger, more able-bodied men."

Logan scoffed at Drew's words. "Able-bodied? You mean those darkies you got with you? Half of them ain't never even fired a rifle."

Jack intervened once again. "I hate it had to come to this, boys," he said. "I truly do. But it looks like this meeting is over."

As we turned to leave, Jack's voice followed us. "It's not too late to change your mind," he said. "Pack up your camp, ride away, and I'll let you go."

Smiling Jack's words hung in the air like smoke from a dying campfire and carried about as much purpose. As we rode away from the gathering ground, I knew running wouldn't be an option. The wheels were turning, and the only path forward was directly through Logan Ashbourne and Smiling Jack.

"I don't like those men," Two Feathers said, offering his only thoughts on the matter.

CHAPTER 61

The unease around camp that night was as palpable as the chill in the air. The quiet was unnerving as the sun sank beneath the horizon, and the flickering firelight cast shadows on the tired faces of my friends. We were a determined yet realistic bunch, and we knew our options were few. But I couldn't have asked for a better group of men and women to trust. Drew, Skillet, Nellie, Two Feathers, Fisher, Tate, Titus, Charity, and I gathered in a tight circle, trying to decide the immediate fate of our band of outcasts.

Fisher was the first to speak, recounting what he and Tate saw while scouting my ranch earlier that day. "There's a dozen of 'em, at least. Big, rough-lookin' fellas. Sho' didn't look the type to shy away from a fight."

Tate nodded. "We got the numbers on 'em, but they got the knowhow. Plus, if they shoot as mean as they look, we in trouble. Goin' in there on 'em won't be easy."

Charity, who'd ventured into Virginia City earlier that day, had more unsettling news to offer. "I heard talk in town," she said, keeping her voice low. "The menfolk said there's at least two dozen more comin'. They said Smilin' Jack would have 'em here by the end of the week."

It was as if a heavy, collective sigh came from our group. "We can't fight men like that," Fisher said. "There's too many of 'em. Our folks is soft when it comes to fightin' and killin'."

Tate agreed. "If what ma heard is true, we ain't no match for that. They might as well be an army. We go chargin' in there, and they'll swat us away like grasshoppers."

"What do you think, Moses?" Nellie added. "Should we take it to them or start lookin' for another place to settle? I'm sure there's land out there we could –"

Drew slammed his fist into his palm, his frustration boiling over. "Are we seriously sittin' here talking about whether or not to give up? We can't just run away like a bunch of chicken-hearted cowards. I don't know about the rest of you, but that ain't me."

Some dropped their heads in shame, but Drew's words stirred me. "Drew's right," I said firmly. "Runnin' ain't in my nature. Not no more. Every man and woman here is free to do as they see fit, and I ain't gonna judge nobody for it, but I ain't running. I'm staying and fighting with Drew, even if we have to do it alone."

Titus spoke next, standing as he cleared his throat. He battled with unspoken misgivings that had him shaken, but he stood there as solid as ever. "It feels like I've spent most of my life decidin' whether to run or hide from devils," Titus said. Though he fought back tears, his voice remained strong and steady. "I've made my share of mistakes. There was times I likely shoulda' run but didn't. And then there was times I regret not standin' up and fightin' back." He paused. "But this here is different. We all know it. We got each other. We in it together, and, live or die, this devil's worth fightin'. I don't believe the good Lord brought us all the way here to turn His back on us.

"You ain't gonna be alone, Moses. You either, Drew. I'll fight with you, and I'll make sure every man we got is standin' with us. This here is our land now. It's our home. The Lord went through a heap of trouble to give it to us. I'll be damned if we let it go without a fight." Titus glanced at Nellie and Charity. "Pardon the language, ladies."

When he finished, Titus sat down and returned to sipping his coffee. It was as if he had no realization of the fiery resolve his words ignited within us. The air itself changed. A fresh breeze of hope comforted our spirits, and fear gave way to determination. Skillet slapped his hand against his knee and cracked a rare smile. "I can get rifles for anybody who needs 'em. If we're goin' out, we'll go out shootin'. How 'bout you, Two Feathers? You in?" Skillet said. "You've saved our bacon plenty of times, but we all know this ain't your fight. If you want to walk away now, we'll wish you well, but we sure could use your help."

Two Feathers stared at the fire momentarily before returning Skillet's gaze. "Those men know only greed. They choose fighting over peace. I choose standing with you. Those men do not scare me."

The decision was made then and there. We would take back my ranch or die trying. We agreed to move at sunrise before Smiling Jack's reinforcements showed up and tipped the scales in his and Ashbourne's favor.

Despite their protests, Nellie and Skillet were responsible for moving the women and children as far away from the action as possible.

"No," Nellie said, her fierce spirit undeterred by the gravity of our situation. "We want to fight. Skillet spent more time on the battlefield than all of us put together. And don't you dare say anything about me bein' a woman. I can outshoot most men I know, present company included. Skillet and I are strong, and we want to fight."

"You will fight," I attempted to assure her. "You're gonna fight to keep these families safe. I know you both want to be out there with us, but this is a job I need my best folks on." I glanced from Nellie to Skillet. "I trust you both more than you know. And if anyone tracks this wagon train down while we're away, I need fighters to stand against them. These folks need you here more than I need you out there. Help me with this. Please."

They didn't like it, but Skillet and Nellie knew there was truth in my words. With heaviness in their hearts and grumbling on their lips, they ultimately agreed.

I grabbed a stick and began drawing up plans in the dirt. We all chimed in, debated, discussed, and revised until reaching a consensus. Two Feathers, Fisher, and Tate, would lead a contingent to flank the ranch from the east, using the cover of the terrain to their advantage. I knew Two Feathers could get close without being seen, and I had no doubt he was itching to set things right. Drew and Titus would take a smaller group to create a diversion. They'd ride right up to the front gate, hopefully drawing attention rather than gunfire. With the eyes of Smiling Jack's men fixed on Drew, I would attack from the west with a dozen or so men. At the same time, Two Feathers' crew would move in from the east. If all went well, we'd have them surrounded. They'd have to decide whether to surrender or go out shooting. At this point, either way was fine with me.

As our campfire burned down to embers and the stars filled the sky, we decided we'd done all we could do. For better or worse, our fates would be decided by the end of the day tomorrow. We'd either settle into our new home or get lowered into the dirt.

We parted ways that night with somber faces, each of us lost in our racing thoughts. Our minds swirled with images of the looming battle and the reality that some of us probably wouldn't make it out alive. Still, we were united in purpose, bound by a common thread of faith. Despite being pensive, we were firm in our conviction.

As I laid down, I prayed that night – something I'm ashamed to say didn't happen often enough. I prayed for safety and protection, for strong will, and true aim. I prayed the Lord would see us through this ordeal and that the men and women under my care would finally be safe. Surprisingly enough, I also prayed for Logan Ashbourne and Smiling Jack Davis. Regardless of all that had happened, I didn't hate the men, even though they seemed to have no lack of hatred for me. I prayed the Lord would siphon that bitterness from their hearts and that they'd finally be free from whatever hold their greed and anger had on them. Truth be told, I had my doubts about whether it was even possible. But, after all I'd witnessed the past few weeks, I supposed anything was possible.

The night passed slowly. Like most of the men in camp, I was restless and anxious, but I knew we'd be up and moving well before sunrise. At some point, I managed to drift off, but I didn't dream of gunshots, powder smoke, living or dying. I dreamed of Elise.

CHAPTER 62

E ven in my dreams, seeing Elise's smile brought me happiness. Elise Higgins was certainly attractive – pretty enough that I deliberately kept my distance and spoke very little to her initially. I constantly reminded myself that my role was simply to escort this young woman to her aunt, nothing more. God willing, I'd get her there safely and then figure out what to do with the rest of my life. Part of me knew it was only a dream and that Elise wasn't actually with me, but I didn't want it to end. Whether real or imagined, I found comfort in spending time with her.

My dream took me back to when Elise and I had been on the trail for over a week, leaving her father's ranch behind. The journey was arduous and slow. We wound through rugged terrain and kept watch for the Sioux, always doing our best to cover our tracks. I knew our efforts to stay hidden were likely futile – if the Sioux were determined to find us, they would. However, I had no intention of making it easier for them. If they tracked us down, I wanted them to work for it. Thankfully, there had been no signs of Indians or any indication that Smiling Jack and his crew were following us. With some luck, we might make it to Wyoming without incident.

Elise did most of the talking along the way, filling the silence with stories of her life. She spoke of growing up in Boston, with its bustling streets, fine foods, and culture, the dinner parties she used to attend, and the life she left behind. She also spoke of how her mother had died a couple of years earlier and how her father had grown restless living in the city. I listened, riding alongside her, offering the occasional nod or grunt to show I was paying attention. Mostly, I kept my thoughts to myself. A cultured woman like Elise would have no interest in the thoughts of a wandering degenerate.

"Why do you keep so quiet, Moses?" Elise finally asked one afternoon as we neared Fort Laramie. "Don't you think the time would go quicker if you spoke up a bit more?"

I shrugged, annoyed that I was uncomfortable being under her gaze. "I guess I ain't much for talkin'," I said. "Never have been, really."

Elise laughed a little, but more in a teasing way than a mocking one. "Well, you'll have to learn to hold a conversation if you ever hope to find a wife. Women don't much care for a man who can't speak his mind."

I couldn't help but bristle at the comment. "Maybe not women back east, but we ain't in Boston. Besides, I don't recall sayin' I was lookin' for a wife." My words came out more forcefully than I intended. "And I ain't even sure why you care. It ain't like we'd ever be courting one another."

Elise's own defensiveness rose up in her response. "By the look of things, I'd say you don't have to concern yourself with such thoughts," she said. She paused, huffing for a moment and looking for the right words. "And just what's wrong with me anyway? I can't see why a man such as yourself wouldn't be interested in courting a girl like me." She paused again, but I chose not to respond. "Not that it matters much. Before long, I'll be living in Cheyenne with good old Aunt Hilda."

On several occasions, Elise had made it clear she held little affection for her Aunt Hilda, describing her as wretched and overbearing. "The only reason I'm going to Wyoming in the first place is because my father practically forced me," she went on. "But it *is* a city, at least. I plan on finding a nice man to settle down with so I can move out of Aunt Hilda's home as quickly as possible." She glanced at me. "I'll find a man soon enough, you know. A good man. One who understands the importance of good conversation."

I kept my eyes on the trail. "Good luck with that."

"And what about you?" she went on, undeterred. "What do you plan on doing after you've fulfilled your noble duty? If what my father said is true, I don't suspect you'll be running back to your old friends."

"I'm not sure yet," I said. "I heard there's land for sale not far from here near Virginia City. It might be worth lookin' into."

She perked up at that. "Virginia City? Hunting gold, are you?"

"No," I replied firmly. "Gold ain't for me. As far as I'm concerned, huntin' gold ain't no different than huntin' trouble. I'm done with trouble. The only thing I'm huntin' now is a peaceful life."

That seemed to resonate with Elise, and a smile touched her lips for a moment. Or perhaps she was simply satisfied with herself for getting more than a handful of words out of me.

Our time at Fort Laramie was brief and brought grim news. Elise learned that her father had been shot and killed by a group of outlaws trying to take his land – my group of outlaws. In the days that followed, the brightness that had once filled her voice was replaced by a silence that weighed heavily between us. Elise never cried in front of me, but I was familiar enough with hardship to know that tears don't always accompany grief. Still, at night, when all was calm and we'd settled in to rest, I could hear her quiet sniffles and knew she was hurting.

The days that followed were somber. Our talks were strained and infrequent as Elise wrestled with her loss. Yet, in those quiet moments, a bond slowly formed between us. We shared the hardships of the trail and an unspoken understanding of one another's pain.

As we continued to Wyoming, I found myself opening up more. I shared bits and pieces of my life and my dream of having a home far from the turmoil and violence that had dogged me for so many years. Before long, Elise, in her resilience and strength, began to come around. She shared her dreams of the future and how much she longed to have a family of her own.

By the time we reached Cheyenne, our thoughts toward one another had changed. We were no longer people who tolerated each other's company. We were companions, fellow travelers, and friends who shared their sorrows and dreams.

As we rode into Cheyenne, I asked her where her aunt lived because I intended to deliver her right to the front door. To my surprise, Elise didn't answer right away, and when I glanced at her, I saw those big blue eyes welling up with tears. "Moses, I can't stay here," she said, her voice cracking. "I don't want to be in this city, and I don't want to live with such a despicable old woman."

"Elise, I promised your pa that I'd –"

"Well, my father is dead," she said flatly. "I don't reckon he cares too much about whether or not you fulfill your obligation."

"I can't just leave you here," I said. "You already told me you don't have any other family and nowhere to go. What will you do?"

Elise's eyes darted frantically as she searched for an answer. "I'll go with you," she finally said. "I'll go with you to Virginia City, and we'll buy a ranch, raise sheep or something, and live there in peace."

I shook my head. "Elise, talk like that ain't proper for a lady such as yourself. We can't move into a place together. It ain't how respectable women live."

"Then we'll get married," she said, staring straight into my eyes. "Everything will be nice and proper for you, and you won't have to be concerned with my honor."

I was shocked to hear a woman speak in such a manner, but then again, I hadn't spent much time talking to women. Maybe this was how all of them spoke.

"You don't wanna marry someone like me."

"Why not?" she said with a spark in her eyes. "You're as good as any other man – better than most I've met. Do you believe in God?"

I didn't know how to answer, so I went with the first thing that came into my head. "I suppose so," I said. "At least...I suppose it's just as likely he's up there as he's not."

"That's exactly what an honest man would say," she added. "I feel good about this, Moses. This can work for us."

"I don't know, Elise, I just –"

"What's not to know?" she said. "I'm a good woman. I work hard. I tell the truth. And I have no problem cooking, cleaning, or raising children. And not to be too forward, but I ain't so bad to look at either, Moses Colter. Unless you think you could do better."

She stood there staring at me, and I couldn't help but chuckle. "You are something else, Elise Higgins," I said. Her assertive nature intimidated me, but I had to admit she made some fair points. "I'll tell you what," I went on. "I won't leave you here if you don't wanna be left. You can ride with me to scout out some land around Virginia City, and we'll talk about all this marriage business later."

She grinned. "You've got yourself a deal." And with that, Elise spun her horse around, put her heels to him, and left Cheyenne, Wyoming behind her.

Chapter 63

The early morning air was sharp, carrying the bite of an approaching winter. We gathered quietly under the predawn stars, with the gravity of our mission now a reality. All told, Titus had managed to muster forty-eight souls to our cause. Strong and willing, they were men with years of pent-up anger, tired of bowing to the abuse of others. They gathered in a tight bunch, awaiting instruction, their smoky breath visible in the air.

As expected, Skillet delivered on his promise. Rifles, no doubt procured under questionable circumstances, were placed into shaky hands. I didn't ask questions because I'd learned to trust Skillet. He could be an ornery old cuss, but he never failed to find whatever we needed. The men clutched their weapons, some with novice awkwardness and others with cold determination. We were not soldiers. We were men driven to action, willing to stand on the edge of life and death to do what's right.

Though we'd been up for a while, it was still dark and cold as we moved out. There weren't near enough horses for everyone, and we didn't want to take mules away from the wagons. Drew, Two Feathers, and I were mounted while the others joined us on foot. It was a somber procession with little to no interaction. We moved like a company of ghosts across the valley with only the sound of scraping and shuffling feet and hooves against cold earth.

As the first light of dawn painted the sky purple and orange, we halted our march a good quarter mile from the ranch. The land lay quiet, deceptively peaceful, and a bit too still for my liking. No birds sang, no critters scrambled around in the brush, and no wind blew.

The men from Ivywood were scared. They stood there wide-eyed and shivering, but despite their fear, there was a hunger in their eyes. Looking at them staring up at me with stern, fearful faces, I knew they'd fight until their last breath. The lives and futures of those they loved depended upon it.

"The plan is still the plan," I said in a low voice. The men drew in tighter, their faces barely visible in the struggling sunlight. "Divide into your groups."

Two Feathers, alongside Fisher and Tate, had selected the most agile men to circle the perimeter unseen and sneak into the ranch from the east.

With his typical bravado, Drew took command of those willing to confront the danger head-on. He'd selected the largest, most intimidating men of the bunch. "We'll draw some eyes for you," he said, clapping one of the bigger men on the shoulder. His crew nodded with steely eyes and gripped their rifles tight.

I was with Titus, accompanied by our best marksmen. "We strike all together," I said. "Be patient. Don't get antsy and make a mistake. Sit tight until Drew, Two Feathers, or I take the first shot like we planned. No matter who takes it, us or them, as soon as you hear a shot, we all rush the place at once."

A murmur of agreement passed through the group of men. It was a fleeting moment of peaceful unity amidst the fear and impending chaos.

"We're with you, Moses," Titus said as he glanced around the circle of men. "All of us. Ain't one of us that don't appreciate what all you and Drew done for us. We'll be with you to the end."

"No man should have to live in fear," I replied. "You all deserve this as much as anyone. You've worked for it, and you've earned it. No matter how it all plays out, we do this together."

"Together," Drew addressed the men with a smirk. "Old Jack's boys won't know what hit 'em. Now, as much as I appreciate this demonstration of brotherly love, it's all a bit melancholy for my taste. This here's a gunfight, boys, not a funeral. Let's get down there and get this over with. Then we can have a proper celebration in our new home. Drinks on me tonight, fellas."

The men grinned and chuckled, grateful for a touch of levity in the moment's heaviness. As we prepared to move out, Cali's head rose quickly, and her ears perked up. She and I noticed it at the same time. My attention snapped to a sudden glint of light on the hillside to our west. I recognized it immediately – sunlight reflecting off metal. A surge of dread washed through my veins like ice water.

"Sniper!" I barely had time to call out a warning before it happened.

The shot cracked through the silence of the morning, rolling across the hills like a clap of thunder. Pain erupted in my gut, an intense, searing shock. I was thrown from Cali before I knew what was happening. The ground rushed up to meet me, and I landed hard on my back.

The air was knocked from my lungs, and a spreading warmth began to soak into my shirt. My vision narrowed, and my breath was ragged and labored. For a moment, everything around me seemed distant and hollow. The shouts of men, the scrambling of boots, the whinnying of horses, and Drew calling my name as if he were miles away.

Through a hazy blur of pain, I watched our men scatter, heading for the trees. Their initial formations were thrown into chaos by the sniper's bullet. As I was all too aware, the best-laid plans, no matter how ironclad, could unravel with frightening speed. These men needed someone to take control, to tell them what to do. I groped at the ground, digging my fingers into the dirt, trying to push myself upright. But each movement brought a fresh wave of agony, like someone pressing a red-hot poker into my side.

Suddenly, Drew was there, his face twisted with concern as he knelt beside me. "Moses, stay down," he said. "I'll get you out of here."

"No. You gotta get moving, Drew," I gasped through my labored breath. "Don't give Jack any more time. We don't stand a chance if you don't hit him now."

Drew nodded, his expression instantly hardening. "Sit tight, brother. I'll take care of you in a minute." He turned, shouting orders and rallying the men like a battle-hardened general. Despite their fear, the men responded to his call and quickly gathered, glancing over their shoulders and breathing heavily.

"Listen to me," Drew called out. "The plan is still the plan. Get with your groups and go now. I'll get Moses to a safe place and then catch up to you.

"Fisher, Tate, you take the lead for your group. Get into position, and don't let them see you." Drew went on. "Two Feathers, it was Sutton that took the shot. I'm sure of it. Can you find him?"

Two Feathers gazed at Fisher and Tate. "You can do this alone?" he said.

Fisher and Tate nodded in unison. "We know what to do," Fisher said.

With one last glance at Drew, Two Feathers simply nodded. "I will end him," he said as he raced away, disappearing into the treeline.

The Montana ground felt like a block of ice beneath me, the only hint of warmth being the blood pooling around me. In an instant, Drew returned. "I've gotta get you up, Moses," he said. "It's gonna hurt like hell, but I gotta get you somewhere safe, and I gotta do it fast."

"Leave me here and come back when it's done," I said as I shifted around, looking for a way to ease the searing pain. "Don't waste time with me."

Drew shook his head. "Sorry, but I ain't leaving my brother on the side of the road to get shot again. Just grit your teeth and hang on."

Drew sprang into action. He ripped up some cloth from what looked like an old shirt and began wrapping it tightly around my stomach, attempting to keep my insides in their proper place. He grabbed my hand and placed it over the gunshot wound.

"Press down hard and hold it there," Drew said. "Can you ride?"

"I'll try," I answered.

A moment later, Drew lifted me from the ground and pushed me into the saddle. Cali stood perfectly still as Drew got me situated. Pain like I'd never felt before tore through my body and escaped my lips in agonizing groans. Drew moved quickly. He climbed onto Stormy and grabbed Calli's reins as I slumped over the saddle. My right hand was pressed firmly over the wound in my gut, and my left grasped onto a fistful of Cali's mane.

Each step the horses took fired a fresh jolt of burning pain through me as Drew led us up to a hillside overlooking the ranch. An unending barrage of involuntary grunts and whines flowed as freely from me as the blood trickling down my leg.

I lost consciousness for a moment. I came back around as my back thudded against the rocky earth once more.

"You're alright, Moses," Drew said. "You'll be safe here." He took the saddlebags from Cali, swatted her on the rear, and shooed her away.

I tried to speak but had difficulty getting the words out. "Drew, I – You have to –"

"Save your breath," Drew cut in. He reached into the saddlebag and pulled out my spyglass. "Take this," he said, pressing it into my hands. "You sit here and watch. Watch us take your land back. Don't think about the pain, and don't you dare die on me, Moses Colter. I'll take care of everything and then get you to a doctor."

I was surprised by the laugh that escaped my lips. "I'm afraid it's a little late for that," I said through gritted teeth. "Just take care of them."

"I will," Drew said soberly. "And it's not too late. I'll be back for you."

Drew leaped onto Stormy and whirled around to take one last look at me. "I *will* come back," he said as if trying to convince himself.

"I know," I answered weakly. "Now get outta here. The men can't do this without you."

Drew nodded stiffly and tore down the hillside, kicking up dirt and rocks behind him. I watched as he raced to catch up with his crew, and I couldn't help but think it was the last time I'd ever see Drew. I'd seen enough shooting in my time to know mine wasn't the type of wound a doctor could repair. Drew would come back for me. I didn't have a single doubt about it. Only I knew it wouldn't be the reunion he wanted.

Drew and Stormy raced out of sight, and it felt as if my soul went with them. What they left behind wasn't much more than the shell of a man clinging to life. Drew and I were family, and it grieved me that I wasn't able to help him – to be there for him like he had been for me. "I love you, brother," I whispered.

Chapter 64

I lay there propped up against a large rock, struggling to stay alive. Each breath was a strain, sending fresh waves of pain through the gaping wound in my gut. The cold Montana ground beneath me was stained with a growing pool of crimson. I did my best to keep pressure on the wound – tried to slow the steady trickle of life seeping from my veins. With each passing moment, I felt the icy grip of darkness tightening around me, and I knew my time was nearly up.

My thoughts drifted like cottonwood seeds floating on a spring breeze. Memories and stories flashed through my consciousness, coming and going at will. The idea of everything I'd be leaving unfinished troubled me. I promised the Ivywood workers I would see them safely to their new home. And though I'd done my best, it was now out of my hands. That promise meant as much to me as it did to them. Keeping my word allowed me to make amends – to clean up a life stained by sin and regrets. All of this had been a chance to start anew. But the Lord, it seemed, had different plans for me.

Summoning what little strength remained, I reached for my spyglass and trained it on the scene unfolding before me. Drew and his comrades approached the ranch gate just as the rising sun cleared the mountain peaks. They moved steadily forward, with confidence in their steps. The men at the entrance were immediately on guard, their weathered faces hard and unfeeling. They were armed to the teeth, and their steely gazes showed no hint of mercy or trace of decency.

Drew reined in his stallion and offered a disarming smile. "Mornin' fellas," he greeted them. They said nothing. "There's a rumor goin' around that old Smiling Jack and Logan Ashbourne hired some stone killers to protect this place. You wouldn't know anything about that, would you?"

One of the men turned his head and spit before responding. "Funny," he said, his voice gruff and abrasive. "I heard the same. Now, what you want?"

"See there, boys," Drew said to his men, "I told you it was true." He turned his attention back to the spokesman for the group. "You wouldn't mind going to fetch them killers for me, would you? I'd love to have a chat with them."

The air was charged with tension as Jack's men exchanged amused glances, their laughter tinged with menace. "You're talkin' to 'em, dummy," the man said. He paused to spit again. "And if you got a lick of sense, you best be movin' on."

Drew's brow furrowed. "Wait just a minute," he said, feigning confusion. "You mean to tell me that *you* fellas are the killers I heard talk of?" He shook his head and scratched the back of his neck. "Well, no offense, gentlemen, but you boys don't look near as tough as I had you pegged. Maybe you ought to run along and get Jack and Ashbourne before this all goes sideways for you."

At that, the men moved in unison, pulling their weapons and taking aim at Drew. "How 'bout we just fill you and these darkies with holes instead. Save us all some time."

No further words were exchanged before a crack of gunfire from the far end of the ranch shattered the stillness. All eyes flashed in the direction of the gunfire, and Drew and his companions sprang into action. Their movements were swift and decisive as they raced for cover, filling the quiet morning air with shots and powder smoke. Men on both sides fell, their cries of pain lost in the chaos of battle.

I lowered the spyglass as my senses began to dull. The world around me faded into shadow, and memories flooded my mind. I was taken back to a time long since passed, to the day Elise and I first laid eyes on this land. Our dreams were born here, and here they'd remain forever.

Elise and I cleared a rise just a few miles outside Virginia City and laid eyes on a beautiful expanse of land before us. The large, green valley was nestled among mountain ranges surrounding it on all sides. The gentle light of the morning sun bathed the land in a soft, golden glow. The rich, fertile land, seemingly untouched by the ever-present greed of men, captured our hearts. A thin creek wound its way through the property. It babbled over sturdy rocks and fallen tree limbs, singing along with the soothing rustle of cottonwood trees in the breeze. Elise immediately fell in love with the place. I couldn't blame her. There was something special about this land. I couldn't place a finger on it, but I felt it just the same. A sense of awe washed over us as if we were staring at a tiny slice of heaven.

Turning to Elise, I couldn't help but voice my concerns. "It sure is pretty here," I said, "but...I don't know."

"You don't know?" she said, her eyes lit with determination. "What's not to know? This place is as close to perfect as anywhere I've ever seen." She began pointing around the valley. "We can put our house right there, build a corral or a barn there, and I'm sure we could raise some sheep on this land if we –"

"Elise," I cut in, "You're right about this place. It may be the most beautiful stretch of land I've ever seen. But I ain't got near enough money for this. I mean, I could work for it, but it'd take me years to save up."

"Then it's a good thing you're not in this alone," she said, her eyes latching onto mine. "My father's land in Colorado rightfully belongs to me now, and I've decided I don't want it anymore. That ranch was his dream, not mine. I say we sell it, combine our money, and use it to buy this place. It's beautiful, close to a city, and looks perfect for raising a family."

It was a simple yet profound proposal. We could do this together.

"Maybe we should talk about gettin' married first," I said. "Then we can discuss buying land together and raising up kids and sheep."

Elise smiled, and at that moment, amidst the tranquility around us, I resigned myself to the fact that something good was happening to me.

I came back around, unsure of exactly how long I'd been unconscious. I found my spyglass and lifted it to my eye. The battle had erupted, and the valley was filled with the thunderous roar of gunfire and the primal cries of men charging into the fray. Drew, Titus, Fisher, and Tate led their respective groups, advancing upon the ranch with the ferocity of an Indian war party. I always knew ours were bold, strong men, but I never realized they had such fire in their bellies.

It was unlike anything I'd ever seen. The coordinated assault, the sight of my friends fighting for their freedom, and the passion they displayed stirred something within my failing body. I was proud. Grateful. And I knew that regardless of whether I lived or died, these men would be fine. They were survivors, warriors in their own way, and their courage knew no bounds.

As the combined force of those free men descended upon the ranch, Smiling Jack's men found themselves faced with formidable opposition. It was a threat that had been both disregarded and unanticipated. Jack's hired guns had been caught off guard by the sheer tenacity of their adversaries. As a result, Smiling Jack's men faltered, their bravado soon giving way to panic. They were outnumbered and nearly surrounded.

With little option, Smiling Jack's men abandoned the fight and ran. They mounted their frenzied horses and fled the valley, firing shots behind them as they went.

It took a moment for my friends to realize what had happened. They stood there, looking for someone to shoot at, but no one was left. In that instant, they froze where they stood. The gunfire ceased, and the valley was quiet once more. Drew lifted his rifle above his head and cried out in victory. The men joined in, and I dropped my head and closed my eyes.

The sun was directly overhead, shining down on the horseshoe bend in the creek where Elise and I chose to exchange our vows. It was a tranquil spot, shaded and cool, with a bright blue sky above and rolling hills in the distance. We had done just as we'd planned. Elise sold her father's land in Colorado, and she and I purchased the property outside of Virginia City. It all happened much quicker than we imagined, and I proposed to Elise as soon as the deed was signed. Time was a luxury neither of us intended to squander, so we celebrated by exchanging vows on the land where our future was to be built.

Only a handful of people were present for the ceremony since neither of us had any family to speak of. A few townsfolk showed up, mostly out of curiosity, and Reverend Phillips officiated. We exchanged vows, each of us dressed in fancy new clothes we'd bought in town, and began our lives together.

After the ceremony ended and everyone returned to their lives, we were alone, sitting on a couple of makeshift chairs outside a tent that would be our home until we built the house. Elise and I talked for hours about the future and our dreams. I didn't have much to say because it felt like I was already living my dream. I never expected to find a wife, let alone have discussions about my future.

"I want three or four children," Elise said. "Maybe a girl, and the rest can be boys. The girl is so I can have another woman around the house, and the boys can help you with the chores on the ranch."

"Sounds like you got it all figured out," I said with a grin. "But what about you? Is there anything you want to do before you start havin' all those youngins? Is there any place you want to see?"

Elise dropped her head and smiled shyly. "It may sound silly to you, but I've always wanted to see California. I read about San Francisco when I was a girl, and it sounded so amazing to me. It has theaters, opera houses, artists, and musicians. It seems like a wonderful place to visit."

"Then we'll visit," I said. "There's nothin' stopping us. We need to make it happen before all those boys you're gonna have show up expecting to eat."

"Boys and a *girl*," Elise said with a chuckle. "Don't forget the girl." She paused. "What do you think about the name Cali? You know, like California?"

"I think it's a beautiful name."

"Well, look what we have here," a spiteful voice called out. I forced my heavy eyes open, foggy as my vision was, to see a pistol pointed directly at me. The hand that held it and the hateful eyes behind it belonged to Logan Ashbourne.

Chapter 65

Drew and the Ivywood workers reveled in their victory. Joyful voices, laughter, and celebration echoed throughout the valley. The tension that had gripped us all for weeks dissipated almost instantly. They had done it. They had taken back the land and secured their new home.

Drew's voice cut through the hoopla as he returned to reality. "I'll be back, fellas," he announced, his tone growing serious. "I've gotta check on Moses and get him into town. He needs a doctor."

Drew raced toward Stormy, and just as his foot found the stirrup, a commanding voice rang out from across the ranch, halting him in his tracks. It was Harold Gullet. He stepped out of the barn, shotgun in hand, a vision of menace and hatred. "Drew Harlan, I'm callin' you out," he declared, his eyes burning with resolve. "It's time we settle this for good."

Drew clenched his jaw, and his gaze flickered briefly toward the distant hillside where Moses lay waiting for him. "I ain't got time to fight you, Gullet," Drew called out, his voice laced with weariness. "You lost. That's all there is to it. Now, get on out of here and leave us be."

Harold stood his ground. "You *will* fight," he said. "You'll fight, or you'll die. I'll be satisfied either way." The Ivywood workers looked on in stunned silence. Harold Gullet was a man they had learned to fear – the one responsible for carrying out all of the vicious punishments dreamed up by Logan Ashbourne over the years.

With a resigned sigh, Drew stepped forward, steeling himself for the inevitable. "Fine," he conceded. "We'll finish this for good. But we do it without guns. Best man wins."

Harold smiled and leaned his shotgun against the barn, his gaze fixed on Drew. "The best man will be the one left breathin'."

Drew glanced at Titus, who simply nodded stiffly. It wasn't much of a gesture, but enough to remind Drew of the terrible things Harold

Gullet had done. Memories raced through his mind like flipping through a stack of photographs. Memories of Gullet's cruel taunts and punishments, years of him lording over innocent folks through fear and intimidation, his vicious treatment of Titus, and his cold-blooded killing of Carl Bancroft.

Then there was the horse. The trusting eyes of the Thoroughbred Gullet forced Drew to kill when he was just a boy invaded his mind, and a fierce rage ignited within him. Drew dropped his gunbelt and launched himself at Harold Gullet, quickly closing the distance between them. He collided with Gullet, grabbed him around the waist, and drove him to the ground. They groaned and grappled with each other, rolling around in the dirt, neither gaining the upper hand, until they managed to scramble to their feet. The others gathered around as they fought, determined to ensure the fight was fair, knowing neither man would yield.

Harold was an imposing figure, large and strong. However, Drew possessed a fierce tenacity and lightning-fast reflexes that made up for his lack of size. As the Ivywood workers circled around them, Drew unleashed a barrage of punches, landing a flurry of blows to Harold's body. Despite Drew's ferocity, Harold Gullet was undeterred by the onslaught. He retaliated with several powerful blows of his own, each strike landing with incredible force and a sickening thud.

Drew swung wildly at Gullet's jaw, but Gullet slipped the punch and landed a heavy blow to Drew's ribcage. Drew dropped to one knee, and Gullet saw his opportunity to end the fight quickly. He kicked Drew in the side of the head, knocking him to his hands and knees and sending a stream of spit and blood flying from Drew's mouth. He kicked at Drew again, this time aiming for his side. But Drew caught Gullet's leg under his left arm and began jabbing wildly at him with his right. Drew's punches seemed to have little impact, and Gullet delivered what appeared to be the finishing blow. His thick fist landed just above Drew's jaw on the side of his head, and Drew collapsed. He was still conscious, though barely, and he coughed and wheezed as blood trickled down his face. Harold turned and walked toward the barn – toward his shotgun. "Get up, Drew," Titus said forcefully. "Don't you quit on us now."

Titus' words echoed in Drew's mind, and the thought of his friend bleeding out on the hillside gave him the resolve he needed. Drew made it to his feet. He staggered a bit but soon regained his composure. "Gullet," he called out with a guttural groan. "We ain't done yet."

Gullet stopped and turned to look at Drew, a disgusted look on his face. Gullet didn't reply but raced back toward his unsteady opponent. Drew stood his ground and let him come, watching intently as the large man raced forward. Just as Gullet reached him, arm pulled back, Drew lunged forward, and his fist collided with Gullet's nose. Blood exploded, and Gullet stumbled backward, dropping to a knee. Drew saw his opportunity and acted. He stepped up and began landing punches to Gullet's head and face. Gullet did his best to protect himself, but Drew was too fast despite his injuries.

Just as it seemed that Drew might have gained the advantage, Harold Gullet's hand darted to his belt, and he pulled out a large gleaming knife. In one swift motion, Gullet slashed out wildly, slicing a deep gash across Drew's neck and chest.

Shock and rage coursed through Drew as he staggered away, his eyes darting to the blood that soaked through his shirt. The world around him grew still; the pain left his body, and he felt strong again. With a primal roar, Drew charged at Harold Gullet like a man possessed, hurling himself at him with a fury that took the larger man by surprise. Drew pummeled Gullet relentlessly, his fists raining down upon him with unbridled rage. Harold was entirely caught off guard and fell to the ground, floundering helplessly beneath the barrage of blows. Drew climbed on top of Gullet, punching his head and face until there was no fight left in Gullet. Blow after blow landed, and it was only when Fisher and Tate intervened, pulling Drew clear of his fallen foe, that the onslaught finally ceased.

Breathless and bloodied, Drew stood over Harold Gullet, his chest heaving with exertion. "Damn you, Gullet," he spat, his voice shaking with anger. He snatched the rifle away from Titus and pointed it directly at Gullet's head. "I outta put a bullet in your skull." No one protested. No man there would have tried to prevent it, but a wave of doubt crept over him even as he spoke.

Gullet, battered and defeated, struggled to his knees. His face was a swollen, bloodied mess. "Do it," he said, his voice as defiant as ever. "Put a bullet in me, Drew Harlan. If you've got the stones for it."

Drew's grip tightened on the rifle, the urge to exact vengeance warring with his sense of justice. In the end, mercy prevailed, and Drew slowly lowered the rifle. "Get him out of here," he ordered, his voice firm and commanding. "Killin' him would be doing him a favor. He ain't worth the bullet."

Titus and another man pulled Gullet to his feet, leading him away. Another of the workers brought Gullet's horse over. "No," Drew said. "The horse stays here. It belongs to me now."

Gullet looked back at Drew. "You're gonna send a man out into the wilderness without a horse or a gun?" Harold said, laboring to get the words out.

"That's right," Drew replied coolly. "I'll leave it up to the Lord to decide whether you live or die."

Harold shook his head. "Then I ain't leavin'," he said, pushing away from Titus. "I'd rather die here than out there."

"Titus, please escort this degenerate off our land," Drew said. "And if he refuses to walk away, shoot him in the leg. If he don't wanna walk away, he can crawl." Harold Gullet cursed at Drew but ultimately accepted his fate and staggered off, leaving the ranch and the Ivywood workers for good. Drew called out to him as he went. "Don't come back here, Gullet. You come anywhere near here; I'll let these fellas deal with you as they see fit."

CHAPTER 66

"**Y**ou don't look so good, Moses," Logan Ashbourne taunted, gesturing toward my wound with his pistol. "I bet that hurts like hell." I lay there on the ground, my breaths ragged and shallow, each slight movement sending bolts of pain through my stomach. Logan towered over me, the familiar self-satisfied smirk on his face.

My voice was strained, barely a whisper, as I managed to speak. "What is wrong with you, Logan? Can't you let me die in peace?" I struggled to keep my composure. My words were a feeble attempt to mask the agony coursing through my body.

"Oh, I'm sorry, little brother," Logan said, feigning concern. "Please pardon my cheerfulness. It's just...seeing you here in such a state. Well, I've waited a long time for this day."

Suddenly, a triumphant shout erupted from the valley below. Logan's gaze hardened, and his anger boiled over at what I assumed to be a victory cry. "Looks like your friends managed to scare off Jack Davis' two-bit gunmen," he said with disdain. "I should've never trusted Davis with such a job. I knew he was all hot air and bluster."

Logan dropped to his knees beside me. "Let me ask you something, Moses." His voice was low and quiet. "Why'd you do it? And don't give me any story about God or destiny. Why'd you steal my workers from me?"

I met his gaze, my resolve unwavering despite my pain. "They don't belong to you, Logan. They never did. And I didn't steal them. They don't belong to me either. If you want the truth, I believe the Lord sent me to get them out. To get them away from you and Harold Gullet."

Logan's laughter echoed through the hills. "So that's how it is, huh?" He waved his pistol over my body, taking in my injuries. "What about all of this? Did your Lord want this, too?"

"I suppose we'll all find out soon enough," I said just before breaking into a coughing fit.

"I suppose you're right," Logan said, kneeling beside me. "But, what if I decide I'm tired of the Lord making all the decisions? Why should He get the pleasure of ushering you through those pearly gates? I could just do it myself?" Logan pressed the barrel of the pistol against my temple. If he was hoping to see some sort of fear in my eyes, he was sorely disappointed. I figured I was already closer to heaven and Elise than I was to this world anyway.

"You know, Moses, we could've gotten along as kids," Logan said. "As adults even. But I never trusted you. I could read you like a book right from the start. You wanted what I had. Ever since we were young boys, you always wanted what was mine. You see, I believe *that's* why you stole those men from me. The Lord had nothing to do with it. It was all you."

I shook my head. "You're wrong, Logan. I never wanted anything of yours. You can kill me, but it won't make it true."

"I reckon it won't matter much in a few minutes," Logan replied flatly. "All I know is, it didn't have to be this way."

"Those are the truest words you've said yet."

"Alright, enough of this," Logan said, rising to his feet. "I'm sure good old Drew Harlan will come riding in here to your rescue soon like some redneck cavalry. So I think I'll just be on my way." He aimed his pistol at me. "Close your eyes, Moses. This will be quick."

I closed my eyes, resigning myself to whatever fate awaited me. But as darkness threatened to consume me, a sudden, dull thud came in place of gunfire, followed by the weight of someone collapsing onto me. I cried out in pain as I forced my eyes open.

"Moses, are you okay, son?" a man said. "Can you hear me? Oh, what has he done to you, Moses." It took a moment, but when I eventually forced my eyes to focus, I saw Smiling Jack Davis. His face was weathered with concern as he pulled Logan's unconscious body from me.

"He didn't do it, Jack," I said, "it was your man, Sutton."

Jack sank to his knees. "I'm so sorry, Moses," he said as he gently inspected the rifle wound. "I never wanted this. Sutton acted on his own. All I wanted to do was scare you boys."

"You tried to steal my land, Jack," I said, trying to direct my weakening gaze. "We made a deal. We still had time. I had your money."

Jack dropped his head, and his eyes welled up. "I know, Moses. I know, and I am deeply sorry. None of this should have happened." His eyes lit up with determination. "Let's get you up. I can get you to a doctor." He began to ready himself to lift me. "I can get you on my horse, and it won't take long for us to –"

"No, Jack," I said, taking him by the wrist. "It's too late for that, now."

"But, Moses, there's still a chance I can help you. Maybe I can fix things."

Staring up into the desperate eyes of my one-time mentor, I was struck with an overwhelming sense of compassion. With my dying words, I could curse Smiling Jack Davis. I could rightfully blame him for a significant amount of pain and confusion that I'd lived through for years. I could blame him for my death. I could lash out with words that would haunt him for the rest of his life. But when I looked into his tear-filled eyes, I saw a broken man – an imperfect soul plagued by demons of his own. So, instead of cursing him, I said the words I never imagined speaking to Smiling Jack Davis.

"I forgive you."

"I have to do something to try and make this right, Moses," Smiling Jack said as he sniffed and wiped the tears from his face. He reached into his pocket and pulled out an envelope. "Here," he said, tucking the envelope into my shirt. "This is the deed to your land. I'm sorry for the hurt I've caused, but at least you can die knowing that those men and women will have a home."

I smiled, though nothing in me felt joyful. The pain in my belly had become a dull ache, and I was shivering. "You better go now, Jack," I said through labored breath. "Drew will be on his way up here. He may not see things like I do."

Smiling Jack nodded solemnly. "Is there anything I can do to ease your mind before...?"

"There's one more thing," I said, motioning for Jack to come close. I whispered into his ear, and Jack nodded and smiled.

"True to the end," he said with a chuckle as he rose. "You're a good man, Moses Colter." Smiling Jack took one last, long look at me as I lay there with what little life I possessed draining from my body. Jack removed two pearl-handled Colt revolvers from the holsters he wore on each hip. They were the same revolvers Jack had taken from Drew when we met him in Bozeman. He placed the revolvers on my chest, and I held them tightly so Drew would be sure to find them.

Afterward, Smiling Jack lifted the still unconscious Logan Ashbourne and laid him across the back of his horse. "Goodbye, son," Jack said as he climbed into the saddle. "Put a good word in for me up there, will you?" Smiling Jack Davis rode away, and I listened for a moment as the heavy steps of his horse faded into the distance.

With my last bit of strength, I reached into my pack and pulled out a book. Drew's old book – the one he gave me when we were just kids, *A Practical Guide to Horse Breeds of the World*. I cracked it open and smiled at the photograph of a strong black stallion with the words of young Drew scrawled on the page. "*I figured you needed this more than me. This here is my horse, so you'll need to pick another one. Make sure it's fast. One day I'll show up to get you and we'll take off! Your pal, Drew.*"

With my last few breaths, I stared at the clear blue sky. "Thank you, Lord," I whispered as I heard the faint sound of Drew calling out to me.

"We did it, Moses. " His voice was a muffled echo miles away. "We really did it." Then I closed my eyes and was gone.

Epilogue
DREW HARLAN: ONE YEAR LATER

The ranch house was too quiet. I never liked it when things were too quiet. It made me uneasy, like something terrible might happen. Maybe that sounds foolish, but we've all got our quirks. The floorboards creaked as I walked to the kitchen, where the smell of coffee stirred me to life. I wasn't used to staying in one place for so long. Matter of fact, I wasn't even used to sleeping inside. An open trail in front of me, the stars overhead at night, and the excitement of meeting new folks was more my style. Truthfully, I was still trying to decide if I wanted to stay at the ranch or if it was time to move on.

Since Moses died, the place had changed in many ways. The men and women from Tennessee were turning this ranch into a respectable business. We decided to name it Colter Ranch, to honor Moses. It felt like the right thing to do, but it sure was ironic. For one, Moses hated the name Colter. I don't know if he ever made peace with it. Still, whether he liked it or not, he *was* Moses Colter – my friend and brother. Speaking of irony, the Colter River, which had been such an obstacle to us, wasn't near what it used to be. Soon after we'd left Tennessee, a severe drought hit. It was so bad that the Colter River nearly dried up entirely and never recovered. I'd be surprised if it were little more than a trickling stream by now. But it was fitting in a way, like the river itself mourned Moses' passing.

I took one last sip of coffee, grabbed my coat, and stepped outside into the cool morning. Even if it wasn't the same without him, this was still the home Moses had dreamed of.

The sun wasn't fully up yet, but the sounds of life already stirred on the ranch. Titus was busy extending the corral with his sons, Fisher and Tate. The three of them waved and greeted me as I passed nearby.

Soon after we took the land back, everyone voted for Titus to be the ranch foreman, which he reluctantly accepted. It was a good choice, even though Titus didn't feel qualified. He'd always worked in the tobacco fields, but the men and women of Colter Ranch decided we'd raise horses.

Most of the workers had experience with horses, and the idea of growing any sort of crop no longer appealed to them. I couldn't blame them. The land was better suited for grazing than for planting anyway. Besides the horses, we had a small herd of sheep to keep the old legacy alive. Not many, just enough to honor Moses' and Elise's vision for the place.

Stormy, my black stallion, and Moses' Palomino, Cali, grazed out in the field. Hurley, the sturdy old mule, trailed behind them. There was something special about those horses. Every time I saw them, I thought of my good friend and how, as long as Cali was alive, a part of Moses would live on as well.

It was Saturday, which meant I'd need to saddle Stormy and head into Virginia City. One of the fellas rounded him up for me, which wasn't too much of a challenge. Stormy liked getting out and moving as much as I did, so he quickly raced for the barn. I saddled Stormy, feeling the excitement and warmth of the sturdy old boy.

The sun came up and cast a soft light over the land. Stormy and I slowly made our way through the ranch, admiring the shades of red and gold leaves fluttering in the breeze. Breathing deeply, I let the chilly air fill my lungs.

My mind wandered as we eased toward town, and I thought about everything we'd all been through for the past year and a half. I was glad to be a part of this new thing we were doing, but I couldn't help but wonder what we had really accomplished. The ranch was thriving, but was that enough? Was that what Moses wanted? The workers were free, but free to do what exactly? Would they all stay here, content with their new lives, or would they eventually leave? And what about me? What was my role in all of this? What was I supposed to do now that things were finally stable?

There was movement in the bushes to my right. It was likely a squirrel or rabbit, but I thought of Two Feathers for some reason. I'd sent him to find Gregory Sutton after the coward sniped Moses. Two Feathers missed the battle at the ranch, but he showed up a few days after Moses' funeral. He gave no details on hunting down Sutton. I asked him how it went, and he simply nodded. But the stern look in his eyes told me everything I needed to know, not to mention the shiny new rifle Two Feathers had tied to his saddle. Sutton was gone. Two Feathers had dealt with him. And after that, he left. Two Feathers disappeared without so much as a goodbye. I didn't hold it against him, though. It was just his way. Two Feathers had his own path to follow, and I felt sure we'd see him again.

As I reached the edge of town, I could sense the energy. Virginia City had grown in the past year, and the town was full of folks trading goods, laughing, and chatting about the weather. It all rang in my ears at once like a living melody. Life had moved on.

I hitched Stormy to the post outside of the Rusty Nail Saloon, which was under new ownership. When Smiling Jack left without the five thousand dollars, I gave it to Skillet to pay him back for funding the trip to Tennessee. He and Nellie used the cash to buy the Rusty Nail, which no one saw coming. Skillet cooked and worked in the back while Nellie manned the bar and chatted up the locals. They lived upstairs in separate rooms, and even though they owned the place, I still had to pay for every drink.

"Mornin', Drew," Nellie called out as I pushed through the front doors. "Is it Saturday already?"

"Yes, ma'am, it is," I said. "I just thought I'd stop in and see how you all were gettin' along."

Skillet yelled from the kitchen. "Is that Drew? Tell him to go pick up some flour for me, will you?"

"He does know I don't work for him, right?" I said.

Nellie rolled her eyes. "Skillet thinks whenever he opens his mouth, the world should stop everything to listen."

I laughed at Nellie's comment. "I figured you and Skillet would be married by now. You two have been livin' together for a year. It's time he made an honest woman of you before folks start talkin'."

Nellie propped her hands on her hips and raised an eyebrow. "Drew Harlan, you better take that back. You know as well as I do there's two bedrooms upstairs, and that is as close as Skillet will ever sleep to me." She paused while I chuckled. "I mean it," she went on. "I'll live here for a while, work the bar, and run the saloon, but anything other than that? He can forget it."

Skillet entered from the kitchen, sweating and wiping his forehead with a bandana. "There he is," he said when he saw me. "It must be Saturday."

I sat, and we shot the breeze for a while, but I didn't stay long. Nellie sneaked a biscuit for me when Skillet wasn't looking, and I made for the door.

"It's good to see you, Drew," Nellie said with a hint of concern. "Are you doin' alright? Like really?" I nodded, though unconvincingly. "Well, you hang in there. I know you feel a little lost right now, but things have a way of workin' out. The Lord didn't bring you this far to let you go now."

Nellie was right. I was all mixed up. My mind was wrestling itself over what came next. I had a responsibility to the men and women of Colter Ranch, but something inside of me was chomping at the bit to get moving again.

With a final wave, I stepped outside and walked down the street to the small church cemetery. I never was one for keeping routines, but visiting Moses had become a weekly habit. I knelt and wiped away the fallen leaves from all three gravestones. I had two made when Moses died – one for him and another for his daughter, Cali. The way I saw it, he, Elise, and Cali deserved to be remembered. And since Moses had no family to keep their gravesites looking nice and clean, I decided to take on the job. I was there every Saturday.

"Hey, Moses," I said as I crouched there on my heels. "How you gettin' along, old friend?" Though I did the same thing each week, there was always a part of me that felt foolish for carrying on a conversation with someone who'd been dead for over a year.

"I know I've said it before," I went on, "but you'd be real proud of how everything's been goin' at the ranch. We're makin' real progress gatherin' up horses. It's mostly wild Mustangs, but we caught a few Appoloosas, too. The fellas have been breakin' them, and we've been breedin' the strongest ones. We'll be a legitimate horse ranch before you know it." I paused. "I sure wish you could see it."

It was a quiet morning, with only the rustling of dry leaves in the wind and the faint call of songbirds in the distance. I took a deep breath and sat on the ground in front of Moses' grave. "I'm havin' some troubles, Moses," I said, battling the guilt of admitting it. "I need to talk to you. And I know you won't answer, but still."

I sat there for a moment, picking dirt from my boots. A cool wind blew, and I pulled my coat tight. A short, sad laugh escaped my lips. "I used to think it was funny, you know? The way you'd just handle problems that came up. I never thought too much about it because you did it so easy-like. You were so calm and in control that I didn't notice how you were always workin' things out. I mean, how many times did I come to you all excited about some hairbrained mess of an idea? And I'll admit, my ideas weren't fully formed most of the time, but you never made me feel dumb about it. You'd listen and ask me questions until I worked out a decent plan that looked much better than when it started. You made it look so easy that I didn't really notice it happening. More times than not, you had me believin' I had a great idea the whole time. I sure could use one of those talks now."

My voice was shaking a bit, so I stopped and swallowed the lump growing in my throat. "That's one of the things I always liked about you, Moses. You just did and said what needed to be done or said. Even when you were droppin' some terrible news on me, I knew everything was gonna work out. You always told me the truth, and you'd help me make things right even when it was me that caused the trouble. It's like you had a way of makin' a big mess seem like something worth cleanin' up." I paused. "You'd probably say I'm ramblin' now and that I need to just go ahead and say what I need to say."

I felt like a buffoon sitting there afraid to talk to someone who couldn't talk back. I glanced at the mountains in the distance and felt small and weak. "First off, I'm not ready to give up on this place. These men and women aren't just strangers we agreed to help and look after. They're more than that. They're family now, and I can't turn my back on family. It's not even about the ranch. I mean, let's be honest, I don't know nothin' about runnin' a ranch. But they do. And it was always more for them anyway. The trouble is, they all look to me to hold everything together. That was more your job, Moses, but I'm doin' my best.

"Still, there's this part of me," I continued, "always feelin' like there's something more. It's not that I don't care about Titus, Charity, and everyone else. It's just that...I got a visit a while back from a man named Amos Turner. He's the sheriff out of Bozeman. Turner said he'd been lookin' for a deputy, and Marshal Wesley put in a good word for me. Apparently, they were old friends back in Tennessee before this Turner fella joined the army and moved away. I had a good laugh over it and ended up tellin' him, 'Thanks but no thanks.' But I ain't been able to stop thinkin' about it ever since. What if I took him up on it? What if I could go legit just like we always talked about? Think about it, Moses – me, a real lawman. I bet I'd be good at it too, even though I spent most of my life runnin' from the law.

Hell, Moses, who knows, I might even arrest old Smiling Jack one day." I chuckled, thinking about how Moses would've reacted to that.

"Problem is, part of me feels guilty about leaving. I wanna do right by you and these folks we brought here. It's all mixed up in my head, and I don't know how to sort it out."

I was caught off guard by a single tear that slipped from my eye and ran down my cheek before I could catch it. I quickly sucked in and pushed down those emotions. Now wasn't the time to cry. Now was the time to get things settled.

"I guess that's what I'm tryin' to ask you, Moses. You always knew what to do. But me? All these years, and I'm still tryin' to figure out whether to stay put or go. It seems like that's what I'm always tryin' figure out. I don't want to leave these folks; it's just...I don't – I'm not sure I'm built for all of this ranching life. It's been gnawin' at me 'cause I don't think I can be both things. How can I be a lawman over in Bozeman and protect the ranch at the same time?" I took a settling breath. "You knew this was comin', didn't you? You probably figured I'd be stuck tryin' to decide what to do after you were gone."

The wind picked up again, carrying the threat of winter. It was hard for everyone, but we made it through that first Montana winter, and they learned how to survive. They could do this without me. They could make it. I thought so, anyway.

"Moses, I need you to tell me it's okay. I need to know whether it's fine to leave or if I need to stick around and make sure these folks make this ranch work. I don't know how to do this without you. And I can't live with myself if I think I'm lettin' you down. So, I don't know how it works up there, but if you can send me some sort of message or sign, I'd appreciate it." I sat there for a moment, just staring at the sky.

"But you'd probably say, *Why are you askin' me, Drew? If you need some sort of sign, do what I did. Ask the Lord for it.* Well, I don't know how that works either, so this is officially me askin' you, the Lord, or whoever else up there wants to tell me what to do. Just let me know." Then I remembered what Moses used to tell me. *Sometimes, you don't know which way to turn, and the only thing you can do is walk the path that's in front of you until you figure it out.*

"Alright, then, Moses," I said, rising to my feet. "That's enough of that for now. I ain't one to sit around cryin' in a graveyard, and you ain't too quick to speak up. I suppose I'll just wait and trust that I'll know what to do when the time is right." I smiled and brushed away a single leaf that landed on top of Moses' gravestone. "Thanks for listenin' to me, old friend. You rest well."

I lingered there for a few more minutes, soaking in the solitude of the morning and filling my lungs with cool mountain air. For a moment, the silence felt less heavy, and my shoulders relaxed.

"Drew Harlan," a voice called from behind me. "I thought I'd find you here." It was Reverend Phillips, a friend of Moses' but someone I barely knew. "It's very generous of you to take care of the family plot."

"I suppose so, Reverend," I answered. "I ain't never been labeled a good Samaritan, but if I don't do it, I don't know who would?"

Reverend Phillips smiled kindly. "I understand that," he said, "but still, there are plenty of plots around here that no one cares for. The church looks after things as best as possible, but no one cares as much as family."

"Maybe so," I said. "Well, I'd best be goin' now."

"You know, Drew," Reverend Phillips said as I turned to leave, "I'm surprised you've stuck around here so long. I figured you'd be back out there on the trail somewhere, living the life of a true adventurer."

"I can't say I haven't thought about it," I said, "but there's a ton of folks back at Colter Ranch who need me. I have to make sure they're okay."

"That's kind of you, Drew," Reverend Phillips said with a puzzled brow. "But you're not alone in this, you know? Plenty of good people here want to see those families do well. We're all willing to pitch in and help however we can. Maybe it's time – well, maybe it's time you let us help you."

"Help me?" I said. "I appreciate the sentiment, but I don't know what you can do. I don't want these folks gettin' mixed up with bad men who'll try to take what they have. No offense, but that don't seem like a job for church folk."

Reverend Phillips grinned. "That is a valid point, but pardon me for saying it isn't your job either."

"How do you figure?"

"It's the Lord's job to care for and provide for his people," Reverend Phillips said. "He's done it all along. Sure, the Lord used you and Moses to get those good people out of a bad situation, but it was His doing, not yours."

"I'm not sure I'm followin' you, Reverend," I said.

"I'm trying to say, God will care for you just as He cared for them. He has a plan for them, but He also has one for you. Sometimes those plans cross paths, but at other times they don't." I tried to interrupt, but the reverend kept going. "Listen, Drew, God made you with a penchant for adventure and travel. He made you tough but caring. He made you to look out for others. He put all of those things in you. That's who you are. I'm not tellin' you what to do, but I feel like you need someone to tell you it's okay to be who God made you to be. If you want to roam, then roam. When you want to come back, come back. Above all, be who you were meant to be and look for ways to help and care for others."

"Well, you just said a mouthful, Reverend," I said. "I appreciate that, and I'll think on it."

Truthfully, I didn't need to think about it at all. I asked for direction and it smacked me right in the face. I loved the men and women at Colter Ranch, and I'd always help them when they needed it. But, as the reverend said, I was made to be me. And who knows, maybe other folks out there need my help. I could go, and I could come back. It didn't have to be either/or. The Reverend was right. Providing for those folks was God's responsibility, but I had a responsibility, too. I'd always look out for them, but I couldn't ignore the stirring in my soul.

There were more questions than answers for now, and I didn't see that changing anytime soon. I said goodbye to the reverend, returned to Stormy, and climbed into the saddle. I'd ride back to Colter Ranch, tell everyone I'd be leaving for a while, and then be on my way. I didn't know what the future held, but I knew there was more to come. Whatever was in store for my family from Tennessee, they'd never have to face it alone.

Thank you for reading *Moses of the Colter*. If you enjoyed this story, please consider leaving a review on Amazon or wherever you purchased this book. Even a short review or a 5-star rating can make a world of difference finding a wider audience.

If you'd like to hear about upcoming projects, join my mailing list at mknobles.com and stay in the loop. Until next time, keep walking the path in front of you.

Acknowledgements

Writing *Moses of the Colter* has been a deeply personal and rewarding journey. Under the pen name "M.K. Nobles," we have worked together to craft a story that reflects our love for the Western genre, as well as the growth and healing we've experienced in our own lives. This book has been a process of laughter, tears, and the occasional grumble. Above all, it is a testament to the Lord's work in our lives and the incredible people who have supported us along the way.

To our **family and friends,** thank you for your unwavering support. Time and again, we have learned that navigating life's challenges is impossible without faith and family. Your prayers, encouragement, and steadfast belief in us have been indispensable throughout this process.

We approached writing this novel the same way we approach life — one day at a time, one page at a time, and, on tougher days, one word at a time. We are grateful for the opportunity to collaborate, honor God through our writing, and encourage one another throughout the journey. While writing this story wasn't always easy, it was always fulfilling. We hope these pages inspire others to trust God's plan and keep moving forward, even in difficult times.

To our **advanced readers**, your feedback has been invaluable. Having you read through our unedited work was both humbling and nerve-wracking, but your insights helped shape this story into something even better than we initially imagined. A special thank you to **Kathy Rath, Sarah Rath, Denita James, Jaime Jirikowic, Lauren Robinson, Ronald Robinson, R.P. Robinson, Kevin Remde, Anne Hays, Kelsey Broome, Bubba Spickler, Kent Ellis, and Mikela King-Cesare,** your contributions have made a lasting impact on this book, and we are so appreciative of your help. To **Kate Griffin and Sara Griffith,** thank you for your help with our horse-related details.

A heartfelt thank you to **Tanya Snoddy** and **Kristina Dodson** for their exceptional work in editing and proofreading. Your enthusiasm and attention to detail has truly been a blessing to us.

And to **Nell Nobles**, thank you for your loving support, countless prayers, and for inspiring the resilient, caring, and sassy character of Nellie. Your love and encouragement have guided us throughout this process.

To **Peter and Caroline O'Connor** from **Bespoke Author,** thank you for designing a beautiful cover that perfectly brought our vision to life. Your patience and talent made the process so much easier, and we're thankful for your willingness to help us "get it right."

Finally, and most importantly, we thank God for His guidance, patience, and abundant grace. This book, inspired by the biblical story of Moses, reflects much of what we've learned about growth, faith, trust, and redemption. Moses Colter's journey, his thoughts, struggles, and regrets, echo our own experiences. Growth can be painful, change can be stressful, and pruning can be brutal, but we trust the Lord to accomplish His purpose through us. We hope this story is a blessing to others, just as we've been blessed through its creation.

To the authors, novels, and life experiences that have inspired us, thank you for sparking our imagination and passion for storytelling. Writing in the Western genre has been an incredible adventure, and we have done our best to draw from the greats to bring this world to life.

With humble and grateful hearts,
M.K. Nobles (Ken and Gretchen Nobles)

Notes from the Author

One of the most rewarding aspects of writing *Moses of the Colter* was combining historical inspiration with our own creative vision. We have long been fascinated by the western frontier, and we aimed to capture the grit, beauty, and complexity of the late 1800s in a vivid and engaging manner. While we took care to research and accurately reflect the time period, this is ultimately a work of fiction, and we allowed ourselves the creative freedom to shape the story.

The Colter River:

A key element in the story, the Colter River, is entirely fictional. It never existed, but we created it as a central feature of the landscape to help develop the narrative and provide a meaningful backdrop for Moses Colter's journey.

Business/Settlement Names:

Some businesses and settlements mentioned in the novel are authentic, while others were invented for narrative purposes. While readers may recognize historical references to certain establishments and settlements, others, like general stores and saloons in our fictional towns, were created to better serve the plot and atmosphere of the story.

Fictional Characters:

The characters in Moses of the Colter are products of our imagination, with one notable exception: Smiling Jack Davis. Smiling Jack was an actual person who lived during the portrayed time, but the details of his actions and personality in our story are fictional. We drew inspiration from historical accounts to bring him to life in an authentic way that best served the story.

Biblical Inspiration:

This novel is inspired by the Biblical story of the Exodus, particularly Moses's journey leading the Israelites to freedom. While the themes of deliverance, faith, and perseverance are central to our story, we took many creative liberties to modernize and adapt the narrative for a Western setting. These changes allowed us to explore the parallels between Moses Colter's journey and the timeless struggles of leadership, redemption, and trust in God's plan.

A Blend of History and Imagination:

Writing this novel was a journey of discovery in both the research we conducted and the creative choices we made to bring this story to life. We hope our readers enjoy the blend of historical accuracy, literary fiction, and the themes that guide the narrative.

Thank you for being part of this experience. It is a privilege to share this story with you; we hope it inspires and encourages you.

Made in the USA
Columbia, SC
09 June 2025

59111161R00207